War of the Worlds:

GLOBAL DISPATCHES

Bantam Books
New York • Toronto • London • Sydney • Auckland

War of the Worlds:
GLOBAL DISPATCHES

Edited By
KEVIN J. ANDERSON

WAR OF THE WORLDS: GLOBAL DISPATCHES

A Bantam Spectra Book / June 1996

Spectra and the portrayal of a boxed "s" are trademarks of Bantam Books, a division of Bantam Doubleday Dell Publishing Group, Inc.

War of the worlds : global dispatches : anthology / edited by Kevin J. Anderson.
p.   cm.
ISBN 0-553-10353-9
1. Science fiction, American. 2. Imaginary wars and battles—Fiction. 3. Mars (Planet)—Fiction. 4. War stories, American. I. Anderson, Kevin J.
PS648.S3W374   1996
813'.0876208358—dc20   95-45125
                                                              CIP

Published simultaneously in the United States and Canada

Bantam Books are published by Bantam Books, a division of Bantam Doubleday Dell Publishing Group, Inc. Its trademark, consisting of the words "Bantam Books" and the portrayal of a rooster, is Registered in U.S. Patent and Trademark Office and in other countries. Marca Registrada. Bantam Books, 1540 Broadway, New York, New York 10036.

PRINTED IN THE UNITED STATES OF AMERICA

BVG   10   9   8   7   6   5   4   3   2   1

DEDICATION

To H. G. Wells
George Pal
and Jeff Wayne

whose separate versions of THE WAR OF THE WORLDS have
proved immensely inspirational to me, each in their own way.

ACKNOWLEDGMENTS

Special thanks to all the individual authors for their excitement over doing stories for this anthology; to my editor, Tom Dupree, for his enthusiasm over the concept; to my wife, Rebecca Moesta Anderson, for her support in this and all my other projects; and to Daniel Keys Moran and Heather McConnell, who were there to watch the expression on my face when I stopped dead in my tracks on a hiking trail in the redwood forests of California with the sudden idea for this book.

CONTENTS

FOREWORD

No one would have believed, in these first few decades of the Twentieth Century, how vastly human affairs could have been altered by a terrible invasion from space. That terrible onslaught from our planetary neighbors, our enemies the Martians, has left great scars and wrought great changes upon this green and blue world we call home.

My own chronicle of the Martian invasion that took place at the turn of our century is well known and, I suspect, familiar to all readers. In this retrospective, however, I have compiled several reports from other notables whose experiences during the Martian attacks may prove interesting and enlightening to students of mankind's first interplanetary war.

Because of the great turmoil of the time, some of the dates contradict, as do some of the events depicted here. (Messrs. Verne and Picasso have refused to speak with each other further on account of the discrepancies in their accounts of the sacking of Paris.) Due to the literary stature of Mr. Henry James, I have also included his account of the siege of London, though I question his interpretation of events; his journals are purported to have been written at the time, but I have no recollection of his keeping any written record during our excursions.

As it has been through the ages, history lives in the memories of the survivors, and sometimes those memories contain flaws. Nevertheless, these accounts deserve to be published—and let the future decide their worth.

Finally, I must thank my good friend, Monsieur Jules Verne, for his assistance in obtaining several of these manuscripts, as well as providing an Afterword to this volume.

—H. G. Wells

Teddy Roosevelt

THE ROOSEVELT DISPATCHES

MIKE RESNICK

Excerpt from the diary of Theodore Roosevelt (volume 23):

July 9, 1898:

Shot and killed a most unusual beast this afternoon. Letters of inquiry go off tomorrow to the various museums to see which of them would like the mounted specimen once I have finished studying it.

Tropical rain continues unabated. Many of the men are down with influenza, and in the case of poor Westmore it looks like we shall lose him to pneumonia before the week is out.

Still awaiting orders, now that San Juan Hill and the surrounding countryside is secured. It may well be that we should remain here until we know that the island is totally free from any more of the creatures that I shot this afternoon.

It's quite late. Just time for a two-mile run and a chapter of Jane Austen, and then off to bed.

Letter from Theodore Roosevelt to F. C. Selous, July 12, 1898:

My Dear Selous:

I had the most remarkable experience in Cuba this week, one that I feel compelled to share with you.

I had just led my Rough Riders in a victorious campaign in Cuba. We were still stationed there, awaiting orders to return home. With nothing better to do, I spent many happy hours bird-watching, and the event in question occurred late one afternoon when I was making my way through a riverine forest in search of the Long-billed Curlew.

Afternoon had just passed into twilight, and as I made my way through the dense vegetation I had the distinct feeling that I was no longer alone, that an entity at least as large as myself was lurking nearby. I couldn't imagine what it might be, for to the best of my knowledge the tapir and the jaguar do not inhabit the islands of the Caribbean.

I proceeded more cautiously, and in another twenty yards I came to a halt and found myself facing a *thing* the size of one of our American grizzlies. The only comparably sized animal within your experience would probably be the mountain gorilla, but this creature was at least thirty percent larger than the largest of the silverbacks.

The head was round, and was totally without a nose! The eyes were large, dark, and quite widely spread. The mouth was V-shaped and lipless, and drooled constantly.

It was brown—not the brown of an impala or a koodoo, but rather the slick moist brown of a sea-slug, its body glistening as if greased. The thing had no arms as such, but it did have a number of long, sinewy tentacles, each seemingly the thickness and strength of an elephant's trunk.

It took one look at me, made a sound that was half-growl and half-roar, and charged. I had no idea of its offensive capabilities, but I didn't like the look of those tentacles, so I quickly raised my Winchester to my shoulder and fired at almost point-blank range. I could hear the *smack!* of the bullet as it bounced off the trunk of the beast's body. The creature continued to approach me, and I hurled myself aside at the last instant, barely avoiding two of its outstretched tentacles.

I rolled as I hit the ground, and fired once more from a prone position, right into the open V of its mouth. This time there was a reaction, and a violent one. The thing hooted noisily and began tearing up pieces of the turf, all the while shaking its head vigorously. Within seconds it was literally uprooting large bushes and shredding them as if they were no more than mere tissue paper.

I waited until it was facing in my direction again and put a bullet into its left eye. Again, the reaction was startling: the creature began ripping apart nearby trees and screaming at such a pitch that all the nearby bird life fled in terror.

By that point I must confess that I was looking for some means of retreat, for I know of no animal that could take a rifle bullet in the mouth and another in the eye and still remain not just standing but aggressive and formidable. I trained my rifle on the brute and began backing away.

My movement seemed to have caught its attention, for suddenly it ceased its ravings and turned to face me. Then it began advancing slowly and purposefully—and a moment later it did something that no animal anywhere in the world has ever done: it produced a weapon.

The thing looked like a sword, but when the creature pointed it at me, a beam of light shot out of it, missing me only by inches, and instantly setting the bush beside me ablaze. I jumped in the opposite direction as it fired its sword of heat again, and again the forest combusted in a blinding conflagration.

I turned and raced back the way I had come. After perhaps sixty yards I chanced a look back, and saw that the creature was following me. However, despite its many physical attributes, speed was not to be counted among them. I used that to my advantage, putting enough distance between us so that it lost sight of me. I then jumped into the nearby river, making sure that no water should invade my rifle. Here, at least, I felt safe from the indirect effects of the creature's heat weapon.

It came down the path some forty seconds later. Rather than shooting it immediately, I let it walk by while I studied it, looking for vulnerable areas. The thing bore no body armour as such, not even the type of body plating that our mutual friend Corbett describes on the Indian rhino, yet its skin seemed impervious to bullets. Its body, which I now could see in its entirety, was almost perfectly spherical except for the head and tentacles, and there were no discernible weak or thin spots where head and tentacles joined the trunk.

Still, I couldn't let it continue along the path, because sooner or later it would come upon my men, who were totally unprepared for it. I looked for an earhole, could not find one, and with only the back of its head to shoot at felt that I could not do it any damage. So I stood up, waist deep in the water, and yelled at it. It turned toward me, and as it did so I put two more bullets into its left eye.

Its reaction was the same as before, but much shorter in duration. Then it regained control of itself, stared balefully at me through both eyes—the good one and the one that had taken three bullets—and began walking toward me, weapon in hand . . . and therein I thought I saw a way in which I might finally disable it.

I began walking backward in the water, and evidently the creature felt some doubt about the weapon's accuracy, because it entered the water and came after me. I stood motionless, my sights trained on the sword of heat. When the creature was perhaps thirty yards from me, it came to a halt and raised its weapon—and as it did so, I fired.

The sword of heat flew from the creature's hand, spraying its deadly light in all directions. Then it fell into the water, its muzzle—if that is the right word, and I very much suspect that it isn't—pointing at the creature. The water around it began boiling and hissing as steam rose, and the creature screeched once and sank beneath the surface of the river.

It took about five minutes before I felt safe in approaching it—after all, I had no idea how long it could hold its breath—but sure enough, as I had hoped, the beast was dead.

I have never before seen anything like it, and I will be stuffing and mounting this specimen for either the American Museum or the Smithsonian. I'll send you a copy of my notes, and hopefully a number of photographs taken at various stages of the postmortem examination and the mounting.

I realize that I was incredibly lucky to have survived. I don't know how many more such creatures exist here in the jungles of Cuba, but they are too malevolent to be allowed to survive and wreak their havoc on the innocent locals here. They must be eradicated, and I know of no hunter with whom I would rather share this expedition than yourself. I will put my gun and my men at your disposal, and hopefully we can rid the island of this most unlikely and lethal aberration.

Yours,
Roosevelt

Letter to Carl Akeley, hunter and taxidermist, c/o The American Museum of Natural History, July 13, 1898:

Dear Carl:

Sorry to have missed you at the last annual banquet, but as you know, I've been preoccupied with matters here in Cuba.

Allow me to ask you a purely hypothetical question: could a life-form exist that has no stomach or digestive tract? Let me further hypothesize that this life-form injects the blood of its prey—other living creatures—directly into its veins.

First, is it possible?

Second, could such a form of nourishment supply sufficient energy to power a body the size of, say, a grizzly bear?

I realize that you are a busy man, but while I cannot go into detail, I beg you to give these questions your most urgent attention.

Yours very truly,
Theodore Roosevelt

Letter to Dr. Joel A. Allen, Curator of Birds and Mammals, American Museum of Natural History, July 13, 1898:

Dear Joel:

I have a strange but, please believe me, very serious question for you.

Can a complex animal life-form exist without gender? Could it possibly reproduce—don't laugh—by budding? Could a complex life-form reproduce by splitting apart, as some of our single-celled animals do?

Please give me your answers soonest.

Yours very truly,
Theodore Roosevelt

Excerpts from monograph submitted by Theodore Roosevelt on July 14, 1898, for publication by the American Museum of Natural History:

. . . The epidermis is especially unique, not only in its thickness and pliability, but also in that there is no layer of subcutaneous fat, nor can I discern any likely source for the secretion of the oily liquid that covers the entire body surface of the creature.

One of the more unusual features is the total absence of a stomach, intestine, or any other internal organ that could be used for digestion. My own conclusion, which I hasten to add is not based on observation, is that nourishment is ingested directly into the bloodstream from the blood of other animals.

The V-shaped mouth was most puzzling, for what use can a mouth be to a life-form that has no need of eating? But as I continued examining the creature, I concluded that I was guilty of a false assumption, based on the placement of the "mouth." The V-shaped opening is not a mouth at all, but rather a breathing orifice, which I shall not call a nose simply because it is also the source of the creature's vocalizations, if I may so term the growls and shrieks that emanate from it. . . .

Perhaps the most interesting feature of the eye is not the multifaceted pupil, nor even the purple-and-brown cornea, which doubtless distorts its ability to see colors as we do, but rather the birdlike nictitating membrane, (or haw, as this inner eyelid is called in dogs) which protects it from harm. Notice that although it could not possibly have known the purpose or effects of my rifle, it nonetheless managed to lower it quickly enough to shield the eye from the main force of my bullet. Indeed, as is apparent from even a cursory examination of the haw, the healing process is so incredibly rapid that although I shot it three times in the left eye, the three wounds are barely discernible, even though the bullets passed entirely through the haw and buried themselves at the back of the eye.

I cannot believe that the creature's color can possibly be considered protective coloration . . . but then, I do not accept the concept of protective coloration to begin with. Consider the zebra: were it brown or black, it would be no easier to spot at, say, a quarter mile, than a wildebeest or topi or pronghorned deer—but because God saw fit to give it black and white stripes, it stands out at more than half a mile, giving notice of its presence to all predators, thereby negating the notion of protective coloration, for the zebra's stripes are, if anything, anti-protective, and yet it is one of the most successful animals in Africa. Thus, while the creature I shot is indeed difficult to pick out in what I assume to be its natural forest surroundings, I feel that it is brown by chance rather than design.

. . . Field conditions are rather primitive here, but I counted more than one hundred separate muscles in the largest of the tentacles, and must assume there are at least another two hundred that I was unable to discern. This is the only section of the body that seems criss-crossed with nerves, and it is conceivable that if the creature can be slowed by shock, a bullet placed in the cluster of nerves and blood vessels where the tentacle joins the trunk of the body will do the trick. . . .

The brain was a surprise to me. It is actually three to four times larger and heavier, in proportion to the body, than a man's brain is in proportion to his body. This, plus the fact that the creature used a weapon (which, alas, was lost in the current of the river), leads me to the startling but inescapable conclusion that what we have here is a species of intelligence at least equal to, and probably greater than, our own.

Respectfully submitted on this 14th day of July, 1898, by

Theodore Roosevelt, Colonel
United States Armed Forces

Letter to Willis Maynard Crenshaw, of Winchester Rifles, July 14, 1898:

Dear Mr. Crenshaw:

Enclosed you will find a sample of skin from a newly discovered animal. The texture is such that it is much thicker than elephant or rhinoceros hide, though it in no way resembles the skin of either pachyderm.

However, I'm not asking you to analyze the skin, at least not scientifically. What I want you to do is come up with a rifle and a bullet that will penetrate the skin.

Just as importantly, I shall need stopping power. Assume the animal will weigh just under a ton, but has remarkable vitality. Given the terrain, I'll most likely be shooting from no more than twenty yards, so I probably won't have time for too many second shots. The first shot *must* bring it down from the force of the bullet, even if no vital organs are hit.

Please let me know when you have a prototype that I can test in the field, and please make no mention of this to anyone except the artisans who will be working on the project.

Thank you.

Yours very truly,
Theodore Roosevelt

Private hand-delivered message from Theodore Roosevelt to President William McKinley, July 17, 1898:

Dear Mr. President:

Certain facts have come to my attention that make it imperative that you neither recall the Rough Riders from the Island of Cuba, nor disband them upon signing the Armistice with Spain.

There is something here, on this island, that is so evil, so powerful, so inimical to all men, that I do not believe I am exaggerating when I tell you that the entire human race is threatened by its very existence. I will make no attempt to describe it, for should said description fall into the wrong hands we could start a national panic if it is believed, or become figures of public ridicule if it is not.

You will simply have to trust me that the threat is a very real one. Furthermore, I urge you not to recall *any* of our troops, for if my suspicions are correct we may need all of them and still more.

Col. Theodore Roosevelt
"The Rough Riders"

Letter to Secretary of War Russell A. Alger, July 20, 1898:

Dear Russell:

McKinley is a fool! I warned him of perhaps the greatest threat yet to the people of America, and indeed to the world, and he has treated it as a joke.

Listen to me: it is essential that you cancel the recall order immediately and let my Rough Riders remain in Cuba. Furthermore, I want the entire army on standby notice, and if you're wise you'll transfer at least half of our forces to Florida, for that seems the likeliest spot for the invasion to begin.

I will be coming to Washington to speak to McKinley personally and try to convince him of the danger facing us. Anything you can do to pave the way will be appreciated.

Regards, Roosevelt

Speech delivered from the balcony above the Columbia Restaurant, Tampa, Florida, August 3, 1898:

My fellow Americans:

It has lately come to your government's attention that there is a threat to the national security—indeed, to the security of the world—that currently lurks in the jungles of Cuba. I have seen it with my own eyes, and I assure you that no matter what you may hear in the days and weeks to come, the danger is real and cannot be underestimated.

Shortly after my Rough Riders took San Juan Hill, I encountered something in the nearby jungle so incredible that a description of it would only arouse your skepticism and your disbelief. It was a creature, quite probably intelligent, the like of which has never before been seen on this Earth. I am and always have been a vociferous Darwinian, but despite my knowledge of the biological sciences, I cannot begin to hazard a guess concerning how this creature evolved.

What I *can* tell you is that it has developed the ability to create weapons unlike any we have seen, and that it has no compunction about using them against human beings. It is an evil and malevolent life-form, and it must be eradicated before it can turn its hatred loose against innocent Americans.

I was fortunate enough to kill the one I encountered in Cuba, but where there is one there will certainly be more. The United States government was originally dubious about the veracity of my claim, but I gather that recent information forwarded to the White House and the State Department from England, where more of these creatures have appeared, has finally convinced them that I was telling the truth.

Thus far none of the creatures has been discovered in the United States, but I say to you that it would be foolhardy to wait until they are found before coming up with an appropriate response. Americans have always been willing to make sacrifices and take up arms to defend their country, and this will be no exception. These creatures may have had their momentary successes against Cuban peasants and an unprepared Great Britain, but I tell you confidently they have no chance against an army of motivated Americans, driven by the indomitable American spirit and displaying the unshakable courage of all true Americans.

To us as a people it has been granted to lay the foundations of our national life on a new continent. We are the heirs of the ages, and yet we have had to pay few of the penalties which in old countries are exacted by the bygone hand of a dead civilization. We have not been obliged to fight for our existence against any alien challenge—until now. I believe we are up to the challenge, and I am convinced that you believe so too.

I am leaving for Miami tomorrow, and from there I will be departing for Cuba two days later, to lead my men into battle against however many of these creatures exist in the dank rotting jungles of that tropical island. I urge every red-blooded able-bodied American among you to join me on this greatest of adventures.

Letter to Kermit, Theodore Junior, Archie, and Quentin Roosevelt, August 5, 1898:

Dear Boys:

Tomorrow I embark on a great and exciting safari. I'm sure the details will be wired back to the newspapers on a daily basis, but I promise that when I return we'll sit around a campfire at Sagamore Hill and I'll tell you all the stories that the press never reported. Not only that, but I will bring back a trophy for each and every one of you.

School will be starting before I return. I expect each of you to go to class prepared for his lessons, and to apply your minds as vigorously as you apply your bodies to the games you play at home. Had I been slow of wit *or* of body I would not have survived my initial encounter with the creatures I shall be hunting in the coming days and weeks. Always remember that *balance* is the key in all things.

Love,
Father

Letter (#1,317) to Edith Carow Roosevelt, August 5, 1898:

My Dearest Edith:

My ship leaves tomorrow morning, so it will perhaps be some weeks before I have the opportunity to write to you again.

Shortly I shall be off on the greatest hunt of my life. Give my love to the children. I wish the boys were just a little bit older, so that I could take them along on what promises to be the most exciting endeavor of my life.

I am still trying to rid myself of the cold I picked up when I plunged into that river in Cuba, but other than that I feel fit as a bull moose. It will take a lot more than a strange beast and a runny nose to bring a true American to his knees. The coming days should be just bully!

Your Theodore

Percival Lowell

CANALS IN THE SAND

KEVIN J. ANDERSON

Under the sweltering heat of the Sahara, Percival Lowell stood beside his own tent at the center of the camp and reveled in the clamor of his vast construction site. The excavations extended beyond the vanishing point of the flat desert horizon. Thousands of sweating workers—who worked for mere pennies a day—moved like choreographed machinery as they dug monumental trenches according to Lowell's commands, scribing a long line in the sand.

Lowell had seen the same on Mars, long canals, straight lines extending thousands of miles across the rusted desert. His own observations had absolutely convinced him that such markings must be indicative of surface life on a dying world.

Other astronomers claimed not to see the network of canals, that the lines on the disk of Mars were not there. It reminded him of the trial of Galileo, when the high church officials and Pope Paul V had refused to see the moons of Jupiter through the astronomer's "optick glass," denying the evidence of their own eyes. Lowell couldn't decide if his own contemporaries were similarly bullheaded, or just plain blind.

He took a deep breath, ignoring the pounding sun. The fiery heat and dust and petroleum stench practically curled the hairs in his mustache. With recently washed hands, he fished inside the front pocket of his cream jacket and withdrew his special pair of pince-nez with lenses made of red-stained glass. Through the copper oxide tint, he could look out at the blistering and dead Sahara, seeing instead the scarlet sands of Mars. *Mars.*

How could one stand out here in the desert and not intuitively understand why the Martians would need to construct an extravagant set of canals to transport precious water from the melting ice caps down to their ancient cities? Water covered sixty percent of the Earth's surface, while Mars remained one vast planetary wasteland. The Martians' magnificent canals had endured as their world grew parched and withered with age, as their civilization mummified. By this time, those once glorious minds must be desperate, ready to grasp at any hope.

Lowell strolled out along the well-packed path from the encampment to the long ditch his army of workers had dug in the shifting sands. Compared to what the Martians had accomplished, it seemed a child's futile effort, and it certainly wouldn't endure long—but then Lowell's canal was not required to.

It must remain only long enough to send a signal.

If Ogilvy's calculations were correct, Lowell had little time. He prayed his Bedouin workers would be fast enough. But he vowed nothing would deter him. After all, he had built his great Arizona observatory in a mere six weeks from groundbreaking to first light. He could certainly handle digging a ditch, even if it was ten miles long out in the middle of the Sahara.

Night on Mars Hill in the Arizona Territory, at an elevation of seven thousand feet, with clear skies far from the smoke of men. The big refractor and the observatory dome had been completed just in time to allow observations of the 1894 opposition of Mars.

Lowell spent his every free moment at the telescope.

His fellow Bostonian William H. Pickering, an astronomer for Harvard, and his assistant Andrew Ellicott Douglass both stood inside the chill, echoing dome of the Flagstaff Observatory, waiting for Lowell to relinquish the eyepiece. The wooden-plank walls of the observatory dome exuded a resinous scent. From where he sat in the uncomfortable chair, porkpie hat turned backward on his head and sketch pad in his lap, Lowell could sense their impatience.

"It is *my* telescope, gentlemen, and *I* will do the observing," Lowell said, not removing his eye from the wavering disk of the ruddy world, where fine lines appeared and disappeared as the seeing shifted in the Earth's atmosphere.

"Mister Lowell, sir," Pickering said, clearing his throat, "I understand your eagerness to use the refractor, but *we* are your professional astronomers, with the proper qualifications—"

Lowell finally turned, feeling annoyance heat his skin. "Qualifications, Mr. Pickering? I have exceptionally keen eyesight—and an exceptionally large fortune, which has built this telescope and pays your stipend. Therefore I am fully qualified."

He snorted, looking down from his seat on the padded ladder and adjusting the porkpie hat on his head. "Perhaps if your Harvard had agreed to engage in a joint venture with me, Pickering, rather than calling me 'egoistic and unreasonable,' I would be more inclined to share. But instead, my own alma mater could not be convinced to do more than give you two gentlemen leave to work here, and then lease— *lease!*—me one of their small telescopes."

Douglass took a step back and looked to Pickering for his cue. Pickering, as always, cleared his throat and searched in vain for words.

Lowell's nostrils flared over his mustache. "You gentlemen are welcome to devote your nights to the study of the heavens at any other time, but this is *Mars* and it is at opposition. Please indulge this unworthy amateur." He turned back to the telescope, while the others shuffled their feet uncomfortably and continued to wait. Within moments, Lowell had become totally engrossed in the view, his universe shrunk down to the tiny circle visible through the eyepiece.

Tact was a commodity that served little purpose when time was short. Lowell had selected Pickering, in part, because of his successful studies of Mars in 1892 at Arequipa in Peru. Pickering, a decent though somewhat stuffy administrator, had spent the winter of '93 in Boston supervising the design and construction of this observatory, which had been shipped out piece by piece to Flagstaff the following spring. Every bit of the project was a rush, because Lowell demanded that the telescope absolutely must be functional by the time of the planetary opposition. Such a close encounter with Mars would not come again for many years.

Lowell drew a deep breath, shifted himself in his seat high above the observatory floor, and craned his neck. He fiddled with the eyepiece, and Mars stared back at him. He had the strangest sensation of being on the opposite end of a microscope, as if some immense being from across the cosmos were watching *him,* as someone with a microscope studied creatures that swarmed and multiplied in a drop of water.

His hands working independently, guided by the information channeled through the refractor tube, Lowell deftly sketched Mars, copying the lines he saw on the face of the planet. He had never been an armchair astronomer and would go blind before he ever allowed himself to be considered one. He and his staff had already recorded some four hundred canals on Mars—canals that other observers preposterously refused to see!

Lowell's outspoken beliefs had earned him much scorn, but no descendant of the great Boston family could remain quiet about deep convictions. In this case, and in many others, Percival Lowell knew he was right and the rest of the world was wrong—and he had proved it.

Well after midnight, his eyes burned. He flipped over the page in his sketch pad to where he had already scribed another perfect circle for a new map. Daylight hours were best used to prepare for the next clear night's observing.

Lowell noted that Douglass and Pickering had left unobtrusively, and he hoped they were at least doing work at the other telescopes, since the seeing was so extraordinary this evening. He blinked, oriented his hand and a newly sharpened pencil on the map pad, then pressed against the eyepiece again.

A brilliant green flash leaped from the surface of Mars.

Lowell barely restrained himself from crying out. The flame had been a vivid emerald, a jet of fire as of a great explosion or some kind of immense cannon shot, a huge mass of luminous gas, trailing a green mist behind it.

Once previously, Lowell had seen the glint of sunlight on the Martian ice caps, which had fooled him into seeing a dazzling message—but it had not been like this. Not so green, so violent, so prominent.

Before long he witnessed another green flash, and quickly noted the exact time on the pad in his lap. His excitement grew as he formulated his own explanation for the phenomenon. . . .

Several days later he received a telegram from Ogilvy, a prominent London astronomer, confirming the green flashes from Mars. Ogilvy himself had counted flashes on ten nights, while Lowell had recorded several others, which had occurred during the daylight hours in England.

Lowell knew exactly what the flashes must be, and he exhibited no reluctance whatsoever in telling others about his theories. Obviously, these brilliant flares were indications of stupendous launches, a fleet of ships exploding away from Martian gravity into space.

There could be no other explanation. The Martians were coming!

Work crews toiled day and night to move the sand: some complaining, some happy for the meager pay, some shaking their sweat-dripping heads at the insanity of this loud American and his incomprehensible obsession.

The Bedouins thought he was mad, as did many of Lowell's colleagues. But the superstitious Bedouins understood nothing of the universe . . . nor, for that matter, did most other astronomers.

He allowed no slacking in the construction for any reason. Shovels tossed sand up over the walls of the ditches; half-naked boys ran with ladles and buckets, while camels strained to drag barrels of warm water along the length of the dry canal. Lowell supervised here, and he could only hope that the other two trenches would be completed in time to intersect with this one.

When the teams grew too tired to continue, he hired more. Lowell had spread his funds as far as Cairo and Alexandria. He had bribed port officials, paid for the construction of a new railroad out into the desert, leading nowhere, so that a private train could deliver supplies and workers to Lowell's canals.

The sand hissed in the breeze, glittering in the sun. A drummer pounded a cadence to keep the workers in a steady rhythm, like galley slaves. But they were being paid for this labor, and they had volunteered, so Lowell felt no sympathy for them.

Smoke curled into the air, carrying an acrid, sulfurous stench as brown-skinned men dumped wagonloads of hot bitumen into the newly dug trench. The sticky black mass would hold the sands in place, bind them into a thick, flammable mass. Still the walls shifted, and the bitumen ran black and sticky in the heat of the day.

Grumbling, Lowell doubted the sloping walls of sand would hold if one of the great dust storms of the Sahara swept across the dunes. With one mighty breath, God could erase all of Lowell's handiwork, the fruits of years of labor and a squandered family fortune.

If only luck could hold until he sent his signal . . .

The great Suez Canal had been completed three decades earlier. For years the United States had discussed excavating a canal across Central America, as soon as the government found some way to grab the necessary land. Lowell's own project was not impossible. It could not be impossible.

He strutted up and down the edge of the ditch, a dusty bandanna wrapped over his mouth, nose, and mustache. He recalled the ancient Hebrew slaves, erecting immense monuments for the pharaohs. But the pharaohs had had decades, even generations, to complete their enormous projects. Lowell had no such luxury.

The line in the sand stretched into a shimmer of mirage in the wavering air. Just a ditch, many miles long, extending to meet two other ditches in what his surveyors guaranteed would be a perfect equilateral triangle.

Back home in Boston, leaving the Flagstaff Observatory in the hands of Pickering and Douglass for the autumn, Lowell had calculated the absolute limit of his financial resources, determining the largest excavation he could complete, since the governments of the world refused to help in what they called his "crackpot scheme."

And still Percival Lowell had accomplished little more than a gnat, compared to Martian accomplishments, even allowing for the fact that their task would have been simpler, given that Martian gravity was only a third of Earth's. He had postulated Martian beings, therefore, three times the size of a human; in their reduced gravity, such Martians could be twenty-one times as efficient and have eighty-one times the effective strength of an earthbound man. For such a species, the project of planetary canals seemed not unlikely.

Lowell's notebooks lay in the tent, but he had done the mathematics himself, letting the engineers double-check his work. Three trenches, each ten miles long, five yards wide, filled with liquid to a depth of an inch or so, equaled thousands and thousands of gallons of petroleum distillate, naphtha, kerosene. The convoys traveled endlessly across the Sahara: an impossible task, made possible—just barely—through the use of his great fortune.

It was a huge investment, but what better way could Lowell spend his money?

Douglass and Pickering had squawked when he had cut his generous allowance of funding for the Flagstaff Observatory down to a maintenance stipend. "How are we to continue our research?" their plaintive telegram had wailed.

"Come to the Sahara," he had replied, "and I will show you."

If Lowell succeeded in signaling the Martians, here and now, astronomical observatories around the world would never again lack for funding.

But they had to hurry. Hurry.

A blustery man, not intimidated by challenge, Lowell nevertheless found himself stuttering in awe when he met in Milan with the great

Giovanni Schiaparelli—discoverer of asteroids and the original cartographer of the canals of Mars.

After spotting the green flashes, then laying plans for his great project to signal back to the Martians, Lowell had allotted himself half a year to travel to Europe and generate support. He had taken a first-class cabin on a steamer bound for England. Reaching London, he had sought out Ogilvy and immediately enlisted his aid.

The other astronomer had at first been skeptical that there could be any living thing on that remote, forbidding planet. Lowell, however, had been very persuasive.

Obtaining leave from his observatory, Ogilvy accompanied Lowell on his travels. Ogilvy's friend, a journalist named Wells, also asked to travel with them in hopes of getting a good story for his newspaper, but Lowell would have none of it. The newspapers had resoundingly ridiculed Lowell's theories about the Martian canals, and he wanted nothing further to do with reporters, not in the initial stages of a project of such importance.

The two men proceeded across the Channel and thence to Paris for an excellent dinner and conversation with the well-known French writer and astronomer Camille Flammarion, who gave Lowell's idea a favorable reception. He beamed with pleasure to hear the Frenchman proclaim that Lowell's own theories about the canals and life on Mars had been "ascertained indubitably."

By train and private carriage, Lowell and a wide-eyed Ogilvy—who had never previously visited the Continent—traveled to Italy to meet with Schiaparelli in his small villa.

Schiaparelli had been director of the Milan Observatory since 1862, where he had discovered the asteroid Hesperia, written a brilliant treatise on comets and meteors, and created his original maps of the Martian *canali* in 1877, only a year after Lowell himself had graduated with honors from Harvard. During that same opposition, the American astronomer Asaph Hall had discovered the two tiny moons of Mars, Phobos and Deimos—Fear and Dread. But using only an eight-inch telescope, Schiaparelli had exposed a more profound cosmic secret.

"When I originally drew my maps," the old astronomer said, struggling with his English, "I meant to represent the lines merely as channels or cracks in the surface. I understand that *canali* implies a different thing to non-Italian ears, suggesting man-made canals—"

"Not *man*-made," Lowell interrupted, extracting his pipe from its case and tamping a load of sweet tobacco from his pouch, "but made by intelligent beings, whose minds may be immeasurably superior to ours. Extraterrestrial life does not mean extraterrestrial human life. Under changed conditions, life itself must take on other forms."

"Yes, yes." Schiaparelli nodded, took a sip of his deep red wine, then a bigger gulp. He blinked his rheumy eyes. "But your subsequent observations have convinced even me, my friend."

Lowell leaned forward intently, lacing his fingers together over his knees. "I wish you could see what I have seen on the red disk of the Great God of War, Schiaparelli. Such wonders."

The old astronomer sighed. His rooms were filled with books, oil lamps, and melted lumps of candles in terra-cotta dishes. A pair of spectacles lay on an open tome, while an enormous magnifying glass rested in easy reach on another stack of books.

"I can only imagine them. My own eyesight has grown so poor that I must now occupy my mind and my time with the study of history. Though I can no longer study comets or meteors or planets, even an old man with dim vision can make astute observations of history."

"Tell him about Mars, Lowell, my good man," Ogilvy said, searching for something else to eat, and finally settling on some water crackers and old cheese left out on the sideboard in the Italian's dim rooms.

Lowell opened his mind's eye wide as he spoke in an oddly quiet and reverent voice, totally distinct from his usual booming, commanding tone. Thoughts of Mars still made him breathless with astonishment.

"You drew the canals yourself, Schiaparelli—narrow dark lines of uniform width and intensity, perfectly straight. Some even compose portions of great circles across the globe. As I view them from Flagstaff in my best refractor, they look to be gossamer filaments, cobwebs on the face of the Martian disk, threads to draw your mind after them, across millions of miles of intervening void."

Schiaparelli rubbed his eyes. "In my youth I, myself, never conceived them to be more than blemishes."

Lowell raised his eyebrows dubiously. "Geometrical precision on a planetary scale? What else can it be but the mark of an intelligent race? If we could respond in kind, would we not be morally obligated to do so, in the name of humanity?"

Ogilvy coughed on his cracker and looked about for something to drink, finally settling on a wicker-wrapped bottle of Chianti that Schiaparelli had opened for them. He poured sloppily into a glass on the sideboard, then took a quick swallow, only to renew his coughing fit. Lowell scowled at the British astronomer for shattering his spell of imagination.

He puffed on his pipe and settled back in the fine leatherbound chair.

Outside on the open balcony, pigeons fluttered in the sunlight. Schiaparelli still watched him with an intent stare. Ogilvy began to page through one of the open history books.

"Imagine it, Schiaparelli," Lowell continued. "Think of a parched, dying world inhabited by a once marvelous civilization, beings with the science and ingenuity to keep themselves alive at all costs. Why, the very existence of a planetwide system of canals implies a world order that knows no national boundaries, a society that long ago forgot its political disputes and racial animosity, uniting the populace in a desperate quest for water. Water . . ."

"And the dark spots, Lowell?" Ogilvy asked, turning back to the conversation. Schiaparelli drank more of his Chianti, amused and fascinated by the description. "Tell him about the oases."

Lowell stood up to stretch, placed his hands behind his back, and turned to the balcony to watch the pigeons. "Pumping stations, obviously."

The old Italian astronomer stared at where the walls of his villa met the ceiling, but he seemed to see nothing, perhaps only a blur with his used-up eyes. Lowell felt a rare flash of sympathy—losing one's eyesight must be the greatest hell a dedicated astronomer could imagine.

"But if Mars is so arid, Lowell, surely all the water would evaporate from these open canals long before it reaches its destination . . . if the temperature is much above freezing, that is—and it *must* be above freezing in order for the water to be in its liquid state." Schiaparelli's forehead creased in a frown.

Ogilvy piped up, pacing the room. "And don't forget, my good man, the astronomical distances involved. If these canals were simple waterways or aqueducts, we would never be able to see them from Earth. They would be much too narrow. How do you account for that?"

Annoyed, Lowell turned to the Englishman. He and Ogilvy had already had this discussion in earnest several times, and again on the train ride to Milan. But he saw Ogilvy's raised eyebrow and understood that the other man had raised the question just to give Lowell a chance to explain.

"Ah, there is a simple answer for both questions," Lowell said, then paused to draw deeply from his pipe. "Almost certainly the lines we see are aqueducts with lush vegetation growing in irrigated croplands along the borders. The only remaining forests on Mars, towering high in the low gravity, sipping precious water from the fertile soil—much as the Egyptians grow their crops in the plains around the Nile. I estimate the darkened fringes of the aqueducts to be about thirty miles wide. This vegetation would not only emphasize the lines of the canals, but would also shield the open water from rapid evaporation. Simple, you see? It is quite clear."

Ogilvy nodded, and Schiaparelli gave a distant smile. The old astronomer seemed more amused than impassioned by the concepts. Lowell came closer to his host, barely controlling his own enthusiasm. "My proposed plan follows a similar principle, Schiaparelli. The project I have conceived will take place on a much smaller scale, naturally, since I am but one man and, alas, our own earthly civilization has no stomach for such dreams.

"I have already dispatched surveyors and work teams to the Sahara, in the flat desert in western Egypt. I will excavate three canals of my own, each ten miles long, across an otherwise featureless basin, to form a perfect equilateral triangle. A geometrical symbol impossible to explain with random natural processes, and therefore a clear message that intelligent life inhabits this world. To make them more visible, I must emphasize my puny canals with lines of fire, by filling the trenches with petroleum products and igniting them. It will be a brief but dramatic message, blazing into the night." His eyes sparkled, his voice rose in volume.

"But why this tremendous effort, my friend?" Schiaparelli asked. "Why now?"

Promptly, he and Ogilvy described the repeated green flashes, the launches of enormous vehicles, ships sent to Earth. Based on Ogilvy's observations and calculations derived from a careful scrutiny of celestial mechanics, Lowell believed he knew the travel time the Martians required to reach Earth.

Lowell's voice became husky. "As you can see, the Martians are on their way. We must show them where to land, where they will meet with an openhearted welcome from earthbound admirers of their past triumphs and their current travails."

Lowell took a deep breath and spoke with absolute confidence. "Gentlemen, I intend to lead that party. I will be the first man to shake hands with a Martian."

Finally.

Finally. Lowell had never been a man of extraordinary patience, but the last week of waiting for the three trenches to join at precise corners had been the most interminable time of his life.

Now, under the starlight and the residual heat that wafted off the baked sands, Lowell stood with his torch in hand, feeling like a tribal shaman, ready to ignite his weapon against the darkness, his symbol of welcome to aliens from another world.

The stench of petroleum distillates stung his eyes and nostrils. The chemical smell had driven off the camels and most of the workers, save those few foremen—mostly Europeans—who intended to watch the spectacle. On high dunes in the distance, the curious Bedouins had gathered by their own tents to observe. This would be an event for their storytellers to repeat for generations.

Working with his reluctant assistants, Pickering and Douglass, Lowell had gone to a great deal of trouble to calculate the best time when the Sahara night would face Mars, so that his transient shout into the universe had the best chance of being seen—if not from the inbound Martian emissary ships, then from those survivors who had remained on the red planet.

Lowell turned to the telegraph operator beside him. Miles of overland cable had been run to the other vertices of the great triangle in the sand, so that the teams could communicate with each other. "Signal Pickering and Douglass at the other two intersections. Tell them to light their channels."

The telegraph operator pecked away at his key, sending a brief message. When the clicks fell into silence, Lowell stepped to the brink of his canal in the sand. He stared down into the bitumen-lined trench, the foul-smelling black mass that was now pooled with kerosene and gasoline dumped from enormous tanks that had been hauled across the desert by his private railroad.

Lowell tossed his torch into the fuel, then watched the fire spread like a hungry demon, rushing down the channel. The inferno devoured the dumped petroleum, hot enough to ignite the sticky bitumen liner so that the triangular symbol would burn for a long time.

Across the desert into the night, rifle shots rang out, signaling to other torchbearers stationed along the ten miles of each canal, who also tossed their burning brands into the ditch so that the fire could engulf the entire triangle. Martians and fire, Lowell thought—what a strange combination.

Lowell's family had already made its mark on the world. Towns had been named after the Lowells and the Lawrences; his maternal grandfather was Abbott Lawrence, minister to Britain. His father, Augustus Lowell, was descended from the early Massachusetts colonists. His family had amassed its fortune in textiles, in landholdings, in finance. But Percival himself would make the greatest mark—on *two* worlds instead of one.

An unbroken wall of flame roared up into the night. He prayed the Martians were watching. He had so much to say to them.

Lowell found it difficult to sleep even long after the inferno had died down. He lay on his cot in his tent, smelling the dying smoke and harsh fumes, listening to the whisper of settling sand sloughing into the bottom of the trench from the burned walls. Far off in the Bedouin camp a pair of camels belched at each other.

In only a year or two, the shifting desert would erase most of his line in the sand, leaving only a dark scar. But if his intended audience received the message, Earth would be a dramatically changed place in that time, and his effort would not be in vain.

Lowell found his situation incredibly strange: he, a wealthy Boston Brahmin, now resting fitfully in an austere tent in the middle of a vast desert that had been made even more unpleasant by his own construction work.

Summoning images of beauty to his mind, he recalled his experiences in Japan, as much an alien world as this Sahara, perhaps even as alien as Mars. He thought of colors bright as enamel and lacquer, gold filigree and cloisonné, the heady perfumes of peonies and burning incense. He remembered being escorted along narrow avenues of carefully tended trees where an explosion of white petals drifted on the winds for the annual cherry blossom festival. He recalled the delicate ritual of a tea ceremony, and the thin atonal melody plucked out on a *biwa* as spiced morsels sizzled on a small hibachi.

During those years as ambassador to Japan, Lowell had lugged his six-inch refractor with him, staring, staring, seeing the Earth but watching the stars. . . .

He had graduated from Harvard with distinction in mathematics at the age of twenty-one, and he had received the Bowdoin Prize for his essay, "The Rank of England as a European Power Between the Death of Elizabeth and the Death of Anne." He had traveled the world, studied the classics, experienced numerous foreign cultures, proved his facility in languages, even tried to join the fighting in the Serbo-Turkish War. What did he care that mere astronomers scorned his ideas?

Lowell had sailed for Japan in 1883, where he was asked to serve as foreign secretary for a special diplomatic mission from Korea to the United States—though at the time he had never even seen Korea. Returning to Tokyo, he had later been asked to help write Japan's new constitution.

Lying sleepless on his cot, he spoke aloud to the apex of his tent, where the canvas rippled in a faint breeze. "I have experience as an ambassador to foreign cultures. I have diplomatic credentials. How could the Martians be stranger than what I have already seen?"

The cylinder screamed through the air with the wailing of a thousand lost souls, trailing behind it a tongue of fire from atmospheric friction and a bright green mist from outgassing extraterrestrial substances.

Lowell burst out of his shaded tent to see the commotion under the midday sun. A burnt smudge of smoke smoldered like a scar across the ceramic-blue sky. Booms of sound thundered in waves as the gigantic ship/projectile crossed overhead.

"It's the emissaries from Mars!" Lowell shouted, raising his hands in the air. "The Martians!"

Like an exploding warship, the cylinder crashed into the desert with a spewed plume of sand and dust. Lowell felt the tremor of impact in his knees, despite the cushioning desert. He laughed aloud, yelling for Douglass and Pickering to join him.

After the burning of the enormous triangle, most of the workers had returned to their widely scattered lands, leaving only a few team bosses to tidy up the loose ends of the construction. Lowell had sold his now useless railroad for scrap steel, giving the salvagers a decent percentage of the profits. The place rapidly turned into a ghost town, which some of the European bosses had quietly begun calling "Lowell's Folly." Pickering and Douglass had returned from the other two base camps to join him here. To wait . . .

Now, as the dust settled in the distance, the other two astronomers ran up, their faces ruddy with sunburn and excitement. "We are vindicated!" Lowell cried. He clapped them each on the shoulder. "The Martians are here!"

The remaining Bedouin helpers fled the camp in panic, thrashing their camels to an awkward gallop across the dunes. *Idiots,* he thought. *Fools.* They did not realize the honor that had been bestowed here.

"The world as we know it is about to change. Come, let us put together an expedition. We must welcome our visitors from space."

The heat from the pit rose up in a tremendous wave, overwhelming even the blistering daytime pounding of the Sahara. Pickering dropped back, coughing, but Lowell plodded forward, hunched over, shielding his watering eyes. On an impulse, he reached into the pocket of his cream-colored suit jacket and withdrew his bright red spectacles, placing them over his eyes, seeing the world as a Martian would, the better to understand them.

Because of the residual heat, he could not get close to the crash site, and he felt a terrible dread that the Martian ship had exploded when it struck the ground, that all the interplanetary ambassadors had been obliterated by fire.

But then he heard faint pounding sounds within the metal-walled cylinder, mechanical noises, a soft unscrewing. . . .

Finally, Douglass dragged him back. "It's too hot, Mister Lowell! We must wait."

With savage disappointment, Lowell stumbled away, keeping his head turned to stare at the smoldering crater through his red-lensed spectacles. "I have waited years for this moment. I can tolerate a few more hours—but not much longer than that."

His eyes stinging from tears not entirely caused by the blistering heat, he followed the other two men back to the main camp.

Douglass fetched some water, toiletries, and fresh clothes after sweaty hours spent in the dim shelter of their tents. He and Pickering ate ravenously of a quickly prepared meal, though Lowell himself felt no hunger. His stomach tied itself in knots as he felt his life's work coming to its climax.

Lowell used some of the tepid water to shave, leaning over a small mirror. Then he changed into a fine new suit and straightened his collar, keeping his gaze intent on the still-glowing pit visible through the propped-open tent flap. Finally, in the cool of the desert night, he told his two companions to wait behind.

"You can't go alone, man," Pickering said, after clearing his throat again.

"Nonsense." Lowell brushed the other astronomer's grasp from his arm. "It was my money that brought the Martians to this landing site, and I claim the right."

"That's the same argument you used with your damned telescope," Pickering muttered, but did not pursue the discussion. Douglass hunkered down, looking forlorn.

Lowell strode across the surrounding dunes in his black leather shoes, mulling over an appropriate speech, wondering if by some miracle the Martians might speak English. No matter, he thought. He had a knack for languages, and would manage to communicate somehow.

Looking dapper, he approached the edge of the pit. He noted with fascination that the heat of the impact had been great enough to fuse some of the sand grains into lumps of glass. If the Martians could survive that, they must be prime specimens indeed.

He stood on the brink, looking down into the glow that lit up the crater as if it were day. A long shiny lid had been unscrewed from the large pitted cylinder and lay on the blasted sands. Below, he saw clanking machines stirring, odd tentacled creatures moving about, exhibiting an industriousness no doubt born of their dire circumstances on Mars. Most remarkable, he saw, was a tall, newly assembled construction rising up on stiltlike tripod legs. The heat was still incredible.

Magnificent! Lowell felt proud and overwhelmed to be mankind's emissary. Now that they had reached Earth, though, the poor Martians could be saved.

Lowell hurried forward to greet the Martians. The wonders of the universe awaited him.

Dowager Empress of China

FOREIGN DEVILS

WALTER JON WILLIAMS

There is no longer anyone alive who knows her name.

She has always been known by her titles, titles related to the role she was expected to play. When she was sixteen and had been chosen as a minor concubine for the Son of Heaven, she had been called Lady Yehenara, because she was born in the Yehe tribe of the Nara clan of the great Manchu race. Later, after her husband died and she assumed the regency for their son, she was given the title Tzu Hsi, Empress of the West, because she once lived in a pavilion on the western side of the Forbidden City.

But no one alive knows her real name, the milk-name her mother had given her almost sixty-five years ago, the name she had answered to when she was young and happy and free from care. Her real name is unimportant.

Only her position matters, and it is a lonely one.

She lives in a world of imperial yellow. The wall hangings are yellow, the carpets are yellow, and she wears a gown of crackling yellow brocade. She sleeps on yellow brocade sheets, and rests her head on pillows of yellow silk beneath embroidered yellow bed curtains.

Now Peking is on fire, and the hangings of yellow silk are stained with the red of burning.

She rises from her bed in the Hour of the Rat, a little after midnight. Her working day, and that of the Emperor, begins early.

A eunuch braids her hair while her ladies—all of them young, and all of them in gowns of blue—help her to dress. She wears a yellow satin gown embroidered with pink flowers, and a cape ornamented with four thousand pearls. The eunuch expertly twists her braided hair into a topknot, and fits over it a headdress made of jade adorned on either side with fresh flowers. Gold sheaths protect the two long fingernails of her right hand, and jade sheaths protect the two long fingernails of her left. Her prize black lion dogs frolic around her feet.

The smell of burning floats into the room, detectable above the scent of her favorite Nine-Buddha incense. The burning scent imparts a certain urgency to the proceedings, but her toilette cannot be completed in haste.

At last she is ready. She calls for her sedan chair and retinue—Li Lien-Ying, the Chief Eunuch, the Second Chief Eunuch, four Eunuchs of the Fifth Rank, twelve Eunuchs of the Sixth Rank, plus eight more eunuchs to carry the chair.

"Take me to the Emperor's apartments," she says.

The sedan chair swoops gently upward as the eunuchs lift it to their shoulders. As she leaves her pavilion, she hears the sound of the sentries saluting her as she passes.

They are not *her* sentries. These elite troops of the Tiger-Hunt Marksmen are not here to keep anyone *out*. They are in the employ of ambitious men, and the guards serve only to keep her a prisoner in her own palace.

Despite her titles, despite the blue-clad ladies and the eunuchs and the privileges, despite the silk and brocade and pearls, the Empress of the West is a captive. She can think of no way that she can escape.

The litter's yellow brocade curtains part for a moment, and the Empress catches a brief glimpse of the sky. There is Mars, glowing high in the sky like a red lantern, and below it streaks a falling star, a beautiful ribbon of imperial yellow against the velvet night. It streaks east to west, and then is gone.

Perhaps, she thinks, it is a hopeful sign.

———

The audience room smells of burning. Yellow brocade crackles as the members of the family council perform their ritual kowtows before the Son of Heaven. Before they present their petitions to the Emperor they pause, as they realize from his flushed face and sudden intake of breath that he is having an orgasm as he sits in his dragon-embroidered robes upon his yellow-draped chair.

The Emperor Kuang Hsu is twenty-eight years old and has suffered from severe health problems his entire life. Sometimes, in moments of tension, he succumbs to a sudden fit of orgasm. The doctors claim it is the result of a kidney malady, but no matter how many Kidney Rectifying Pills the Emperor is made to swallow, his condition never improves.

The illness is sometimes embarrassing, but the family has become accustomed to it.

After the Emperor's breathing returns to normal, Prince Jung Lu presents his petition. "Your Majesty," he says, "for three days the Righteous Harmony Fists have rioted in the Tatar City and the Chinese City. There are no less than thirty thousand of these disreputable scoundrels in Peking. They have set fire to the home of Grand Secretary Hsu Tung and to many others. Grand Secretary Sun Chia-nai has been assaulted and robbed. As the Supreme Ones of the past safeguarded the tranquillity of the realm by issuing edicts to suppress rebellion and disorder, and as the Righteous Harmony Fists have shown themselves violent, disorderly, and disrespectful of Your Majesty's servants, I hope that an edict from Your Majesty will soon be forthcoming that allows this unworthy person to use the Military Guards Army to suppress disorder."

Prince Tuan spits tobacco into his pocket spittoon. "I beg the favor of disagreeing with the esteemed prince," he says. Other officials, members of his Iron Hat Faction, murmur their agreement.

The Dowager Empress, sitting on her yellow cushion next to the Emperor, looks from one to the other, and feels only despair.

Jung Lu has been her friend from childhood. He is a moderate and sensible man, but the situation that envelops them all is neither moderate nor sensible.

It is Prince Tuan, a younger man, bulky in his brocade court costume and with the famous Shangfang Sword strapped to his waist, who is in command of the situation. He and his allies—Tuan's brother Duke Lan, Prince Chuang of the Gendarmerie, the Grand Councillor Kang I, Chao Shu-chiao of the Board of Punishments—form the core of those Iron Hats who had seized power two years ago, at the end of the Hundred Days' Reform.

It is Tuan who has surrounded the Dragon Throne with his personal army of ten thousand Tiger-Hunt Marksmen. It is Tuan who controls the ferocious Muslim cavalry of General Tung, his ally, camped in the gardens south of the city. It is Tuan who extorted the honor of carrying the Shangfang Sword in the imperial presence, and with it the right to use the sword to execute anyone on the spot, for any reason. And it is Tuan's son, Pu Chun, who has been made heir to the throne.

It is Prince Tuan, and the others of his Iron Hat Faction, who have encouraged the thousands of martial artists and spirit warriors of the Righteous Harmony Fists to invade Peking, to attack Chinese Christians and others against whom they have a grudge, and who threaten to envelop China in a war with all the foreign powers at once.

The young Emperor Kuang Hsu opens his mouth but cannot say a word. He has a bad stammer, and in stressful situations he cannot speak at all.

Prince Tuan fills the silence. "I am certain that should the Son of Heaven deign to address us, he would assure us of his confidence in the patriotism and loyalty of the Righteous Harmony Fists. His Majesty knows that any disorders are incidental, and that the Righteous Harmony Fists are united in their desire to rid the Middle Kingdom of the Foreign Devils that oppress our nation. In the past," he continues, getting to his point—for in the Imperial Court, one always presented conclusions by invoking the past—"In the past, the great rulers of the Middle Kingdom established order in their dominions by calling upon their loyal subjects to do away with foreign influences and causes of disorder. If His Majesty will only issue an edict to this effect, the Righteous Harmony Fists can use their martial powers and their invincible magic to sweep the Foreign Devils from our land."

The Emperor attempts again to speak and again fails. This time it is the Dowager Empress who fills the silence.

"Will such an edict not bring us to war with all the Foreign Devils at once? We have never been able to hold off even one foreign power at a time. The white ghosts of England and France, and even lately the dwarf-bandits of Japan, have all won concessions from us."

Prince Tuan scowls, and his hand tightens on the Shangfang Sword. "The Righteous Harmony Fists are not members of the imperial forces. They are merely righteous citizens stirred to anger by the actions of the Foreign Devils and the Secondary Foreign Devils, the Christian converts. The government cannot be held responsible for their actions. And besides—the Righteous Harmony Fists are invulnerable. You have seen yourself, a few weeks ago, when I brought one of their members into this room and fired a pistol straight at him. He was not harmed."

The Empress of the West falls silent as clouds of doubt enter her mind. She had seen the pistol fired, and the man had taken no hurt. It had been an impressive demonstration.

"I regret to report to the Throne," Jung Lu says, "of an unfortunate incident in the city. The German ambassador, Von Ketteler, personally opened fire on a group of Righteous Harmony Fists peacefully exercising in the open. He killed seven and wounded many more."

"An outrage!" Prince Tuan cries.

"Truly," Jung Lu says, "but unfortunately the Righteous Harmony Fists proved somewhat less than invulnerable to Von Ketteler's bullets. Perhaps their invincibility has been overstated."

Prince Tuan glares sullenly at Jung Lu. He bites his lip, then says, "It is the fault of wicked Chinese Christian women. The Secondary Foreign Devils flaunted their naked private parts through windows, and the Righteous Harmony Fists lost their strength."

There is a thoughtful pause as the others absorb this information. And then the Emperor opens his mouth again.

The Emperor has, for the moment, mastered his speech impediment, though his gaunt young face is strained with effort and there are long, breathy pauses between each word. "Our subjects depend on the Dragon Throne for their safety," he gasps. "Prince Jung Lu is ordered to restore order in the city and to stand between the foreign legations and the Righteous Harmony Fists . . . to prevent further incidents."

Kuang Hsu falls back on his yellow cushions, exhausted from the effort to speak. "The Son of Heaven is wise," Jung Lu says.

"Truly," says Prince Tuan, his eyes narrowing.

Using appropriate formal language, and of course invoking the all-important precedents from the past, court scribes write the edict in Manchu, then translate the words into Chinese. The Dowager Empress holds the Chinese translation to her failing eyes and reads it with care. As a female, she had not been judged worthy of education until she had been chosen as an imperial concubine. She has never learned more than a few hundred characters of Chinese, and is unable to read Manchu at all.

But whether she can read and write or not, her position as Dowager Empress gives her the power of veto over any imperial edict. It is important that she view any document personally.

"Everything is in order," she ventures to guess.

The Imperial Seal Eunuch inks the heavy Imperial Seal and presses it to the edict, and with ceremony the document is presented to Prince Jung Lu. Prince Tuan draws himself up and speaks. "This unworthy subject must beg the Throne for permission to deal with this German, Von Ketteler. This white ghost is killing Chinese at random, for his own amusement, and in the confused circumstances none can be blamed if there is an accident."

The Empress of the West and the Emperor exchange quick glances. Perhaps, thinks the Empress, it is best to let Prince Tuan win a point. It may assuage his bloodlust for the moment.

And she very much doubts anyone will miss the German ambassador.

She tilts her head briefly, an affirmative gesture. The Emperor's eyes flicker as he absorbs her import.

"We leave it to you," he says. It is a ritual form of assent, the Throne's formal permission for an action to take place.

"The Supreme One's brilliance and sagacity exceeds all measure," says Prince Tuan.

The family council ends. The royal princes make their kowtows and leave the chamber.

The Dowager Empress leaves her chair and approaches her nephew, the Emperor. He seems shrunken in his formal dragon robes—he has twenty-eight sets of robes altogether, one auspicious for each day of the lunar month. Tenderly the Dowager dabs sweat from his brow with a handkerchief. He reaches into his sleeve for a lighter and a packet of Turkish cigarettes.

"We won't win, you know," he sighs. His stammer has disappeared along with his formidable, intimidating relations. "If we couldn't beat the Japanese dwarf-bandits, we can't beat anybody. We're just going to lose more territory to the Foreign Devils, just as we've already lost Burma, Nepal, Indochina, Taiwan, Korea, Hong Kong, all the treaty ports we've had to cede to Foreign Devils. . . ."

"You don't believe the spirit fighters' magic will help us?"

The Emperor laughs and draws on his cigarette. "Cheap tricks to impress peasants. I have seen that bullet-catching trick done by conjurors."

"We must delay. Delay as long as possible. If we delay, the correct path may become clearer."

The Emperor flicks cigarette ash off his yellow sleeve. His tone is bitter. "Delay is the only possible course for those who have no power. Very well. We will delay as long as possible. But delay the war or not, we will still lose."

Tears well in the old woman's eyes. It is all, she knows, her fault.

Her husband, the Emperor, had died of grief after losing the Second Opium War to the Foreign Devils. Their child was only an infant at the time. She did her best to bring up her son, engaging the most rigorous and moral of teachers, but after reigning for only a few years her son had died at the age of eighteen from exhaustion brought on by unending sexual dissipation.

Since then she has devoted her life to caring for her nephew, the new Emperor. She had rescued Kuang Hsu from her sister, who had beaten him savagely and starved him—one of his brothers had actually been starved to death—but she had erred again in choosing the young Emperor's companions. He had been so bullied by eunuchs, so plagued by ill health, and so intimidated by his tutors and the blustering royal princes, that he had remained shy, hesitant, and self-conscious. He had only acted decisively once, two years ago, during the Hundred Days' Reform, and that had ended badly, with the palace surrounded by Prince Tuan's Tiger-Hunt Marksmen and the Emperor held captive.

"I will leave Your Majesty to rest," she says. He looks at her, not unkindly.

"Thank you, Mother," he says.

Tears prickle the Dowager's eyes. Even though she has betrayed him, still he calls her "mother" instead of "aunt."

She walks from the room, and with her twenty-four attending eunuchs returns to her palace.

Alone in the darkness of the litter, no one sees the tears that patter on the yellow brocade cushions.

"All the news is good," Prince Tuan says. "One of our soldiers, a Manchu bannerman named Enhai, has shot the German ambassador outside the Tsungli Yamen. Admiral Seymour's Foreign Devils, marching up the railway line from Tientsin, have turned back after a battle with the Righteous Harmony Fists."

"I had heard the Righteous Harmony Fists had all been killed," says Jung Lu. "Where was their bullet-catching magic?"

"Their magic was sufficient to turn back Admiral Seymour," Prince Tuan retorts.

"He may have just gone back for reinforcements. More and more foreign warships are appearing off Tientsin."

It is the Hour of the Ox, just before dawn. Several days have passed since Prince Jung Lu was ordered to seal off the foreign legations. This has reduced the number of incidents in the city, though the Foreign Devils continue their distressing habit of shooting any Chinese they see, sometimes using machine guns on crowds. Since no one is attacking them, the foreigners' behavior is puzzling. Jung Lu sent several peace delegations to inquire their reasons, but the delegates had all been shot down as soon as they appeared in sight of the legations. Jung Lu has been forced to admit that the foreigners may no longer be behaving rationally.

"In the past," Prince Tuan says, "Heaven made known its wishes through the movements of the stars and planets and through portents displayed in the skies. This unworthy servant reminds the Throne that this is a year with an extra intercalary month, and therefore a year that promises unusual occurrences. This is also a Kengtze year, which occurs only every ten years. Therefore the heavens demonstrate the extraordinary nature of this year, and require that all inhabitants of the Earth assist Heaven in creating extraordinary happenings."

"I have not heard that Kengtze years were lucky for the Pure Dynasty," Jung Lu remarks. But Prince Tuan doesn't even slow down.

"There are other indications that war is at hand," he says. "The red planet Mars is high in the heavens, and the ancients spoke truly when they declared, 'When Mars is high, prepare for war and civil strife; when Mars sinks below the horizon, send the soldiers home.'

"But there is another indication more decisive than any of these. Heaven has declared its will by dropping meteors upon the Middle Kingdom. Three falling stars have landed outside of Tientsin. Another three landed south of the capital near Yungtsing. According to the office of Telegraph Sheng, three have also landed in Shantung, three more southwest of Shanghai, and three near Kwangtung."

The Dowager Empress and the Emperor exchange glances. Several of these falling meteors have been observed from the palace, and their significance discussed. But reports of meteors landing in threes throughout eastern China are new.

"Heaven is declaring its will!" Prince Tuan says. "The meteors have all landed near places where there are large concentrations of Foreign Devils! Obviously Heaven wishes us to exterminate these vermin!"

Tuan gives a triumphant laugh and draws the Shangfang Sword. The Emperor turns pale and shrinks into his heavy brocade robes.

"I demand an edict from the Dragon Throne!" Tuan shouts. "Let the Son of Heaven command that all Foreign Devils be killed!"

The Emperor tries to speak, but terror has plainly seized his tongue. Choosing her words carefully, the Dowager Empress speaks in his place. *Delay*, she thinks.

"We will consult the auspices and act wisely in accordance with their wishes."

Prince Tuan gives a roar of anger and brandishes the sword. "No more delay! Heaven has made its will clear! If you don't issue the edicts, I'll do it myself!"

There is a moment of horrified silence. The Emperor's face turns stony as he looks at Prince Tuan. Sweat pops onto his brow with the effort to control his tongue.

"W-w-why," he stammers, "don't you go k-k-k-kill yourself?"

There is another moment of silence. Prince Tuan coldly forces a smile onto his face.

"The Son of Heaven makes a very amusing witticism," he says.

And then, at swordpoint, he commands the Imperial Seal Eunuch to bring out the heavy seal that will confirm his edicts.

Watching, the Dowager Empress's heart floods with sorrow.

It is the Hour of the Tiger, two days after Prince Tuan seized control. A red dawn provides a scarlet blush to the yellow hangings. Tuan and his allies confer before the Dragon Throne. Tuan has brought his son, the imperial heir Pu Chun, to watch his father as he commands the fate of China. The boy spends most of his time practicing martial arts, pretending to skewer Foreign Devils with his sword.

The Emperor, disgusted, smokes a cigarette behind a wall hanging. No one bothers to ask his opinion of the edicts that are going out under his seal.

The Righteous Harmony Fists have all been drafted into the army and sent to reinforce General Nieh standing between Tientsin and the capital. Governors have been ordered to defend their provinces against attack. Jung Lu's army has been ordered to wipe out the foreigners in the legation quarter, but so far he has found reason to delay.

Can China fight the whole world? the Dowager Empress wonders.

But she sits on her yellow cushion, and smokes her water pipe, and plays with her little lion dogs while she pretends unconcern. It is all she can do.

A messenger arrives and hands to Jung Lu a pair of messages from the office of Telegraph Sheng, and Jung Lu reads them with a puzzled expression. He approaches the Empress, leans close, and speaks in a low tone.

"The Foreign Devils off Tientsin have ordered our troops to evacuate the Taku Forts by midnight—that is midnight yesterday, so the ultimatum has already expired."

Anxiety grips the Empress's heart. "Can our troops hold the forts?"
Jung Lu frowns. "Their record is not good."

If the Taku Forts fall, the Empress knows, Tientsin will fall. And once
Tientsin falls, it is but a short march from there to Peking. It has all
happened before.

Sick at heart, the Empress remembers the headlong flight from the
capital during the Second Opium War, how her happy, innocent little
lion dogs had been thrown down wells rather than let the Foreign
Devils capture them.

It is going to happen again, she thinks.

Prince Tuan marches toward them. Hearing his steps, Jung Lu's face
turns to a mask. He hides the first message in his sleeve.

"This unworthy servant hopes the mighty commander of the Military Guards Army will share his news," Tuan says.

Jung Lu hands Tuan the second of the two messages. "Confused
news of fighting south of Tientsin. Some towns have been destroyed—
the message says by monsters that rode to earth on meteors, but obviously the message was confused. Perhaps he meant to say that meteors
have landed on some towns."

"Were they Christian towns?" Tuan asks. "Perhaps Heaven's vengeance is falling on the Secondary Foreign Devils. There are many
Christians around Tientsin."

"The message does not say."

Prince Tuan looks at the message and spits into his pocket spittoon.
"It probably doesn't matter," he says.

It is the Hour of the Snake. Bright morning sun blazes on the room's
yellow hangings. A lengthy dispatch has arrived from the office of Telegraph Sheng. Prince Tuan reads it, then laughs and swaggers toward
the captive Emperor.

"This miserable one regrets to report to the Throne that last night
an allied force of Foreign Devils captured the forts at Taku," he says.

Then why are you smiling? the Empress wonders, and takes a slow,
deliberate puff of smoke from her water pipe while she strives to control
her alarm.

"Are steps being taken to rectify the situation?" asks the Emperor.

Tuan's smile broadens. "Heaven, which is just, has acted on behalf of
the Son of Heaven. The Foreign Devils, their armies, and their fleets
have been destroyed!"

The Empress exchanges glances with her nephew. The Emperor

gives a puzzled frown as he absorbs the information. "Please tell us what has occurred," he says.

"The armies of the Foreign Devils were preparing to advance on Tientsin from Taku," Prince Tuan says, "when a force of metal giants appeared from the south. The Foreign Devils were obliterated! Their armies were destroyed by a blast of fire, and then their warships!"

"I fail to understand . . . ," the Empress begins.

"It's obvious!" Prince Tuan says. "The metal giants rode from heaven to earth on meteors! The Jade Emperor must have sent them expressly to destroy the Foreign Devils."

"Perhaps our information is incomplete," Jung Lu says cautiously.

Prince Tuan laughs. "Read the dispatch yourself," he says, and carelessly shoves the long telegram into the older man's hands.

The Emperor looks from one to the other, suspicion plain on his face. He clearly does not know whether to believe the news, or whether he wants to believe.

"We will wait for confirmation," he says.

More dispatches arrive over the course of the day. The destruction of the foreign armies and fleets is confirmed. Confused news of fighting comes from other areas where meteors are known to have landed. Giants are mentioned, as are bronze tripods. Prince Tuan and other members of his Iron Hat Faction swagger in triumph, boasting of the destruction of all the Foreign Devils. Pu Chun, the imperial heir, skips about the room in delight, pretending he is a giant and kicking imaginary armies out of his path.

It is the Hour of the Monkey. Supper dishes have been brought into the audience chamber, and the council members eat as they view the dispatches.

"The report from Tientsin says that the city is on fire," Jung Lu reports. "The message is unfinished. Apparently something happened to the telegraph office, or perhaps the wires were cut."

Kuang Hsu scowls. His face is etched with tension, and he speaks only with difficulty. "Tientsin is a city filled with our loyal subjects. If they are on our side, how is it that the Falling Star Giants are destroying a Chinese city?"

"There are many Foreign Devils in Tientsin," Prince Tuan says. "Perhaps it was necessary to destroy the entire city in order to eradicate the foreign influence."

A look of disgust passes across the Emperor's face at this casual attitude toward his subjects. He opens his mouth to speak, but then a spasm crosses his face. He flushes in shame.

The others in the room politely turn their gaze to the wall hangings while the Emperor has an orgasm.

Afterward he cannot speak at all. He fumbles with his soiled dragon robes as he walks behind the hangings in order to smoke a cigarette.

Watching his attempt to regain his dignity, the Dowager Empress feels her heart flood with sorrow.

Over the next two days, messages continue to arrive. Telegraph offices in the major cities are destroyed, and soon the only available information comes from horsemen galloping to the capital from local commanders and provincial governors.

General Nieh's army, stationed between Peking and Tientsin, has been wiped out by Falling Star Giants, along with most of the Righteous Harmony Fists that had been sent as reinforcements. Their spirit magic has proved inadequate to the occasion. From the information available it would seem that Shanghai, Tsingtao, and Canton have been attacked and very possibly destroyed. Just south of Peking, in Hopeh, three Falling Star Giants have been causing unimaginable destruction in one of China's richest provinces, and Hopeh's governor has committed suicide after admitting to the Throne his inability to control the situation.

The Dowager Empress notes that the Iron Hats' swaggering is noticeably reduced.

"Perhaps it is time," says Jung Lu, "to examine the possibility that the Falling Star Giants are just another kind of Foreign Devil, as rapacious as the first, and more powerful."

"Nonsense," says Prince Tuan automatically. "Heaven has sent the Falling Star Giants to aid us." But he looks uncertain as he says it.

It is the Hour of the Sheep. The midday sun beats down on the capital, turning even the shady gardens of the Forbidden City into broiling ovens.

The Emperor struggles with his tongue. "W-we desire that the august prince Jung Lu continue."

Jung Lu is happy to oblige. "This unworthy servant begs the Throne to recall that General Nieh and the Righteous Harmony Fists were neither Foreign Devils nor Christians, and they were destroyed. There are few Foreign Devils or Secondary Foreign Devils in Hopeh, but the massacres there have been terrible. And everywhere the Falling Star Giants appear, many more Chinese than Foreign Devils have been killed." Jung Lu looks solemn. "I regret the necessity to alert the Throne to a dangerous possibility. If the Falling Star Giants advance west up the railway line from Tientsin, and simultaneously march north from Hopeh, Peking will be caught between two forces. I must sadly recommend that we consider the defense of the capital."

The Dowager Empress glances at Prince Tuan, expecting him to contradict this suggestion, but instead the prince only gnaws his lip and looks uncertain.

A little flame of hope kindles in the Empress's heart.

The Emperor also sees Tuan's uncertainty and presses his advantage while he can. "Has the commander of the Military Guards Army any suggestions to make?" he asks.

"From the reports available," Jung Lu says, "it would seem that the Falling Star Giants have two weapons. The first is a beam of heat that incinerates all that it touches. This we call the Fire of the Meteor, from the flame of a falling star, and it is used to defeat armies and fleets. The second weapon is a poison black smoke that is fired from rockets. This we call the Tail of the Meteor, from a falling star's smoky tail, and it is used against cities, smothering the entire population."

"These weapons are not new," says a new voice. It is old Kang I, the Grand Councillor.

Kang I is a relic of a former age. In his many years he has served four emperors, and in his rigid adherence to tradition and hatred of foreigners has joined the Iron Hats from pure conviction.

Kang I spits into his pocket spittoon and speaks in a loud voice. "This worthless one begs the Throne to recall the Heng Ha Erh Chiang, the Door Gods. At the famous Battle of Mu between the Yin and the Chou, Marshal Cheng Lung was known as Heng the Snorter, because when he snorted, two beams of light shot from his nostrils and incinerated the enemy. Likewise, Marshal Ch'en Chi was known as Ha the Blower, because he was able to blow out clouds of poisonous yellow gas that smothered his foe.

"Thus it is clear," he concludes, "that these weapons were invented centuries ago in China, and must subsequently have been stolen by the Falling Star Giants, who are obviously a worthless and imitative people, like all foreigners." He falls silent, a superior smile ghosting across his face.

The Empress finds herself intrigued by this anecdote. "Does the esteemed councillor know if the historical records offer a method of defeating these weapons?"

"Indeed. Heng the Snorter was killed by a spear, and Ha the Blower by a magic bezoar spat at him by an ox-spirit."

"We have many spears," Jung Lu says softly. "But this ignorant one confesses his bafflement concerning where a suitable ox-spirit may be obtained. Perhaps the esteemed Grand Councillor has a suggestion?"

The smile vanishes from Kang I's face. "All answers may be found in the annals," he says stonily.

The Emperor, admirably controlling any impulse to smile at the Iron Hat's discomfort, turns again to Jung Lu. "Does the illustrious prince have any suggestions?"

"We have only three forces near Peking," Jung Lu says. "Of these, my Military Guards Army is fully occupied in blockading the foreign legations here in Peking. General Tung's horsemen are already in a position to move eastward to Tientsin. This leaves our most modern and best-equipped force, the Tiger-Hunt Marksmen, admirably suited to march south to stand between the capital and the Falling Star Giants of Hopeh. May this unworthy one suggest that the Dragon Throne issue orders to the Tiger-Hunt Marksmen and to General Tung at once?"

The Empress, careful to keep her face impassive, watches Prince Tuan as Jung Lu makes his recommendations. The ten thousand Tiger-Hunt Marksmen and General Tung's Muslim cavalry are Prince Tuan's personal armies. All his political power derives from his military strength. To risk his forces in battle is to endanger his own standing.

"What of the Throne?" Tuan asks. "If the Tiger-Hunt Marksmen march south, who will guard His Majesty? The Imperial Guard are only a few hundred men—surely their numbers are inadequate."

"The Throne may best be guarded by defeating the Falling Star Giants," Jung Lu says.

"I must insist that half the Tiger-Hunt Marksmen be left in the capital to guard the person of the Son of Heaven," Tuan says.

The Empress and Emperor look at one another. Best to act now, the Empress thinks, before Prince Tuan regains his confidence. Half the Tiger-Hunt Marksmen are better than all.

Kuang Hsu turns back to the princes. "We leave it to you," he says.

In the still night the tramp of boots echoes from the high walls of the Forbidden City. Columns of Tiger-Hunt Marksmen, under the command of Tuan's brother Duke Lan, are marching off to meet the enemy. In the Hour of the Dog, after nightfall, one of the Empress's blue-gowned maidens escorts Prince Jung Lu into her presence. He had avoided the Tiger-Hunt Marksmen by using the tunnels beneath the Forbidden City—they were designed to help servants move unobtrusively about their duties, but over the years they have been used for less licit purposes.

"We are pleased to express our gratitude," the Empress says, and takes from around her neck a necklace in which each pearl has been carved into the likeness of a stork. She places the necklace into the hands of her delighted maid.

Sad, she thinks, that it is necessary to bribe her own servants to encourage them to do what they should do unquestioningly, which is to obey and keep silent.

The darkness of the Empress's pavilion is broken only by starlight reflected from the yellow hangings. The odor of Nine-Buddha incense floats in the air.

"My friend," she tells Jung Lu, and reaches to touch his sleeve. "You must survive this upcoming battle. You and your army must live to rescue the Emperor from the Iron Hats."

"My life is in the hands of Fate," Jung Lu murmurs. "I must fight alongside my army."

"I *order* you to survive!" the Empress demands. "His Majesty cannot spare you."

There is a moment of silence, and then the old man sighs.

"This unworthy one will obey Her Majesty," he says.

Irrational though it may be, the Empress begins to glimpse a tiny, feeble ray of hope.

Hot western winds buffet the city, and the sky turns yellow with loess, dust blown hundreds of *li* from the Gobi Desert. It falls in the courtyards of the Forbidden City, on the shoulders of the black-clad eunuchs as they scurry madly through the courtyards with arms full of valuables or documents. Hundreds of carts jam the byways. The Imperial Guard, in full armor, stand in disciplined lines about the litters of the royal family. Prince Tuan stands in the yard, waving the Shangfang Sword and shouting orders. Nobody obeys him, least of all his own son, Pu Chun, the imperial heir who crouches in terror beneath a cart.

The court is fleeing the city. Yesterday, the Falling Star Giants finally made their advance on Peking. At first the news was all bad, horsemen riding into the city with stories of entire regiments being incinerated by the Fire of the Meteor.

After that it was worse, because there was no news at all.

In the early hours of the morning an order arrived from Jung Lu to evacuate the court to the Summer Palace north of the city. Since then, all has been madness.

It is the Hour of the Hare, early in the morning. The Empress's blue-clad maidservants huddle in knots, weeping. The Empress, however, is made of sterner stuff. She has been through this once before. She picks up one of her little lion dogs and thrusts it into the arms of one of her maids.

"Save my dogs!" she orders. She can't stand the idea of losing them again.

"Falling Star Giants seen from the city walls!" someone cries. There is no telling whether or not the report is true. Servingwomen dash heedlessly about the court, their gowns whipped by the strong west wind.

"Flee at once!" Prince Tuan shrieks. "The capital is lost!" He runs for his horse and gallops away. His son, screaming in terror, follows on foot, waving his arms.

The Emperor appears, a plain traveling cloak thrown over his shoulders. "Mother," he says, "it is time to go."

The Empress carries two of her favorite dogs to the litter. Her eunuchs hoist her to their shoulders, and the column begins to march for the Chienmen Gate. The western wind rattles the banners of the guard, but over the sound of the wind the Empress can hear a strange wailing sound, like a demon calling out to its mate. And then a wail from another direction as the mate answers.

"Faster!" someone calls, and the litter begins to jounce. The guardsmen's armor rattles as they begin to jog. The Empress braces herself against the sides of the litter.

"Black smoke!" Another cry. "The Tail of the Meteor!"

Women scream as the escort breaks into a run. The Empress's lion dogs whimper in fear. She clutches the curtains and peers anxiously past the curtains. The black smoke is plain to see, a tall column billowing out over the walls. As she watches, another rocket falls, trailing black.

But the strong west wind catches the top of the dark, billowing column and tears the smoke away, bearing it to the east.

As the column flees to safety, loess covers the city in a soft blanket of imperial yellow.

Much of the disorganized column, including most of the wagon train with its documents and treasure, is caught in the black smoke and never escapes the capital. Half the Tiger-Hunt Marksmen are dead or missing.

The terror and confusion make the Empress Dowager breathless, but it is the missing lion dogs that make her weep.

The column pauses north of the city at the Summer Palace only for a few hours, to beat some order into the chaos, then sets out into the teeth of the gale to Jehol on the Great Wall. In the distance the strange wailings of the Falling Star Giants are sometimes heard, but streamers of yellow dust conceal them.

By this time Prince Tuan has found his courage, his son, and his troops, the few thousand Tiger-Hunt Marksmen to have survived the fall of the capital. He calls a family conference in a requisitioned mansion, and issues edicts under the Imperial Seal calling for the extermination of all foreigners and Chinese Christians.

"Who will obey you?" the Emperor shouts at him. His hopelessness has made him fearless, has caused his stammer to disappear. "You have lost all China!"

"Heaven will not permit us to fail," Tuan says.

"I command you to kill yourself!" cries the Emperor.

Tuan turns to the Emperor and laughs aloud. "Once again His Majesty makes a witticism!"

But as news trickles in over the next few days, Tuan's belligerence turns sullen. A few survivors from a Peking suburb tell of the city's being inundated by black smoke after a second attack. Tuan's ally Prince Chuang is believed dead in the city, and old Kang I was found stone dead in his cart in Jehol, apparently having died unnoticed in the evacuation. Tuan's great ally General Tung has been killed along with his entire army. And his brother Duke Lan, after losing his entire division of Tiger-Hunt Marksmen to the Fire of the Meteor, committed suicide by drinking poison. There is no word from any of the great cities where meteors were known to have landed. No messages have come from Jung Lu, and he is believed dead.

"West!" Prince Tuan orders. His son Pu Chun stands by his side. "We will go west!"

"Kill yourself!" cries the Emperor. Pu Chun laughs.

"Somebody just farted," he sneers.

It is the Hour of the Horse, and the hot noon sun shortens tempers. The Dowager Empress holds her favorite lion dog for comfort. The dog whimpers, sensing the tension in the room.

"We will move tomorrow," Tuan says, and casts a cold look over his shoulder as he marches away from the imperial presence.

Kuang Hsu slumps defeated in his chair. The old lady rises, the lion dog still in her arms, and slowly walks to her nephew's side. Tears spill from her eyes onto his brocade sleeve.

"Please forgive me," she says.

"Don't cry, Mother," he says. "It isn't your fault that Foreign Devils have learned to ride meteors."

"I don't mean that," the Empress says. "I mean two years ago, during the Hundred Days' Reform."

"Ahh," the Emperor sighs. He turns away. "Let us not speak of it."

"They frightened me, Prince Tuan and the others. They said your reforms were destroying the country. They said the Japanese were using you. They said the dwarf-bandits were plotting to kill us all. They said if I didn't come out of retirement, we would be destroyed."

"The Japanese modernized their country." Kuang Hsu speaks unwillingly. His eyes rise to gaze into the past, at his own dead hopes. "I asked for advice from Ito, who had written their constitution. That was all. There was no danger to anyone."

"The Japanese had just killed the Korean Empress! I was afraid they would kill me next!" The old woman clutches at the Emperor's hand. "I was old and afraid!" she says. "I betrayed you. Please forgive me for everything."

He turns to her and raises a hand to her cheek. His own eyes glitter with tears. "I understand, Mother," he says. "Please don't cry."

"What can we do?"

He sighs again and turns away. "Ito told me that I could accomplish nothing as long as I was in the Forbidden City. That I could never truly be an emperor with the eunuchs and the princes and the court in the way. Well—now the Forbidden City is no more. The eunuchs' power is gone, and there is no court. There are only a few of the princes left, and only one of those is important."

He wipes tears from his eyes with his sleeve, and the Empress sees cold determination cross his face. "I will wait," he says. "But when the opportunity comes, I will act. I must act."

The royal column continues its flight. There seems no purpose in its peregrinations, and the Empress of the West cannot tell if they are running away from something, or toward something else. Possibly they are doing both at once.

Apparently the Falling Star Giants have better things to do than pursue. Exhausted and with nowhere else to go, the royal family ends up in the governor's mansion in the provincial capital of T'ai-yüan. The courtyard is spattered with blood because the governor, Yu Hsien, had dozens of Christian missionaries killed here, along with their wives and children. Their eyeless heads now decorate the city walls.

One afternoon the Empress looks out the window and sees Pu Chun practicing martial arts in the court. In his hands is a bloodstained beheading sword given him by Governor Yu.

She never looks out the window again.

All messages from the east are of death and unimaginable suffering. Cities destroyed, armies wiped out, entire populations fleeing before the attackers in routes as directionless as that of the court.

There is no news whatever from the rest of the world. Apparently all the Foreign Devils have been afflicted by Foreign Devils of their own.

And then, in the Hour of the Rooster, word comes that Prince Jung Lu has arrived and requests an audience, and the Empress feels her heart leap. She had never permitted herself to hope, not once she heard of the total destruction of Peking.

At once she convenes a family council.

The horrors of war have clearly affected Jung Lu. He walks into the imperial presence with a weary tread and painfully gets on his knees to perform the required kowtows.

"This worthless old man begs to report to the Throne that the Falling Star Giants are all dead."

There is a long, stunned silence. The Emperor, flushed with sudden excitement, tries to speak but trips over his own tongue.

Joy floods Tzu Hsi's heart. "How did this occur?" she asks. "Did we defeat them in battle?"

"They were not defeated," Jung Lu says. "I do not know how they died. Perhaps it was a disease. I stayed only to confirm the reports personally, and then I rode here at once with all the soldiers I could raise. Five thousand Manchu bannermen await the imperial command outside the city walls."

The Empress strokes one of her lion dogs while she makes a careful calculation. Jung Lu's five thousand bannermen considerably outnumber Prince Tuan's remaining Tiger-Hunt Marksmen, but Tuan's men have modern weapons and the bannermen do not. And these bannermen are not likely to be brave, as they probably survived the Falling Star Giants only by fleeing at the very rumor of their arrival.

She sees the relieved smile on Prince Tuan's face. "Heaven is just!" he says.

All turn at a noise from the Emperor. Kuang Hsu's hands clutch the arms of his chair, and his face twists with the effort to speak. Then he gasps and has an orgasm.

An hour ago he was a ghost-emperor, nothing he did mattered, and he spoke freely. Now that he is the Son of Heaven again, his stammer and his nervous condition have returned.

A few moments later he speaks, his head turned away in embarrassment.

"Tonight we will thank Heaven for its mercy and benevolence. Tomorrow, at the Hour of the Dragon, we will assemble again in celebration." He looks at Pu Chun, who stands near Prince Tuan. "I have observed the Heir practice wushu in the courtyard. I hope the Heir will favor us with a demonstration of his martial prowess."

Prince Tuan flushes with pleasure. He and his son fall to their knees and kowtow.

"We will obey the imperial command with pleasure," Tuan says.

The Emperor turns his head away as he dismisses the company. At first the Empress thinks it is because he is shamed by his public orgasm, but then she sees the tight, merciless smile of triumph on the Emperor's lips, and a cold finger touches the back of her neck.

In the next hours the Empress of the West tries to smuggle a message to Jung Lu in hopes of seeing him privately, but the situation is so confusing that the messenger cannot find him. She decides to wait for a better time.

With the morning the Hour of the Dragon arrives, and the family council convenes. The remaining Iron Hats cluster together in pride and triumph. It is clearly their hour—the Falling Star Giants have abdicated, as it were, and left the nation to the mercies of the Iron Hats. As if in recognition of this fact, the Emperor awards Prince Tuan the office of Grand Councillor in place of the late Kang I.

Then Pu Chun is brought forward to perform wushu, and the Emperor calls the Imperial Guard into the room to watch. The imperial heir leaps about the room, shouting and waving the blood-encrusted sword given him by Governor Yu as he decapitates one imaginary Foreign Devil after another. The Empress has seen much better martial art in her time, but at the end of the performance, all are loud in their praise of the young heir, and the Emperor descends from his chair to congratulate him.

Fighting his tongue—the Emperor seems unusually tense today—he turns to the heir and says, "I wonder if the Heir has learned a sword technique called The Dragon in Flight from Low to High?"

Pu Chun is reluctant to admit that he is not a complete master of the sword, but with a bit of paternal prodding he admits that this technique seems to have escaped him.

Kuang Hsu's stammer is so bad he can barely get the words out. "Will the Heir permit me to teach?"

"Your Majesty honors us beyond all description," Prince Tuan says. Despite his lifelong ill health, the Emperor, like every Manchu prince, practiced *wushu* since he was a boy, and always received praise from his instructors.

The Emperor turns to Prince Tuan, his face red with the struggle to speak. "May . . . I . . . have the honor . . . to use . . . the Shangfang Sword?"

"The Son of Heaven does his unworthy servant too much honor!" Prince Tuan eagerly strips the long blade from its sheath and presents it on his knees to the Emperor.

The Emperor strikes a martial pose, sword cocked, and Pu Chun imitates him. Watching from her chair, the Empress feels her heart stop. Terror fills her. She knows what is about to happen.

The movement is too swift to follow, but the Shangfang Sword whistles as it hurtles through air, and its blade is sharp and true. Suddenly Prince Tuan's head rolls across the floor. Blood fountains from the headless trunk.

Fury blazes from Kuang Hsu's eyes, and his body, unlike his tongue, has no stammer. His second strike crushes the skull of Tuan's ally, Governor Yu. His third kills the president of the Board of Punishments. And his fourth—the Empress cries out to stop, but is too late—the fourth blow strikes the neck of the boy heir, Pu Chun, who is so stunned by the unexpected death of his father that he doesn't think to protect himself from the blade that kills him.

"Protect the Emperor!" Jung Lu cries to his guardsmen. "Kill the traitors!"

Those Iron Hats still breathing are finished off by the Imperial Guard. And then the Guard rounds up the Iron Hats' subordinate officers, and within minutes their heads are struck off.

The Emperor dictates an order to open the city gates, and the order is signed with the Imperial Seal. Jung Lu's loyal bannermen pour into the city and surround the Throne with a wall of guns, swords, and spears.

Only then does the Emperor notice the old woman, still frozen in fear, who sits on her throne clutching her whimpering lion dogs.

Kuang Hsu approaches, and the Empress shrinks from the blood that soaks his dragon-embroidered robes.

"I am sorry, Mother, that you had to watch this," he says.

The Empress manages to find words within the cloud of terror that fills her mind.

"It was necessary," she says.

"The Foreign Devils have been destroyed," the Emperor says, "and so have the Falling Star Giants. The Righteous Harmony Fists are no more, and neither are the Iron Hats. Now there is much suffering and loss of life, but China has survived such catastrophes before."

The Empress looks at the blood-spattered dragons on the Emperor's robes. "The Dragon has flown from Low to High," she says.

"Yes." The Emperor looks at the Shangfang Sword, still in his hand. "The Falling Star Giants have landed all over the world," he says. "For many years the Foreign Devils will be busy with their own affairs. While they are thus occupied we will take control of our own ports, our own laws, the railroads, industries, and telegraphs. By the time they are ready to deal with us again, the Middle Kingdom will be strong and united, and on its way to being as modern as any nation in the world."

Kuang Hsu looks up at the Empress of the West.

"Will you help me, Mother?" he asks. "There will be need of reform—not just for a Hundred Days, but for all time. And I promise you—" His eyes harden, and for a moment she sees a dragon there, the animal that according to legend lives in every emperor, and which has slumbered in Kuang Hsu till now. "I promise you that you will be safe. No one will be in a position to harm you."

"I am old," the Empress says, "but I will help however I can." She strokes the head of her lion dog. Her heart overflows. Tears of relief sting her eyes. "May the Hour of the Dragon last ten thousand years," she says.

"Ten thousand years!" the guards chorus, and to the cheers the Emperor walks across the bloodstained floor to the throne that awaits him.

Pablo Picasso

BLUE PERIOD

DANIEL MARCUS

Charcoal was good. Pablo liked the simplicity of it, the challenge of coaxing subtlety from the purest of elements. You begin with nothing. White paper. Black lump of coal. And like God shaping the Earth from light and void, you create a world.

Sometimes.

He had been working since early afternoon. A woman in the market giving an apple to her half-wit son. Something about the two of them, the set of her shoulders toward the boy, the way the light touched his hair, suggesting that some measure of divinity lay in him and that she was the one saddled with infirmity. But Pablo wasn't getting it. The thing emerging from the rough paper was a cartoon, a grotesque joke.

The shadows in the studio lengthened until the sun fell behind the buildings across the rue Gabrielle. Pablo took no notice, working until it was almost too dark to see. Finally, when the charcoal smudges began to flow of their own accord into the unmarked whiteness of the paper, he stepped back and stretched his cramped shoulders.

He lit a lamp and the studio filled with warm yellow light. The large room looked like it had been visited by a whirlwind with an artistic fetish. Canvases in various stages of completion were scattered about; rough sketches littered the floor. To the left of the wide bay windows, to catch the light of afternoon, a raised platform for the models. Heavy-breasted cows, most of them, but what could you do? Pablo loved Paris, but the women were pigs.

On a table near the door, a loaf of bread, three days old and hard as stone, a bottle of rough burgundy, a bowl of apples. And leaning against the south wall of the studio, about twenty finished canvases, Pablo's portfolio. They were set apart from the clutter as if a protective wall had been erected around them. His ticket to greatness. Nineteen years old and already he was breaking new ground, surpassing the work of the established masters. After all, he had been chosen to represent his native Spain at the Paris Exhibition! The canvases he saw in the Montmartre galleries would be better suited to wrap liver. Monet should have been smothered as a child. Smothered in flowers. Who cared a dog's teat about flowers? Even the best of the new ones, Denis, say, or Vuillard, couldn't paint their way out of a burlap sack. Dragon-flies! Lilies! Swirling hair! It was crap, all of it.

The Spanish upstart, they were calling him. Dismissing him as if he were an insect. Deft but morbid, one review said. Uneven, said another. He would show those symbolist faggots what a real artist could do. He turned back to the sketch of the woman and the idiot boy.

But not tonight, he thought. This is shit.

Pablo tore the page from the easel and ripped it in half, then in half again. He let the pieces fall to the floor and walked across the room to the table. He uncorked the burgundy and raised it to his lips, taking a long draught. It was rough but good, leaving a warm glow in his gullet. The French peasants were all right for something. He raised the bottle to his lips again when suddenly, a bright green flash lit the sky outside his window. It was gone in an instant, but it was so intense that the afterimage of the silhouetted buildings across the street stayed pulsing in his vision.

What the hell was that? He ran to the window and looked out. A few souls on the street, looking up. He scanned the horizon. There, beyond the Basilica of Sacré-Coeur, a greenish glow pushing into the twilight, just beginning to recede.

Even as his eyes began to adjust, another green flash lit the sky. This time, Pablo could see its trail, like a shooting star but brighter, lancing downward to the west. It was accompanied by a roaring sound, some-thing like thunder but with an edge to it, as if the sky were made of cloth and somebody was ripping it in two. There was a moment of preternatural quiet, the world itself holding its breath, then a flickering orange glow began to lick at the bottom of the sky. The Bois de Boulogne? It was hard to tell. Pablo was still new to Paris and didn't quite have his bearings yet. In fact, he hardly ever left Montmartre.

His countryman Casagemas had said he'd be at Le Ciel on the boulevard Clichy, fondling women, no doubt, and getting drunk. Pablo felt a sudden need for his companionship. He grabbed his jacket and cap and began to head out the door.

Then, as if he'd forgotten something but wasn't quite sure what, he stopped, turned, and looked around the room. His eyes lingered on the stack of canvases leaning against the wall. His mind filled with an unfocused dread, almost crushing him under its sudden weight. With an effort of will, he pushed it aside. Everything was all right. Shooting stars. Big deal. God taking potshots at the lame and unrepentant. Pablo knew that God had other plans for him.

The streets were buzzing with energy. People clustered in front of shops, talking, gesturing up at the sky. As Pablo passed one such group in front of a pâtisserie on the rue Saint-Vincent, he overheard someone say, "Men from Mars, I'm telling you! They've landed!"

Pablo approached the group. "Excuse me, my French still isn't very good. Did you say 'men from Mars'?"

"Yes!" The speaker grabbed Pablo by the lapels. He was drunk; his breath would have knocked over a horse. "A cylinder landed at Royaumont this morning and vile *things* crawled out. Gargoyles! The monastery is in ruins!"

Pablo pried the man loose and backed away. One of his companions laughed. "The monastery is seven hundred years old. It's already in ruins."

"Laugh all you want," the drunk said. "We aren't the only creatures in the cosmos God has graced with intelligence. They're here to test us, and we'd better be ready!"

Another of the man's companions winked at Pablo and pantomimed drinking from a bottle. Pablo walked away. Their voices faded behind him, drifting up into the warm night air.

Men from Mars! Pablo had read in *Le Figaro* about the recent volcanic activity on Mars, jets of gas shooting out from the planet's surface, visible from Earth with even a modest telescope. Forty million miles away. Pablo shook his head. What did numbers like that mean? And now men. No, *monsters*! Gargoyles sent by the God of War! He laughed. Casagemas was really going to get a kick out of this. He quickened his pace.

He cut through the Montmartre Cemetery on his way to the boulevard Clichy, and quiet surrounded him like a velvet glove. Gnarled oak trees cast a protective canopy, muffling the street sounds. Neat rows of headstones, pale in the moonlight, followed the gentle, hilly contours like cultivated crops. The sky above the trees to the south was bleeding orange at the bottom.

Inside Le Ciel, the smoky air was charged with reassuring chaos. An acrobat tumbled across the stage, flanked on one side by a dwarf in formal evening attire and on the other by a grinning pinhead in a flowered nightshirt. A mustached pianist played a lively accompaniment. Near the bar, two men shouted at each other at the top of their lungs. It was business as usual at Le Ciel, Martians or not.

He scanned the tables for Casagemas. There, near the front, his friend's broad back and shaggy black hair. He was leaning over to whisper something into his companion's ear. She threw back her head and laughed. Pablo stared. This one was beautiful. Not painted like a whore, but flush with the bloom and innocence of youth. Casagemas was moving up in the world!

Pablo pushed through the maze of tables and wedged a chair between the two of them.

"Ho, Carles!" he said. "What have you been keeping from me?" Up close, the woman was even more lovely than he'd thought. Curly brown tresses framed a heart-shaped face. Cool blue-green eyes, like the ocean under a tropical sun. "Casagemas and I are the best of friends," he said to her. "We share everything, you know."

She blushed and smiled, but Pablo saw first a flicker of anger pass across her face. Passion, too! Good!

"Hey, Pablo, behave yourself," Casagemas said. He turned to his companion. "He doesn't know how to act around a real woman. Just the whores. Germaine, this is Pablo Ruiz Picasso, the greatest painter in Paris, only nobody knows it but him. Nineteen years old and already he is a legend in his own mind."

"Yes, well, one day Carles will shock us all and sell one of his own paintings," Pablo said. He took Germaine's hand and brought it to his lips. "I am not only charmed," he said, in Spanish, "but stricken with envy that this pig will be taking you home tonight and not I."

Her eyes flashed again with anger, and she blushed a deeper red. She started to say something, glared at Casagemas, pushed back her chair, and stalked away.

Casagemas glared at Pablo. "Her father is Spanish, you fool. She speaks it like a native. You've really done it this time."

He got up and hurried after Germaine. Pablo grinned and watched him weave through the crowd, narrowly missing a collision with a waiter carrying a tray laden with bottles and glasses.

He picked up his friend's glass, still half full of ruby burgundy, took a healthy sip, and turned his attention to the stage. The dwarf was balanced on the acrobat's shoulders, juggling a wicked-looking knife, an empty wine bottle, and a flaming torch. The pinhead looked on, his mouth hanging open. In the light from the stage lamps, his lips were shiny with drool.

After a few moments, Casagemas and Germaine returned to the table.

"Germaine has consented to stay if you will apologize to her, Pablo," Casagemas said.

She was glaring down at Pablo so hard that he had to look away to keep from smiling.

"I'm sorry," he said. That you're with Casagemas, he added to himself. "We've gotten off on the wrong foot. Please stay."

She smiled, a little stiffly, though, to be sure, and sat. Casagemas did likewise. Pablo motioned a waiter over and ordered a bottle of wine and a plate of bread and hard cheese.

"So," he said when they were settled. "What do you think about the men from Mars?"

Casagemas laughed. "It's the Germans. Von Bülow's ambition has finally gotten the better of his common sense. We'll crush them like insects."

"The Germans!" Germaine said. "We're at war, then?"

"No, I'm kidding." Casagemas held up a hand. "But it seems more likely an explanation than men from outer space."

"Well, something is going on," Pablo said. "There were two explosions—at least two—and I think the Bois de Boulogne is burning."

"Burning!" Germaine said. "Maybe we should try to find out what's happening."

"Maybe we should have some more wine," Casagemas said.

Pablo thought for a moment, then grabbed the bottle and stood up. "Maybe we should do both. It's better to know what's going on than to be left in the dark."

He wrapped the bread and cheese in a napkin and stuffed it in his jacket pocket. Germaine and Casagemas looked up at him from the table.

"Well, what are you waiting for?" Pablo asked. "Let's go!"

They looked at each other. Casagemas shrugged and reluctantly pushed back his chair. He offered his hand to Germaine.

"I have a bad feeling about this, Pablo. If there was something wrong, the authorities would notify us. This is another one of your crazy expeditions."

Back in Barcelona, Pablo had persuaded Casagemas to come with him to the recent scene of an anarchist bombing. An outdoor café, reduced to rubble in the middle of the afternoon. Two hours later, it was still a charnel house, debris everywhere, a row of bodies in the street covered with bloody tablecloths. Due to their scruffy looks, Pablo and Casagemas were arrested at the scene and detained for several hours. Eventually, they were released, but not before some very rough questioning. It was all fuel for Pablo's artistic drive; he filled a whole notebook with sketches. Casagemas had nightmares for weeks. Disembodied hands, flesh cracked and burned, reached for him in the dark while faceless inquisitors hurled nonsense questions at him.

"Don't worry, Carles," Pablo said. "Germaine and I will protect you."

Germaine smiled uneasily.

Pablo took a last look across the room at the stage. The pinhead was looking directly at him. His eyes, which Pablo had first thought glazed with idiocy, burned, full of suffering and grace, into his own. Pablo turned away.

Traffic was heavy on the boulevard Clichy; horses, carriages, the occasional motorcar, wove through the thickening crowd of pedestrians. A tradesman, still in work clothes, had his wife and two beribboned girls in tow. A trio of drunken soldiers passed a bottle back and forth, laughing. The overall mood was almost that of a holiday. It was as if they were saying, "This is Paris, after all, the center of the civilized world! What could possibly happen?"

Pablo thought back to Barcelona again, to Death himself laying waste upon the languid peace of an afternoon. *Anything* could happen. Anything. God is a cruel prankster and these Parisians are fools.

When he could get a glimpse of the sky to the west, Pablo saw that it was still tinged with flickering red at the bottom, but the crowd was moving in the opposite direction, toward the center of the city.

He stopped a young man in a blue watch cap. "What's going on?"

"Something crashed in the Seine, near the Île de la Cité! The river is boiling!"

Germaine and Casagemas clung tightly together to avoid being separated in the thickening crowd. She reached out her hand to Pablo and he took it. It was warm, soft, and strong.

Pablo heard several different stories, each of them more fantastic than the last. Notre-Dame had been leveled. A great crater had been plowed into the Jardin du Luxembourg and grotesque things were crawling out. Another variation of the Royaumont story, only this time the Martians, after destroying the monastery, began striding across the land in great cowled vehicles hundreds of feet high, setting fire to everything in their path.

The crowd had a life of its own now, sweeping them down the rue de Rivoli. When they reached the Pont d'Arcole, Pablo shouted to his companions, "Let's stay on the bridge and let the crowd pass. We can see everything from here."

They pushed their way to the side of the bridge, buffeted by passing bodies. When they reached the railing they held on. Soon, the mob thinned.

Something *was* going on in the river. Just beyond the tip of the Île de la Cité, a circular patch of water ten meters across pulsed a luminous green, the glow intensifying to eye-searing brightness and fading to cool chartreuse within a period of roughly thirty seconds. As the glow intensified, the water in the affected region bubbled furiously. Wraiths of steam floated above the river.

"This must be where one of the shooting stars landed," Pablo said.

A pair of barges bristling with grappling equipment floated on either side of the glowing area. Men clustered on the decks.

There was something wrong with the outline of Notre-Dame Cathedral. As his eyes adjusted, Pablo saw that one of the towers was gone, sheared off near the top leaving a jagged silhouette. The shooting star must have grazed the old cathedral in its descent.

A black tentacle broke the roiling surface of the water. Its motions were flexible, but it was clearly a mechanical contrivance, composed of a series of articulated segments. Tentative at first, it waved this way and that, as if sniffing the air, extending itself all the while above the river like a metallic beanstalk.

It stopped its weaving motion, leaned toward one of the barges, and struck with reptilian speed. The tentacle wrapped itself around the barge and, in an instant, dragged it down into the turbulent, glowing water.

Bits of debris floated to the surface. A few men struggled briefly, but they were being boiled alive like crabs in a pot. Soon their motions ceased.

Another tentacle, or perhaps it was the same one, broke through the water's surface. This time there was no hesitation; it went directly for the other barge, pulling it under in the blink of an eye.

All was quiet. The luminous patch faded to a dull, pulsing glow. A few scraps of wood bobbed in the water.

Pablo looked at Casagemas. His friend's face was pale. Germaine clung tightly to his arm.

"What *was* that?" she asked.

Casagemas shook his head. "I don't know."

"Germans, eh?" Pablo asked. He was badly shaken, but he didn't want his friend or Germaine to know just how badly. "Germans from outer space!"

He realized that he still held the wine bottle by its neck. He lifted it to his lips, took a long pull, and offered the bottle to Germaine.

She shook her head, and Casagemas shot him an annoyed look. "Don't be flip, Pablo. People are *dead*. What sort of horror *is* this?"

Pablo shrugged. "Maybe it's true. Men from Mars bearing the judgment of a cruel, stupid God." He took another pull of wine and winked at Germaine. "Or maybe they come to Paris for the women."

Germaine looked away.

Suddenly, the water began bubbling furiously again, and a rounded shape broke through the roiling surface. It continued to rise; sheets of water cascaded off its surface. As it cleared the water Pablo saw that it was supported by three jointed legs. Curled tentacles dangled from its flat bottom. One such tentacle was wrapped around a box, affixed to one end of which was a shape like the funnel of a Victrola.

At its full height, the thing towered above the river, balanced on spidery tripod legs. The cowled head was level with the turrets of Notre-Dame. It looked this way and that in a manner that was almost human.

Surely *this* thing is not one of the Martians, Pablo thought. It must be some sort of vehicle, with the creatures themselves inside.

Whatever it was, intelligence and malice guided its motions. It stepped out of the river onto the quay, raised the funneled box, and pointed it at Notre-Dame Cathedral.

A deep thrumming sound seemed to emanate from the device. Suddenly, a ghostly green beam, almost too faint to see, leapt from the box, and the face of the great cathedral exploded. Stone shattered, stained glass glowed and ran like wax. The remains of the south tower began to collapse, as if in slow motion.

It took Pablo a moment to realize that what he was seeing was the effect of great heat, but when the Martian swept the beam across the roofs of the surrounding buildings, there was no doubt. As soon as the beam touched them, they burst into flames as if ignited by a torch.

The crowd, so anxious a little while ago to get close to the spectacle, began flowing back across the Pont d'Arcole. It was a brainless mob; Pablo saw at least one person trampled under its relentless, panicked flight.

"Hold tightly to the railing!" he shouted to his companions.

As they were buffeted in the sea of bodies, trying to keep from being swept downstream, a ragged line of soldiers appeared on the quay from the nearby *préfecture de police*. They raised their rifles at the great machine towering above them.

Pablo could see muzzle flashes, like tiny fireflies in the night. Their effect upon the leviathan was little more than that. It swept the beam across the pitiful rank of soldiers, and one by one as it touched them they burst into flame.

The machine swept the beam across the river, leaving a violent wake of hissing steam, and as it touched buildings on the Rive Gauche, they exploded into fiery blossoms. The beam cut a swath across the mob on the Pont d'Arcole, not twenty feet away from Pablo and his companions. Pablo felt the heat on his face; it was like standing too close to a furnace.

Each person the heat-ray touched instantly became a wick encased in a billowing column of fire. One man was looking in Pablo's direction as the beam touched him. Time slowed to a halt; every detail imprinted itself on Pablo's vision. The dark hollows of his eyes in the flickering inferno, his skin peeling, blackening, cracking, his mouth open to scream, consumed by the fire before he could utter a sound.

Pablo ducked down, seeking the meager protection of the stone fence. Casagemas and Germaine stood clutching each other, frozen with fear.

"Get down, you idiots!" Pablo grabbed Germaine by the hem of her coat, pulling her down. She pulled Casagemas down with her to the stone walkway.

They huddled together, leaving as little exposed as possible to the panic of the mob and the return of the heat-ray. Countless feet kicked their hunched backs in passing flight. They huddled closer.

A deafening screech filled the air, exultant and alien.

"Aloo! Aloo!"

Pablo looked up. Almost directly in front of him, one of the tripod legs rose out of the water. Its strangely scaled surface held a dull sheen. Impossibly far above them, the cowled head swept back and forth. Suddenly, a jet of bright green steam hissed from one of the joints, and the leg lifted out of the water. It passed over their heads, gone in an instant. The alien howl cut through the night again, fading as the thing strode west along the river toward the flickering glow in the sky.

Pablo was hyperaware of his surroundings—the smell of Germaine's perfume, her rapid breathing. The scratchy feel of Casagemas's over-coat on his cheek, more real than the Bosch-like image of a three-legged monster towering above the river, laying swaths of destruction across the City of Light.

Soon, relative calm descended upon the bridge. The cries of those touched by the edge of the beam floated toward them. A greasy, burned smell hung in the air, singed hair mixed with meat left too long on a spit. Wisps of smoke rose from the pathetic charred hulks that had once been human beings. Scattered groups of survivors began looking dazedly around. A few began seeing to the injured.

"What are we going to do?" Casagemas asked. They had retreated to the safety of an alley on the Rive Gauche side of the Pont d'Arcole. In the distance, they could hear the hollow boom of artillery.

"My parents live in Versailles," Germaine said. "I have to get out there."

"I will accompany you, of course," Casagemas said. Germaine touched his arm gratefully. He looked at Pablo.

Pablo thought of the stack of canvases in his studio. His portfolio, the sum total of his work to date. It would be easy to dismount them and roll them up. He could no more abandon them than he could leave an arm or a leg behind.

Pablo nodded toward the orange glow in the western sky.

"That's probably Versailles," he said. "I don't know if there's anything left."

Germaine began to weep.

"Pablo, you are such an asshole sometimes," Casagemas said.

Pablo shrugged. "Do what you must. I have to go back to the studio and get my paintings. It would be a disaster if they were destroyed."

"A disaster!" Casagemas said. "What do you think is happening here? Your paintings mean nothing, Pablo. We have to survive, help if we can. Our chances are better if we stick together."

Pablo stiffened. "You are a woman, Carles. Go then. Run. Survival is nothing without art. Otherwise, we are no better than dogs pissing in the street."

Casagemas glared at Pablo and pulled Germaine closer. Without a word, he turned and walked out of the alley, his arm around her shoulders.

Pablo watched them turn the corner and disappear. His soul was filled with blackness. A part of him wanted to chase after them, to throw in his lot with them, flee the city and find a safe haven somewhere far away. But Casagemas was a fool. There was no safety anywhere. It was the Apocalypse. Grace had passed Man by and thrown open the Gates of Hell in her passage. The Beast was loose upon the world.

Pablo wandered the streets, trying to make his way back to the rue Gabrielle. He quickly became lost. A detachment of mounted cavalry appeared out of nowhere and all but ran him down.

The sound of distant artillery shook the warm night air. Above it floated the sharp staccato of rifle fire. If he stopped to listen, he could sometimes hear the deep thrumming of the terrible ray. Several times, the uncanny cries of the Martian machines pierced the night.

Knots of people stood on street corners, talking and gesturing. Others huddled together in alleyways, passing bottles of wine and bits of food back and forth. The stories of destruction he heard were similar to what he'd witnessed from the Pont d'Arcole. Paris was being crushed under the weight of the Martians' onslaught.

The things weren't unstoppable, though. An artillery battery near the Bois de Boulogne had shot one of a tripod's legs out from under it and the thing toppled, sending a ball of flame hundreds of feet into the sky when the cowled head hit the ground. But for the most part, the resistance offered the Martians was sporadic and ineffective.

Somewhere near the rue de Rivoli, Pablo came upon a small mob smashing windows and ransacking shops. A handful of soldiers appeared on the other end of the block and began firing into the crowd. Pablo ran.

The sky was beginning to segue through lightening shades of gray. He emerged from a labyrinthine tangle of streets onto the Quai d'Orsay. A bloody, swollen sun hung low in the sky over the Seine, peering through a haze of smoke.

Across the river, the spire of the Eiffel Tower scratched the bottom of the sky. Pablo loved Eiffel's creation. The juxtaposition of fluid curvature and implacable Cartesian logic epitomized for him Mankind's emergence into the new century.

A pair of tripods approached the tower from either side. They were dwarfed by the structure, their heads rising only to the second tier. They moved in and backed away, giving the appearance of nothing so much as a pair of dogs investigating a particularly troublesome artifact.

A bundle of tentacles descended from the belly of one of the machines and wrapped itself around the tower's leg. Its fellow likewise approached the adjacent leg. The machines pulled and strained at the structure, clearly trying to bring it down, but without success.

Then, the nearest machine stepped back and lifted one of the funneled boxes high in the air. Its companion stepped back and pointed its own device at the tower. In the daylight, Pablo couldn't see the heat-rays, but their effect was immediately apparent. Currents tore at the air above the tower. Soon the entire structure was glowing cherry red. The Martians swept their beams up and down its length, and the bottom arches began to sag. Suddenly, it folded over upon itself and collapsed onto the Champ-de-Mars.

Champ-de-Mars! Pablo began to laugh. Champ-de-Mars! He looked around for Casagemas to share the joke with, but there was nobody. Pablo shook his head, remembering. Casagemas was gone. Fatigue descended upon him like a dark, heavy cloak. Gone, his friend and countryman. Gone, his beloved tower. All gone.

The machines stood above it for a moment, like hunters gloating over a kill, then they strode off to the west, crossing the Seine and disappearing into morning haze made thick by the smoke of many fires.

Witnessing the tower's ruin tore at Pablo's heart, but it had a sobering effect as well. He resolved to get back to his studio. He wasn't sure, but he thought that Montmartre was vaguely north, so he walked with the rising sun at his right, trying to avoid the major thoroughfares.

The streets were strangely quiet. He could hear the distant sound of fighting, but it hadn't yet spread to this part of the city. He guessed that people had either left the city or were cowering in their apartments. He was grateful that he'd had the foresight to stuff some bread and cheese in his pocket back at Le Ciel, and he gnawed at them as he walked.

He turned a corner onto the boulevard de Magenta, and everything clicked into place. The dome of Sacré-Coeur rose above the rooftops. Almost home.

His studio was just as he left it. Morning light cast stripes of light and shadow across the floor. His paintings leaned in a stack against the far wall, but his eyes were drawn to an unfinished canvas propped up in a corner, a commission from the Church of St. Geneviève. It was a standard Crucifixion scene. So far, he'd just sketched in the cross and the outline of a man upon it.

Pablo stared at it for what seemed like a long time. Then, moving as if he were in a trance, he dragged his easel into the light and placed the framed canvas on it.

He used oil, thick, viscous gobs of it. At first, he applied it with a knife, but before long he was using his hands, his fingers, the end of a smock, anything that would serve the image emerging onto the canvas.

Shadows crawled across the floor. The sound of artillery grew closer for a time, then began to recede. Smoke drifted in through the open window.

Pablo stepped back, wiping the sweat from his forehead with a stained sleeve. He was done.

There, the vacant idiot eyes and glistening lips. Slack-jawed, full of grace and pain. Behind Him, Judgment rose above the smooth, tawny hills of Calvary on spindly tripod legs.

Henry James

THE MARTIAN INVASION
JOURNALS OF HENRY JAMES

ROBERT SILVERBERG

Editor's Note:

*Of all the treasures contained in the coffin-shaped wooden sea chest at Harvard's Widener Library in which those of Henry James's notebooks and journals that survived his death were preserved and in the associated James archive at Harvard, only James's account of his bizarre encounter with the Martian invaders in the summer of 1900 has gone unpublished until now. The rest of the material the box contained—the diaries and datebooks, the notes for unfinished novels, the variant drafts of his late plays, and so forth—has long since been made available to James scholars, first in the form of selections under the editorship of F. O. Matthiessen and Kenneth B. Murdock (*The Notebooks of Henry James, *Oxford University Press, 1947), and then a generation later in the magisterial full text edited by Leon Edel and Lyall H. Powers (*The Complete Notebooks of Henry James, *Oxford University Press, 1987).*

Despite the superb latter volume's assertions, in its title and subtitle, of being "complete," "authoritative," and "definitive," one brief text was indeed omitted from it, which was, of course, the invasion journal. Edel and Powers are in no way to be faulted for this, since they could not have been aware of the existence of the Martian papers, which had (apparently accidentally) been sequestered long ago among a group of documents at Harvard associated with the life of James's sister Alice (1848–1892) and had either gone unnoticed by the biographers of Alice James or else, since the diary obviously had been composed some years after her death, had been dismissed by them as irrelevant to their research. It may also be that they found the little notebook simply illegible, for James had suffered severely from writer's cramp from the winter of 1896–97 onward; his handwriting by 1900 had become quite erratic, and many of the (largely pencilled) entries in the Martian notebook are extremely challenging even to a reader experienced in Henry James's hand, set down as they were in great haste under intensely strange circumstances.

The text is contained in a pocket diary book, four and a half inches by six, bound in a green leatherette cover. It appears that James used such books, in those years, in which to jot notes that he would later transcribe into his permanent notebook (Houghton Journal VI, 26 October 1896 to 10 February 1909); *but this is the only one of its kind that has survived. The first entry is undated, but can be specifically identified as belonging to mid-May of 1900 by its references to James's visit to London in that month. At that time James made his home at Lamb House in the pleasant Sussex town of Rye, about seventy miles southeast of London. After an absence of nearly two years he had made a brief trip to the capital in March 1900, at which time, he wrote, he was greeted by his friends "almost as if I had returned from African or Asian exile." After seventeen days he went home to Lamb House, but he returned to London in May, having suddenly shaven off, a few days before, the beard that he had worn since the 1860s, because it had begun to turn white and offended his vanity. (James was then fifty-seven.) From internal evidence, then, we can date the first entry in the Martian journals to the period between May 15 and May 25, 1900.*

[Undated]

Stepped clean-shaven from the train at Charing Cross. Felt clean and light and eerily young: I could have been forty. A miraculous transformation, so simply achieved! Alas, the sad truth of it is that it will always be I, never any younger even without the beard; but this is a good way to greet the new century nevertheless.

Called on Helena De Kay. Gratifying surprise and expressions of pleasure over my rejuvenated physiognomy. Clemens is there, that is, "Mark Twain." He has aged greatly in the three years since our last meeting. "The twentieth century is a stranger to me," he sadly declares. His health is bad: has been to Sweden for a cure. Not clear what ails him, physically, at least. He is a dark and troubled soul in any case. His best work is behind him and plainly he knows it. I pray whatever God there be that that is not to be my fate.

To the club in the evening. Tomorrow a full day, the galleries, the booksellers, the customary dismaying conference with the publishers. (The war in South Africa is depressing all trade, publishing particularly badly hit, though I should think people would read more novels at a time of such tension.) Luncheon and dinner engagements, of course, the usual hosts, no doubt the usual guests. And so on and on the next day and the next and the next. I yearn already for little restful, red-roofed, uncomplicated Rye.

June 7, LH [Lamb House, Rye]

Home again at long last. London tires me: that is the truth of things. I have lost the habit of it, *je crois.* How I yearned, all the while I was there, for cabless days and dinnerless nights! And of course there is work to do. *The Sacred Fount* is now finished and ready to go to the agent. A fine flight into the high fantastic, I think—fanciful, fantastic, but very close and sustained. Writing in the first person makes me uneasy—it lends itself so readily to garrulity, to a fluidity of self-revelation—but there is no questioning that such a structure was essential to this tale.

What is to be next? There is of course the great Project, the fine and major thing, which perhaps I mean to call *The Ambassadors.* Am I ready to begin it? It will call for the most supreme effort, though I think the reward will be commensurate. A masterpiece, dare I say? I might do well to set down one more sketch of it before commencing. But not immediately. There is powerful temptation to be dilatory: I find a note here from Wells, who suggests that I bicycle over to Sandgate and indulge in a bit of conversation with him. Indeed it has been a while, and I am terribly fond of him. Wells first, yes, and some serious thought about my ambassadors after that.

June 14, Sandgate.

I am at Wells's this fine bright Thursday, very warm even for June. The bicycle ride in such heat across Romney Marsh to this grand new villa of his on the Kentish coast left me quite wilted, but Wells's robust hospitality has quickly restored me.

What a vigorous man Wells is! Not that you would know it to look at him; his health is much improved since his great sickly time two years ago, but he is nonetheless such a flimsy little wisp of a man, with those short legs, that high squeaky voice, his somewhat absurd moustaches. And yet the mind of the man burns like a sun within that frail body! The energy comes forth in that stream of books, the marvelous fantastic tales, the time-machine story and the one about Dr. Moreau's bestial monsters and the one that I think is my favorite, the pitiful narrative of the invisible man. Now he wants to write the story of a journey to the Moon, among innumerable other projects, all of which he will probably fulfill. But of course there is much more to Wells than these outlandish if amusing fables: his recent book, *Love and Mr. Lewisham,* is not at all a scientific romance but rather quite the searching analysis of matters of love and power. Even so Wells is not just a novelist (a *mere* novelist, I came close to saying!); he is a seer, a prophet, he genuinely wishes to transform the world according to his great plan for it. I doubt very much that he will have the chance, but I wish him well. It is a trifle exhausting to listen to him go on and on about the new century and the miracles that it will bring, but it is enthralling as well. And of course behind his scientific optimism lurks a dark vision, quite contradictory, of the inherent nature of mankind. He is a fascinating man, a raw, elemental force. I wish he paid more attention to matters of literary style; but, then, he wishes that I would pay *less.* I dare say each of us is both right and wrong about the other.

We spoke sadly of our poor friend and neighbor, Crane *[Stephen Crane, the American novelist]* whose untimely death last week we both lament. His short life was chaotic and his disregard for his own health was virtually criminal; but *The Red Badge of Courage,* I believe, will surely long outlive him. I wonder what other magnificent works were still in him when he died.

We talk of paying calls the next day on some of our other literary friends who live nearby, Conrad, perhaps, or young Hueffer, or even Kipling up at Burwash. What a den of novelists these few counties possess!

A fine dinner and splendid talk afterward.

Early to bed for me; Wells, I suppose, will stay awake far into the night, writing, writing, writing.

June 14, Spade House, Sandgate.

In mid-morning after a generous late breakfast Wells is just at the point of composing a note to Conrad proposing an impromptu visit—Conrad is still despondently toiling at his interminable *Lord Jim* and no doubt would welcome an interruption, Wells says—when a young fellow whom Wells knows comes riding up, all out of breath, with news that a falling star has been seen crossing the skies in the night, rushing high overhead, inscribing a line of flame visible from Winchester eastward, and that—no doubt as a consequence of that event—something strange has dropped from the heavens and landed in Wells's old town of Woking, over Surrey way. It is a tangible thunderbolt, a meteor, some kind of shaft flung by the hand of Zeus, at any rate.

So, *instanter,* all is up with our visit to Conrad. Wells's scientific curiosity takes full hold of him. He must go to Woking this very moment to inspect this gift of the gods; and, willy-nilly, I am to accompany him. "You must come, you *must!*" he cries, voice disappearing upward into an octave extraordinary even for him. I ask him why, and he will only say that there will be revelations of an earthshaking kind, of planetary dimensions. "To what are you fantastically alluding?" I demand, but he will only smile enigmatically. And, shortly afterward, off we go.

June 14, much later, Woking.

Utterly extraordinary! We make the lengthy journey over from Sandgate by pony carriage, Wells and I, two literary gentlemen out for an excursion on this bright and extravagantly warm morning in late spring. I am garbed as though for a bicycle journey, my usual knickerbockers and my exiguous jacket of black and white stripes and my peaked cap; I feel ill at ease in these regalia but I have brought nothing else with me suitable for this outing. We arrive at Woking by late afternoon and plunge at once into—what other word can I use?—into madness.

The object from on high, we immediately learn, landed with an evidently violent impact in the common between Woking, Horsell, and Ottershaw, burying itself deep in the ground. The heat and fury of its impact have hurled sand and gravel in every direction and set the surrounding heather ablaze, though the fires were quickly enough extinguished. But what has fallen is no meteorite. The top of an immense metallic cylinder, perhaps thirty yards across, can be seen protruding from the pit.

Early this morning Ogilvy, the astronomer, hastened to inspect the site; and, he tells us now, he was able despite the heat emanating from the cylinder's surface to get close enough to perceive that the top of the thing had begun to rotate—as though, so he declares, there were creatures within attempting to get out!

"What we have here is a visitation from the denizens of Mars, I would hazard," says Wells without hesitation, in a tone of amazing calmness and assurance.

"Exactly so!" cries Ogilvy. "Exactly so!"

These are both men of science, and I am but a *littérateur*. I stare in bewilderment from one to the other. "How can you be so certain?" I ask them, finally.

To which Wells replies, "The peculiar bursts of light we have observed on the face of that world in recent years have aroused much curiosity, as I am sure you are aware. And then, some time ago, the sight of jets of flame leaping up night after night from the red planet, as if some great gun were being repeatedly fired—in direct consequence of which, let me propose, there eventually came the streak of light in the sky late last night, which I noticed from my study window—betokening, I would argue, the arrival here of this projectile—why, what else can it all mean, James, other than that travelers from our neighbor world lie embedded here before us on Horsell Common!"

"It can be nothing else," Ogilvy cries enthusiastically. "Travelers from Mars! But are they suffering, I wonder? Has their passage through our atmosphere engendered heat too great for them to endure?"

A flush of sorrow and compassion rushes through me at that. It awes and flusters me to think that the red planet holds sentient life, and that an intrepid band of Martians has ventured to cross the great sea of space that separates their world from ours. To have come such an immense and to me unimaginable distance—only to perish in the attempt—! Can it be, as Ogilvy suggests, that this brave interplanetary venture will end in tragedy for the voyagers? I am racked briefly by the deepest concern.

How ironic, I suppose, in view of the dark and violent later events of this day, that I should expend such pity upon our visitors. But we could tell nothing, then, nor for some little while thereafter. Crowds of curiosity seekers came and went, as they have done all day; workmen with digging tools now began to attempt to excavate the cylinder, which had cooled considerably since the morning; their attempts to complete the unscrewing of the top were wholly unsuccessful. Wells could not take his eyes from the pit. He seemed utterly possessed by a fierce joy that had been kindled in him by the possibility that the cylinder held actual Martians. It was, he told me several times, almost as though one of his own scientific fantasy books were turning to reality before his eyes; and Wells confessed that he had indeed sketched out the outline of a novel about an invasion from Mars, intending to write it some two or three years hence, but of course now that scheme has been overtaken by actual events and he shall have to abandon it. He evidences little regret at this; he appears wholly delighted, precisely as a small boy might be, that the Martians are here. I dare say that he would have regarded the intrusion of a furious horde of dinosaurs into the Surrey countryside with equal pleasure.

But I must admit that I am somewhat excited as well. Travelers from Mars! How extraordinary! *Quel phénomène!* And what vistas open to the mind of the intrepid seeker after novelty! I have traveled somewhat myself, of course, to the Continent, at least, if not to Africa or China, but I have not ruled such farther journeys completely out, and now the prospect of an even farther one becomes possible. To make the Grand Tour of Mars! To see its great monuments and temples, and perhaps have an audience at the court of the Great Martian Cham! It is a beguiling thought, if not a completely serious one. See, see, I am becoming a fantasist worthy of Wells!

(*Later. The hour of sunset.*) The cylinder is open. To our immense awe we find ourselves staring at a Martian. Did I expect them to be essentially human in form? Well, then, I was foolish in my expectations. What we see is a bulky ungainly thing; two huge eyes, great as saucers; tentacles of some sort; a strange quivering mouth—yes, yes, an alien being *senza dubbio*, preternaturally *other*.

Wells, unexpectedly, is appalled. "Disgusting . . . dreadful," he mutters. "That oily skin! Those frightful eyes! What a hideous devil it is!" Where has his scientific objectivity gone? For my part I am altogether fascinated. I tell him that I see rare beauty in the Martian's strangeness, not the beauty of a Greek vase or of a ceiling by Tiepolo, of course, but beauty of a distinct kind all the same. In this, I think, my perceptions are the superior of Wells's. There is beauty in the squirming octopus dangling from the hand of some grinning fisherman at the shore of Capri; there is beauty in the *terrifiant* bas-reliefs of winged bulls from the palaces of Nineveh; and there is beauty of a sort, I maintain, in this Martian also.

He laughs heartily. "You are ever the esthete, eh, James!"

I suppose that I am. But I will not retreat from my appreciation of the strange being who—struggling, it seems, against the unfamiliar conditions of our world—is moving about slowly and clumsily at the edge of its cylinder.

The creature drops back out of sight. The twilight is deepening to darkness. An hour passes, and nothing occurs. Wells suggests we seek dinner, and I heartily agree.

(Later still.) Horror! Just past eight, while Wells and I were dining, a delegation bearing a white flag of peace approached the pit, so we have learned—evidently in the desire to demonstrate to the Martians that we are intelligent and friendly beings. Ogilvy was in the group, and Stent, the Astronomer Royal, and some poor journalist who had arrived to report on the event. There came suddenly a blinding flash of flame from the pit, and another and another, and the whole delegation met with a terrible instant death, forty souls in all. The fiery beam also ignited adjacent trees and brought down a portion of a nearby house; and all those who had survived the massacre fled the scene in the wildest of terror.

"So they are monsters," Wells ejaculates fiercely, "and this is war between the worlds!"

"No, no," I protest, though I too am stunned by the dire news. "They are far from home—frightened, discomforted—it is a tragic misunderstanding and nothing more."

Wells gives me a condescending glance. That one withering look places our relationship, otherwise so cordial, in its proper context. He is the hardheaded man of realities who has clawed his way up from poverty and ignorance; I am the moneyed and comfortable and overly gentle literary artist, the *connoisseur* of the life of the leisured classes. And then too, not for the first time, I have failed to seize the immediate horrific implications of a situation whilst concentrating on peripheral pretty responses. To brusque and self-confident Wells, in his heart of hearts, I surely must appear as something charming but effete.

I think that Wells greatly underestimates the strength of my fibre, but this is no moment to debate the point.

"Shall we pay a call on your unhappy friends from Mars, and see if they receive us more amiably?" he suggests.

I cannot tell whether he is sincere. It is always necessary to allow for Wells's insatiable scientific curiosity.

"By all means, if that is what you wish," I bravely say, and wait for his response. But in fact he is *not* serious; he has no desire to share the fate of Ogilvy and Stent; and, since it is too late now to return to Sandgate this night, we take lodgings at an inn he knows here in Woking. Clearly Wells is torn, I see, between his conviction that the Martians are here to do evil and his powerful desire to learn all that a human mind can possibly learn about these beings from an unknown world.

June 15, Woking and points east.

Perhaps the most ghastly day of my life.

Just as well we made no attempt last evening to revisit the pit. Those who did—there were some such foolhardy ones—did not return, for the heat-ray was seen to flash more than once in the darkness. Great hammering noises came from the pit all night, and occasional puffs of greenish-white smoke. Devil's work, to be sure. Just after midnight a second falling star could be seen in the northwest sky. The invasion, and there is no doubt now that that is what it is, proceeds apace.

In the morning several companies of soldiers took possession of the entire common and much of the area surrounding it. No one may approach the site and indeed the military have ordered an evacuation of part of Horsell. It is a hot, close day and we have, of course, no changes of clothing with us. Rye and dear old Lamb House seem now to be half a world away. In the night I began to yearn terribly for home, but Wells's determination to remain here and observe the unfolding events was manifest from the time of our awakening. I was unwilling to be rebuked for my timidity, nor could I very well take his pony carriage and go off with it whilst leaving him behind, and so I resolved to see it all out at his side.

But would there be any unfolding events to observe? The morning and afternoon were dull and wearying. Wells was an endless fount of scientific speculation—he was convinced that the greater gravitational pull of Earth would keep the Martians from moving about freely on our world, and that conceivably they might drown in our thicker atmosphere, et cetera, and that was interesting to me at first and then considerably less so as he went on with it. Unasked, he lectured me interminably on the subject of Mars, its topography, its climate, its seasons, its bleak and forlorn landscape. Wells is an irrepressible lecturer: there is no halting him once he has the bit between his teeth.

In mid-afternoon we heard the sound of distant gunfire to the north: evidently attempts were being made to destroy the second cylinder before it could open. But at Woking all remained in a nerve-wracking stasis the whole day, until, abruptly, at six in the evening there came an explosion from the common, and gunfire, and a fierce shaking and a crashing that brought into my mind the force of the eruption of Vesuvius as it must have been on the day of the doom of Pompeii. We looked out and saw treetops breaking into flame like struck matches; buildings began to collapse as though the breath of a giant had been angrily expended upon them; and fires sprang up all about. The Martians had begun to destroy Woking.

"Come," Wells said. He had quickly concluded that it was suicidal folly to remain here any longer, and certainly I would not disagree. We hastened to the pony carriage; he seized the reins; and off we went to the east, with black smoke rising behind us and the sounds of rifles and machine guns providing incongruous contrapuntal rhythms as we made our way on this humid spring evening through this most pleasant of green countrysides.

We traveled without incident as far as Leatherhead; all was tranquil; it was next to impossible to believe that behind us lay a dreadful scene of death and destruction. Wells's wife has cousins at Leatherhead, and they, listening gravely and with obvious skepticism to our wild tales of Martians with heat-rays laying waste to Woking, gave us supper and evidently expected that we would be guests for the night, it now being nearly ten; but no, Wells had taken it into his head to drive all night, going on by way of Maidstone or perhaps Tunbridge Wells down into Sussex to deliver me to Rye, and thence homeward for him to Sandgate. It was lunacy, but in the frenzy of the moment I agreed to his plan, wishing at this point quickly to put as much distance between the invaders and myself as could be managed.

And so we took our hasty leave of Leatherhead. Glancing back, we saw a fearsome scarlet glow on the western horizon, and huge clots of black smoke. And, as we drove onward, there came a horrid splash of green light overhead, which we both knew must be the third falling star, bringing with it the next contingent of Martians.

Nevertheless I believed myself to be safe. I have known little if any physical danger in my life and it has a certain unreal quality to me; I cannot ever easily accept it as impinging on my existence. Therefore it came as a great astonishment and a near unhinging of my inner stability when, sometime past midnight, with thunder sounding in the distance and the air portending imminent rain, the pony abruptly whinnied and reared in terror, and a moment later we beheld a titanic metal creature, perhaps one hundred feet high, striding through the young forest before us on three great metal legs, smashing aside all that lay in its way.

"Quickly!" Wells cried, and seized me by the wrist in an iron grasp and tumbled me out of the cart, down into the grass by the side of the road, just as the poor pony swung round in its fright and bolted off, cart and all, into the woods. The beast traveled no more than a dozen yards before it became fouled amidst low-lying branches and tumbled over, breaking the cart to splinters and, I am afraid, snapping its own neck in the fall. Wells and I lay huddled beneath a shrub as the colossal three-legged metal engine passed high above us. Then came a second one, following in its track, setting up a monstrous outcry as it strode along. "Aloo! Aloo!" it called, and from its predecessor came back an acknowledging "Aloo!"

"The Martians have built war machines for themselves," Wells murmured. "That was the hammering we heard in the pit. And now these two are going to greet the companions who have just arrived aboard the third cylinder."

How I admired his cool analytical mind just then! For the thunderstorm had reached us, and we suddenly now were being wholly drenched, and muddied as well, and it was late at night and our cart was smashed and our pony was dead, the two of us alone out here in a deserted countryside at the mercy of marauding metal monsters, and even then Wells was capable of so cool an assessment of the events exploding all around us.

I have no idea how long we remained where we were. Perhaps we even dozed a little. No more Martians did we see. A great calmness came over me as the rain went on and on and I came to understand that I could not possibly get any wetter. At length the storm moved away; Wells aroused me and announced that we were not far from Epsom, where perhaps we might find shelter if the Martians had not already devastated it; and so, drenched to the bone, we set out on foot in the darkness. Wells prattled all the while, about the parchedness of Mars and how intensely interested the Martians must be in the phenomenon of water falling from the skies. I replied somewhat curtly that it was not a phenomenon of such great interest to me, the rain now showing signs of returning. In fact I doubted I should survive this soaking. Already I was beginning to feel unwell. But I drew on unsuspected reservoirs of strength and kept pace with the indomitable Wells as we endlessly walked. To me this excursion was like a dream, and not a pleasing one. We tottered on Epsomward all through the dreadful night, arriving with the dawn.

June 20? 21? 22? Epsom.

My doubt as to today's date is trivial in regard to my doubt over everything else. It seems that I have been in a delirium of fever for at least a week, perhaps more, and the world has tottered all about me in that time.

Wells believes that today is Thursday, the 21st of June, 1900. Our innkeeper passionately insists it is a day earlier than that. His daughter thinks we have reached Saturday or even Sunday. If we had today's newspaper we should be able to settle the question easily enough, but there are no newspapers. Nor can we wire Greenwich to learn whether the summer solstice has yet occurred, for the Observatory no doubt has been abandoned, as has all the rest of London. Civilization, it appears, has collapsed utterly in this single week. All days are Sundays now: nothing stirs, there is no edifying life.

I too collapsed utterly within an hour or two of the end of our night's march to Epsom, lost in a dizzying rhapsody of fatigue and exposure. Wells has nursed me devotedly. Apparently I have had nearly all of his meager ration of food. There are five of us here, the innkeeper and his wife and daughter and us, safely barricaded, so we hope, against the Martian killing machines and the lethal black gas that they have been disseminating. Somehow this town, this inn, this little island within England where we lie concealed, has escaped the general destruction—thus far. But now comes word that our sanctuary may soon be violated; and what shall we do, Wells and I? Proceeding eastward to our homes along the coast is impossible: the Martians have devastated everything in that direction. "We must to London," Wells insists. "The great city stands empty. Only there will we find food enough to continue, and places to hide from them."

It is a source of wonder and mystery to me that all has fallen apart so swiftly, that—in southern England, at least—the comfortable structures of the society I knew have evaporated entirely, within a week, vanishing with the speed of snowflakes after a spring storm.

What has happened? *This* has happened:

Cylinders laden with Martians have continued daily to arrive from the void. The creatures emerge; they assemble their gigantic transporting carriages; the mechanical colossi go back and forth upon the land, spreading chaos and death with their heat-rays, their clouds of poisonous black vapor, and any number of other devices of deviltry. Whole towns have been charred; whole regiments have been dropped in their tracks; whole counties have been abandoned. The government, the military, all has disintegrated. Our leaders have vanished in a hundred directions. Her Majesty and the Members of Parliament and the entire authority-wielding apparatus of the state now seem as mythical as the knights of the Round Table. We have been thrown back into a state of nature, every man for himself.

In London, so our hosts have told us, all remained ignorantly calm through Sunday last, until news came to the capital from the south of the terror and destruction there, the giant invulnerable spiderlike machines, the fires, the suffocating poisonous gas. Evidently a ring of devastation had been laid down on a great arc south of the Thames from Windsor and Staines over through Reigate, at least, and on past Maidstone to Deal and Broadstairs on the Kentish coast. Surely they were closing the net on London, and on Monday morning the populace of that great city commenced to flee in all directions. A few of those who came this way, hoping to reach friends or kin in Kent or East Sussex—there were many thousands—told Wells and the innkeeper of the furious frantic exodus, the great mobs streaming northward, and those other desperate mobs flooding eastward to the Essex shore, as the methodical Martians advanced on London, exterminating all in their path. The loss of life, in that mad rush, must have been unthinkably great.

"And we have had no Martians here?" I asked Wells.

"On occasion, yes," he replied casually, as though I had asked him about cricket matches or rainstorms. "A few of their great machines passed through earlier in the week, bound on deadly business elsewhere, no doubt; we called no attention to ourselves, and they took no notice of us. We have been quite fortunate, James."

The landlord's daughter, though—a wild boyish girl of fourteen or fifteen—has been out boldly roving these last few days, and reports increasing numbers of Martians going to and fro to the immediate south and east of us. She says that everything is burned and ruined as far as she went in the directions of Banstead and Leatherhead, and some sort of red weed, no doubt of Martian origin, is weirdly spreading across the land. It is only a matter of time, Wells believes, before they come into Epsom again, and this time, like the randomly striking godlike beings that they seem to be, they may take it into their minds to hurl this place into ruin as well. We must be off, he says; we must to London, where we will be invisible in the vastness of the place.

"And should we not make an attempt to reach our homes, instead?" I ask.

"There is no hope of that, none," says Wells. "The Martians will have closed the entire coast, to prevent an attack through the Strait of Dover by our maritime forces. Even if we survived the journey to the coast, we should find nothing there, James, nothing but ash and rubble. To London, my friend: that is where we must go, now that you are sturdy again."

There is no arguing with Wells. It would be like arguing with a typhoon.

June 23, let us say. En route to London.

How strange this once-familiar landscape seems! I feel almost as though I have been transported to Mars and my old familiar life has been left behind on some other star.

We are just outside Wimbledon. Everything is scorched and blackened to our rear; everything seems scorched and blackened ahead of us. We have seen things too terrible to relate, signs of the mass death that must have been inflicted here. Yet all is quiet now. The weather continues fiercely hot and largely dry, and the red Martian weed, doubtless finding conditions similar to those at home, has spread everywhere. It reminds me of the enormous cactus plants one sees in southern Italy, but for its somber brick-red hue and the great luxuriance of its habit of growth: it is red, red, *red,* as far as the eye can see. A dreamlike transformation, somber and depressing in its morbid implications, and of course terrifying. I am certain I will never see my home again, which saddens me. It seems pure insanity to me to be going on into London, despite all the seemingly cogent reasons Wells expresses.

And yet, and yet! Behind the terror and the sadness, how wonderfully exhilarating all this is, really! Shameful of me to say so, but I confess it only to my notebook: this is the great adventure of my life, the wondrous powerful action in which I have ever longed to be involved. At last I am fully *living*! My heart weeps for the destruction I see all about me, for the fall of civilization itself, but yet—I will not deny it—I am invigorated far beyond my considerable years by the constant peril, by the demands placed upon my formerly coddled body, above all, by the sheer *strangeness* of everything within my ken. If I survive this journey and live to make my escape to some unblighted land I shall dine out on these events forever.

We are traveling, to my supreme astonishment, by *motorcar*. Wells found one at a house adjacent to the inn, fully stocked with petrol, and he is driving the noisy thing, very slowly but with great perseverance, with all the skill of an expert *chauffeur*. He steers around obstacles capably; he handles sharp and frightening turns in the road with supreme aplomb. It was only after we had been on the road for over an hour that he remarked to me, in an offhand way, "Do you know, James, I have never driven one of these machines before. But there's nothing at all to it, really! Nothing!" Wells is extraordinary. He has offered to give me a chance at the wheel; but no, no, I think I shall let him be the driver on this journey.

(*Later.*) An astonishing incident, somewhere between Wimbledon and London, unforgettably strange.

Wells sees the cupola of a Martian walking machine rising above the treetops not far ahead of us, and brings the motorcar to a halt while we contemplate the situation. The alien engine stands completely still, minute after minute; perhaps it has no tenant, or possibly even its occupant was destroyed in some rare successful attempt at a counterattack. Wells proposes daringly but characteristically that we go up to it on foot and take a close look at it, after which, since we are so close to London and ought not to be drawing the Martians' attention to ourselves as we enter a city which presumably they occupy, we should abandon our motorcar and slip into the capital on foot, like the furtive fugitives that we are.

Naturally I think it's rash to go anywhere near the Martian machine. But Wells will not be gainsaid. And so we warily advance, until we are no more than twenty yards from it; whereupon we discover an amazing sight. The Martians ride in a kind of cabin or basket high up above the great legs of their machines. But this one had dismounted and descended somehow to the ground, where it stands fully exposed in a little open space by the side of a small stream just beyond its mechanical carrier, peering reflectively toward the water for all the world as though it were considering passing the next hour with a bit of angling.

The Martian was globular in form, a mere ambulatory head without body—or a body without head, if you will—a yard or more in diameter, limbless, with an array of many whiplike tentacles grouped in two bunches by its mouth. As we breathlessly watched, the creature leaned ponderously forward and dipped a few of these tentacles into the stream, holding them there a long while in evident satisfaction, as though it were a Frenchman and this was a river of the finest claret passing before it, which could somehow be enjoyed and appreciated in this fashion. We could not take our eyes from the spectacle. I saw Wells glance toward a jagged rock of some size lying nearby, as though he had it in mind to attempt some brutal act of heroism against the alien as it stood with its back to us; but I shook my head, more out of an unwillingness to see him take life than out of fear of the consequences of such an attack, and he let the rock be.

How long did this interlude go on? I could not say. We were rooted, fascinated, by our encounter with *the other*. Then the Martian turned—with the greatest difficulty—and trained its huge dark eyes on us. Wells and I exchanged wary glances. Should we finally flee? The Martian seemed to carry no weapons; but who knew what powers of the mind it might bring to bear on us? Yet it simply studied us, dispassionately, as one might study a badger or a mole that has wandered out of the woods. It was a magical moment, of a sort: beings of two disparate worlds face-to-face (so to speak) and eye-to-eye, and no hostile action taken on either side.

The Martian then uttered a kind of clicking noise, which we took to be a threat, or a warning. "Time for us to be going,"

Wells said, and we backed hastily out of the clearing. The clicking sound, we saw, had notified the Martian's transport mechanism that it wished to be reseated in the cupola, and a kind of cable quickly came down, gathered it up, and raised it to its lofty perch. Now the Martian was in full possession of its armaments again, and I was convinced that my last moments had arrived. But no; no. The thing evinced no interest in murdering us. Perhaps it too had felt the magic of our little encounter; or it may be that we were deemed too insignificant to be worth slaughtering. In any event the great machine lumbered into life and went striding off toward the west, leaving Wells and me gaping slack-jawed at each other like two men who had just experienced the company of some basilisk or chimera or banshee and had lived to tell the tale.

The following day, whichever one that may be.

We are in London, having entered the metropolis from the south by way of the Vauxhall Bridge after a journey on foot that makes my old trampings in Provence and the Campagna and the one long ago over the Alps into Italy seem like the merest trifling strolls. And yet I feel little weariness, for all my hunger and the extreme physical effort of these days past. It is the strange exhilaration, still, that drives me onward, muddied and tattered though I am, and with my banished beard, alas, re-emerging in all its dread whiteness.

Here in the greatest of cities the full extent of the catastrophe comes home with overwhelming impact. There is no one here. We could not be more alone were we on Crusoe's island. The desolation is magnified by the richness of the amenities all about us, the grand hotels, the splendid town-houses, the rich shops, the theatres. Those still remain: but whom do they serve? We see a few corpses lying about here and there, no doubt those who failed to heed the warning to flee; the murderous black powder, apparently no longer lethal, covers much of the city like a horrid dark snowfall; there is some sign of looting, but not really very much, so quickly did everyone flee. The stillness is profound. It is the stillness of Pompeii, the stillness of Agamemnon's Mycenae. But those are bleached ruins; London has the look of a vibrant city, yet, except that there is no one here.

So far as we can see, Wells and I are the only living things, but for birds, and stray cats and dogs. Not even the Martians are in evidence: they must be extending their conquests elsewhere,

meaning to return in leisure when the job is done. We help ourselves to food in the fine shops of Belgravia, whose doors stand
mostly open; we even dare to refresh ourselves, guiltlessly, with a
bottle of three-guinea Chambertin, after much effort on Wells's
part in extracting the cork; and then we plunge onward past Buck-
ingham Palace—empty, empty!—into the strangely bleak pre-
cincts of Mayfair and Piccadilly.

Like some revenant wandering through a dream-world I revisit
the London I loved. Now it is Wells who feels the outsider, and I
who am at home. Here are my first lodgings at Bolton St., in
Piccadilly; here are the clubs where I so often dined, pre-eminent
among them for me the Reform Club, my dear refuge and sanctuary in the city, where when still young I was to meet Gladstone
and Tennyson and Schliemann of Troy. What would Schliemann
make of London now? I invite Wells to admire my little
pied-à-terre at the Reform, but the building is sealed and we move
on. The city is ours. Perhaps we will go to Kensington, where I
can show him my chaste and secluded flat at De Vere Mansions
with its pretty view of the park; but no, no, we turn the other way,
through the terrifying silence, the tragic solitude. Wells wishes to
ascertain whether the British Museum is open. So it is up Charing
Cross Road for us, and into Bloomsbury, and yes, amazingly, the
museum door stands ajar. We can, if we wish, help ourselves to the
Elgin Marbles and the Rosetta Stone and the Portland Vase. But
to what avail? Everything is meaningless now. Wells stations himself before some battered pharaoh in the hall of Egyptian sculp-
ture and cries out, in what I suppose he thinks is a mighty and
terrible voice, "I am Ozymandias, King of Kings! Look on my
works, ye mighty, and despair!"

What, I wonder, shall we do? Wander London at will, until the
Martians come and slay us as they have slain the others? There is a
certain wonderful *frisson* to be had from being the last men in
London; but in truth it is terrible, terrible, terrible. What is the
worth of having survived, when civilization has perished?

Cold sausages and stale beer in a pub just off Russell Square.
The red weed, we see, is encroaching everywhere in London as it
is in the countryside. Wells is loquacious; talks of his impoverished
youth, his early ambitions, his ferociously self-imposed education,
his gradual accretion of achievement and his ultimate great triumph as popular novelist and philosopher. He has a high opinion

of his intellect, but there is nothing offensive in the way he voices it, for his self-approbation is well earned. He is a remarkable man. I could have done worse for a companion in this apocalypse. Imagine being here with poor gloomy tormented Conrad, for example!

A terrifying moment toward nightfall. We have drifted down toward Covent Garden; I turn toward Wells, who has been walking a pace or two behind me peering into shop windows, and suggest that we appropriate lodgings for ourselves at the Savoy or the Ritz. No Wells! He has vanished like his own Invisible Man!

"Wells?" I cry. "Wells, where are you?"

Silence. *Calma come la tomba*. Has he plunged unsuspecting into some unguarded abyss of the street? Or perhaps been snatched away by some silent machine of the Martians? How am I to survive without him in this dead city? It is Wells who has the knack of breaking into food shops and such, Wells who will meet all the practical challenges of our strange life here: not I.

"Wells!" I call again. There is panic in my voice, I fear.

But I am alone. He is utterly gone. What shall I do? Five minutes go by; ten, fifteen. Logic dictates that I remain right on this spot until he reappears, for how else shall we find each other in this huge city? But night is coming; I am suddenly afraid; I am weary and unutterably sad; I see my death looming before me now. I will go to the Savoy. Yes. Yes. I begin to walk, and then to run, as my terror mounts, along Southampton Street.

Then I am at the Strand, at last. There is the hotel; and there is Wells, arms folded, calmly waiting outside it for me.

"I thought you would come here," he says.

"Where have you been? Is this some prank, Wells?" I hotly demand.

"I called to you to follow me. You must not have heard me. Come: I must show you something, James."

"Now? For the love of God, Wells, I'm ready to drop!" But he will hear no protests, of course. He has me by the wrist; he drags me *away* from the hotel, back toward Covent Garden, over to little Henrietta Street. And there, pushed up against the facade of a shabby old building—Number 14, Henrietta Street—is the wreckage of some Martian machine, a kind of low motorcar with metallic tentacles, that has smashed itself in a wild career through the street. A dead Martian is visible through the shattered window of the passenger carriage. We stare awhile in awe. "Do you see?" he asks, as though I could not. "They are not wholly invulnerable, it seems!" To which I agree, thinking only of finding a place where I can lie down; and then he allows us to withdraw, and we go to the hotel, which stands open to us, and ensconce ourselves in the most lavish suites we can find. I sleep as though I have not slept in months.

A day later yet.

It is beyond all belief, but the war is over, and we are, miraculously, free of the Martian terror!

Wells and I discovered, in the morning, a second motionless Martian machine standing like a sentinel at the approach to the Waterloo Bridge. Creeping fearlessly up to it, we saw that its backmost leg was frozen in flexed position, so that the thing was balanced only on two; with one good shove we might have been able to push the whole unstable mechanism over. Of the Martian in its cabin we could see no sign.

All during the day we roamed London, searching out the Martians. I felt strangely tranquil. Perhaps it was only my extreme fatigue; but certainly we were accustomed now to the desolation, to the tangles of the red weed, the packs of newly wild dogs.

Between the Strand and Grosvenor Square we came upon three more Martian machines: dead, dead, all dead. Then we heard a strange sound, emanating from the vicinity of the Marble Arch: "Ulla, ulla, ulla," it was, a mysterious sobbing howl. In the general silence that sound had tremendous power. It drew us; instead of fleeing, as sane men should have done, we approached. "Ulla, ulla!" A short distance down the Bayswater Road we saw a towering Martian fighting machine looming above Hyde Park: the sound was coming from it. A signal of distress? A call to its distant cohorts, if any yet lived? Hands clapped to our ears—for the cry was deafening—we drew nearer still; and, suddenly, it stopped. There seemed an emphatic permanence to that stoppage. We waited. The sound did not begin anew.

"Dead," Wells said. "The last of them, I suspect. Crying a requiem for its race."

"What do you mean?" I asked.

"What our guns could not do, the lowly germs of Earth have achieved—I'll wager a year's earnings on that! Do you think,

James, that the Martians had any way of defending themselves against our microbes? I have been waiting for this! I knew it would happen!"

Did he? He had never said a word.

July 7, Lamb House.

How sweet to be home!

And so it has ended, the long nightmare of the interplanetary war. Wells and I found, all over London, the wrecked and useless vehicles of the Martians, with their dead occupants trapped within. Dead, all dead, every invader. And as we walked about, other human beings came forth from hiding places, and we embraced one another in wild congratulation.

Wells's hypothesis was correct, as we all have learned by now. The Martians have perished in mid-conquest, victims of our terrestrial bacteria. No one has seen a living one anywhere in the past two weeks. We fugitive humans have returned to our homes; the wheels of civilization have begun to turn once more.

We are safe, yes—and yet we are not. Whether the Martians will return, fortified now against our microorganisms and ready to bend us once more to their wishes, we cannot say. But it is clear now to me that the little sense of security that we of Earth feel, most especially we inhabitants of England in the sixty-third year of the reign of Her Majesty Queen Victoria, is a pathetic illusion. Our world is no impregnable fortress. We stand open to the unpredictable sky. If Martians can come one day, Venusians may come another, or Jovians, or warlike beings from some wholly unknown star. The events of these weeks have been marvelous and terrible, and without shame I admit having derived great rewards even from my fear and my exertions; but we must all be aware now that we are at great risk of a reprise of these dark happenings. We have learned, now, that we are far from being the masters of the cosmos, as we like to suppose. It is a bitter lesson to be given at the outset of this glorious new century.

I discussed these points with Wells when he called here yesterday. He was in complete agreement.

And, as he was taking his leave, I went on, somewhat hesitantly, to express to him the other thought that had been forming in my mind all this past week. "You said once," I began, "that you had had some scheme in mind, even before the coming of the Martians, for writing a novel of interplanetary invasion. Is that still your intent now that fantasy has become fact, Wells?"

He allowed that it was.

"But it would not now be," I said, "your usual kind of fantastic fiction, would it? It would be more in the line of *reportage,* would you not say? An account of the responses of certain persons to the true and actual extreme event?"

"Of course it would, of necessity," he said. I smiled expressively and said nothing. And then, quickly divining my meaning, he added: "But of course I would yield, *cher maître,* if it were *your* intention to—"

"It is," I said serenely.

He was quite graceful about it, all in all. And so I will set to work tomorrow. *The Ambassadors* may perhaps be the grandest and finest of my novels, but it will have to wait another year or two, I suppose, for there is something much more urgent that must be written first.*

---

* [James's notebooks indicate that he did not actually begin work on his classic novel of interplanetary conflict, *The War of the Worlds,* until the 28th of July, 1900. The book was finished by the 17th of November, unusually quickly for James, and after serialization in *The Atlantic Monthly* (August–December 1901) was published in England by Macmillan and Company in March 1902 and in the United States by Harper & Brothers one month later. It has remained his most popular book ever since and has on three occasions been adapted for motion pictures. Wells never did write an account of his experiences during the Martian invasion, though those experiences did, of course, have a profound influence on his life and work thereafter.

—The Editor.]

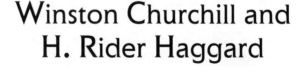

Winston Churchill and H. Rider Haggard

THE TRUE TALE
OF THE FINAL BATTLE
OF UMSLOPOGAAS THE ZULU

JANET BERLINER

Bear with me, please. What I have to say really does relate to the story you are about to read.

I was born and raised in what was, then, the Union of South Africa—a bilingual country where learning to speak and read Afrikaans was mandatory. At the age of thirteen, I was forced to read H. Rider Haggard's King Solomon's Mines *as a setwork book in Afrikaans. The language being what it is, a bland porridge of kitchen Dutch and kitchen German, it remains amazing to me that I not only enjoyed the book, but was turned on to Haggard.*

A few years ago, I discovered that Haggard's She *was based on the Lovedu, a tribe extant even now in the Drakensberg Mountains. I decided to start researching a novel about immortality, using the real descendant of Haggard's white queen, Ayesha, as my protagonist. In order to complete my research, I contacted the chief minister of the queen, and arranged to visit the tribal village.*

This being the nineties, we corresponded via fax and then spoke on the phone. I was treated most graciously. When I asked what gift I should bring to the queen—knowing this to be a tradition—I was informed that a blanket was still the best received present.

Sadly, I had to cancel my trip, but I nevertheless sent the gift of several American Indian blankets. Staying with the old tradition, I received a present in return—one thought to be appropriate to a writer.

The gift sent to me by the Modjadji, as the queen calls herself, was a notebook, an exercise book such as we children used for exams in Standards One and Two in our South African schools. When I opened it up, I found that I held in my hands a yellowed, handwritten chronicle by Winston S. Churchill. I thought of annotating the chronicle here and there, to show you, the reader, where it coincides with historical fact. Upon reconsideration, since most of it is, indeed, verifiable, I decided to leave that for you to discover.

And that is all I have to say for now, except to add that tucked inside the notebook was a handwritten letter addressed to H. Rider Haggard, Esq., Ditchingham House, Norfolk, England, and that the chronicle was dated only with the year—1899. . . .

Dear Mr Haggard,

Shortly before leaving Sandhurst, I read *Allan Quatermain* for a second time, mostly, I confess, to distract myself from the examinations that were looming in my immediate future. It was then that I decided that I would grasp the first opportunity to go to Southern Africa and seek out the Zu-Vendis of your book, so that I could discover the true tale of the death of Umslopogaas, the Zulu.

I have not yet sought out the tribe, so I have no answers. However, I shall make every attempt to find a time for digression into what you call Zu-Vendi territory. I am more than ever determined to do that, for reasons you will understand when you read the chronicle which I will begin when I have completed this letter to you.

Whatever I find, I will write down and send into your hands. Make use of what you read as you see fit.

I remain, Yours truly,
Winston S. Churchill

God knows I love adventure and seek it out, else why would I have been so delighted when, at twenty-four and not an hour after the Boers had delivered their ultimatum regarding the withdrawal of British forces from their frontiers, Oliver Borthwick offered me the post of principal war correspondent there for *The Morning Post*. I could hardly wait to board the *Dunottar Castle* and take passage for my first assignment.

Now that I am here, I find myself fascinated by this country, with its infinite variety of people and terrain, and would likely choose to live here, had I (and my family) not settled upon another, greater design.

However, fervently as I might desire to live in this country, I have no particular reason to wish to die here. Yet, die I could—and soon—which is why I have begun this chronicle of the strange events that are befalling me. So, while I shall continue to chronicle the twists and turns of this war in Southern Africa, and to send them in dispatches to my editor at *The Morning Post*, I will write here of these other things.

This night, sitting with coffee and rusks at the campfire on the outskirts of Estcourt, within the smell of horses and urine and the sounds of preparations for battle, I chanced to look up at the heavens. The moment was propitious, for it served to warn me that something was amiss, and that I should be on the lookout for strange happenings.

What I saw was a red flash, followed by a green flash, followed by a trail of brilliant white light making its way toward the earth. I reached for my companion's flask of good South African brandy, drank long and hard, and retired to my wagon for the night. When I found that I could not sleep, I put match to a candle and penned the letter addressed to Mr H. Rider Haggard which opens this chronicle. I first wrote to him when I was at Harrow and but a boy of thirteen. In that letter, I thanked him for the enjoyment he had given me with his fiction, *Allan Quatermain*, a letter to which he graciously responded.

While at Sandhurst, I read the book again. This second reading left me with an unsettled feeling, for, being now an adult, I became convinced that something was askew with the book's ending. I could not believe that a warrior of the fiber of Umslopogaas, the Zulu, would end his life in wanton destruction of what was holy and sacred to the natives.

Umslopogaas was a warrior and a man of honor. That is enough to label him Christian. His axe, *Inkosi-kaas*, was bloodied honorably in battle. Why then, having defended the temple of the Zu-Vendis with his life, would he make his final act that of lifting his famous battle-axe in the destruction of the black marble block which reputedly fell from the sun and lay at the center of the tradition of the sun worshipers he was giving his life to defend? It makes no sense. And it especially makes no sense when the inscription contains a prophecy which warns that,

". . . when it is shattered into fragments a king of alien race should rule over the land."

In fact, his supposed actions distressed me in much the same manner as those of which I wrote when I talked about Kitchener's actions in my book, *The River War*. I had fought the Dervishes with the 21st Lancers; we defeated them and I was happy of it. Still I saw no merit to the destruction of the Mahdi's tomb, as I see no merit in any such flagrantly un-Christian act of wantonness.

Moreover, and again I refer to Mr Haggard's fiction, the queen whose region (and life) Umslopogaas saved offered so glib an answer to Quatermain's inquiry as to the identity of the king of the alien race (stating almost without deliberation that the reference was to Sir Henry Curtis, her Regent—alien only in that he was a Brit rather than an African) that her reply seemed to me to amount to no less than a *deus ex machina*.

Having written now to Mr Haggard, and having just seen a sight as might have blinded a lesser man, I will take a second swig of brandy— my pay as a field journalist for *The Morning Post* is accumulating at home and my subaltern's pay of two hundred and fifty pounds a month allows for some small luxuries such as brandy and cigars. I must try to sleep, for early in the morning I depart on an armoured train along with a company of Dublin Fusiliers and Durban Light Infantry, and a six-pointer naval gun, all under the command of the formidable Captain Haldane. Should sleep elude me, I will go outside into the soft mid-November rain which has doubtless washed away the nightly influx of glowworms, and walk until I am tired enough to fall into slumber.

A month has passed since my last entry in this chronicle which, happily, was never meant to be one of those day-by-day diaries which I abhor because of the guilt one endures when circumstances force one to miss an entry. Generally speaking, those missed entries point to uneventful days. In this case, my month of pencil-silence stems from nothing if not the opposite case.

On the morning after I saw the heavens lit by what appeared to be an explosion in the sky—being no astronomer, I cannot be entirely sure of the location—I awoke into the sultry Natal morning with a giant hangover. Judging by the state of emptiness of my brandy flask, I took that to mean that what I had seen was hallucination caused by the purity of the South African brew.

Much to my own surprise, I managed to make the train on time.

Before embarking, we were given our instructions. They were, quite simply, to reconnoiter.

Unfortunately, the Boers appeared to have been given much the same instructions. They rained fire upon our armoured train. Since my head was, at the time, above the armour, I caught a piece of shrapnel.

While I know that what I am about to relate happened, it may differ significantly from what history tells of it. I can foresee that people will say that I was adversely affected by the shrapnel, and that I dreamed what I saw. I have tried to tell myself the same thing, but it remains impossible to delude myself.

You may read *their* histories, and decide for yourself. I give you permission, Mr Haggard, should this chronicle fall into your hands, to use it as the base of one of your fictions, though perhaps it is better suited to the pen of Mr Wells. I might even have sent it to him, had I not so roundly and publicly criticized his *Russia in the Shadows* in *The Daily Express*.

In any event, let me return to my adventure on the train.

We were travelling forward at no less than forty miles an hour when I heard a whining noise, loud even above the sound of gunfire. It was followed almost immediately by the appearance of a massive object which seemed to fall from the heavens and embed itself into the ground, creating a huge crater which bellowed forth black smoke and the occasional flash of red and green fire.

I immediately thought of the flashes I had seen in the sky, some one month earlier—those of which I have already written and bethought were born of drunken imaginings.

The train went instantly into reverse. Minutes later, it humped into the air like a caterpillar, as a single truck derailed and impeded its backward progress. Not half a mile away, there lingered a cloud of smoke, hanging in the humid air. Though I longed to investigate, I set about to calm the driver, help the injured, and avoid the rifle shots which came from the Boers who were well situated on a hill above us and kept up a steady stream of fire.

Having cleared the debris of the derailment, we placed the injured in the engine and proceeded again backward along the track. Once having reached a margin of safety, I instructed the driver, jumped from the train, and started back toward Captain Haldane and the others—motivated as much by a curiosity about the large object embedded in the earth, as by what I saw as my duty.

Not far from the Blue Krantz River, I encountered two riflemen, but their appearance before me was overshadowed by that of a mechanical being which loomed behind them, looking as if it had been constructed out of the combined nightmares of Messrs Wells and Verne.

I did not linger long enough to be able to provide here a detailed description. What had started as a beautiful, if hot and humid summer day, had turned dark and scowling. The air was filled with black smoke, and my head hurt from a combination of gunshot grazing, heat, and tension. Still I saw what I saw—a walking metal tripod, it was, spewing red and green flames from a device it held in what, I suppose, was its hand.

Fortunately for me, I had dropped my Mauser at the site of the train crash, else I might have made some foolish attempt at bravery. Instead, choosing discretion above valour, I jumped over a bank and fell to the bottom of a dip in the ground, thus escaping the fate of the riflemen whose ashes I found later when I emerged from my hiding place. It occurred to me as I mumbled a prayer over the ashes—Boer enemy or not, they deserved that much respect—that the metal thing I had seen might simply have been the mechanical servant of the intelligence that had brought the large object, the Thing, to earth. I knew it was my duty to investigate, for there might be other such objects hurtling toward us.

I was torn. As a journalist and humanitarian, my duty lay in investigating this phenomenon so that I could tell the world of what I had seen. But selfishly my concern was for myself, for I had no wish to end up like that pile of ashes, nor did I relish the idea of being taken prisoner by the Boers—a fate, I had been warned, that was almost inevitably followed by death.

Perhaps fortunately for my conscience, the decision was made for me. I was captured almost immediately by a horse-borne rifleman who turned out to be none other than the Boer leader, Louis Botha.

Thus it was that I languished in a Pretoria prison for the better part of a month. I tried to talk about what I had seen, but was dismissed by some as a madman, and by others as a man so desperate to escape that I would pretend lunacy.

I have no reason to detail my escape from prison. Suffice it to say that I *did* escape, and found myself at large, with seventy-five pounds and a few slabs of chocolate in my pocket. I knew that I must head for the safety of Delegoa Bay, three hundred miles away in Portuguese East Africa. I must get clear of town and jump a freight train headed in the right direction, something I could gauge by instinct alone. I found a track, but when no train passed and I had grown hungry and tired, I wandered toward the only lights I could see in the distance.

As luck would have it, I found myself in the hands of a miner who pronounced himself friend. I told him about the explosion in the sky, the landing of the Thing, and the incineration of the two riflemen at the mechanical hands of what I had taken to calling the metal man.

The implacable miner listened without batting an eye and responded by saying that all of that notwithstanding, I was a hunted man with a price on my head. He gave me rations and hid me in the pit, where I remained for several days with nothing but pink-eyed rats as my companions, while he enlisted the help of a friendly Dutchman who agreed to transport me to a freight train, load me onto it, and hide me under a tarpaulin amidst a large shipment of bales of wool.

Safely back in Durban, I found that I had gained some notoriety and was being both lauded and damned by the press. To some, I was the Scarlet Pimpernel, to others, I was a prisoner on the run.

To *The Morning Post*, I was a reporter who must needs continue to do his job. This was made more difficult by the fact that a new mandate—apparently in large part due to my own escapades—precluded officers from also being reporters. Luckily for me, Sir Redvers Buller was willing to give me an unpaid commission in one of the irregular volunteer corps, "Bungo's Regiment," commanded by Colonel Byng, Lord Byng of Vimy.

So I became a lieutenant in the South African Light Horse—the Cockyolibirds. I was, in essence, an unpaid volunteer, but there were advantages to this, particularly when Colonel Byng appointed me his assistant-adjutant and gave me leave to wander where I pleased except when there was need to be involved in physical combat. I acquired the long plume of tail feathers from a *sakabula* bird, placed the feathers in my hat, donned my khaki coat, and might have been perfectly happy had I not remained haunted by what I was sure I had seen on that fateful day of the train crash. This event I continued to mention to as many people as I could. When they dismissed me as suffering from delusions, I visited a doctor who conducted a variety of tests, dismissed my shrapnel wound as a mere scratch, talked about the emotional results of what he called the rigours of being under fire—and pronounced me in perfect health.

Should I return home in one piece, I will write of my involvement in the first attempt at the Relief of Ladysmith. That, combined with the dispatches I have already sent to my editor at *The Morning Post*, will cover my view of the events that took place during the two months of my involvement. This chronicle remains a more personal one, in that it deals with my perceptions of events which, or so it appeared at the time, only I could see.

With Ladysmith over, my greatest pleasure lay in the company of my brother Jack. I intended to show him as much as I could of Southern Africa and, perhaps, to take him with me to visit the Zu-Vendis of Mr Haggard's novel. My pleasure in him was, however, short-lived. He was injured—a bullet to the calf—and was, by strange coincidence, taken aboard the hospital ship *Maine*. I say coincidence because that was the very ship which my mother, the invincible Jennie, had obtained from an American millionaire, equipped with the use of charitable funds, and brought to Southern Africa.

I took three days off and visited with my mother and my brother. I went on to Cape Town, where I dined at the famous Mount Nelson Hotel, an event clouded by the criticism coming my way from England as a result of some of the statements in my dispatches. Despite the beauties of Cape Town, I was not sorry to move on to Bloemfontein, and from there to travel Southeast via Edenburg to Dewetsdorp. By now it was mid-April. On the night of the 19th, I joined the 8th Division, and rode on the next morning to join Brabazon and prepare to do battle with the Boers.

I write all of this as a preamble to what happened next when I rode on reconnaissance, together with Angus McNeill and the late Montmorency's Scouts, into a brigade of Boers who were guarding the kopje which stood before Dewetsdorp.

We arrived at a wire fence which was a little more than a hundred yards from the kopje, and were cutting the wire when twelve or so large and powerful Boers appeared over the rise. Not fast enough to remount and escape with the others, I found myself horseless and vulnerable. Though this time I had my pistol, I was certain that the end had come. Whispering a short prayer of supplication to my Maker, I turned to face the enemy.

At that, riding from the left, came a tall, speckle-bearded, all but naked man wielding a battle-axe. Crying "I Ringed Man, I of the royal blood of Chaka," he pulled me onto his mount, and delivered me safely to within a mile of camp, depositing me unceremoniously upon the ground before he galloped away.

I was escorted into camp by a tall scout who wore a skull-and-crossbones badge and rode a bleeding horse which keeled over and lay dead at journey's end.

I put this encounter with what was surely the ghost of Umslopogaas—though a strong and mighty smell arose from his sweat unlike that of any ghost of my imaginings—down to the nearness of Death, and put all thoughts of it aside. In spanning my four-horse wagon, I prepared for a forty-mile journey through Boer-infested terrain and ultimately found myself at the Vaal River, ready to assist with the evacuation of Johannesburg.

After a harebrained bicycle ride through a mostly evacuated Johannesburg, I delivered a report to my father's old friend, the Commander-in-Chief, Lord Roberts, and remained with him until Pretoria capitulated. I took part, four days after that, in the action of Diamond Hill which drove the Boers farther from Pretoria. That over, I resumed full civilian status. I had decided to return to England, for which journey I had to travel by rail to the port of Cape Town.

Just beyond Kopjes Station, some one hundred miles out of Johannesburg, the train I was travelling in came to a sudden halt. With a dreadful sense of déjà vu, I heard a loud whining sound overhead, followed by an explosion of huge dimension that came from near us on the embankment. Black smoke filled the air, broken by flashes of green and red fire.

I raced along the track to the engine driver and ordered him upon the instant to steam the train in a backwards direction while I stood on the footplate to make sure that no one had been left behind.

That was when I saw, not a hundred yards from me in the dry watercourse under a burning bridge, a cluster of figures whom I took to be Boer guerrillas. Scrambling to get out before the flames took them, they neglected to see the walking metal tripod, identical to the one I had seen before.

Red and green flames enveloped them as, in my horror, I lost my grip and tumbled from the train.

In my fright, I felt no pain of impact with the ground. Curling into a ball like a hedgehog, I summoned all the force my muscles could muster and threw myself down the embankment in the opposite direction to the oncoming danger. I came to rest against the hind legs of a horse and, looking up, saw again my previous rescuer. This time, seeing him face-to-face, I knew beyond all doubt that the towering black man with the grey-speckled beard was the Zulu warrior, Umslopogaas.

"How do you do, Umslopogaas," I said in Zulu, as Allan Quatermain had done in the book that bore his name.

The Zulu smiled and touched first the battle-axe, *Inkosi-kaas*, which was tucked into the band of his *moocha*, then the large gold ring which distended his earlobe almost to his shoulder, and lastly the deep, triangular hole that marred his forehead.

———————

We have reached the bottom of the mountain of the Temple of Gold and are resting for the ascent. Since I have no idea whether or not I will survive this adventure, I have determined to write what I can now of what has befallen me since I met up with Umslopogaas for the second time, and of my intentions.

When in the face of the oncoming danger of the flame-spewing metal man the Zulu stretched out his hand to help me onto the horse, I obeyed without question. For one thing, despite my curiosity about the intelligence that powered it, I wanted to leave behind the metal creature, and the crater from which he had emerged, with as much rapidity as possible; for another, I knew without being told that I was finally going to see the Zu-Vendi Temple of the Sun for myself.

The journey to the Temple was a long and silent one, with little to eat but what Umslopogaas plucked from bushes along the way, but plenty of water to drink from the many streams we passed. We stopped often, to rest and water the steed whose strength Umslopogaas guarded by running easily alongside for hours at a stretch.

Through all of this, the Zulu uttered no word. This silence did not trouble me, for my mind was roaring with all manner of speculations. I went over the prophetic inscription on the marble block again and again.

". . . when it is shattered into fragments a king of alien race should rule over the land."

In the eye of my mind, I saw the page in his fiction where Mr Haggard described the shattering of the marble block, and came at last to the conclusion that the block had indeed been destroyed and the alien ruler, whatever intelligence lay behind the metal man, had simply not, until now, come to claim his territory.

But that still did not explain *why* Umslopogaas had smashed the marble into fragments, nor did it account for his being here with me when he was said to have died, been tied up according to Zulu custom with his knees beneath his chin, and wrapped in a sheet of beaten gold. Then, embalmed with spices, placed facing Zululand in an airtight stone coffer beneath the spot where he had played out his so-called final battle. It was said that at night his ghost rose and shook the phantom of his battle-axe at equally phantom foes.

And, too, a new prophecy had arisen, that if he were to be removed from that place, or if his bones should crumble, ". . . the Nation of the Zu-Vendi shall cease to be a Nation."

I shall reach the Temple and find the answers I seek. Meanwhile, I confess here that contemplation of all this, and knowing the man who was my guide to be of considerable flesh, has sent me into a state of mental confusion. This is compounded by the fact that, as I lie here and peer into the distance from whence we have come, I see every now and then flashes of green and red which grow steadily larger. In the last moments, I have heard the now-familiar heavy clank of metal, carried upon the wind.

This hastily scribbled note, written in the semi-darkness of the cavity beneath the Temple's white marble stairs, will doubtless be my final entry in this chronicle. There is no coffer here containing the embalmed body of Umslopogaas. Above me, he stands with battle-axe raised, facing an enemy such as he nor anyone else can know how to vanquish.

I remain, Yours truly, Winston S. Churchill.

To this chronicle, the minister of the queen added the following note, which I have at no inconsiderable expense, had translated from his native tongue: "The Modjadji and I have read the enclosed chronicle. She has instructed me to inform you of the subsequent happenings which legend has it complete the true tale of the final battle of Umslopogaas the Zulu. It is said that a furious battle ensued, for Umslopogaas had determined to gain the forgiveness of his gods for having destroyed the black marble block, by slaying the alien pretender. In that manner only could his soul finally rest in peace among his ancestors. With such strength did he wield Inkosi-kaas, that though he died in a burst of red and green flame, his battle-axe opened the armour of the metal creature which died that night upon the throne it had come to claim.

"As for the white man beneath the stairs, it appears he was made unconscious by the fumes emitted by the creature in dying. In that state, he was strapped to the horse that had brought him to the Temple and returned to the place where he had fallen from the iron caterpillar.

"Please to come and visit us and, the Queen says, bring more blankets."

Texas Rangers

NIGHT OF THE COOTERS

HOWARD WALDROP

This story is in memory of Slim Pickens (1919–1983)

Sheriff Lindley was asleep on the toilet in the Pachuco County courthouse when someone started pounding on the door. "Bert!" the voice yelled as the sheriff jerked awake.

"Goldang!" said the lawman. The Waco newspaper slid off his lap onto the floor.

He pulled his pants up with one hand and the toilet chain on the water box overhead with the other. He opened the door. Chief Deputy Sweets stood before him, a complaint slip in his hand.

"Dang it, Sweets!" said the sheriff. "I told you never to bother me in there. It's the hottest Thursday in the history of Texas! You woke me up out of a hell of a dream!"

The deputy waited, wiping sweat from his forehead. There were two big circles, like half-moons, under the arms of his blue chambray shirt.

"I was fourteen, maybe fifteen years old, and I was a Aztec or a Mixtec or somethin'," said the sheriff. "Anyways, I was buck naked, and I was standin' on one of them ball courts with the little bitty stone rings twenty foot up one wall, and they was presentin' me to Moctezuma. I was real proud, and the sun was shinin', but it was real still and cool down there in the Valley of the Mexico. I look up at the grandstand, and there's Moctezuma and all his high muckety-mucks with feathers and stuff hangin' off 'em, and more gold than a circus wagon. And there was these other guys, conquistadors and stuff, with beards and rusty helmets, and I-talian priests with crosses you coulda barred a livery-stable door with. One of Moctezuma's men was ex-plainin' how we was fixin' to play ball for the gods and things. I knew in my dream I was captain of my team. I had a name that sounded like a bird fart in Aztec talk, and they mentioned it and the name of the captain of the other team, too. Well, everything was goin' all right, and I was prouder and prouder, until the guy doing the talkin' let slip that whichever team won was gonna be paraded around Tenochtitlán and given women and food and stuff like that; and then tomorrow A.M. they was gonna be cut up and simmered real slow and served up with chilis and onions and tomatoes.

"Well, you never seed such a fight as broke out then! They was a-yellin', and a priest was swingin' a cross, and spears and axes were flyin' around like it was an Irish funeral. Next thing I know, you're a-bangin' on the door and wakin' me up and bringin' me back to Pachuco County! What the hell do you want?"

"Mr. De Spain wants you to come over to his place right away."

"He does, huh?"

"That's right, Sheriff. He says he's got some miscreants he wants you to arrest."

"Everybody else around here has desperadoes. De Spain has miscre-ants. I'll be so danged glad when the town council gets around to movin' the city limits fifty foot the other side of his place, I won't know what to do! Every time anybody farts too loud, he calls me."

Lindley and Sweets walked back to the office at the other end of the courthouse. Four deputies sat around with their feet propped up on desks. They rocked forward respectfully and watched as the sheriff went to the hat pegs. On one of the dowels was a sweat-stained hat with turned-down points at front and back. The side brims were twisted in curves. The hat angled up to end in a crown that looked like the busi-ness end of a Phillips screwdriver. Under the hat was a holster with a Navy Colt .41 that looked like someone had used it to drive railroad spikes all the way to the Continental Divide. Leaning under them was a ten-gauge pump shotgun with the barrel sawed off just in front of the foregrip. On the other peg was an immaculate new round-top Stetson of brown felt with a snakeskin band half as wide as a fingernail running around it.

The deputies stared.

Lindley picked up the Stetson.

The deputies rocked back in their chairs and resumed yakking.

"Hey, Sweets!" said the sheriff at the door. "Change that damn calendar on your desk. It ain't Wednesday, August seventeenth; it's Thursday, August eighteenth."

"Sure thing, Sheriff."

"And you boys try not to play checkers so loud you wake the judge up, okay?"

"Sure thing, Sheriff."

Lindley went down the courthouse steps onto the rock walk. He passed the two courthouse cannons he and the deputies fired off three times a year—March second, July fourth, and Robert E. Lee's birthday. Each cannon had a pyramid of ornamental cannonballs in front of it.

Waves of heat came off the cannons, the ammunition, the telegraph wires overhead, and, in the distance, the rails of the twice-a-day spur line from Waxahachie.

The town was still as a rusty shovel. The forty-five-star United States flag hung like an old, dried dishrag from its stanchion. From looking at the town you couldn't tell the nation was about to go to war with Spain over Cuba, that China was full of unrest, and that five thousand miles away a crazy German count was making airships.

Lindley had seen enough changes in his sixty-eight years. He had been born in the bottom of an Ohio keelboat in 1830; was in Bloody Kansas when John Brown came through; fought for the Confederacy, first as a corporal, then a sergeant major, from Chickamauga to the Wilderness; and had seen more skirmishes with hostile tribes than most people would ever read about in a dozen Wide-Awake Library novels.

It was as hot as under an upside-down washpot on a tin shed roof. The sheriff's wagon horse seemed asleep as it trotted, head down, puffs hanging in the still air like brown shrubs made of dust around its hooves. There were ten, maybe a dozen people in sight in the whole town. Those few on the street moved like molasses, only as far as they had to, from shade to shade. Anybody with sense was asleep at home with wet towels hung over the windows, or sitting as still as possible with a funeral-parlor fan in their hands.

The sheriff licked his big droopy mustache and hoped nobody nodded to him. He was already too hot and tired to tip his hat. He leaned back in the wagon seat and straightened his bad leg (a Yankee souvenir) against the boot board. His gray suit was like a boiling shroud. He was too hot to reach up and flick the dust off his new hat. He had become sheriff in the special election three years ago to fill out Sanderson's term when the governor had appointed the former sheriff attorney general. Nothing much had happened in the county since then.

"Gee-hup," he said.

The horse trotted three steps before going back into its walking trance.

Sheriff Lindley didn't bother her again until he pulled up at De Spain's big place and said, "Whoa, there."

The black man who did everything for De Spain opened the gate.

"Sheriff," he said.

"Luther," said Lindley, nodding his head.

"Around back, Mr. Lindley."

There were two boys—raggedy town kids, the Strother boy and one of the poor Chisums—sitting on the edge of the well. The Chisum kid had been crying.

De Spain was hot and bothered. He was only half dressed, with suit pants, white shirt, vest, and stockings on but no shoes or coat. He hadn't macassared his hair yet. He was pointing a rifle with a barrel big as a drainpipe at the two boys.

"Here they are, Sheriff. Luther saw them down in the orchard. I'm sure he saw them stealing my peaches, but he wouldn't tell me. I knew something was up when he didn't put my clothes in the usual place next to the window where I like to dress. So I looked out and saw them. They had half a potato sack full by the time I crept around the house and caught them. I want to charge them with trespass and thievery."

"Well, well," said the sheriff, looking down at the sackful of evidence. He turned and pointed toward the black man. "You want me to charge Luther here with collusion and abetting a crime?" Neither Lindley's nor Luther's face betrayed any emotion.

"Of course not," said De Spain. "I've told him time and time again he's too soft on filchers. If this keeps happening, I'll hire another boy who'll enforce my orchard with buckshot, if need be."

De Spain was a young man with eyes like a weimaraner's. As Deputy Sweets said, he had the kind of face you couldn't hit just once. He owned half the town of Pachuco City. The other half paid him rent.

"Get in the wagon, boys," said Lindley.

"Aren't you going to cover them with your weapon?" asked De Spain.

"You should know by now, Mr. De Spain, that when I wear this suit I ain't got nothin' but a three-shot pocket pistol on me. Besides"—he looked at the two boys in the wagon bed—"they know if they give me any guff, I'll jerk a bowknot in one of 'em and bite the other'n's ass off."

"I don't think there's a need for profanity," said De Spain.

"It's too damn hot for anything else," said Lindley. "I'll clamp 'em in the *juzgado* and have Sweets run the papers over to your office tomorrow mornin'."

"I wish you'd take them out one of the rural roads somewhere and flail the tar out of them to teach them about property rights," said De Spain.

The sheriff tipped his hat back and looked up at De Spain's three-story house with the parlor so big you could hold a rodeo in it. Then he looked back at the businessman, who'd finally lowered the rifle.

"Well, I know you'd like that," said Lindley. "I seem to remember that most of the fellers who wrote the Constitution were pretty well off, but some of the other rich people thought they had funny ideas. But they were really pretty smart. One of the things they were smart about was the Bill of Rights. You know, Mr. De Spain, the reason they put in the Bill of Rights wasn't to give all the little people without jobs or money a lot of breaks with the law. Why they put that in there was for if the people without jobs or money ever got upset and turned on *them*, they could ask for the same justice everybody else got."

De Spain looked at him with disgust. "I've never liked your home-spun parables, and I don't like the way you sheriff this county."

"I don't doubt that," said Lindley. "You've got sixteen months, three weeks, and two days to find somebody to run against me. Good evening, Mr. De Spain."

He climbed onto the wagon seat.

"Luther."

"Sheriff."

He turned the horse around as De Spain and the black man took the sack of peaches through the kitchen door into the house.

The sheriff stopped the wagon near the railroad tracks where the houses began to deviate from the vertical.

"Jody. Billy Roy." He looked at them with eyes like chips of flint. "You're the dumbest pair of squirts that *ever* lived in Pachuco City! First off, half those peaches were still green. You'd have got bellyaches, and your mothers would have beaten you within an inch of your lives and given you so many doses of Black Draught you'd shit over ten-rail fences all week. Now listen to what I'm sayin', 'cause I'm only gonna say it once. If I ever hear of *either* of you stealing anything, anywhere in this county, I'm going to put you *both* in school."

"No, Sheriff, please, no!"

"I'll put you in there every morning and come and get you out seven long hours later, and I'll have the judge issue a writ keeping you there till you're *twelve years old*. And if you try to run away, I'll follow you to the ends of the earth with Joe Sweeper's bloodhounds, and I'll bring you back."

They were crying now.

"You git home." They were running before they left the wagon.

Somewhere between the second piece of corn bread and the third helping of snap beans, a loud rumble shook the ground.

"Goodness' sakes!" said Elsie, his wife of twenty-three years. "What can that be?"

"I expect that's Elmer, out by the creek. He came in last week and asked if he could blast on the place. I told him it didn't matter to me as long as he did it between sunup and sundown and didn't blow his whole family of rug rats and yard apes up."

"Jake, down at the mercantile, said Elmer bought enough dynamite to blow up Fort Worth if he'd a mind to—all but the last three sticks in the store. Jake had to reorder for stump-blowin' time."

"Whatever could he want with all that much?"

"Oh, that damn fool has the idea the vein in that old mine that played out in '83 might start up again on his property. He got to talking with the Smith boy, oh, hell, what's his name—?"

"Leo?"

"Yeah, Leo, the one that studies down in Austin, learns about stars and rocks and all that shit. . . ."

"Watch your language, Bertram!"

"Oh, hell, anyway, that boy must have put a bug up Elmer's butt about that—"

"Bertram!" said Elsie, putting down her knife and fork.

"Oh, hell, anyway. I guess Elmer'll blow the side off his hill and bury his house before he's through."

The sheriff was reading a week-old copy of the *Waco Herald* while Elsie washed up the dishes. He sure missed *Brann's Iconoclast,* the paper he used to read, which had ceased publication when the editor was gunned down on a Waco street by an irate Baptist four months before. The Waco paper had a little squib from London, England, about there having been explosions on Mars ten nights in a row last month, and whether it was a sign of life on that planet or some unusual volcanic activity.

Sheriff Lindley had never given volcanoes (except those in the Valley of the Mexico) or the planet Mars much thought.

Hooves came pounding down the road. He put down his paper. *"Sheriff, Sheriff!"* he said in a high, mocking voice.

"What?" asked Elsie. Then she heard the hooves and began to dry her hands on the towel on the nail above the sink.

The horse stopped out front; bare feet slapped up to the porch; small fists pounded on the door.

"Sheriff! Sheriff!" yelled a voice Lindley recognized as belonging to either Tommy or Jimmy Atkinson.

He strode to the door and opened it.

"Tommy, what's all the hooraw?"

"Jimmy. Sheriff, something fell on our pasture, tore it all to hell, knocked down *the tree,* killed some of our cattle, Tommy can't find his dog, Mother sent—"

"Hold on! Something fell on your place? Like what?"

"I don't know! Like a big rock, only sparks was flyin' off it, and it roared and blew up! It's at the north end of the place, and—"

"Elsie, run over and get Sweets and the boys. Have them go get Leo Smith if he ain't gone back to college yet. Sounds to me like Pachuco County's got its first shootin' star. Hold on, Jimmy, I'm comin' right along. We'll take my wagon; you can leave your pony here."

"Oh, hurry, Sheriff! It's big! It killed our cattle and tore up the fences—"

"Well, I can't arrest it for *that,*" said Lindley. He put on his Stetson. "And I thought Elmer'd blowed hisself up. My, my, ain't never seen a shooting star before. . . ."

"Damn if it don't look like somebody threw a locomotive through here," said the sheriff. The Atkinson place used to have a sizable hill and the tallest tree in the county on it. Now it had half a hill and a big stump and beyond, a huge crater. Dirt had been thrown up in a ten-foot-high pile around it. There was a large, rounded, gray object buried in the dirt and torn caliche at the bottom. Waves of heat rose from it, and gray ash, like old charcoal, fell off it into the shimmering pit.

Half the town was riding out in wagons and on horseback as the news spread. The closest neighbors were walking over in the twilight, wearing their go-visiting clothes.

"Well, well," said the sheriff, looking down. "So that's what a meteor looks like."

Leo Smith was in the pit, walking around.

"I figured you'd be here sooner or later," said Lindley.

"Hello, Sheriff," said Leo. "It's still too hot to touch. Part of a cow's buried under the back end."

The sheriff looked over at the Atkinson family. "You folks is danged lucky. That thing coulda come down smack on your house or, worse, your barn. What time did it fall?"

"Straight up and down six o'clock," said Mrs. Atkinson. "We was settin' down to supper. I saw it out of the corner of my eye; then all tarnation came down. Rocks must have been falling for ten minutes!"

"It's pretty spectacular, Sheriff," said Leo. "I'm going into town to telegraph off to the professors at the university. They'll sure want to look at this."

"Any reason other than general curiosity?" asked Lindley.

"I've only seen pictures and handled little bitty parts of one," said Leo, "but it doesn't look usual. They're generally like big rocks, all stone or iron. The outside of this one's soft and crumbly. Ashy, too."

There was a slight pop and a stove-cooling noise from the thing.

"Well, you can come back into town with me if you want to. Hey, Sweets!"

The chief deputy came over.

"A couple of you boys better stay here tonight, keep people from falling in the hole. I guess if Leo's gonna wire the university, you better keep anybody from knockin' chunks off it. It'll probably get pretty crowded. If I was the Atkinsons, I'd start chargin' a nickel a look."

"Sure thing, Sheriff."

"I'll be out here tomorrow mornin' to take another gander. I gotta serve a process paper on old Theobald before he lights out for his chores. If I sent one 'a' you boys, he'd as soon shoot you as say howdy."

"Sure thing, Sheriff."

He and Leo and Jimmy Atkinson got in the wagon and rode off toward the quiet lights of town far away.

There was a new smell in the air.

The sheriff noticed it as he rode toward the Atkinson ranch by the south road early the next morning. There was an odor like when something goes wrong at the telegraph office. Smoke was curling up from the pasture. Maybe there was a scrub fire started from the heat of the falling star.

He topped the last rise. Before him lay devastation the likes of which he hadn't seen since the retreat from Atlanta.

"Great gawd ahmighty!" he said.

There were dead horses and charred wagons all around. The ranch house was untouched, but the barn was burned to the ground. There were crisscrossed lines of burnt grass that looked like they'd been painted with a tarbrush.

He saw no bodies anywhere. Where was Sweets? Where was Luke, the other deputy? Where had the people from the wagons gone? What had happened?

Lindley looked at the crater. There was a shiny rod sticking out of it, with something round on the end. From here it looked like one of those carnival acts where a guy spins a plate on the end of a dowel rod, only this glinted like metal in the early sun. As he watched, a small cloud of green steam rose above it from the pit.

He saw a motion behind an old tree uprooted by a storm twelve years ago. It was Sweets. He was yelling and waving the sheriff back. Lindley rode his horse into a small draw, then came up into the open.

There was movement over at the crater. He thought he saw something. Reflected sunlight flashed by his eyes, and he thought he saw a rounded silhouette. He heard a noise like sometimes gets in bob wire on a windy day. He heard a humming sound then, smelled the electric smell real strong. Fire started a few feet from him, out of nowhere, and moved toward him.

Then his horse exploded. The air was an inferno, he was thrown spinning—

He must have blacked out. He had no memory of what went next. When he came to, he was running as fast as he ever had toward the uprooted tree.

Fire jumped all around. Luke was shooting over the tree roots with his pistol. He ducked. A long section of the trunk was washed with flames and sparks.

Lindley dove behind the root tangle.

"What the dingdong is goin' on?" he asked as he tried to catch his breath. He still had his new hat on, but his britches and coat were singed and smoking.

"God damn, Bert! I don't know," said Sweets, leaning around Luke. "We was out here all night; it was a regular party; most of the time we was up on the lip up there. Maybe thirty or forty people comin' and goin' all the time. We was all talking and hoorawing, and then we heard something about an hour ago. We looked down, and I'll be damned if the whole top of that thing didn't come off like a mason jar!

"We was watching, and these damn things started coming out—they looked like big old leather balls, big as horses, with snakes all out the front—"

"What?"

"Snakes. Yeah, tentacles Leo called them, like an octy-puss. Leo'd come back from town and was here when them boogers came out. Martians he said they was, things from Mars. They had big old eyes, big as your head! Everybody was pushing and shoving; then one of them pulled out one of them gun things, real slow like, and just started burning up everything in sight.

"We all ran back for whatever cover we could find—it took 'em a while to get up the dirt pile. They killed horses, dogs, anything they could see. Fire was everywhere. They use that thing just like the volunteer firemen use them water hoses in Waco!"

"Where's Leo?"

Sweets pointed to the draw that ran diagonally to the west. "We watched awhile, finally figured they couldn't line up on the ditch all the way to the rise. Leo and the others got away up the draw—he was gonna telegraph the university about it. The bunch that got away was supposed to send people out to the town road to warn people. You probably would have run into them if you hadn't been coming from Theobald's place. Anyway, soon as them things saw people were gettin' away, they got mad as hornets. That's when they lit up the Atkinsons' barn."

A flash of fire leapt in the roots of the tree, jumped back thirty feet into the burnt grass behind them, then moved back and forth in a curtain of sparks.

"Man, that's what I call a real smoke pole," said Luke.

"Well," Lindley said. "This won't do. These things done attacked citizens in my jurisdiction, and they killed my horse."

He turned to Luke.

"Be real careful, and get back to town, and get the posse up. Telegraph the Rangers and tell 'em to burn leather gettin' here. Then get aholt of Skip Whitworth and have him bring out The Gun."

Skip Whitworth sat behind the tree trunk and pulled the cover from the six-foot rifle at his side. Skip was in his late fifties. He had been a sniper in the War for Southern Independence when he had been in his twenties. He had once shot at a Yankee general just as the officer was bringing a forkful of beans up to his mouth. When the fork got there, there were only some shoulders and a gullet for the beans to drop into.

That had been from a mile and a half away, from sixty feet up a pine tree.

The rifle was an .80-caliber octagonal-barrel breechloader that used two and a half ounces of powder and a percussion cap the size of a jawbreaker for each shot. It had a telescopic sight running the entire length of the barrel.

"They're using that thing on the end of that stick to watch us," said Lindley. "I had Sweets jump around, and every time he did, one of those cooters would come up with that fire gun and give us what-for."

Skip said nothing. He loaded his rifle, which had a breechblock lever the size of a crowbar on it, then placed another round—cap, paper cartridge, ball—next to him. He drew a bead and pulled the trigger. It sounded like dynamite had gone off in their ears. The wobbling pole snapped in two halfway up. The top end flopped around back into the pit.

There was a scrabbling noise above the whirring from the earthen lip. Something round came up.

Skip had smoothly opened the breech, put in the ball, torn the cartridge with his teeth, put in the cap, closed the action, pulled back the hammer, and sighted before the shape reached the top of the dirt.

Metal glinted in the middle of the dark thing. Skip fired. There was a *squeech;* the whole top of the round thing opened up; it spun around and backward, things in its front working like a daddy longlegs thrown on a roaring stove.

Skip loaded again. There were flashes of light from the crater. Something came up shooting, fire leaping like hot sparks from a blacksmith's anvil, the air full of flames and smoke. Skip fired again.

The fire gun flew up in the air. Snakes twisted, writhed, disappeared.

It was very quiet for a few seconds.

Then there was the renewed whining of machinery and noises like a pile driver, the sounds of filing and banging. Steam came up over the crater lip.

"Sounds like a steel foundry in there," said Sweets.

"I don't like it one bit," said Lindley. "Be danged if I'm gonna let 'em get the drop on us. Can you keep them down?"

"How many are there?" asked Skip.

"Luke and Sweets saw four or five before all hell broke loose this morning. Probably more of 'em than that was inside."

"I've got three more shots. If they poke up, I'll get 'em."

"I'm goin' to town, then out to Elmer's. Sweets'll stay with you awhile. If you run outta bullets, light up out the draw. I don't want nobody killed. Sweets, keep an eye out for the posse. I'm telegraphing the Rangers again, then goin' to get Elmer and his dynamite. We're gonna fix their little red wagon for certain."

"Sure thing, Sheriff."

The sun had just passed noon.

Leo looked haggard. He had been up all night, then at the telegraph office sending off messages to the university. Inquiries had begun to come in from as far east as Baton Rouge. Leo had another, supposedly from Percival Lowell out in Flagstaff, Arizona Territory. "Everybody at the university thinks it's wonderful," said Leo.

"People in Austin would," said Lindley.

"They're sure these things are connected with Mars and those bright flashes of gas last month. Seems something's happened in England, starting about a week ago. No one's been able to get through to London for two or three days."

"You telling me Mars is attacking London, England, and Pachuco City, Texas?" asked the sheriff.

"It seems so," said Leo. He took off his glasses and rubbed his eyes.

" 'Scuse me, Leo," said Lindley. "I got to get another telegram off to the Texas Rangers."

"That's funny," said Argyle, the telegraph operator. "The line was working just a second ago." He began tapping his key and fiddling with his coil box.

Leo peered out the window. "Hey!" he said. "Where's the three-fourteen?" He looked at the railroad clock. It was 3:25. In sixteen years of rail service, the train had been four minutes late, and that was after a mud slide in the storm twelve years ago.

"Uh-oh," said the sheriff.

They were turning out of Elmer's yard with a wagonload of dynamite. The wife and eleven of the kids were watching.

"Easy, Sheriff," said Elmer, who, with two of his boys and most of their guns, was riding in back with the explosives. "Jake sold me everything he had. I just didn't notice till we got back here with that stuff that some of it was already sweating."

"Holy shit!" said Lindley. "You mean we gotta go a mile an hour out there? Let's get out and throw the bad stuff off."

"Well, it's all mixed in," said Elmer. "I was sorta gonna set it all up on the hill and put one blasting cap in the whole load."

"Jesus. You woulda blowed up your house and Pachuco City too."

"I was in a hurry," said Elmer, hanging his head.

"Well, can't be helped. We'll take it slow."

Lindley looked at his watch. It was six o'clock. He heard a high-up, fluttering sound. They looked at the sky. Coming down was a large, round, glowing object throwing off sparks in all directions. It was curved with points, like the thing in the crater at the Atkinson place. A long, thin trail of smoke from the back end hung in the air behind it. They watched in awe as it sailed down. It went into the horizon to the north of Pachuco City.

"One," said one of the kids in the wagon, "two, three—"

Silently they took up the count. At twenty-seven there was a roaring boom, just like the night before.

"Five and a half miles," said the sheriff. "That puts it eight miles from the other one. Leo said the ones in London came down twenty-four hours apart, regular as clockwork." They started off as fast as they could under the circumstances.

There were flashes of light beyond the Atkinson place in the near dusk. The lights moved off toward the north where the other thing had plowed in.

It was the time of evening when your eyes can fool you. Sheriff Lindley thought he saw something that shouldn't have been there sticking above the horizon. It glinted like metal in the dim light. He thought it moved, but it might have been the motion of the wagon as they lurched down a gully. When they came up, it was gone.

Skip was gone. His rifle was still there. It wasn't melted but had been crushed, as had the three-foot-thick tree trunk in front of it. All the caps and cartridges were gone.

There was a monstrous series of footprints leading from the crater down to the tree, then off into the distance to the north where Lindley thought he had seen something. There were three footprints in each series. Sweets's hat had been mashed along with Skip's gun. Clanging and banging still came from the crater.

The four of them made their plans. Lindley had his shotgun and pistol, which Luke had brought out with him that morning, though he was still wearing his burned suit and his untouched Stetson.

He tied together the fifteen sweatiest sticks of dynamite he could find.

They crept up, then rushed the crater.

"Hurry up!" yelled the sheriff to the men at the courthouse. "Get that cannon up those stairs!"

"He's still coming this way!" yelled Luke from up above.

They had been watching the giant machine from the courthouse since it had come up out of the Atkinson place, before the sheriff and Elmer and his boys made it into town after their sortie.

It had come across to the north, gone to the site of the second crash, and stood motionless there for quite a while. When it got dark, the deputies brought out the night binoculars. Everybody in town saw the flash of dynamite from the Atkinson place.

A few moments after that, the machine had moved back toward there. It looked like a giant water tower with three legs. It had a thing like a teacher's desk bell on top of it, and something that looked like a Kodak roll-film camera in front of that. As the moon rose, they saw the thing had tentacles like thick wires hanging from between the three giant legs.

The sheriff, Elmer, and his boys made it to town just as the machine found the destruction they had caused at the first landing site. It had turned toward town and was coming at a pace of twenty miles an hour.

"Hurry the hell up!" yelled Luke. "Oh, shit—!" He ducked. There was a flash of light overhead. The building shook. "That heat gun comes out of the box on the front!" he said. "Look out!" The building glared and shook again. Something down the street caught fire.

"Load that son of a bitch," said Lindley. "Bob! Some of you men make sure everybody's in the cyclone cellars or where they won't burn. Cut out all the damn lights!"

"Hell, Sheriff. They know we're here!" yelled a deputy. Lindley hit him with his hat, then followed the cannon up to the top of the clock-tower steps.

Luke was cramming powder into the cannon muzzle. Sweets ran back down the stairs. Other people carried cannonballs up the steps to the tower one at a time.

Leo came up. "What did you find, Sheriff, when you went back?"

There was a cool breeze for a few seconds in the courthouse tower. Lindley breathed a few deep breaths, remembering. "Pretty rough. There was some of them still working after that thing had gone. They were building another one just like it." He pointed toward the ma-

chine, which was firing up houses to the northeast side of town, swinging the ray back and forth. They could hear its hum. Homes and
chicken coops burst into flames. A mooing cow was stilled.

"We threw in the dynamite and blew most of them up. One was in a
machine like a steam tractor. We shot up what was left while they was
hootin' and a-hollerin'. There was some other things in there, live
things maybe, but they was too blowed up to put back together to be
sure what they was, all bleached out and pale. We fed everything there a
diet of buckshot till there wasn't nothin' left. Then we hightailed it
back here on horses, left the wagon sitting."

The machine came on toward the main street of town. Luke finished
with the powder. There were so many men with guns on the building
across the street it looked like a brick porcupine. It must have looked
this way for the James gang when they were shot up in Northfield,
Minnesota.

The courthouse was made of stone. Most of the wooden buildings in
town were scorched or already afire. When the heat gun came this way,
it blew bricks to dust, played flame over everything. The air above the
whole town heated up.

They had put out the lamps behind the clockfaces. There was nothing but moonlight glinting off the three-legged machine, flames of
burning buildings, the faraway glows of prairie fires. It looked like Pachuco City was on the outskirts of hell.

"Get ready, Luke," said the sheriff. The machine stepped between
two burning stores, its tentacles pulling out smoldering horse tack,
chains, kegs of nails, then heaving them this way and that. Someone at
the end of the street fired off a round. There was a high, thin ricochet
off the machine. Sweets ran upstairs, something in his arms. It was a
curtain from one of the judge's windows. He'd ripped it down and tied
it to the end of one of the janitor's long window brushes.

On it he had lettered in tempera paint COME AND TAKE IT. There was a
ragged, nervous cheer from the men on the building as they read it by
the light of the flames.

"Cute, Sweets," said Lindley, "too cute."

The machine turned down Main Street. A line of fire sprang up at the
back side of town from the empty corrals.

"Oh, shit!" said Luke. "I forgot the wadding!" Lindley took off his
hat to hit him with. He looked at its beautiful felt in the mixed moonlight and firelight.

The thing turned toward them. The sheriff thought he saw eyes way up in the bellthing atop the machine, eyes like a big cat's eyes seen through a dirty windowpane on a dark night.

"Goldang, Luke, it's my best hat, but I'll be damned if I let them cooters burn down my town!"

He stuffed the Stetson, crown first, into the cannon barrel. Luke shoved it in with the ramrod, threw in two thirty-five-pound cannonballs behind it, pushed them home, and swung the barrel out over Main Street.

The machine bent to tear up something.

"Okay, boys," yelled Lindley. "Attract its attention." Rifle and shotgun fire winked on the rooftop. It glowed like a hot coal from the muzzle flashes. A great slather of ricochets flew off the giant machine.

It turned, pointing its heat gun at the building. It was fifty feet from the courthouse steps.

"Now," said the sheriff.

Luke touched off the powder with his cigarillo. The whole north side of the courthouse bell tower flew off, and the roof collapsed. Two holes you could see the moon through appeared in the machine: one in the middle, one smashing through the dome atop it. Sheriff Lindley saw the lower cannonball come out and drop lazily toward the end of burning Main Street.

All six of the tentacles of the machine shot straight up into the air, and it took off like a man running with his arms above his head. It staggered, as fast as a freight train could go, through one side of a house and out the other, and ran partway up Park Street. One of its three legs went higher than its top. It hopped around like a crazy man on crutches before its feet got tangled in a horse-pasture fence, and it went over backward with a shudder. A great cloud of steam came out of it and hung in the air. No one in the courthouse tower heard the sound of the steam. They were all deaf as posts from the explosion. The barrel of the cannon was burst all along the end. The men on the other roof were jumping up and down and clapping each other on the back. The COME AND TAKE IT sign on the courthouse had two holes in it, neater than you could have made with a biscuit cutter. First a high whine, then a dull roar, then something like normal hearing came back to the sheriff's left ear. The right one still felt like a kid had his fist in there.

"Dang it, Sweets!" he yelled. "How much powder did Luke use?"

"Huh?" Luke was banging on his head with both his hands.

"How much powder did he use?"

"Two, two and a half cans," said Sweets.

"It only takes half a can a ball!" yelled the sheriff. He reached for his hat to hit Luke with, touched his bare head. "I feel naked. Come on, we're not through yet. We got fires to put out and some hash to settle."

Luke was still standing, shaking his head. The whole town was cheering.

It looked like a pot lid slowly boiling open, moving just a little. Every time the end unscrewed a little more, ashes and cinders fell off into the second pit. There was a piled ridge of them. The back turned again, moved a few inches, quit. Then it wobbled, there was a sound like a stove being jerked up a chimney, and the whole back end rolled open like a mad bank vault and fell off. There were 184 men and 11 women all standing behind the open end of the thing, their guns pointing toward the interior. At the exact center were Sweets and Luke with the other courthouse cannon. This time there was one can of powder, but the barrel was filled to the end with everything from the blacksmith-shop floor—busted window glass, nails, horseshoes, bolts, stirrup buckles, and broken files and saws.

Eyes appeared in the dark interior.

"Remember the Alamo," said the sheriff.

Everybody, and the cannon, fired.

When the third meteor came in that evening, south of town at thirteen minutes past six, they knew something was wrong. It wobbled in flight, lost speed, and dropped like a long, heavy leaf.

They didn't have to wait for this one to cool and open. When the posse arrived, the thing was split in two and torn. Heat and steam came up from the inside.

One of the pale things was creeping forlornly across the ground with great difficulty. It looked like a thin gingerbread man made of glass with only a knob for a head.

"It's probably hurting from the gravity," said Leo.

"Fix it, Sweets," said Lindley.

"Sure thing, Sheriff."

There was a gunshot.

No fourth meteor fell, though they had scouts out for twenty miles in all directions, and the railroad tracks and telegraph wires were fixed again.

"I been doing some figuring," said Leo. "If there were ten explosions on Mars last month, and these things started landing in England last week Thursday, then we should have got the last three. There won't be any more."

"You been figurin', huh?"

"Sure have."

"Well, we'll see."

Sheriff Lindley stood on his porch. It was sundown on Sunday, three hours after another meteor should have fallen, had there been one.

Leo rode up. "I saw Sweets and Luke heading toward the Atkinson place with more dynamite. What are they doing?"

"They're blowing up every last remnant of them things—lock, stock, and asshole."

"But," said Leo, "the professors from the university will be here tomorrow, to look at their ships and machines! You can't destroy them!"

"Shit on the University of Texas and the horse it rode in on," said Lindley. "My jurisdiction runs from Deer Piss Creek to Buenos Frijoles, back to Olatunji, up the Little Clear Fork of the North Branch of Mud River, back to the creek, and everything in between. If I say something gets blowed up, it's on its way to kingdom come."

He put his arms on Leo's shoulders. "Besides, what little grass grows in this county's supposed to be green, and what's growing around them things is red. I *really* don't like that."

"But Sheriff! I've got to meet Professor Lowell in Waxahachie tomorrow. . . ."

"Listen, Leo. I appreciate what you done. But I'm an old man. I been kept up by Martians for three nights, I lost my horse and my new hat, and they busted my favorite gargoyle off the courthouse. I'm going in and get some sleep, and I only want to be woke up for the Second Coming, by Jesus Christ himself."

Leo jumped on his horse and rode for the Atkinson place.

Sheriff Lindley crawled into bed and went to sleep as soon as his head hit the pillow.

He had a dream. He was a king in Babylon, and he lay on a couch at the top of a ziggurat, just like the Tower of Babel in the Bible. He surveyed the city and the river. There were women all around him, and men with curly beards and big headdresses. Occasionally someone would feed him a large fig from a golden bowl. His dreams were not interrupted by the sounds of dynamiting, first from one side of town, then another, and then another.

Albert Einstein

DETERMINISM AND THE MARTIAN WAR, WITH RELATIVISTIC CORRECTIONS

DOUG BEASON

When the train crashed, Albert Einstein was thinking how glorious it was to be twenty-one and finished with school.

His memories of Zurich's Eidgenössische Technische Hochschule were shattered by a shrill train whistle, screams from outside his compartment, and the sickening, high-pitched sound of the train's locked wheels as they screeched to a halt.

Albert shoved out his hand to stop himself from being thrown across the rich leather-clad compartment. But in the same instant that he tried to save himself, he knew that he could not stop his body's momentum, for his thin-boned arm would snap like a piece of chalk, ramrodded by his sixty-kilogram body mass.

The calculation came quickly to Albert: With his body traveling at a hundred kilometers an hour, his arm would be broken by over twenty thousand joules of stopping energy.

Time passed slowly during the collision. Where most people might have experienced their past flashing in front of their eyes, Albert imagined a thought experiment, a *Gedanken* that he so often used to gain deep understanding of a subtle point.

The train compartment was tiny, just enough room for two people to sit comfortably. If his traveling companion, Marcel Grossmann, had not gone to the water closet, then the train crash would have been more than an experiment for Albert. It would have included the impact of the two young men, along with the sound of bones snapping, heads crushing, yelling, and the cursing that came with the impact.

But as it was, he watched as two frames of reference hurtled toward each other: himself and the opposite wall.

Albert realized that he could consider himself to be in either of the two frames. It wasn't only that he was being thrown against the stationary wall; rather, an equally valid frame of reference was that he was stationary and the wall was moving toward him.

He pulled in his arm and balled himself up, attempting to absorb the impact of the crash. The passenger car started to roll to the side. Blue curtains on the window hid the ground from him as he fell. His latest copies of *Annalen der Physik* flew with him to the opposite wall.

Did it make a difference that the wall was accelerating toward me, or that the journals and I were accelerating toward the wall? he thought. It shouldn't make any difference, for the two frames of reference should be identical. . . .

But even as he hit he realized his mistake: The wall had undergone a negative acceleration, suddenly stopping after moving one hundred kilometers an hour. And *that* was the difference between the two frames of reference: He was still moving and had not yet stopped.

And of course, he suffered the consequence of being in the unaccelerated frame as he hit the opposite wall.

"Albert. Albert—are you all right?"

Albert Einstein tried to open his eyes. It was difficult, and he felt as though he had been sleeping for a long time. A blurry shape moved in and out of focus as he forced his eyes open. He was lying on forest ground, evergreen trees towered above him. Among the scent of pine and fresh air, he smelled wood burning and heard moans from injured people.

Somewhere next to him a young boy cried out for his mother. *What happened?* thought Albert.

The round, dark features of Marcel Grossmann moved into his line of sight. His friend nervously wet his lips and spoke in a low voice. "So, once again the mathematician comes to the physicist's rescue. Another triumph of theory over the experiment! For the past four years I've pulled you out of trouble at Eidgenössiche Technische Hochschule, and even now you need me to help you."

Albert pushed up on one elbow. His friend's attempt at humor sounded weak. Albert tried to speak, but his mouth felt cottony, dry. He felt a stiff soreness as he sat up; he remembered colliding with the wall, and discovering the difference between accelerated reference frames. . . .

He lay just inside the tree line, a good hundred meters from the train. Smoke roiled up from the passenger cars. They lay in a crumpled jumble, smashed on the track. Burned spots dotted the grass around the train like oversized polka dots. People lay throughout the woods around him, some unconscious. Other people walked quietly among the wounded, kneeling down to speak a word, or tend to a request. It almost looked as if they were in hiding. . . .

Marcel turned and brought a wet cloth up to Albert's mouth. Albert eagerly sucked on the cloth, feeling the cool wetness against his tongue.

Albert coughed, then sucked out some more water before speaking. "You are all right?"

"Of course," Marcel said.

"How did you escape the accident?"

Again Marcel wet his lips as he squatted beside Albert. He looked around and spoke quietly. "The foresight of being in the water closet. I was wedged against the wall. Most of the injuries came from people being thrown across their compartments, and those of us who weren't injured were lucky to escape. We are all fortunate the train wasn't traveling fast."

Albert continued to suck on the wet cloth. He surveyed the accident through the woods and saw that there were two additional trains lying in a wreck in front of their own train. The other trains had long since burned away.

The train they had been on was resting on its side with fire licking at the cars. "This doesn't make sense," Albert said. "What happened? What caused all these accidents?"

Marcel's face tightened. "You heard of the reports coming out of London?"

Albert blinked. He took one last suck of water and put the cloth down. *Of course, who had not read the headlines?* he thought. "The Martian attack? Marcel, surely you do not believe those stories! That damn British humor is tiring—"

Marcel turned while still squatting and nodded toward the train. Smoke boiled up from the passenger cars, burning as though someone had taken a fire-wand and swept it up and down the train. The last train car was a flatbed that held dozens of barrels of petrol and oil; for now, the fire was far away from the car holding the fuel.

Albert's eyes widened as he noticed for the first time that the burned spots on the ground were actually charred bodies. It looked as if they had been engulfed in flames on the spot. Two or three of the bodies were still alive.

"If the Martians didn't do this, then why is the train burning?" said Marcel.

"The collision caused the engine to erupt, of course—"

Marcel swept an arm across the damage. "Do you see anything that could have set the train on fire, Biedermeier?"

Honest John. Albert felt stung. Marcel had not used that nickname for a long time. And the message was clear: Don't dismiss his Martian explanation lightly.

But there had to be a physical explanation!

Albert pushed against a tree and was dizzy as he struggled to his feet. This didn't make any sense to him, and thus was a mystery to be solved, a puzzle whose pieces needed to be found, then placed together to provide the correct answer.

"Trains just don't burst into flames by themselves," Albert said. "Things happen because of a reason. Cause and effect."

"I have given a reason," Marcel said simply.

Albert snorted. He pulled out his watch—it had only been a few hours since they had left Zurich. He pocketed the watch, straightened his tie, pulled down his vest, and started walking stiffly out of the wood and toward the train.

Marcel quickly caught up with him and grabbed him by the arm. "Don't go out of the trees."

Albert tried to shake off his arm. "What are you talking about?"

Marcel tightened his grip on Albert's arm and pointed to the hills beyond the track. Crisp snowcapped mountaintops of the Italian Alps were visible in the distance. At first Albert saw nothing unusual, but when Marcel's grip remained firm, he scanned the tree-lined foothills again.

Just around the bend where the train tracks disappeared, he spotted a glint of silver high up in the trees. It was as if something was set against the foothills . . . waiting.

Albert took a step forward. Squinting, he stared at the spot until he made out a flat piece of metal that looked like a flattened barrel. It was supported by three metallic appendages that stood in the trees. His eyes widened.

"How far away is it?" whispered Albert.

Marcel shrugged. "Five kilometers? That is what the others think."

Albert performed a quick calculation in his head; the answer came slowly because he went through the trigonometry twice. "Then it is more than thirty-five meters high! I came this way to Milan only six months ago, and surely I would have noticed them building such a structure." He tried to think of a rational reason why the metal structure was present. "Is it a water tower?"

Marcel snorted.

Someone screamed as the young boy who had been crying beside them darted out of the wood and ran toward the burning train cars. The boy ran straight for a woman lying in the middle of a circle of burned grass. The woman slowly withered in agony.

As the boy approached the train, the grass behind him suddenly ignited and turned a churning black. Smoke immediately shot into the air. The boy ran a zigzag path toward the woman as the burning swatch of grass followed him.

Albert felt a tightness in his chest; he realized he was holding his breath as he watched the boy's race. As he drew in a deep breath, he saw that the boy's mother lay next to the car that carried barrels of petrol and oil. When the flames reached that car, there would be an explosion that might even kill the people hiding in the wood!

Albert caught motion out of the corner of his eye. The metallic leviathan in the hills moved forward, and now Albert could clearly see that a hatlike feature covered its mechanical head. A gigantic visor was where its eyes should have been.

The gargantuan head swiveled back and forth, like a hose spewing invisible liquid. Fire appeared on the ground, following the head's movement. Fire burst around the boy as he approached the woman lying on the ground.

A man in the woods yelled, "Stop running, you young fool! Play dead or you will kill us all!"

The boy dropped in his tracks, five meters from his injured mother.

The fire-wand immediately stopped moving. Flames crawled out from the place where the wand passed by, but it was no longer directed by the horrible metallic creature.

Two of the train cars near the boy burst into flames. Smoke boiled up into the air. Albert held up a hand to shield the glare, feeling the heat even at a hundred meters away. He saw that the last car loaded with petrol and oil barrels was next in line and would soon ignite in a conflagration.

The boy raised his head and looked wildly around. "Somebody help me!"

"Keep down, you fool!" yelled the man once again.

Albert took a step forward. "Infrared beams!"

"What?" said Marcel. "The reports from London said they used heat-rays—"

"Heat *is* infrared," interrupted Albert impatiently. He stepped to a tree and absently caressed the trunk. He was mesmerized by the sight of the metallic beast.

The boy inched forward on his elbows until he reached the woman. He rolled her over and examined her. Again someone shouted to the boy from the wood. "Your mother is dying, boy! Leave her alone or you will incite the monster!"

As if on cue, the Martian straightened, towering over the trees where it had been stationed. Smoke from the train periodically hid it from view. It seemed to have trouble focusing in on where to direct its infrared beam. It left its nesting place and started clumping toward the encampment. It took small, careful steps on its three long silvery legs to advance through the forest.

People started screaming. The crowd surged back farther into the wood. Several young men ran past Albert, away from the train, followed by older men, women, and children.

The boy tried to drag his mother out of the clearing, but she was too heavy for him to carry. She was limp, and Albert was afraid that the boy might even pull an arm off her burned body. The woman screamed in pain.

The boy looked back desperately to the wood. "Someone, please help me! I cannot leave her here!" Smoke roiled up from the burning train as fire licked at the last car loaded with barrels of petrol.

Marcel placed a hand on Albert's shoulder. "Albert, we have to move back with the others."

Albert shook off his friend's hand as he watched the Martian. The beast seemed confused by the smoke and fire. It did not shoot its infrared beams. "We can help the boy," Albert said. He stepped forward.

"What are you doing?"

Albert thought for a long moment. Then a simple solution popped into his head. But he would need rope. A lot of it. "Come on." He started jogging toward the boy and left the sanctity of the wood.

"Albert, you'll get us killed!"

But Albert didn't heed his friend's pleas and instead ran straight toward the last car filled with barrels of oil and petrol. He heard Marcel running behind him. The smoke rose in front of him, and he lost sight of the Martian, still nearly four kilometers away.

The young boy saw him coming and started screaming. "Over here! Please, you must help my mother!"

Albert motioned for Marcel to help the lad as he continued for the train. The heat grew from the burning train as he approached. Reaching the last car, he began to untie the long cords that bound the barrels of petrol and oil. He would need several hundred meters of the rope to do what he planned, but the heat was almost too unbearable for him to work.

Marcel ran up to him, panting. "Albert, we must leave—"

"Help the boy with his mother!"

"The others are helping. We must get back."

Albert returned to his task. "Untie the rest of these barrels, then tip them on the side to let the oil run free. I need this rope."

"But the oil will further feed the fire!"

Albert strained with the cap on the barrel. The lid gave with a jolt, and dark liquid sloshed from the top. "The smoke and heat will hide us from the Martian. It will provide a shield for people to escape." Albert wrestled the barrel to the ground. Tipping it to its side, he gave it a push to send it rolling slowly down the track. Black oil oozed out, covering the ground in a thick, viscous liquid. The sharp smell of petrochemicals stung his nostrils.

Albert hopped up on the car and grabbed another barrel. His face felt smeared with black oil. "Hurry, we need to get as much oil as we can on the ground before we ignite it. The more the better."

Marcel joined him, and soon the two were popping off the lids and pushing the barrels over the edge of the car. Albert looked over his shoulder. The Martian's silvery head was closer as it moved swiftly toward the train. Spots of fire ignited all around as the Martian fired wildly, disoriented by the heat and boiling smoke.

A man with a bushy beard lumbered out to help the young boy. He knelt and scooped the boy's mother into his arms. He turned back for the wood. A line of fire danced at his feet as he carried the injured woman inside the tree line. The Martian continued to clump toward them.

Albert spotted a gnarled stick burning from where the Martian's heat-ray had swept over the ground. He coiled the long rope that bound the barrels together and tossed it to the ground, then jumped off the car and sprinted toward the burning stick.

Marcel shouted behind him. "Albert!"

Albert grabbed the burning stick and ran to the growing slick of oil. He stopped at the black lake of petrochemicals and held the fire down to the surface—the oil caught fire, and flames quickly spread across the surface. Thick black smoke instantly rolled into the air. Albert coughed and stepped back. The smoke moved down the track, further masking the train and the people in the wood from the Martian.

The heat-rays stopped immediately. Three men raced out from the wood into the clearing and picked up the burned people lying on the ground. Someone cheered from the trees, "That will show the bastard!" Others stepped cautiously from the wood, and the silence in the trees was shattered as people poured out to carry the injured to safety.

Marcel grabbed Albert by the arm. "Let's get out of here!"

Albert turned and picked up the long coil of rope. *Good, he had enough.* The Martian was hidden for the moment by the thick black smoke. Albert coughed, and tears ran from his eyes from the pungent stench.

"Come on, Albert," screamed Marcel. "We can hide in the wood!"

"You saw it waiting in the trees. It will hunt us down unless we stop it."

Marcel looked wildly around. His hair was mussed, and he was covered with soot from fueling the fire that burned around them. "Stop it? Are you crazy in the head? How are we going to stop that thing?"

Albert scanned the area between the train and the approaching Martian. The Martian was moving fast, and had less than two kilometers to go before it reached them. Twenty meters away, on the other side of the fire, a creek paralleled the track. A tree towered over the creek, and some of its leaves had started to catch fire. The creek bank sloped down a good two meters to the water.

If he ran alongside the creek he could keep out of sight and get to the other side of the Martian's path. If he moved fast.

Albert threw Marcel the end of the rope. "Anchor the rope to that tree by the creek—I don't have time to explain. Just make sure it's tied tight."

Marcel moaned, but followed his friend as Albert sprinted for the creek bed.

Running down the bank, Albert played the rope out behind him, crouching low as he followed the creek. He couldn't see the approaching behemoth, but he heard the crashing sound of its spindly legs and a high-pitched chirping coming from its massive head.

Albert splashed in the water as he crossed to the other side. Suddenly the noise stopped, and the grass on the opposite creek bank ignited with fire. *It heard me,* thought Albert. He froze, and the fan of fire ceased as well.

Moments passed, then the high-pitched chirping started again. Albert dropped to the ground and crawled up the side of the creek.

The smoke had thinned, and Albert could see the people in the wood behind him. As if the Martian realized that the smoke had cleared as well, it started striding toward the train.

He didn't have much time. Looking wildly around, he spotted a clump of trees on top of a low hill. The Martian passed the hill and started for the creek bank. He had to move fast.

Still trailing the rope behind him, Albert waited until the behemoth passed by, then sprinted around behind it. The Martian stepped down the creek bank, stopped, and started fanning out fire with its infrared beam.

Albert quickly ran around the Martian, trailing the rope behind him. Within seconds he had passed underneath the towering creature and looped the rope around the Martian's legs. Crouching low, he ran up the rise to the two thickest trees and started to pull. The rope tightened around the Martian's spindly legs.

He heard shouting come from the other side of the train and the sounds of people clanging on metal. He saw Marcel and some of the other people trying to divert attention away from him. As the Martian's heat-ray beamed out, it struck the train and more of the oil that Marcel had poured. Flames and boiling black smoke boiled up, once again hiding the train from view.

The Martian turned its head and started fanning its infrared beam across the ground toward Albert. The leaves on the tree exploded in fire. The Martian tried to pull one leg up and step over the rope, but it was captured by the rope noose.

The heat-ray beamed out, as if it were trying to find the rope and burn it, but the flames only weaved crazily out on the ground, as if directed by a drunkard. The Martian made one final attempt to lift a leg free, then tipped off balance and fell.

The fall seemed to last for minutes. The giant barrellike head twisted back and forth during the fall, high-pitched chirping shrilled from under its hood.

It crashed with a crushing metal sound, and the chirping changed to whimpering.

Exhausted, Albert walked up the rise and watched as the creature lay twitching on the ground. People from the train appeared around the edges of the smoke and fire. Smeared with blackened oil, and with the fire and smoke roiling into the air, Albert watched as the creature jerked sporadically, then stopped moving.

It had been less than a half an hour since he had awakened from the accident—and had stoutly dismissed the notion of an invasion from Mars.

Marcel stepped up beside Albert. Marcel was covered with black soot, and looked more like a chimney sweep than the mathematical genius professors at the Eidgenössiche Technische Hochschule had once lauded.

Albert and Marcel surveyed the fallen monster from afar, knowing that it was dead, but still unable to convince themselves that it wouldn't rise up to attack them. In the distance Albert heard booms of artillery fire; the city of Milan must be under siege.

Marcel spoke in a whisper, as if afraid to disturb the fallen beast. He nervously wet his lips and glanced all around him. "I don't think we can count on anyone coming out here to rescue us. How far is it to Milan from here?"

Albert turned to look down the track. The wreckage of two trains that had come before them littered the tracks. Nothing had been able to stop the Martian. Until now.

"I don't know. Maybe twenty kilometers?" Albert said. "I can hear artillery, so they're probably under attack as well."

"Then we're safe," Marcel said.

Albert shook his head. "Pavia is not far from Milan. My parents are there." *If they are still alive,* he thought. What had happened to his mother and father? His sister Maja? Were they suffering? And what about Uncle Jakob, his mentor who had taught him the Pythagorean theorem . . . ? Albert felt his anger growing toward the Martians.

Albert controlled his voice and said, "If we strike out on foot, it might take us another day to reach Pavia. No telling how bad things are in Milan, especially if the Martians had stationed a sentry to stop the incoming trains."

"Why?" said Marcel. "Are they trying to keep food and supplies from entering Milan? If so, then people on horses, carriages, and those on foot might not have any chance at all. What can we do?"

"I don't know." Albert fingered his mustache, still scrawny after all these years of trying to grow it. But at least his Serbian classmate Mileva Maric had liked it—she was the one bright spot at school, besides Marcel, that he would always remember.

Marcel looked nervously around, as if another Martian would come stalking around the bend to menace the small band of people.

Albert stared at the fallen Martian. It did not look so formidable now that it had fallen. And it might give him a clue as to how it functioned. He started walking briskly toward the head.

Marcel sputtered, then trotted to keep up with him. "Albert, what are you doing? Did the fire give you a heat stroke? What if the Martian is still alive?"

Albert stepped up his pace to the Martian, more determined than ever to investigate the fallen leviathan up close. "This may give us a clue as to how to defeat them."

Marcel moaned. "I think this is a bad idea!"

"Allowing these beasts to ravage my family is worse!"

They reached the metallic head. It was as big as a small house. The metal visor stuck out like an overhanging porch. A stench of chemicals drifted from the barrellike head. The legs extended out thirty meters and were as thick as an old tree.

Albert walked around the huge head, then scrambled up on the metallic body. A horrible smell drifted out from under the visor. Albert rubbed his mustache and wrinkled his nose; the smell reminded him of horse manure thrown in a fire. He tried not to gag as he looked inside.

"Be careful!" warned Marcel from behind him.

The interior was unlighted. Weird shadows clustered against the back of the head, and it took a moment for Albert's eyes to grow accustomed to the dark. Slowly, things came into focus, but Albert couldn't make sense of anything he saw. Glowing rectangles and lighted buttons were set throughout the chamber. His mind could not comprehend the unearthly angles, the grainy material that made up the interior.

He reached inside to get a better grip and pull himself up higher—

Suddenly, the visor swung open. Albert yelped and held on to the top part of the visor as it opened wide like a gate. The visor swung him out over the metallic body, then over the grass. His feet dangled as he held on to the yawning flange.

Marcel screamed, "Albert—drop and run away!"

Sunshine poured into the interior as a gray, limp mass tumbled out of the chamber. The round, soft body of the Martian hit the metallic armor, bounced off, and rolled to the grass. Blue-green liquid oozed from wounds where it had hit.

A crowd of people who had approached gasped in a collective sound. They stepped back as Albert dangled above the ground. Grunting, he tried to swing the visor back to the main part of the head, but could not budge the gatelike structure.

Albert gingerly slid hand over hand down the visor to the main part of the head. He reached out with a foot and, grabbing a toehold, was able to steady himself. He ducked under the visor and pulled himself into the chamber.

The fresh air had cleared some of the stench, but the horse-manure odor still lingered. Marcel yelled from outside. "Albert! Get out of there!"

Albert stepped cautiously until he stood at the center of the chamber. Now that he was inside, he could feel the chamber pulsating with a low vibration.

Panels were set all around the chamber. They were placed on the curving wall about shoulder height.

Movement on the glowing panels caught his attention. Albert could make out tiny figures moving around on the front panel. Stepping closer, he saw that it was a tilted view from outside the metallic structure! He glanced around. The panels were like tiny windows, showing different views; but some of them were focused on scenes far away from the metallic head: streets filled with people running away in mobs, black smoke curling up from burning factories, and scenes of what looked like the Milan Cathedral, then the La Scala opera house, and the Church of Santa Maria delle Grazie—

Albert drew in a breath. The scenes *were* of Milan, but the city was at least twenty kilometers away from here! The images were bright and sharp, as though there were little people moving behind the panel.

Mesmerized, he stepped back. Something didn't feel right. It was time to leave this place. He caught himself as he bumped against a row of glowing lights—

The outside visor swung shut. The motion startled him; the visor moved too quickly for him to try and escape. In an instant he was sealed in the Martian chamber.

Albert kept still. He dared not move close to the glowing lights again.

He stepped slowly to where the visor had closed. It was sealed solidly shut. He ran a hand over the chamber wall and inspected the place where the seams had been, but he couldn't detect any joint at all. It was as if the entire chamber had been formed out of one solid metallic piece.

Albert backed away to the middle of the chamber. What about the air in here? The Martians obviously breathed air, but would there be enough in the chamber for him to survive? He felt suddenly cold, and found himself drawing in several rapid breaths.

A low pulsation. Something was happening in the chamber.

He turned to the panels that showed the outside world—everyone dashed madly about, as if time had been speeded up. From the outside view, the Martian structure appeared to have settled in the ground, as if the weight of the chamber had suddenly increased. And the images were all tinged light blue.

He saw Marcel scurry up to the Martian war machine, only to bounce against some invisible shield surrounding the chamber. Marcel frantically rapped on the metallic legs, a woodpecker in fast motion. His friend could not approach the metallic head.

Albert breathed faster. He scanned the panoramic view from inside of the machine. Everything had the same light blue tint, as if he were looking through a filter.

He saw a boy dash up into a tree. The young lad was not more than ten years old. The boy immediately jumped down from the branches. A crowd of people gathered around the tree. The tree was alive with people scrambling up to look at the Martian, then leaping back down. Up and down. Up and down. Faster and faster.

Two men ran toward the war machine. They held torches. The flames burned as if they were fueled by rapidly burning petrol.

Albert moved to the other panels. He saw images as if he was in another Martian's control chamber, high above the streets of Milan. The monsters swept through the city. Striding along, swinging their views from side to side. Albert saw sheets of fire burst up from the Galleria Vittorio Emanuele. The Martians were training their infrared beams on Milan!

A cloud of blue-tinged smoke oozed from yet another Martian. The cloud slithered down to envelop a crowd of people who had gathered outside of the plaza. With the fast-motion action, when the smoke cleared away, only a powdery dark residue remained . . . and legions of dead bodies. Women, children alongside the men.

Albert heard no sound from the outside world, only the dull throbbing inside the chamber from the hidden machinery. *What is going on?* The world just can't have started moving faster.

He gaped at the scenes around him, a world gone mad. He remembered his teachings, the immutable rules for making sense of the unknown, but ordered universe. *Determinism. Cause and effect—things happen for a reason, and not by magic.*

This absolute didn't change because he was somewhere else, locked up in a Martian war machine. It didn't matter if he was sitting still, or if he had been moving. The physics should remain the same, both inside and outside the chamber.

He wasn't moving now, but it was obvious that time itself had changed. What was different about this damned chamber he was in and the outside world? *The laws of physics must be the same in unaccelerated frames.*

His mind raced back to the morning. He remembered being slammed against the wall during the train crash. He remembered his conjecture about the equivalence of reference frames, but only if they were not accelerating . . . and he wasn't accelerating now.

Was he?

He caught a movement on one of the panels showing another Martian's view. The Martian was heading away from the center of Milan and toward the countryside. It marched three-legged along a set of railroad tracks.

The scene looked chillingly familiar. Albert recognized the countryside outside of Milan. He had ridden past this scenery many times on a train, back to Zurich. Long steel railroad tracks disappeared in the hills. He could see the Italian Alps in the distance. Was the Martian heading to where Albert was?

To help the fallen Martian that Albert had killed?

Albert reached out to the panel. The control chamber seemed to sink deeper into the ground, and the motion outside the chamber speeded up even faster. The panels turned a deep blue, and he could barely make out what was going on outside.

Rapid, jerky movements. The panel that showed the Martian's view heading for the countryside wheeled crazily about. Albert spotted a battery of artillery set above the hills outside Milan. Smoke erupted from where they had shot their weapons at the Martian.

That panel blinked and went blank.

It happened almost too fast for Albert to comprehend. The Martian must have been hit.

Albert was safe for now.

The sun burned as a bright violet ball. The angle of the sun changed, and Albert realized that it was setting . . . darkness fell, and the ice-cold pinpoints of deep blue stars swung around the sky. Within minutes the sun appeared again and started crawling from one panel to another.

Albert watched, bewildered. Time was accelerating for him, and the days raced past. It made no sense.

Suddenly the panels from Milan started blinking. One panel flickered, then went blank. One after another blacked out. Something was happening to the Martians. Within minutes—half a day to the outside world—he lost all the scenes from Milan.

He lost track of how much time had passed outside of his little world. Could years go by? The implications staggered him. What would become of his parents? Uncle Jakob? Of his Serbian classmate, dark-eyed Mileva Maric?

He held out his hands to the lights, and the motion in the main panels slowed. The chamber rocked up from the ground.

He saw that down by the train track people worked to move the overturned train and to clear out the devastation. Workers had erected a tent for food, water, and medical care. Another train chugged in from the city, trailing smoke behind it. Everyone moved at a normal pace.

But what had happened to the Martians? He had seen no activity from them since the other panels had gone blank.

Now unafraid of the consequences, Albert moved to where the visor had sealed into the chamber. Getting on his hands and knees, he inspected the smooth wall. He still couldn't find a seam.

He straightened. A row of lights blinked over a blank area on the opposite wall. It was the same area he had backed into when he first entered the chamber.

He slowly ran his hands over the lights and stepped back as the sound from the machinery changed pitch. With a sudden movement, the visor swung open. Fresh, clean air spilled inside.

Albert blinked at the unexpected light. The low hum of pulsating machinery sighed to a stop. For the first time since he had entered the chamber, Albert heard no sound. He stood at the entrance and stared out at the changes that had occurred around him since he had entered the chamber.

After a few minutes an excited chatter rose from the crowd. Someone shouted in the distance. "Albert!" It was Marcel's voice, calling excitedly from the tent.

Albert reached out to the visor that extended from the chamber and slid hand over hand away from the monstrous head. Once clear of the metallic body, he let go and fell a good three meters to the ground. Landing in the grass, he rolled to the side.

The hills seemed greener, the clouds a more brilliant white, untinged with blue. He stood and blinked in the sunlight.

Marcel ran up to him; he was followed by a group of boys and men. A tall thin man with a white beard accompanied Marcel. Several other men carried rifles and stood warily back, as if they were unconvinced that Albert was not a threat.

"Albert!" His friend Marcel panted as he reached him. He threw his arms around Albert. "Thank God you are alive! The others had given you up for dead."

The tall thin man with Marcel stepped up to Albert. "Are there any Martians inside?" He spoke with a Dutch accent.

Albert shook his head. "One fell out just as I entered. I . . . I was trapped inside."

The man looked disappointed. "The Martian lived for only a short time. It did not have time to disable its machinery, like the others we've found. In fact, this is the only Martian war machine that still has power. We've been waiting a long time to find one that worked." He stepped up on his tiptoes to try and peer inside the chamber.

Albert drew in a deep breath, and felt relieved not to smell any of the alien stench. He felt suddenly hungry. "How long have you waited?"

The man answered over his shoulder. "Two and a half weeks. You're lucky to be alive."

Albert wavered. *Two and a half weeks!* Then it wasn't a dream. He hadn't had any water, much less food, in the chamber.

Marcel stepped up to the two. "Albert, this is Dr. Lorentz. He was visiting in Milan when the Martians landed. He was commissioned by the minister of science to investigate the Martian technology. He's a physicist like yourself—"

Albert's eyes grew wide. Of course he knew of the eminent scholar; at ETH Professor Minkowski had often spoke of Lorentz's work investigating Maxwell's equations and the ether.

With shaky hands Albert pulled out his watch. It read five o'clock. Only seven hours had passed since he had entered the Martian . . . or two and a half weeks, if he could believe Dr. Lorentz.

". . . the Martians succumbed to a disease," said Marcel, still talking. "So I decided to wait here." He looked over to the group of men standing by the clump of trees; they had lowered their weapons, but they still looked ominous. "They were planning to use explosives on the war machine. We had given up all hope of you ever coming out."

Dr. Lorentz dismissed Marcel's comments. "This machine is much too important for me to have allowed that to happen, young man." He looked eagerly at the Martian head. "The device seemed to have become quite massive while you were inside. We were unable to approach it until the visor swung open. Do you know how to work the equipment inside?"

Albert's head was still reeling with the implications of difference in time. "Somewhat. But I think the power has gone off. At least everything fell silent when I opened the visor."

Dr. Lorentz looked disappointed. "I'll speak with you later then." He turned for the metallic body.

"Over here," said Marcel. He steered his friend away from the Martian war machine. "I'll get you some hot tea." He led him to the medical tent.

As Albert rested, he watched the men entering the chamber. The ground around the massive metallic head looked compressed, as if the chamber had once weighed much more than it did now.

"Here," said Marcel, approaching from the canteen. He held out a cup of tea for his friend.

Albert took the drink and gulped it down. He stayed silent when Marcel queried him about his experience. It would be too difficult to explain the passage of time. *Two and a half weeks! What could cause this to happen?* he thought. Was he dreaming?

He absently touched his head. The wound from the train crash was still present. It should have healed after two and a half weeks.

Cause and effect.

Albert looked at the ground around the massive head. What if it *had* tremendously increased in weight? And what if whatever had kept the people away also prevented the chamber from sinking into the ground? Did the increase in weight affect the passage of time?

Reference frames . . .

Maybe the Martians had built a rescue device into the chamber: In an emergency, the visor would seal tight, and with time passing quickly outside the chamber, it would serve as a "lifeboat" until help could come. Albert thought back to the Martian that had attempted to leave Milan. What would have happened if it had arrived, only to find him inside?

Albert's thoughts were interrupted by Marcel, who was clearly agitated that his friend stayed mute. "I think, Biedermeier, that there is more to your adventure than you are willing to tell. Is that not so?"

Biedermeier. Honest John.

Dr. Lorentz had left the chamber and dropped to the ground. He now strode hurriedly to where they sat. No doubt he would be wanting to know how Albert had managed to live for two and a half weeks in the tiny chamber without leaving any crumbs of food, any water . . . or any sign of human waste.

Marcel said, "I telegraphed your parents that I would let them know how you were when the chamber opened. Tell me. Is there more to your story?"

Albert pulled on his mustache, still half immersed in deep thought. Dr. Lorentz looked grim, and he would be demanding an explanation. An explanation based on cause and effect, not magic.

Albert spoke softly as the eminent physicist approached. "It depends on how you look at it, my friend. It all depends." He felt suddenly strengthened with the knowledge that his *Gedanken* experiments with reference frames had something to do with this.

Albert Einstein pushed up to greet Dr. Lorentz. "I'm not sure where this is heading, my friend, but I'm starting to think it's all relative."

Rudyard Kipling

SOLDIER OF THE QUEEN

BARBARA HAMBLY

"Christ if we don't got sufficient to deal wid in this hellacious country, widout rumor and claptrap from down-country." Private Mulvaney stood the butt of his Enfield on the parapet, and spoke at my step, without taking eyes from the blue-black loom of hills and midnight sky. "It is rumor, isn't it, sorr? This fallin' star Colonel Crocker's after findin'?"

"Na, we seen t' fallin' star, sure enough." Scarcely less massive than the Himalaya foothills themselves, Learoyd moved towards us through the wet, breathless dark.

"Hit's allus summat in the marketplace," theorized Ortheris, who by rights should have been half a hundred feet along the wall at the corner of the gatehouse, though nothing had stirred in the darkness for close to four hours. "Meself, I find it 'ard to b'lieve the 'igh-up god Shiva really up an' sent a fallin' star down at Gorakhpur wi' a load of demons to wipe out the gora-log just 'cause the local Brahmin got done out o' two square feet of land and a cow by some Manchester bank."

"Who's saying that?" I asked, startled.

"Every bhisti and punka-wallah in the camp, 'til old Crock quodded the lot."

"Have you heard anythin', sorr?" asked Mulvaney, who had been, I realized, startlingly silent during this interchange. His attention had been fixed on the night beyond the walls, straining to catch some sound beyond the incessant creaking of insects, and the cries of wolves.

"Nothing definite," I said slowly, and stubbed my cigarette against the rough-cast wall of Fort Chopal. And indeed, the telegram from my paper that afternoon had been disparaging in the extreme about the rumors from Surrey. "But it seems this isn't the only falling star to have struck Earth. Two have come down in England since Friday; one in France, and another that we know of in the United States. As for demons . . ."

Cold, keening, and indescribable, a wailing ululation rose out of the dark lowlands that fell away on the other side of the fort. No human throat could have produced it, nor any animal of Earth. In the next moment light flared, like the heat lightning that had already begun to illuminate the dense, hot Indian summer, but infinitely greater. My three friends turned, seizing their rifles, and as blinding dark succeeded blinding light came the awed and frightened outcry from the men on the walls whom Colonel Crocker had left behind when he went down-country to investigate the falling star.

"Gor blimey!"

"Strewth . . ."

"Git back here, y'ill-got clods!" bellowed Mulvaney, as Cockney and Yorkshireman, more by instinct than plan, started to run after me along the parapet to the down-country side of Fort Chopal's parapet. "The good Lord only knows what's snakin' up this side of the wall whilst ye're gawpin' like grannies!"

The Irishman's voice pulled Ortheris and Learoyd up short, but I continued to run. Below me in the compound yard I heard the Hindoos imprisoned in the post jail yammering and beating on the doors of their cells as if certain of imminent liberation.

Green light smote the night again, limning the dark trees like smoke, and the glassy curve of the river, and again the high, metallic wailing lifted the hair from my head. Below it I heard gunshots, the massed firing of half a regiment.

There was another flare of light, and the firing stopped.

Then for an endless time—it must have been ten or fifteen minutes—we stood on the wall, staring into the night. From the direction of Gorakhpur came the orange glare of fires burning uncontrolled, and still we strained our eyes. Beside me Colonel Crocker's adjutant, a very young first-poster named Sotheby, peered through field glasses, muttering, "The Maxim guns, for Heaven's sake! If the Indians think this is some kind of Heavenly intervention, the Maxims'll straighten them out. . . . Good Lord!"

Beyond the trees something flashed, too bright, too glistening in the fire's reflections.

Someone on the wall behind me gave a horrified yell.

What I saw, newspapermen and soldiers had already seen, on Horsell Common and in Woking, and across the green fields of Surrey, though no word of it had reached me or anyone in India at that time. The giant tripod of flashing steel came running at us, racing with the liquid articulation of an animal, clearing fields and huts and trees with long strides of its jointed limbs.

Rifle fire snapped behind me, and from the compound below a cacophony of shouting arose. I turned from the horrifying and unprecedented sight of the first of the Martian war machines, in time to see brown men slipping from shadow to shadow of the courtyard, steel glinting in their hands in the oily lantern light. The men on the walls, save for only a few like Mulvaney, had run to watch the approach of the machine, and in those unguarded minutes the native men had effected their entrance: Thugees, hunters, Pandies, and malcontents of all sorts whose dissatisfaction with the Queen's rule and the Queen's justice had been a slow-simmering constant since the days of Lucknow and Cawnpore. Soldiers crowded either side of me on the walls turned to fight them as they poured up the gangways.

I heard young Captain Sotheby crying "At them, men!" as I was thrust back against the parapet. It was savage work, too close for rifles, though the men of the 14th had stood to that night with bayonets fixed. I was trapped in the midst of it, while men shrieked and stabbed and shoved all about me. And all the time I was conscious of that monstrous Thing below, the chill piercing howls of it as it approached the fort answered by the Indians' wild cries of delight.

There was another bright flash, and I felt the wall crumble beneath us. A sickening lurch, and the stone parapet cracked in two at my back, spilling soldiers, Thugs, and all like ants from a snapped twig into the rocks of the hillside below.

"Goad, sir, Ah'm glad you're alive."

I wasn't. Nor was I sure I still lived, for the heat was theological, the stink of dust and blood suffocating, and my body an armature of pain.

Even the sound of that deep Yorkshire boom, or the light Cockney, "There, what'd Hi tell yer?" that followed, did not reassure me. Could I be assured of any facet of the afterlife, it would be the eventual downward destination of Mulvaney, Ortheris, and Learoyd.

Certainly those two looked like escapees from Gehenna. Soot-blackened, grimy with dust and sweat, they knelt in torn uniforms on either side of me. Morning light, and the dense and breathtaking heat of midmorning, filled the marginal shelter of the stretched bit of canvas under which I lay, in what appeared to be a nullah, or gorge. I could hear the voices of men outside, hushed and arguing anxiously. The air was thick with the smell of burning.

"Hit wiped 'em out, sir." Ortheris clawed the sweat from his face. There was a haunted look in his eyes. "Wiped 'em clean out, like ants frizzlin' up on a griddle, hit did, wi' a beam o' light. Blast me for six if I ever saw such a thing."

A shadow darkened the opening of the shelter. Ortheris and Learoyd got to their feet and saluted. It was the young adjutant Sotheby, who returned the salute punctiliously with his swagger stick, though as torn and dirty as they. "Are you fit to move, sir?" he asked me. "This position is untenable. All communications to district HQ at Patna appear to have been cut. As the fort itself has been destroyed, there is no question of making a stand and awaiting reenforcements. We must fall back."

"The fort destroyed?" I managed to say. My mouth was swollen nearly speechless.

"I'm afraid so," said Sotheby.

"Walls knocked clean acock by yon thing," said Learoyd softly, "Thugees crawlin' through every nook. Ah did go back, sir," he added. "Ah did go back an' look. . . ."

This he said behind me, as he and Ortheris helped me to rise, and the three of us limped out into the brazen glare of the midmorning sun. A straggling group of men in torn and dirty red uniforms were strung out along the thin brown trickle of the nullah among the rocks, engaged in packing up tins of beef and biscuits, or here and there ammunition boxes, or filling canteens. It took me a moment to realize, with slow-dawning horror, that this was in truth all that remained of the 14th ——shires; the sum total of those who had survived the first attack of the Martians, and of the native partisans who followed in their wake.

And as we started off on that long retreat, I could already see that among them there was no sign of Terence Mulvaney.

Of the long retreat of the 14th to Patna—and beyond it to Calcutta, when it became clear that the Martians had reached the district HQ before us and left it a wasteland of cindery death—reports have been written elsewhere. Indeed, it is a story that is repeated many times by other regiments, or the fragments of others. The 7th ——shires journeyed from Kabul almost to Delhi before they were destroyed by Indian partisan bands; ten members of the Black Tyrone fought their way from Lahore to Bombay after all their officers and most of their comrades succumbed to the heat-ray and the black smoke dispensed by the Martians of the second invading vessel, which struck down nearly on top of Lahore Saturday night.

At the time we knew not of the other attacks in India; knew nothing of the catastrophe reaching out to engulf the world. For the fifty-three men of the 14th, the world began and ended with the stifling damp heat of the Bengal jungles; the silent tea plantations where dogs worried at the bodies of the dead. We learned very quickly to distinguish the slumped but unmarked corpses left by the black smoke, covered with their powdery shroud of ebon dust, from those the partisans had killed. Before we reached Patna, even, there were fewer of either sort.

Sufficient praise does not exist for young Captain Sotheby. Less than a year out of Sandhurst, he had a reputation as a martinet. Yet his insistence upon adequate scouting, camp guards, and utter silence in both movement and rest more than once saved our lives. It was he who deduced from the scouts' reports that common water precipitated the harmful elements in the black smoke, and ordered each man to carry a wet shirt when we were in territory held by the Martians, to wrap round the head should we be caught in the discharge of that weapon. Given the quickness with which the black smoke converted to a harmless precipitate in the humidity of the Bengal summer, this too saved many lives, my own among them.

"They'll be holding out in Calcutta," Sotheby said, when dawn showed us what the Martians had left of Patna. "They have artillery there—regular artillery, not just light field cannon and Maxim guns."

"Reg'lar artillery?" demanded Ortheris, turning from the sight of those charred streets and crumbled buildings. We were grouped on a small elevation in what had been a tea plantation, half starved, exhausted, as wild and ragged a band of ruffians as you would care to see. Though the attacks by the Indian partisans had ceased days ago, we had been fighting our way through ever-thickening masses of the pestilent red weed, which grew riotously in the wet climate. I think it was the strangeness of the landscape, as much as the danger of the Martians and the sheer, deadly heat, which drove the little man to the edge of insubordination and despair. "What the 'ell chance you think reg'lar artillery's gonna stand, against them?"

He flung out his arm in a furious gesture toward the distant, gleaming shapes that walked to and fro among the drifting steams and broken houses of what had once been a city of hundreds of thousands. "By Gord, sir, ain't you been watchin'? Ain't you seen what they do with that 'eat-ray of theirs? You think it won't blast a sixteen-inch gun to Jesus just as quick as it'll blow up a Maxim? It's 'opeless, sir! Can't you see?" His voice rose almost to a scream. " 'Opeless!"

Sotheby stood facing him, making no reply for a time, cold and prim and immaculate despite his shirtless raggedness and grubby wisps of pale beard. Ortheris stared at him, panting with despair and rage. Then after a long time he dropped his eyes.

"Shout it a little louder while you're at it, Private Ortheris," said the officer quietly. "Let them really hear you."

In the silence, the distant hoots of the Martian machines were eerily loud.

"And what would your alternative be?" the young man went on after a time. "Creeping away into the hills, to die like a rat? Meeting your end huddled in some native hut gnawing carrion, when the Martians finally find you? Every surviving regiment in the countryside will be making for Calcutta. Some communications will exist there; food supplies, also. It is there that reenforcements will be sent. Do you think Britain's government is helpless? Do you think they'll simply abandon us?"

Ortheris raised his eyes for a moment, and I could see his thoughts were like mine. But like me, he would not speak them, and after a moment he whispered, "No, sir."

"Very well, then." He nodded back toward the ruins of the plantation house. It had been destroyed by Martians, not partisans. All was black with the powder of the black smoke, and the house itself had been trodden flat, wrecked by one of the war machines, but it offered some shelter from the sun. "Two hours' rest before guard duty. We press on as soon as it gets dark tonight."

We reached Calcutta in darkness, and from all that vast city came no light, but only a great smell of charred wood and burnt flesh hanging chokingly in the heavy air. Away toward the west, green and white flares of light spoke of Martian encampments; puffs of smoke shimmered faintly in the light of the waning moon.

Sotheby had reckoned wrong. No other military units in that city had survived.

By the chalky light we made our way to the wreck of the Krishnana-gar Artillery Barracks, and drank greedily of what muddy water remained in its tanks and wells. The barracks stood on ground sufficiently high—and sufficiently clear of running water—to avoid engulfment in the huge tangles of Martian red weed that buried nearly all the plantations in the lower valley. Calcutta itself was an endless morass of the stuff, glowing sickly purple in the blackness. On guard duty that night I looked down from the walls upon the stuff, prey to the queer, ghastly sensation of seeing the world I knew transformed into another world entirely, a world in which we who had conquered this land were now less than even the natives had been in the eyes of these new conquerors. The very speed with which this had taken place rendered the whole experience dreamlike, and I wondered if I might presently wake.

There was a faint sound of scratching among the rocks below me. I brought to my shoulder the rifle I would not have dared to fire, and listened again. It had been nearly two weeks since any of the native partisan bands had molested us, but it was not something to be discounted.

Then a voice, barely a whisper, called out, "Don't shoot, whoever y'are." And I nearly cried out myself, in surprise and delight, for there was no mistaking the mellow County Liffey accents of Terence Mulvaney.

"Close on two thousand of us there are, and that only the one band." Mulvaney shut his eyes and drew hard on the clay pipe, the scent of the barracks commander's tobacco—found intact in the dead man's rooms—like a blessing in the hot morning air. The Indian who'd accompanied Mulvaney to the walls sat in the wide window of the duty room, a brown, nearly naked young man who smelled like a wolf, and his dark eyes followed the talk from myself to Mulvaney to Sotheby and the other two Musketeers and half a dozen of the other men, gathered in the broken shadow and sun-glare.

"I swear I thought I was a goner, for the thing picked me outen the ruins like an elephant'll pick a mahout, an' nary a dint could I make on that metal tentacle of it. What wid the dark an' the shock I musta been off my head for a bit, 'cause next thing I knew I was in the Martian camp, in this metal basket thing on the back o' one o' their blasted machines, wid two or three Indians—brown naked Pandies, two of 'em were, but the third a little skinny slip of a babu lawyer in spectacles, starin' out through the bars at the Martians for all the world as if they was in the zoo, not him.

"Have ye seen the Martian camps at all? Great pits druv in the airth they are, wid embankments, like, raised all round, an' these divilish machines diggin' out dirt an' makin' white metal of it, an' pourin' this powder aside. Aluminium, the babu said; like the princess in the tower spinnin' straw into gold, it looked to me, given it was a damn' ugly princess. I wasn't much interested in the aluminium myself, considerin' what else was goin' on. Have ye seen what the Martians do to a man, when they catch him?"

There was a silence. I said, "We've found bodies."

"Well, then, I won't go into it. They've got other machines besides them war machines, like great glitherin' crabs. One of 'em cranked over an' pulled a Pandy outen the basket, an' him shriekin' an' wavin' his arms about an' tellin' Shiva he'd got the wrong person, most like, for all the good it did him. Every Martian in the camp gathered round for the feed, an' me an' the Pandy crouched back in the corners, wonderin' if we'd be next. But our boy in the specs, he was right on the bars, watchin'—not like a kid at a donnybrook, mind, but like a man tryin' to understand somethin' he couldn't understand.

"Well, durin' the height of teatime, what do we get but my friend over there . . ." He jerked his pipe stem at the guide. ". . . climbin' the outside of the cage, an' flippin' the lock. How he got down inside the embankment wi'out bein' seen I still don't know. They say round our band he was raised in the jungle by wolves, but faith, half the hunters in India say that about theirselves. I believe it of 'em, now. We was out o' that cage like three ferrets outen a bag, an' the four of us skinned up the side o' that embankment as fast as we dared. We was near to the top when one o' the Martians seen us, an' you never heard such a hollerin' an' a whistlin'. But they're slow. By the time they humped theirselves over to them machines we was runnin' down the outside of their redoubt, an' we was in the red weed, out o' sight an' pantin' like conies.

"Fair spitless I was, fearin' to see one o' them war machines come stridin' outen the pit, but old Mowgli just says . . ." He nodded at the guide again, ". . . 'I put that powder they made from the dirt into the leg-joints of their steeds; I do not think they will gallop so fast now.' Leastwise he says this to Mr Gandhi—the babu, y'understand."

"Why dint they use the black smoke on yer?" asked Ortheris, and Mulvaney shook his head.

"One can only surmise," said Sotheby, "that it comes packed in cylinders large enough to annihilate a city. On that first night they can't have known how much of their limited supply they were going to need."

"Fair enough, sorr," agreed Mulvaney. "Whyever they didn't—well, Mowgli here got us back to the partisan camp. Our leader—their leader," he added, rather self-consciously, "—is a woman name of Padmini who looks like your old aunt; she was the one voted not to kill me out of hand, but rather keep me as a kind of slave porter. They figured out pretty quick after that this show wasn't all laid on by Shiva to kick the gora-log out of India, for the Martians was attackin' partisan bands as well as military—attackin' anythin' they found, over a dozen, an' carryin' off whoever they could. There was talk of just splittin' up, disappearin' into the hills. Them machines ain't much in rough country. But I pointed out to Padmini that it stands to reason they'd only come up with some better way to follow, maybe one we couldn't avoid. An' we knew, after that first night, what they wanted of mankind. T'was the first time—the only time—I found meself rejoicin' that Mrs Mulvaney was dead."

He settled his back against the wall, his eyes somber. I saw Ortheris and Learoyd exchange a worried glance, for the death of his wife two years ago had been a terrible blow to Mulvaney, and one of which he never spoke. Like us all, Mulvaney was sunburned, emaciated, and half naked, the only remaining portion of his uniform his ammunition boots and cartridge belt—God knows where he got the ragged cotton trousers he wore. His rusty whiskers were shot through with grey, and there was a grimness to his eyes, a hardness, that had been absent when he had been but a soldier of the Queen.

"They's bands all over the country now," Mulvaney went on slowly. "We've had news—rumor, bush-telegraph . . ." He nodded at his guide again. "They say he talks to kites an' jackals, an' maybe he does. But the Martians can't control up-country. Ground's too rough, an' there's too much territory to cover. God knows, sorr, we never managed it."

Sotheby stiffened. "I venture to say, Private Mulvaney, that Her Majesty's forces did not do so ill."

Ortheris and Learoyd caught each other's eye, with volumes of hill-fighting and badmashes and ambush in their silence, but Mulvaney only said, "Be that as it may, sorr. We brought down two of their machines, the hunters sneakin' into camp an' pourin' that powder that's left over from the aluminium into the joints. Sometimes a hunter would just slip into the camp an' open all the petcocks on their fuel an' water an' oil alike. They're not so good at pinnin' a single man alone. The hunters'd wait 'til the Martians had caught someone, an' were havin' a feed. We'd lose half a dozen men for every one of 'em who succeeded, but with the Martians makin' Earth their huntin' preserve, it's but little odds how you die.

"They're movin' in on Calcutta now, sir. Comin' in from up-country. Calcutta's a swamp now, a choke of red weed crawlin' with people like ants in meadow grass. Even if they used the black smoke, Mr Gandhi been passin' word around among 'em for three days about wrappin' your face in a wet cloth, or gettin' under water for a minute or so; it turns to powder in not much more'n that. An' I don't think they will. We're their food."

He knocked the ashes from his pipe and handed it back to Ortheris, whose property it was. It had been one blessing on the march that though Sotheby enforced silence and caution, it had become quickly clear that the Martians had no sense of smell, nor organs for discriminating one odor from another. The men could smoke whenever they found tobacco in the ruined houses.

"Maybe we can't defeat 'em, but they're an army, when all's said," concluded Mulvaney grimly. "An' they got supply lines a million miles long. Like I says to Padmini, an' that Kim boy that's her second-in-command: All we got to do is make it not worth their while to stay. You've read the papers yourself, sorr, about people wantin' to get the Army out of India. Sooner or later the rate-payers back on Mars'll say, 'Bugger this.' Beggin' your pardon, sorr. 'Let 'em invade Venus instead.'"

Sotheby's breath escaped him in a sigh. "I fear you're correct, Private Mulvaney. But it stands to reason that the Martians would not have undertaken so expensive an invasion in the first place were not their need desperate. And one cannot discount the possibility that they, too, have their national pride. In any case, you have done a hero's work. Welcome back."

Mulvaney looked embarrassed, and scratched at the side of his greying beard. "Well, point of fact, sorr, I'm not back, exactly. This Padmini, she took my parole, an' sent me here as liaison. I'm on duty for her, so to speak. She—we—need your help, sir. We're cookin' up a few little surprises for the Martians when the main force of 'em arrive, bein' as how they only got the machines they brought with 'em, y'understand. We need gunpowder for pit-traps. I know there's some in this fort. There were depots throughout the city; I was hopin' ye'd know where those all were."

"In other words," said Sotheby coldly, "we are being asked to reveal British military secrets to your Padmini's Indian partisans."

"Yes, sorr." Mulvaney looked down at his hands. Then he raised his eyes again. "No, sorr. Padmini's askin' you to join human bein's, as other human bein's, to fight what'll kill us all if we go on each hidin' in our own hole. Sorr."

The young captain fixed the older man with a frozen gaze. "You remember, do you not, Private Mulvaney, that these are the very partisans who sacked and destroyed Fort Chopal? Who laid us open to destruction by the Martians?"

"Beggin' your pardon, sorr," said Mulvaney slowly, "they didn't lay us open to nuthin'. The Martians woulda had the fort in flinders if the partisans had been fightin' alongside us, instead of stabbin' us in the backs. An' . . . well, havin' seen the Martians turnin' our world into a sort of copy of their own with the red weed an' all, an' huntin' us an' usin' us . . . I can't say I agree with the partisans, but I do understand 'em a bit better, sorr."

Sotheby's silence lay heavy on the shadowed room, like the marble hand of Law. "And I suppose," he said at last, "that were I to command you to remain here, you would return to your natives?"

Mulvaney shut his eyes, a look of strain on his already worn features. In time he said softly, "No, sir. I'm a soldier of the Queen."

Sitting silent between Ortheris and Learoyd, I wondered if the Queen were even still alive. Wondered if anyone at home were still alive. If enough of a government remained to dispatch troops to our reenforcement, or if we were destined to perish, at last, like animals in these sodden jungles of Martian weed and black Martian dust.

"Very good," said Sotheby primly. "Then as your commanding officer, Private Mulvaney, I order you to return to Madame Padmini and inform her that we will need a dozen of her best scouts and hunters, if she can spare them, for immediate reconnaissance into the surviving powder depots in the city. Request arrangements for a meeting between herself and me at her earliest convenience. Perhaps I can be of assistance in the placement of pit-traps to the greatest military advantage. Dismissed."

Mulvaney got to his feet and saluted. We had all learned too much in the past weeks to make any kind of noise in the open, but through the arched window I saw Mulvaney, Learoyd, and Ortheris, as they crossed the courtyard, fall into each other's arms, shoving and roughhousing and smiting one another over the back like schoolboys in a paroxysm of soundless delight.

For two days we worked like dogs. Sweaty, filthy, stealthy, we dodged through the charred and reeking alleys of the dead city, ankle deep in sluggish floodwaters and nearly impassable with great, choking forests of red weed. In our arms we carried gunpowder charges, weaponry, whatever we could find. The Indian partisans who helped us— and there must have been seven or eight different bands of them, in addition to the considerable population who still remained in hiding in Calcutta—were for the most part worse off than we were, for while we had been driving straight for Calcutta, they had been harrying the Martians, and being harried in return.

Padmini turned out to be a grey-haired village matron with a soft voice and a wealth of practical cunning; her husband had been a hunter, as had been the husbands of two of her three now-widowed daughters: Lakshmi, Uma, and Chandira. All worked alongside the men—soldiers and partisans both—in digging deadfalls and pits, which were either mined with guncotton and percussion detonators, or flooded, and the thick, sickly jungles of red weed guaranteed that even from above the traps were invisible. Kim, Padmini's second-in-command, spoke English well, having been educated and worked for a time for British Intelligence; it was he who acted as liaison for the most part between troops and partisans. The young lawyer, Mr Gandhi, proved a genius at organizing the population of Calcutta itself, teaching them how to avoid the black smoke, and how to disappear into holes and corners of the crimson jungle when the Martian patrols appeared.

On a grillingly hot afternoon two days later, the rest of the Martians in India came.

We saw them from Fort Krishnanagar, a long line striding through the choking red swamps that had been tea plantations two months before. It seemed to me their dust-covered brazen cowls had lost the bright, deadly flash of their early victories. Many were clearly damaged, their smooth articulation reduced to a juddering limp; while we watched, one of the war machines suddenly ran amok, staggering crazily and cutting huge swatches in the red jungles of weed with its heat-ray until it collapsed like a stricken horse into the river.

"Fever," said Padmini softly, and Kim, beside her, translated for us. "The heat."

"Strewth," muttered Learoyd, "if Ah don't feel for t' poor bugger."

" 'Ave me 'anky," offered Ortheris. "Hi can't stand the sight of sympathetic tears."

We feared the Martians would lay down black smoke, which even with Mr Gandhi's precautions would doubtless kill many, but they did not. Such was their strategy of demoralization, to divide and scatter organized resistance, that they were unfamiliar, it seemed, with resistance that did not gather. They entered Calcutta like lords, and when the ground collapsed beneath their tripods, spilling them into the pit-traps which either drowned their engines or blew up from the percussion detonators, the only humans killed were those who might have been close enough to be caught in the blast of the exploding guncotton.

"Maybe we can't defeat those infernal machines of theirs," Sotheby said, watching from the stumpy ruin of the barracks tower through a dead commander's field glasses. "But we can damn well pick them off one at a time."

"And what else have they done," murmured Mr Gandhi, adjusting his spectacles, "in the villages, in the hills, in the countryside, for so many years?"

Sotheby glanced sharply at him, but said nothing. Indeed, I'm not sure what he could have said.

There was, in the end, no single defeat of the Martians. As all the world knows, they perished of diseases, of infection and fever. The scene we saw enacted upon the Martian entrance, when the war machine ran amok, was repeated a number of times, until at last no machines moved at all, and the oily, brownish corpses lay rotting in their pits in the blistering Indian sun.

"That's what we been fightin'?" demanded Ortheris, shocked.

And Learoyd only said, "Strewth!"

"If it's happening here, it must be happening elsewhere," said Sotheby that night in a general conference with the partisan leaders of all the city. "I don't doubt that in a few weeks, or a few months at most, word will arrive from home. Not reenforcements, of course, but at least some communication to reestablish contact with the home government."

"Ah," said Padmini. "But you see, Captain Sotheby, we are now the home government. We . . ." Her gesture included herself, Kim, and Mr Gandhi, who though he would not raise his hand even against a Martian had turned out to be one of the best organizers of rebuilding in the ravished countryside, and resupplying the city with food. "We are now the government of this, our home."

Sotheby opened his mouth to protest, and then closed it again. At length he said, "That we shall have to see, Madame."

One of the other partisan chiefs began to protest, but Padmini smiled. "Of course," she said—Kim was translating again. "And it is your home, too, Captain Sotheby. Your home, and the home of all your men, for how shall you return to England, now that all the ships are sunk? And to what shall you return? You are educated men. You know science, and how to make governments run. If you cannot return to your own land, then make this new land your home. Be our partners in this new rule, as we were partners in our defeat."

She did not mention, of course, that most surviving Indians had spent the past four weeks acquiring a quite comprehensive expertise in guerrilla-fighting tactics which might easily be put to other uses than resisting Martians.

But Sotheby only pursed his thin lips and said again, "We shall see."

It was nearly six months before the first Committee of Inspection arrived from the tattered and much-restructured government of England. And by then, of course, it was far too late.

The same ship which brought the inspectors—who were politely thanked for their concern and given messages from the Parliament of Indian States to take back to their former Queen-Empress—brought also garbled reports of the destruction of London, the horrible havoc wreaked by the Martians in all corners of the globe. It was nearly a year before word reached me of the survival of my family, whom I had been informed were dead.

My final meeting, therefore, with the Three Musketeers was in the Café Piccadilly. That establishment, wrought from the ruin of some princely palace above the flat brown waters of the Hugli, murmured that night with talk in Hindi and Urdu and English about young Gandhi's motion in the Upper House to ban even experimentation with the salvaged Martian weapons and machines, though the consensus was that since the heat-ray generators had uniformly blown up when tampered with, and the limited stores of fuel for the war machines were already beginning to degrade into unusable components, the point was a moot one.

But for us, sitting by smoky torchlight at a corner table, the talk turned on the cruiser *Victoria,* newly in port, and the offer from the British government to take back all those former members of Her Majesty's forces who wished to return.

"Ah thought on't." Jock Learoyd lifted a great stein of painted native ware to his lips, a ruminative look in his eyes. "Small odds, though, bossin' a buildin' gang here, or a selfsame gang in York. When it comes to it . . . It sounds daft, think on, but Ah'm not ettlin' to see all I knew as a child, broke down an' put together like a child's toy."

"Yer not daft, Jock." Ortheris clapped him on the shoulder. "Hit'll be a fair bit 'fore I walks down Piccadilly again—a fair bit 'fore me mother-in-law'll spare me or anyone else," he added with a rueful grin. "By then I'll 'ave got used to it, that it'll all be changed. Dirty old town, anyway," he added, a little shyly, and under his Cockney brashness I could hear the wistful memory for a London that was no more.

"Here's to 'em, then, them dhirthy old towns." Mulvaney raised his tankard. "You must have a drink for us all, sorr, down on the Embankment. . . . They didn't destroy the Embankment, did they, sorr? They can't have done!"

"I don't know," I said. "And speaking of drinks, Ortheris, my compliments to your mother-in-law—and to yourself—on the beer."

"She's trainin' us, she's trainin' us." The little man grinned. "Lord, what Hi dint know about brewin' when I married Miss Uma . . . But Madame Padmini, hif she could train farmers to be soldiers, an' turn around and make 'ill-fighters into statesmen—near enough, anyway—sure she could make a wastrel boy like me into a beer-brewer. Well, look, lads . . . hit's 'Imself 'imself."

They rose to their feet—old habit—and saluted with their tankards as Sotheby crossed to our table. "At ease, men," he said, as reflexively as the salute, and held out his hand for me to shake. "Bound for London in the morning?"

I said I was.

He lowered his voice. "Might I entrust you with these documents, to be delivered to Her Majesty's Foreign Office? You understand," he added, and I nodded. "I feel certain that when presented in the proper light—as these petitions present it—the case for our government's reopening of negotiations to take back the Indian colonies under our wing will be obvious. My work as liaison between the two governments has convinced me that this is the only viable course."

" 'Course it is, sorr, 'course it is," agreed Mulvaney affably. Sotheby stiffened in his neatly tailored suit—where he found a tailor in Calcutta to make him a black one, rather than the almost universal white, I could not guess—and looked sidelong at the Queen's former soldier to see if he were being jested, but Mulvaney wore an expression of earnest encouragement.

The liaison pursed his thin lips with disapproval, and turned back to me. "You'll deliver them?"

"I will indeed, sir." I took the dispatch case from his hand. "My friends . . ." Turning to the Three Musketeers, one by one I shook their hands, and so left them. As I walked out into the smutted torchlight of the Indian night, I glanced back to see the aproned form of

Mulvaney cross back to his usual position behind the Piccadilly's bar, and heard for the last time that persuasive Irish voice saying,

"Let me draw your attention to the latest batch of beer, sorr. The Minister of Treasury done herself proud on this one, like mither's milk it is . . ."

I wondered if England, and all of those I knew, would be as changed.

Edgar Rice Burroughs

MARS: THE HOME FRONT

GEORGE ALEC EFFINGER

I had just finished cleaning the fish that we'd caught earlier in the day, and I carried them back into the cabin. I opened one of the cupboards, looking for the tin canister of cornmeal and hoping that my partner hadn't forgotten to purchase some the last time he went into the town for supplies. I heard an odd sound behind me, but I didn't immediately turn around. "Turner," I said, "did you remember—"

There came that odd sound again, a good deal louder than before. This time it startled me so that I did turn, whereupon I gave an involuntary cry of alarm at what I then beheld.

It was a creature such as neither I nor anyone else on Earth had ever seen. It was of great size, and of such a fearsome visage that I can honestly say that for a moment I was truly dumbstruck with horror. I could not move, even as I knew that I should be fleeing for my life. I could only stare helplessly and pray to whatever god may be to spare me from a terrible fate.

The monster was about the size of a Shetland pony, yet its head was strangely amphibian, something like a giant frog. It had great jaws, each armed with three rows of long, daggerlike fangs. If I had any doubts that this was not an earthly animal, they were dispelled by the sight of its ten legs, for there are not any higher members of our world's animal kingdom so endowed.

It uttered again its grim, bloodcurdling growl, for such it was that had so surprised me. Then I heard a voice, a human voice, which reassured me that I might, indeed, live to dine upon the fish I had not yet finished preparing. The voice spoke in an unfamiliar language, and I understood but a single word. That word was "Woola," yet hearing it I knew at once that the nightmarish thing that confronted me was a Barsoomian calot, that Woola was its name, and that its master was none other than John Carter, Warlord of Mars.

"Hello, my nephew," he said. "I did not mean to be the cause of such consternation. I had decided that it was appropriate for me to make one more—and perhaps final—journey to Earth, and I brought along my loyal Woola merely as an experiment. I wished to ascertain if I could transport another living being with me across the dark, cold abyss of space that separates your Earth from my beloved Mars."

"And you have succeeded, John Carter," I replied. "Now, what new adventures have you to report?"

"Let us make ourselves comfortable," he said, "and I will tell you of a most urgent and bloody conflict that recently engulfed all of Barsoom, a crisis that surpassed even the desperate rescue of that planet's vital atmosphere plant, the harrowing tale of which I have already unfolded to you."

We seated ourselves at the simple wooden-plank table in the cabin's small kitchen, and as he had promised, my visitor began to relate the bizarre and frightful events that follow. I listened in rapt attention until well after the sun vanished from the Virginia skies, yet so commanding was John Carter's grim demeanor, and so remarkable his tale, that I can still recall his words as if they had been permanently engraved upon the tablets of my memory. I will thus let the hero of this narrative convey his experiences to you just as he told them to me.

The tale begins with treachery and ends with the wreaking of a vengeance terrible enough to change forever the lives of every man and woman upon two planets. It is a history of savage conquest, of horror beyond imagining, and of a worldwide alliance of many races and nations unprecedented in the ancient annals of Barsoom.

Looking back now, I am struck by how curiously serene and peaceful it was in the beginning. It seems strange that we, in our pride and ignorance, were so blissfully unaware of the danger that threatened us even as we slumbered in the false security of our high-walled city of Helium. Nevertheless, morning dawned as it always had, and slave and jeddak alike arose to take up the day's occupations. Children recited their lessons, pampered noblewomen bathed in luxury, and warriors among the red men of Mars practiced their martial skills, little dreaming that very soon their daily drills would turn in earnest to dreadful combat.

In the evening there was a reception at the palace of Mors Kajak, the father of the incomparable Dejah Thoris, the most beautiful woman on Barsoom or Earth, my wife and the mother of my son, Carthoris. I do not attend such formal affairs with quite the same pleasure as she who had grown to maturity as the daughter of the Jed of Lesser Helium. Still, I know that stifling formality and tedious dialogues are the price of what we choose to call "civilization."

I can yet recall the forever-unfinished conversation with Kantos Kan, an officer in the navy of Helium. We spoke of things that seemed important to us then, but in the light of later events those matters seem so trivial as to be almost foolish. And thus it is that fate—howsoever we name it—may relieve us of both our problems and our schemes to solve them, and in turn presents us with new troubles beyond the scope of our imagining.

I noticed that Kantos Kan had raised his eyebrows in puzzlement. "Did you not hear me, John Carter?" he inquired.

"You must forgive me, my friend," I replied. In truth, I had not been listening closely to him. My gaze had wandered across the great room, to a group of people standing near the richly woven arras that hung upon the closely fitted marble blocks of the east wall. Dejah Thoris had been the center of attention there, but no more. I did not see her lovely form by the east wall, or anywhere else in the reception hall.

Kantos Kan read the beginning of apprehension in my expression. "Do you then have some reason to be concerned?" he asked.

"I am no doubt worrying without cause," I said. "There is no purpose in creating vexations where none exist. Yet I would know where our hostess, the Princess of Helium, has gone."

"Yes, of course your fears are groundless!" laughed my companion. "How could the beauteous Dejah Thoris have vanished from our midst? Do you think that some evil power may have spirited her away? It is inconceivable that she could be abducted from the safety of her own father's palace."

"You are doubtless correct, Kantos Kan," I answered. I thought no

more about the matter then, while all about us the guests of Mors
Kajak ate and drank and took pleasure in the company.

Yet ten xats later, approximately half an earthly hour, I still could not
locate my beloved Dejah Thoris. My initial bewilderment turned first to
alarm, and then to a cold dread that centered itself in the pit of my
stomach. I spoke first to her father, who admitted that he had not seen
his daughter since early in the evening; then I approached Tardos Mors,
Jeddak of the empire of Helium, and received from him nothing in the
way of reassurance.

Kantos Kan accompanied me, and his growing anxiety was very
nearly as great as my own, for Dejah Thoris is well loved by all the
citizens of the twin cities, from the highest to the humblest slave. I
hurried from the great hall, forgetting entirely my social duties and
responsibilities. In my mind was only a gnawing fear that some terrible
accident had befallen my princess.

Outside, in the carefully tended gardens that surrounded the palace
of Mors Kajak, I discovered the first clue. The body of a young red man
lay sprawled upon the raked white pebbles of the path, his throat
slashed, his blood glistening darkly in the wan light of Cluros, the
farther moon. Although mortally wounded, yet the fellow was still
alive, and as I did my best to slow his bleeding, he endeavored to speak.

"John Carter," he murmured, "they have taken her."

"Where?" I demanded. "Who were they? How many?"

Kantos Kan placed a hand upon my forearm. "By my first ancestor,
you make demands of a dead man," he said. "It is not seemly."

"What care I for propriety?" I cried. "I would barter my immortal
soul to secure the safety of Dejah Thoris!"

"There," whispered the unfortunate victim. He attempted to lift his
hand. I looked where he pointed, but I saw nothing out of the ordinary. When I turned again to question him, I saw that indeed he had
taken his ultimate breath, and that now he was at last one with the
spirits of his ancestors. I let his corpse fall back gently to the graveled
lane.

"Come," said Kantos Kan. "There may be something further to be
learned up there. I expect that our heroic friend meant for us to examine the docking station on the roof of the palace."

I understood at once that we had little time to squander, and without
further discussion I turned and ran back toward the main entrance to
the jed's residence. I felt a momentary sadness for the unknown young
man who had been unlucky enough to witness the flight of Dejah

Thoris and her captors, but almost instantly my mind turned to thoughts of pursuit.

I never for a moment entertained the idea that some terrible fate had befallen my princess. It seems sometimes that fortune has always been my invisible ally, and I saw no reason to expect that the present circumstance was different in that regard. Thus it was that I planned punishment for those who had taken Dejah Thoris prisoner, but not revenge. I suppose it was impossible for me to imagine great harm coming to her whom I loved most on this or any world.

Kantos Kan and I emerged upon the roof of the palace. Below us, all of Lesser Helium spread out toward the horizon, with the yellow tower of the city stretching up a mile into the thin Martian atmosphere. Some seventy-five miles away, I could see the twin tower of Greater Helium, a vivid scarlet against the midnight-black sky. Many of the city's inhabitants had already sought their sleeping silks, but I knew that for me such respite would be long delayed.

Then I heard the voice of Kantos Kan, raised in excitement. "John Carter!" he called. "The gods favor us, after all!"

"How so?" I asked, hurrying to his side. I saw that a battle had been waged upon that rooftop, for several red men wearing the insignia of Mors Kajak's household militia upon their leather harnesses lay slain, and with them several others. These corpses, which bore no identifying badges of any sort, only deepened the mystery for me.

Not so Kantos Kan. "See here," he said, indicating a flier moored nearby. "Quite evidently, the villains arrived in two or more airships. One party of them managed in some way to gain entrance to the palace and carry off the princess. The others, left here to guard the ships, were surprised by the sentinels posted by Mors Kajak to patrol this rooftop. What these lifeless bodies tell us is that the kidnappers escaped in one flier, leaving behind their fallen comrades, and abandoning this other ship of which they no longer had need."

"Yes, yes!" I cried impatiently. "But all that gets us no nearer to our goal."

Kantos Kan smiled grimly. "On the contrary, John Carter, it does indeed. You do not understand the working of the destination compass. Look at it closely, and you will see that it does not indicate the city of Helium—it is already set for the return voyage! We need but enter the flier and activate its motor, and we will be guided directly to the sanctuary of our enemies!"

I could only utter a brief prayer of thanks. "Blessed be your ancestors, Kantos Kan," I said.

"Come aboard, then," he replied, "and let us be off."

It was the work of but a minute or two to make the flier ready, and then the light craft lifted rapidly above the twinkling city. We headed away from everything we held dear, racing recklessly after the cruel creatures who had stolen from me all that I had worth the stealing. I am a fighting man, and nothing more; perhaps a more thoughtful soul would have considered that two swords might not be sufficient against whatever force we would find arrayed against us at the end of our journey. However, that idle cogitator would not have the advantages that I enjoy, having been born on Earth and possessed of Earthly strength and speed, and moved by the need to protect my loved one, the greatest motivating factor in the world.

We sped across what had once been a great ocean that had lapped the shores of Greater Helium, and was now but a vast plain covered with ocher moss. We were heading eastward, and as we raced along, the thin Barsoomian night air turned cold. We found cloaks in a storage locker and gratefully wrapped them about ourselves for warmth.

Soon Thuria, the nearer moon, rose above the horizon and chased after her cold and distant husband, Cluros. It was very quiet aboard the flier, for neither Kantos Kan nor I was inclined to speak. Hours passed in this silence, and I began to realize that our long flight was taking us into a region of Barsoom I had never before visited, and about which precious little information had been recorded.

When the first bloodred rays of the dawning sun lightened the horizon before us, Kantos Kan marked our position as best he could on the craft's navigational chart. "Observe, John Carter," he exclaimed. "We are flying ever farther from everything familiar." I believe I detected a slight note of alarm in his voice.

I attempted to reassure him. "Yet there is no immediate cause for concern," I said. I studied the map carefully. We were now approaching the vicinity of the walled city of Zodanga, almost two thousand miles from Helium. As the flier neither slowed its headlong rush nor steered nearer to that city, I guessed that our destination lay yet some distance to the east, in uncharted territory south of Kaol, halfway around the globe of Barsoom from our starting point.

If Kantos Kan was, in fact, anxious about our fate, he gave no outward sign of it. He was a courageous fellow, and a more stalwart companion I could not have chosen had I the pick of every sword-wielding red man upon the face of my adopted world. For a moment I regretted bringing him into what might prove to be deadly danger; but, after all, he had not hesitated to join me in my quest, although I am quite certain that he well understood the risks we were taking.

I suppose that at last my weary body betrayed me, because I awoke from a fitful sleep when the craft tilted downward toward the crimson sward, having reached its goal after flying for half a Martian day. I held fast to the guardrail on the deck of the flier and tried to make sense of what I saw below.

There were some two dozen large buildings scattered about an area the size of a large plaza in the city of Helium. I saw no streets or avenues connecting the buildings, and as a matter of fact I recognized not the least sign that the site was presently inhabited by intelligent beings of any sort. The buildings themselves were in good condition, for they did not appear to be the kind of abandoned ruins such as mark many ancient cities upon the face of Barsoom.

More remarkable still, however, was the huge circular well or pit about which the structures were centered. From the air I estimated that the well was between ninety and one hundred sofads in diameter—in earthly measure, about thirty yards across. It was immediately clear to me that this opening in the Barsoomian surface had been artificially constructed, as its circumference was lined with a thick wall of metal of a glistening brightness and color unfamiliar to me. Of its creators and its purpose I could not yet even speculate.

Kantos Kan stood beside me at the railing. "We shall soon have our answers," he remarked.

"And then I shall have back the treasure which was taken from me," I added grimly. Already I held my longsword in my right hand.

The flier touched down upon the short-cropped red grass, and I leaped lightly from the deck. Kantos Kan climbed down beside me. I started toward the nearest building, which was about five stories high and completely without windows. I had covered perhaps half the distance, when I beheld an armed party of red men rushing toward us from the structure's broad main portal. I counted ten of the foe, but I was not dismayed. "We must not slay them all," I told my friend. "There must be one left alive to guide us to Dejah Thoris."

"As you say, John Carter," he replied, drawing his own longsword.

Our welcoming party spread out to surround us, but made no attempt to come near enough to cross swords. I determined that if I must take the fight to them, then so be it; but before I could put my plan into action, one of their number drew a strange hand-weapon and pointed it at me. It made no sound at all, yet instantly I felt a warm, unpleasant sensation throughout my body. Then I learned to my horror that I was unable to move a single muscle. I could yet breathe, but otherwise I was completely paralyzed. I could not even utter a sound, or turn my head to see if the weapon had had the same effect on Kantos Kan.

My sword was ripped from my grasp, and two of the opposing red men lifted me from the ground and carried me toward the building. I was their helpless prisoner, and although my body was for the moment useless, my mind was not so disabled. I carefully noted each detail of my surroundings and of my captors, so that when eventually I regained my freedom, I would know from whom to exact payment for this indignity.

Inside the building it was dark and evil smelling. I was carried up a ramp, past many doors from behind which echoed the cries and pleadings of tormented men. I did not yet understand what sort of place this was, or who for the moment controlled my destiny. Nevertheless, I was coolly confident that in a brief period of time I would again be the master of my own fate, and that I would depart this unknown land with Kantos Kan and my beautiful wife, Dejah Thoris. I knew also that I would leave behind me the bloody bodies of all who would stand between me and my freedom.

Now, however, one of the nameless jailers unlocked one of the doors, and I was rudely thrust into a black and fetid cell. I sprawled helplessly upon the floor, still unable to move even a finger against my enemies. Kantos Kan was thrown in after me, and he fell across my legs. Neither of us was able to speak, and I cannot say how long we lay there in the darkness, listening to the piteous screams of other prisoners in other cells nearby. I suppose that it was well that I did not know what the masters of this awful place planned for myself and my fellow captives, else I had gone mad with futile rage.

It was impossible to mark the passing of time in that cell. There was no window to let in the sunlight or the feeble rays of the Barsoomian moons. It may have been hours or days, but eventually I realized that I was regaining some strength in my hands. At the same time, I slowly recovered the power of speech. My first attempt at communication produced only a thick grunting noise, but I received no reply of any sort from Kantos Kan. I feared that without my Earthborn strength, he had been more strongly affected by the paralysis ray. He might even have perished there in the dank and squalid chamber.

"Kantos Kan," I said, "it will not be long before I am completely free of this hideous paralysis. We must formulate a plan of escape. When you too are able to move, we may work together to overpower our guard, perhaps when he arrives bearing our next meal."

A voice spoke up hoarsely in the stygian blackness. It was not the voice of Kantos Kan. "Then you will have a very long wait indeed, my friend," it said. "They will never feed you. You do not understand. It is we who feed them."

I felt my blood run cold. "Who are you?" I demanded. "And by your first ancestor, what do you mean?"

"My name is Bas-ok, of the city of Gathol. You, your friend, and I are captives of the sarmaks. It is unlikely in the extreme that any of us shall see the light of the sun again."

"The sarmaks?" I asked. "Is that what those villainous red men call themselves? I have never before heard the word. What does it mean?"

My unseen companion made a dry sound that may once have been laughter. "No," he replied, "those men are slaves of the sarmaks, even as are we. They do the creatures' bidding, for they have been promised life in return—a life of nightmarish servitude, but a life nonetheless, at least for a brief period of time. Then, when their usefulness to their masters comes to an end, they too meet the destiny that awaits us all."

"Death, you mean," I said. "I have faced death before, yet I still live."

Bas-ok laughed again. "You may have faced death, brave hero, but you have not yet faced the sarmaks."

I was growing weary of this dialogue. "Then tell me, man of Gathol, what are these sarmaks?"

"They are more than men, yet less than beasts," he said in a strained voice. "They are the evil demons of your most terrible dreams. The sarmaks resemble nothing so much as disembodied heads, huge and glistening like moist brown leather. They have piercing eyes that see into your very thoughts, a ragged, dripping mouth, and a mass of twisting, grasping tentacles."

He paused for breath, then went on. "I have heard of creatures in Bantoom called kaldanes that are truly bodiless heads, which yearn for the day when their evolution leaves them no other function but pure thought; still, those kaldanes are to the sarmaks as your mate's pet sorak is to the magnificent hunting banth of the dead sea bottoms."

I considered his words for a few moments. "You make them sound indeed strange," I said at last. "How, then, are these great thinking monsters a source of peril to us?"

I believed I heard a groan issue from Bas-ok. "You do not understand," he answered. "The sarmaks have no organs of digestion. They must take their nourishment directly, by injecting the blood of a living creature. They prefer . . . human beings."

I felt an involuntary shudder of horror. "Then the prisoners here—"

"They shall be a sarmak's meal before very long," stated Bas-ok. "The monsters employ civilized men to kidnap and transport their fellows here, and those slaves are clever enough to leave sufficient evidence of their crimes to draw still others afterward, who set out to rescue their loved ones but end up in the same sorry state as you and I."

"Yes," I said in a low voice, "it is my dear wife who was abducted."

"Then perhaps if the gods are gracious, you may still see her again before you both shall perish."

Before I could make a reply, there was a gigantic explosion that shook the slabs of the cell's walls and made the paving stones of the floor dance. The thunderous noise echoed deafeningly for what seemed to me many minutes, although in truth it must not have been of so long duration.

At last, when both the din and the violent vibrations had again died away, I heard Kantos Kan speak for the first time. "By the mother of the farther moon, what has happened?" he cried.

"That is the third such detonation I have heard, though I do not know if there were others previous to my capture," Bas-ok replied. "They have occurred about once each day—I know that, because I mark the time by the progression of my hunger and thirst, and by my sleeping periods. It is the great cannon which the sarmaks have designed and built, sinking the shaft of the thing deep into the surface of Barsoom. No doubt you saw the circular mouth of the cannon before you were brought to this place."

"Yes, that is so," I said. "Tell me, against what enemy is that immense weapon directed?"

"It is not a cannon in that sense. It does not fire explosive shells, but large cylinders in which the sarmaks will cross the many karads that separate Barsoom from its nearest planetary neighbor, Jasoom, in an expedition of conquest."

Now, indeed, I had still another urgent reason to escape that noxious stone cell. First, I must find and rescue my princess, Dejah Thoris, and then I had to discover the means to end the sarmak's evil scheme to enslave all of Earth. "Kantos Kan," I said, "are you yet able to move your limbs?"

"My arms and legs have not wholly regained their normal feeling,

John Carter, although I am able to sit up," he answered. "I believe that shortly I will have entirely recovered control of my body."

"That is good," I said. "Now we must begin to take the measure of our prison, so that we may find a weakness that we might exploit to our benefit."

A derisive snort came from Bas-ok. "If you are indeed John Carter, famed even in my city of Gathol, still you will find no such weakness here. I have searched long hours before e'er you arrived, and I discovered nothing."

"I will search anyway," I declared. "While I live, there is hope."

That hope seemed to fade almost immediately. The heavy portal of the cell crashed open, and light from the corridor beyond streamed in. I saw Bas-ok for the first time. He was an old man, well beyond the prime of life, yet he still wore the harness of a fighting man. I saw from his emblems and badges that he was an officer in the army of Gathol, the oldest inhabited city upon the face of Barsoom.

Four armed guards stood in the doorway, their longswords drawn. One of them spoke. "It is your time, unlucky ones," he said in a sneering voice. "The sarmaks will send you to your gods, if you have any. It is a slow death and a horrible one."

"Then slay me now," Bas-ok cried. "You are a red man as am I. How can you do this? How can you serve those abominable creatures?"

The guard uttered a sardonic laugh. "Would that I might grant your wish, but then it would be my blood the sarmaks would drink, not yours. Come along now. There is no escape from your fate."

The guards were confident of their power. After all, they were four against three, and they were armed and we had no weapons but our terror and our fists. Yet sometimes that can be enough, especially so when one of the captives enjoys the greater strength and agility of one whose muscles developed in the greater gravity of Earth. I leaped upon the guard who had spoken, whom I took to be the leader, and Kantos Kan struck a second man, fighting with bare hands and rendering his enemy's sword useless in such close quarters. Bas-ok, for all his military insignia, did not deign to aid us.

I made quick work of the first guard, then swiftly vanquished a second. Kantos Kan defeated his opponent, and together we turned on the remaining guard. That brave stalwart decided to seek the better part of valor, and ran shouting from the cell.

"We must hurry, John Carter," remarked Kantos Kan. "That man will raise a general alarm."

"Yes," I answered. "I will find Dejah Thoris wherever they have imprisoned her. You must hasten to the flier and return to Helium. The sarmaks must be stopped in their unspeakably vile schemes, and moreover they must be destroyed utterly. Tell your tale to Mors Kajak and Tardos Mors, and lead the forces of Helium back to this place of horror. Do so as quickly as may be, for more innocent people will be dreadfully tortured and slain while you linger."

"I will do as you say, John Carter." He placed both hands on my shoulders in a gesture of friendship, and I placed mine on his. Then he was gone, and the hopes of the civilized human beings of two worlds went with him.

The remainder of John Carter's astonishing tale must wait until another occasion: the story of his frantic search for his beloved Dejah Thoris; the treachery of Bas-ok and how that man of Gathol paid dearly for it; the great battle in the feeding room; the rescue of Dejah Thoris and the reunion with her husband; their perilous escape from the prison compound; John Carter's desperate and courageous fight in the cannon control chamber, and his destruction of the cylinder-launching device after the tenth launching; the arrival of Kantos Kan with the navy of Helium, as well as the combined forces of the green men of Thark and Warhoon, the black First Born, and red men from many cities and nations; and finally, the ultimate battle and victory.

The dangers were many and terrible, but the single reward was more than adequate recompense. Thanks to the courage of John Carter and his allies, human beings on both Barsoom and Earth may sleep in peace, their thoughts untroubled by visions of the leathery-skinned monsters that plotted our doom.

"I must return now to my world and to my princess," John Carter explained. "I came to tell you this dire history so that you might publish the story in all the lands of Earth. Your people must understand that there is no longer any need for revenge and violence against Barsoom. The threat of the sarmaks is ended, and our worlds are again at peace."

And so I bid my friend farewell, wondering if ever again I would see him and listen in rapt attention to his tales of love and bloodshed beneath the hurtling moons of Mars.

This story is for four friends who dreamed of Barsoom as often as I. *Kaor,* Mike Resnick, Dick Lupoff, Caz Cazedessus, and John Malin!

Joseph Pulitzer

A LETTER FROM ST. LOUIS

ALLEN STEELE

The following is an annotated letter from Arthur Barnett, a staff reporter for the St. Louis Post-Dispatch, *to his elder sister, Rachel Barnett Simpson, a resident of San Francisco. The original handwritten letter now resides in the archives of the St. Louis Historical Society, which has graciously permitted it to be reprinted here with the approval of Mrs. Simpson's estate.*

July the 24th, 1900

My dearest Rachel,

I wish this note could be written on a happier occasion, since I have seldom found time to write to you in the last few years. Because I know not for certain whether you will receive this correspondence at all, considering the current dire state of affairs, it is one more reason to regret failing to reply to the many letters you have sent me following your marriage to Chet.[1]

---

[1] St. Louis native Rachel Barnett married San Francisco financier Chester J. Simpson on April 20, 1897. They moved to San Francisco shortly thereafter.

By whatever means and time this letter finally reaches you, the good Lord willing, I hope you will forgive my lassitude. I had always thought there would be time for correspondence, once the work was done and there were not so many pressing engagements. Now my labors are at last complete, but I seem to have run out of time as well.

You know of the Martians, of course. I shan't repeat the story of their coming to our world, for if they have bothered to strike at Saint Louis, then there is little doubt that you have witnessed their wrath in San Francisco as well. I can only pray that you and Chet have escaped without harm, and that this missive finds you in good health and spirits. Yet it is necessary for me to relate to you the dire fate which has befallen your native city. As Father used to say (with some scorn, as I recall) I'm a "tattler" by nature . . . although I far prefer to use Mr. Pulitzer's favored term, a "newspaperman."

I finally had the opportunity to meet Mr. Pulitzer, by the way. It occurred only a few days ago, as I write, during which he gave me the greatest compliment of my professional career. Yet I'm getting ahead of myself, and there is much to be told as prelude to this chance encounter.

The first Martian shell in these parts arrived on the evening of July the 5th, as a fireball which crashed to the earth a few miles from East Saint Louis.[2] Although several people witnessed its descent and reported it to the newspaper, the newsroom staff dismissed it as a remnant of the Independence Day fireworks— perhaps a final Chinese rocket sent aloft by some boys who had stolen it from the Veiled Prophet Society parade.

It was not until the following morning that we received a reliable report of what appeared to be a large ballistic shell, half buried in a crater it had carved in a cow pasture not far from the Indian mounds. A small crowd had already gathered around the fallen shell, we were told, and although its surface was much too hot to approach, witnesses claimed to have heard muted sounds from within the thing, along with great puffs of green smoke which rose from the crater.

By this time, we had already received the first telegraph reports of similar occurrences elsewhere in the world, beginning with the

---

[2] East St. Louis is a small city in southwestern Illinois, on the opposite side of the Mississippi River from St. Louis, Missouri.

landing of a shell in Woking, England, courtesy of the international desk at the *World*.[3] I begged the city room editor to be allowed to cover this story, but he reminded me that I was still facing a deadline for another story involving the repainting of the Four Courts Building, and sent McPherson to the scene instead.

I was left at my typewriter, murmuring unseemly oaths beneath my breath. In hindsight, though, it is most fortunate that I was hampered with this trivial assignment, else I might not have survived to write these words. On the other hand, I almost envy McPherson now, for at least his death was quick, and he did not have to witness the terrifying events yet to come.

The next word we received from Illinois was in the middle of the afternoon, when a young farmhand who had ridden his horse in great hurry across the Eads Bridge dashed into the city room with a breathless tale on his lips. At first we were incredulous. Monstrous gray creatures emerging from the shell? A tentacle holding a rotating mirror, which in turn sent forth beams that put everything ablaze? Dozens of bystanders disintegrating within moments? Absurd!

Yet within the hour we received more reports from bystanders who, like the lad, had narrowly escaped death. McPherson himself never returned to our offices. We were finally left with the cold realization that some unearthly horror was indeed upon us.

Nor was East Saint Louis alone. As the afternoon wore on, the telegraph operator received a flurry of dispatches from elsewhere in the country, telling of similar landings throughout the country. Another shell had crashed in Grovers Mills, New Jersey, followed by a similar slaughter of hapless civilians. Local militia were being mobilized in Massachusetts, Pennsylvania, Ohio, Tennessee, Virginia, and Texas where other shells had crashed, usually in rural areas not far from major cities. Later there came disjointed reports of great machines—sometimes described as "walking milk stools" or "three-legged boilers"—that were seen emerging from the craters that the shells had formed upon impact.

We were still attempting to make coherent sense of these reports when the editor was informed that he had a long-distance telephone call awaiting him. He promptly adjourned to his office and closed the door, yet through the glass walls I was able to see him speaking into the instrument. He seemed considerably agi-

[3] The *New York World*, sister newspaper to the *Post-Dispatch*.

tated, and when he returned a few minutes later with a pro-
nouncement, the staff learned the reason why. He had just spoken
with Mr. Pulitzer himself,[4] who had instructed him to compile
whatever reports into an extra edition, which was to be printed as
quickly as it could be set in hot type and rushed onto the street
before the ink was dry on the pages.

By late afternoon, newsboys were hawking the extra on every
street corner, where they were instantly snatched from their hands
by the citizenry. I imagine that many of our readers initially
thought we were engaged in another bout of "yellow press" war-
mongering. Memory of the accusations that Mr. Pulitzer had de-
liberately fostered the Cuban conflict as part of his rivalry with
Mr. Hearst were still fresh, and I must confess that the thought
crossed my mind that we were making too much smoke out of too
little heat. Yet even though we didn't have Stephen Crane's ster-
ling prose as eyewitness testimony, there seemed little doubt that
something of dire importance was indeed occurring.[5]

Once the extra was on the street, I barely had time to hastily
consume half of a grocery sandwich at my desk before the city
editor approached me. "Arthur," he said, "we've received word
that the army is mobilizing and a defensive line is being established at the levee. I need a good man to cover this for as long as it
takes, even if he has to remain there all night. Can you do this?"

I told him that I could, but before I could rise from my chair,
he put a hand on my shoulder. "There is one more thing," he
continued, dropping his voice to a near whisper. "If this is indeed
an invasion of sorts, there may be just cause for you not returning
to the office."

I raised an eyebrow at this stark admission, yet before I could
inquire further, he went on. "If this is the case, you are to go
straight to Union Station, where you will search for a private Pull-
man coach called 'Newport.' If it is there, tell the porter you wish
to speak with Andes. Do you understand? Ask for Andes."

Although mystified, I dutifully repeated the word, and he sent

---

[4] By 1900, Joseph Pulitzer no longer lived in St. Louis. Following the scandal that
resulted from the killing of a local attorney by the previous editor of the *Post-
Dispatch*, he had taken permanent residence in New York City.
[5] Barnett alludes here to the Spanish-American War, which was largely incited by
the *World* and William Randolph Hearst's New York *Journal*. The novelist Stephen
Crane was the Pulitzer newspapers' correspondent during the war.

me off, with little more than pen, notebook, and the other half of my sandwich to sustain me.

I hastened to the levee, where I discovered the riverfront already crowded with soldiers from the Jefferson Barracks. Wagons bearing munitions had just arrived from the city armory, and heavy artillery pieces were being set up in a row along the top of the levee. Army officers were engaged in heated arguments with riverboat captains, trying to get them to move their craft away from the piers so that the guns would be assured of a direct line of fire across the river, while troops positioned Gatling guns upon the floating wharfs. It was rumored that ironclads would soon be arriving, but I was told by a lieutenant that all available gunboats had already been sent farther downriver . . . although for what purpose, no one seemed to know for certain.

Yet, despite the high state of anxiety, there was no sign of enemy movement from the other side of the Mississippi. Some of the soldiers with whom I spoke were convinced that this was an elaborate hoax. Once they were in position behind sandbags and gun emplacements, many settled down to roll cigarettes and enjoy a casual meal from their dinner pails. After a time, curious civilians began to gather along the levee, and several industrious vendors pushed their carts down from Market Street to hawk their wares.

Westbound trains continued to rumble across the Eads Bridge, apparently unscratched from their journey through Illinois, and although most of the river traffic had been cleared away, a few packet steamers and barges continued to cruise down the broad muddy expanse. If this was prelude to war, then it was oddly peaceful.

Nonetheless, I remained on the riverfront all night, composing a quick story in longhand which was sent back to the paper with the copyboy who was sent down to check on me. Although he told me that the telegraph operator had been unable to receive news from anywhere east of Saint Louis, and I spied intermittent flashes of what seemed to be heat lightning from across the eastern horizon, all seemed to be calm. Around midnight I curled up behind a row of barrels and napped for a few hours.

The peace was only temporary, though, and not to last. In hindsight, it's obvious that the Martians were awaiting dawn to make their move.

The eastern sky had just been painted pale red with first light when we were awakened by a string of fires which spontaneously erupted among the buildings of East Saint Louis. As the soldiers, most of whom had been dozing behind their barricades, stumbled to their feet in bleary-eyed confusion, a cry rose from a young sergeant standing watch atop one of the wharfs: "Enemy sighted! Enemy sighted!"

It was then the first of the Martian war machines strode into view. If you haven't seen one of these "tripods" yourself, Rachel, there is little I can say that fully describes the dreadful enormity of this unholy creation. Fully a hundred feet tall, it somewhat resembles a railway water tower, except that its jointed legs move at a fast gait which belies their cumbersome arrangement. Beneath its saucerlike cab, slender tentacles whipped about, swatting aside brick chimneys as if they were stacks of children's blocks.

No sooner had the first tripod appeared when another machine joined it several hundred yards away to the left. Then a third, the same distance to the right, then a fourth following behind it. Finally there was a fifth machine, bringing up the left rear leg of this star-shaped figuration.

As they marched through East Saint Louis, blazes broke out on all sides as buildings exploded into flame. Although we could not see what ignited these fires, they were the work of the awesome "heat-rays" caused by the spinning mirrors carried by the tripods. Despite their invisibility, whatever the heat-rays touched was instantaneously destroyed as the tripods carved their way through the Illinois town.

Above the roar of flames, unearthly sirens wailed from the machines as some sort of signal from one to another. This made the soldiers even more afraid; there was the crack of rifle shots as some opened fire with their carbines, until their commanding officers shouted for them to hold their fire until the tripods were within range.

For a few minutes the tripods disappeared from view within the dense smoke of the burning town. I took the opportunity to dash up to the top of the levee behind the artillery guns, both to obtain a better view of the coming battle and to escape from being caught by the cross fire. In retrospect, that prudent decision may have saved my life.

A few moments later, the foremost tripod lurched out of the smoke and onto the Illinois levee, its massive legs reaching the edge of the river. If anyone thought it would be daunted by the mighty Mississippi, they were proven wrong, for without any apparent hesitation it walked straight into the curling brown water.

At this instant, the army colonel who had previously urged restraint gave the order to open fire, and the gates of Hades swung fully open.

The thunder of a score of artillery guns letting loose was the most deafening sound I have ever heard. It was as if all the world's supply of TNT was being let go at once. Huge gouts of water kicked up as shells impacted the water all around the first tripod; the buildings around its companions to the left and right were ripped asunder as more shells slammed into them. At the same instant, the battery of Gatling guns let loose with all their chattering fury, while individual sharpshooters sought to train their rifles through the fog of combat.

For a few moments, it seemed as if the assault would have no effect. Strange as it seems, it appeared that artillery shells detonated in midair only a few feet from their mark, as if they struck an invisible shield. Then a shell exploded within the hood of the leading war machine. There was a mighty blast and the tripod staggered, then with a slow grind of tortured metal, its legs succumbed to the Mississippi's relentless tide and the tripod toppled into the river.

A great shout rose from the defending army. The damned things weren't invulnerable after all! With great haste, the artillerymen made to reload their guns while the battery gunners shouted for fresh belts, even as the four remaining tripods seemingly hesitated just as they reached the river's edge.

I had just ducked into the open doorway of a warehouse behind me and was reaching for my notebook and pen when the true horror began.

Although I'm a writer by trade, I still cannot find words to describe all that happened next. It almost seems like a madman's hallucination, such was the insane extent of the violence which occurred around me. If I tried to describe all that I saw, I fear I might go mad myself.

Within the next minute, I watched hundreds of men die, although they courageously . . .

No . . . this is a lie. This was no Charge of the Light Brigade, and I am no Lord Tennyson. There was no honor or glory in the way that they fought, for the massacre was so swift that it left no room for such human qualities.

The truth of the matter, dear Rachel, is that these brave men were burned alive, screaming and writhing in mortal agony as their weapons exploded in their hands. Even those who sought refuge behind sandbags perished, for the heat-rays spared nothing and no one. Boats and wharfs went up as massive funeral pyres, incinerating all that stood on their decks, while gun carriages and ammunition stacks detonated before they could be used. The air was filled with the stench of burning gunpowder, wood, and flesh.

Realizing that I was in peril, I dashed from the doorway in which I had been hiding and ran down the levee until I reached the corner of Market Street. Already the avenue was crowded with soldiers and civilians. Hearing an explosion from close behind me, I glanced around just in time to see a waterfront building go up in flames as one of the tripods leveled its heat-ray upon it. Even as brick and plaster rained down around the crowd, I ran as hard as I could, narrowly escaping my own destruction.

Nor did it cease there. One by one, warehouses and factories burst into flames as the beam swept across them. Within minutes, the entire river district had become a raging inferno. As if to spite God Himself, the spire of the Catholic cathedral crumbled beneath the heat-rays, causing debris to rain down upon screaming pedestrians.

I ran straight down Market, pushing my way through mobs of panic-stricken men and women who had filled the street, knocking each other down in their haste, while behind us more buildings were being set afire by the advancing tripods. Although fire companies rushed to the scene, their wagons could not penetrate the crowds; finally, even the firemen were forced to abandon their equipment and flee for their lives.

I finally managed to leap aboard a trolley as it careened down Market Street, jammed with men and women clinging to every seat and railing. Safe for the moment, I briefly considered returning to the office, but realized that this was ludicrous; the newsroom would not protect me, and it was much too close to the waterfront. Besides, what would I do there? I laughed bitterly at the very thought. No, there would not be an extra published this morning!

It was then that I remembered my editor's final words to me the evening before, and I realized that I had one last duty to perform.

I rode the trolley until it reached Union Station, where I

jumped off. The crowds were thinner here, but when I looked back I saw now that the downtown business district had become a vast wall of flame that already had reached the courthouse dome. I couldn't see the tripods, but I knew that they were coming; if the mighty currents of the Mississippi River didn't stop them, then they would soon be marching across the Eads Bridge.

The train shed was packed with citizens, all attempting to force their way aboard coaches. Even the freight cars were packed with refugees; I saw several men wrestling with each other as they tried to struggle on top of a coal carrier. What few policemen were present had already given up attempting to control the mob.

I savaged my way through the mob until I suddenly located a short train parked on a siding. Armed Pinkertons surrounded the four cars, firing rounds into the air to ward off those who attempted to board without presenting identification. Through the windows, I caught a glimpse of faces pressed against the glass while the train's nervous driver watched the confusion from within his cab.

The last car on the train was an ornate private coach, with the word "Newport" inscribed in gold filigree above the curtained windows. One of the Pinkertons leveled his Winchester at me as I approached and told me to back away, but when I told him that I was here to see Mr. Andes, he relented and stood aside, allowing me to climb up the coach's rear steps and push open the door.

The interior of the coach was dimly illuminated by only a couple of gas lamps, but once my eyes adjusted to the gloom I saw that it was as lavishly furnished as a club drawing room. In the quiet of the coach, I saw a handsome woman sitting on a plush settee. She clutched a crying child to her bosom, and she looked up at me in fear when I entered, but before either one of us could say a word, a European-accented voice spoke from farther within the car.

"Yes?" the man inquired. "Who is it?"

I cleared my throat. "Arthur Barnett, from the *Post-Dispatch*. I'm here to see Mr. Andes."

There was a low chuckle; from its location I was finally able to discern its source. I saw a tall gaunt man in his middle years, whose bushy beard had grown silver with age and whose eyes were shadowed by tinted spectacles. He sat alone in an armchair at the far end of the compartment.

"Just Andes, Mr. Barnett," he said. "Like the mountain range.[6] Please, be seated. I'm Joseph Pulitzer."

Mrs. Pulitzer stood up and guided me to a chair next to her husband. As exhausted and fearful as I was, I found myself humbled by the proximity to the great man, yet when I sat down I noticed that he didn't look straight at me until I spoke again.

"Have you visited your newspaper?" he asked.

"No, sir, I haven't," I replied. "I was told that I was to come straight here if I believed . . ."

I hesitated, suddenly unwilling to explain my reasons. It was then that Mr. Pulitzer's face turned in my direction.

"If you believed what, young man?" he demanded. "Why haven't you returned to your office? We've got an evening edition to publish, haven't we?"

I swallowed what felt like a lump of dry lint. "I believe this is no longer possible, sir," I said. "I don't think the *Post-Dispatch* will be published today."

Mr. Pulitzer frowned as he considered that statement for a moment. As he did, he reached down with his left hand and groped along the carpeted floor until he found a silver-headed cane. He picked it up and set it upright on the floor, clasping his hands together atop its crook.

"Tell me everything you have seen," he said.

I began to stammer out the events of the last half hour, but he interrupted me with an impatient shake of his head. "You're a reporter, Mr. Barnett," he said. "Pretend as if I'm your reader and know nothing of the facts. Now, from the beginning . . ."

From outside the coach, I could hear shouting and more gunshots. It all seemed surreal; our world collapsing under the heel of an unearthly invader, and I was being told to deliver a journalistic report. Nonetheless, I did so. Plucking my notebook from my jacket pocket, I quickly delivered the facts as I had witnessed them, beginning with the arrival of the Martian shell the previous morning and ending, finally, with the destruction of the U.S. Army troops on the levee and the torching of the business district.

Throughout it all, Mr. Pulitzer sat quietly and listened, occasionally nodding or shaking his head but otherwise rarely displaying any outward emotion. When I was done, he asked a couple of

---

[6] To ensure privacy, the Pulitzer organization used in-house code words to designate various individuals. "Andes" was Joseph Pulitzer's code name.

minor questions, which I answered as honestly as I could. Then he nodded again in apparent satisfaction.

"You've done well, Mr. Barnett," he said. "If I were able to see, I would want your pair of eyes as my own."

I almost gasped at this admission. Of all the things I had heard about Mr. Pulitzer, the one thing I didn't know was that he had lost his eyesight. He must have picked up on my astonishment, for he smiled. "The curse of all my years of hard work," he said quietly. "I gained great wealth from the newspaper business, but at a sacrifice."

The smile faded, replaced again by the dark frown. "They say I helped instigate a war," he murmured bitterly, more to himself than to me, "and in that they may be right. Hearst and I sold many copies by trumping up charges against the Spaniards. Now we have a real war on our hands, one whose devastation far exceeds that of Havana Harbor and San Juan Hill . . . and the irony of it is that I have no newspapers left to publish the story."

"The *World*?" I asked, quite astonished. "It's gone, too?"

He slowly nodded his head. "The *World*, yes, and New York with it." He pointed toward the front of the train. "If you go up front, you'll find a few of my friends. Morgan, Vanderbilt . . . even Bill himself, damn him! . . . plus assorted sycophants who begged their way aboard at the last moment. . . ."

He emitted a great sigh. "Not that it matters. I had rather hoped Saint Louis would fare better, but now it turns out its fate will be the same, if only delayed. No more editions. No more stories . . ."

Another gunshot from outside. It seemed to awaken the great man. He abruptly stood, using his cane to push himself to his feet. "Time is short," he said. "We must be getting off." He thrust out his hand. "Thank you, Mr. Barnett. You're a first-class journalist. I'm proud to have had you on my staff."

I thought of begging for sanctuary aboard his coach, but that was clearly out of the question. There was no place for me on his train, compliments notwithstanding; only the wealthy and important would ride with Mr. Pulitzer on his westward flight. I shook his hand, then I made my leave from his railcar.

A freight train was beginning to leave the station just then, and I managed to pull myself onto the rear platform of its caboose before it worked up steam. By then, the skies above Saint Louis were turning dark black with a dense smoke that masked even the flames devouring the city. Even without realizing the poisonous nature of those Martian fumes, I intuitively knew that nothing lived beneath that hideous cloud.

I write these words from a farmhouse basement just outside Springfield, where I have sought refuge for the last two days. I thought I would be safe here, but yesterday yet another shell landed only a few miles distant. The evening light is fading now, and since I dare not strike a torch, I cannot spend more time with this letter. I will hide here for as long as I can, but I fear this will be my final dispatch.

If these pages find their way to your hands, please know that I love you, and you have never been far from my mind. And if you remember me for anything, please may it be as a good newspaper-man.

Arthur

This letter was found on Arthur Barnett's body shortly after the fall of the Martian invaders. It is the only known account of the destruction of St. Louis. The letter was delivered to Mrs. Chester Simpson, whose children donated it to the St. Louis Historical Society following her death in 1947.

More than thirty-five thousand people perished during the siege of St. Louis. Joseph Pulitzer, his family, and his entourage were among those listed as missing.

Leo Tolstoy

RESURRECTION

MARK W. TIEDEMANN

From: Karyn Alexander, assistant archivist, Bodleian Library, Oxford University.

To: Pavel Pobodonostsev, deputy archivist, Tolstoy Institute, St. Petersburg University, Tula.

Pav: Here it is, the Document that has everyone all bothered and excited. Before you ask, yes, it is authentic, yes, it was in Chertkov's possession at one time, and no, it was not in the Tuckton Vault with the rest of Chertkov's archive of Tolstoyan writings. It was found among some old papers of John Kenworthy, the founder of the Croyden Brotherhood. Let me know what you think. Maybe we can work on a presentation together. The Conference on Global Synergism is coming up.

My Dear Vladimir Grigoryevich,

There is no way for me to know with certainty that you will ever read this, but, as has been my impulse all my adult life, I must write. Perhaps England has suffered the same fate as Moscow and

Smolensk, and, as I have heard, as St. Petersburg itself. There is, however, much to do, so I will be brief.

My last night in Moscow Strakhov visited us at our house on Dolgo-Khamovnichesky Street and asked whether we had heard of the falling star that had crashed outside Smolensk. "Stars do not fall," I said and waved my cane confidently skyward. "One has to believe that the pale blue sky up there is a solid vault. Otherwise one would believe in revolution."

"Perhaps," said Strakhov, "but nevertheless the reports are that it made an enormous crater and that it is as large as the Tsar's yacht."

After supper he took his leave. As he was about to climb into his carriage, a bright light flared in the sky. A long streak of green fire, behind a bloated head like a ghostly comet, came down on Moscow. After a long silence, Strakhov shook himself and said perhaps the night sky was not so solid as the day, then bade us good night.

I should have stayed, but I do not like Moscow, especially in the summer. The new novel—yes, I had finished it, and Sofya had brought it at once to Moscow—was with the publisher and there were details. Details consume us, Vladimir Grigoryevich, like ants consume a crumb carelessly dropped. At least Strakhov was there to help. I suffered it all impatiently and after that night I left, joyously, to return to the country, to my home, Yasnaya Polyana. Sasha and Masha remained in Moscow with their mother.

The coach took me by the river, past the Kremlin. On the levee soldiers gathered along with workmen and sightseers. The road was puddled and I saw shrouds over corpses. I stopped the coach and asked a subaltern what had happened. The green comet, he told me, had fallen into the Moskva last night and had caused the river to swamp its banks. People had been carried away, drowned or smashed to death against the wall of the Kremlin fortress, and considerable property had been damaged. I looked past him to the river. Warehouses and docks lined the far bank. A barge was capsized.

"It fell in *here*?" I asked.

The subaltern turned to point when the river bubbled. In the center huge domes of air burst through the surface, churning the water violently for several seconds. I thought I saw steam rise. As abruptly as it began, the water stilled. I waited awhile longer, but nothing more happened. I thanked the subaltern and continued on to Kursk Station.

On the train I shared a compartment with a Cossack major on leave, one Yepishka Sekhim, on his way from St. Petersburg to the Caucasus. We talked about his home and I warmed to the remembrance of my time spent there as a young officer, newly commissioned. That, of course, was before the Crimea and Sebastopol and all that my life became afterward. The conversation drifted from the army to war and we spoke about the Boer War then ongoing. I made a comparison between Britain's actions against the Boers and our own lamentable annexation of Manchuria so recently completed, which annoyed him considerably. He defended Russia's move as necessary to our territorial integrity. "What of Manchuria's territorial integrity?" I countered. "Besides, territoriality is an artifice of governments. There is no natural basis for it."

"Oh? You can think of no instance where the natural condition of a people might be one of separateness from others and therefore innately territorial?"

I was delighted. An educated Cossack! But I said, "No, we are all human, and any separateness is the creation of a lie."

"Then," he said with a wide grin, "it is only natural that we annex Manchuria, if only to dissolve such barriers to our common humanity."

And so it went all the way to Tula. It was, in retrospect, the last pleasant time I had for many weeks. I invited the major to Yasnaya Polyana. He accepted, and we continued through Tula and detrained at Shchyokino Station, where my son Ilya waited with a carriage.

On the road, by the old turret that marks the entrance to Yasnaya Polyana, we encountered three large wagons filled with people. They were shabby, mostly peasants, but a few townspeople were mixed among them. Ilya stopped and I stood in the carriage and asked them where they were from and what they wanted.

They all began speaking at once until I insisted they pick a spokesman. One man jumped down from the lead wagon. He was short, wide-shouldered, with a thick mustache and several days' growth of beard. His eyes were set wide apart and, though narrow, were very clear.

"We've been on the road for over three days," he said. "Some are from Orol, but most are from Begichevkaest."

"That is Ivan Ivanovich Rayevsky's estate," I said. "What are you all doing here?"

"Running. As, perhaps, you should, too, old man."

"Muzhik!" the major shouted, stepping down to the road. "He is *dvoryanstvo*! Count Lev Nikolayevitch Tolstoy!"

"Da? Nui chto zh?"

So what indeed, I thought. But Major Sekhim was not amused. "Major, enough," I said. "They are all obviously hungry. Come, eat. You can tell me afterward what you're running from."

We all continued in silence to my home. I told Ilya to take them the last mile to the village and see to food and shelter for the night. Among these prodigal *muzhikii* I heard whispers, words spoken in terror laced with hope. *Shtativii, teplovoy potok, zakhvatchik* . . .

"They speak of invasion," Major Sekhim said. "Tomorrow, with your permission, Lev Nikolayevitch, I'll go back to the station and telegraph Orol and find out what this is all about. When I left St. Petersburg there was no talk of any trouble. How could an invader strike so deep into Russia without warning? We would have been alerted. This is probably just some mischief concocted by anarchists and democrats."

I showed him to his room. I promised the use of a good horse, but I did not believe there was mischief by democrats. I wondered if another pogrom were under way farther south. Perhaps these people had come a greater distance than they claimed. Mikhail came to the house from the fields and I asked him to take a few men in the morning to visit Ivan Ivanovich.

"He won't get through." I turned to find the spokesman standing nearby, eating bread and watching intently.

"Why not? What's to stop him?"

"Vtorzhenie," he said.

"An invasion by who?" I asked.

"Who? Whom? You wouldn't believe me."

"What is your name?"

"Iosef Vissarionovich."

"Are you their leader?"

"The refugees? No. They think I am."

I could never, I decided, like this man, but he impressed me. I asked him to stay in the house. He consented, but it was almost as if he were doing *me* the favor.

The rest of the day passed in seeing to the refugees' needs and telling Tanya, Ilya, and Mikhail the news of their mother and sisters. At dinner I told them about the green comet and what I

saw in the Moskva by the Kremlin. The major seemed unim-
pressed, but Iosef Vissarionovich asked many questions. Major
Sekhim grew irritated again and began questioning him. Where
was he from? Tiflis, but he was born in Gori. Why was he so far
north? He was on his way somewhere. Where? Pskov. Why was he
not still on his way? How does the major know he is not? The
major probed and baited, sometimes clumsily, and Iosef toyed
with him, like a cat with an impudent rat.

I was very tired, but I did not sleep well. In the morning Major
Sekhim rode out one direction and Mikhail the opposite way. An
hour later four more wagons of weary, frightened *muzhikii* arrived. Ilya, Tanya, and I, and then Iosef, worked most of the day
organizing an encampment outside the village. I enjoyed working
among my peasants; I had missed the harvest by being in Moscow. The work distracted me, put me back in good spirits. Iosef
demonstrated a fine head for organization. I commented that we
could have used him back in '92 for the famine relief in Samara.
He seemed uninterested, though, as if he did this only because he
had nothing else to do.

By midday more wagons and people on foot with carts arrived.
It looked like the beginnings of a steady exodus. As I walked
among them, talking to them, I heard stories of fire and destruction. From what? I asked, and the same two words repeated again
and again: *shtativ* and *zakhvatchik*—tripod and invader. What?
cannons on tripods? Machine guns? No, no, only *shtativ, veliki
shtativii,* great tripods. They stuttered over their own fear. They
were hungry and exhausted, so we fed them, gave them a place to
sleep. The imagination of a frightened man is not a reliable source
of information, but the consistency from story to story troubled
me.

Toward evening Major Sekhim returned with a squadron of
soldiers. His face was drawn. "We must speak, Lev Nikolayevitch," he said, and I led him toward the grove of *chepyzh* near
the house, my place of privacy. "Moscow is invaded," he said.
"The garrison at Tula is on alert. There is word that St. Petersburg is also under siege. I telegraphed Orel, but the line no longer
goes through. I began sending messages to other places—Bry-
ansk, Gomel, Mogilev—from Mogilev I received word that Smolensk has been burned."

I took this news calmly, but it was a false calm. Shock? Perhaps,
though I have never been easily shocked. Sofya Andreyevitch and

two of our daughters were in Moscow. My son Sergey was in St. Petersburg, attached to the Ministry of Interior. They appeared in my mind, nebulous and unreal. They seemed somehow safe from danger because, at that moment, they were only ideas. Of all the things I might have asked Major Sekhim at that moment, what I *did* ask was, "What of the Tsar?"

"Escaped on his yacht, *Standart,* into the Gulf of Finland."

"Who is the aggressor?"

He shook his head, his eyes wide, disbelieving. "Great machines rose up out of the Moskva River, near the Kremlin. They possess a weapon that brings fire and instant death, one message called it *teplovoy potok.* I have never heard of such a thing, have you?"

A heat-ray? Perhaps the Germans might invent something like that. They have an intense love of things mechanical. But that seemed unlikely. I said, "More refugees are coming. This will soon be a very crowded camp."

"Why are they coming here?"

"They remember Samara, the famine, what we did then. They come to who will feed them. But that won't be enough. Can you return to Tula and bring supplies? Tents, blankets, whatever food?"

"I can try. But they will be preparing for an attack."

"Do what you can, or this alone will become terrible."

I watched him walk away, back straight, stride firm. He was shaken, but still he would do his best. At that moment I still thought all this news an exaggeration. But it did not matter. There were refugees here and on the way, and the telegraph lines to several cities were down. I thought of the green comet and the bubbling in the Moskva and I shuddered. My son Lev, at least, was away, in Paris, and so, I thought, safe.

I returned to the house to find Major Sekhim and Iosef arguing. The major looked to me for support. "He intends to take men and steal food from other estates!"

"If things are as you say," Iosef said, "that may be our only source of food."

"It is theft!"

"We must do what is necessary," I said. "I'll draft a letter he can take with him, asking the other landlords for help."

This did not improve Major Sekhim's mood, but he relented for the time being.

That night I shall never forget. Major Sekhim had left for Tula again. I sat with Iosef and a few others on the veranda. Tanya had brought us tea and we spoke companionably. Iosef had read me and had questions about my work. He said he admired my radicalism, but did not think much of my solutions. He had attended the seminary in Tiflis, but it had not suited him. I fell into reminiscing again about the Caucasus, about the army, about Chechnya, about the Cossacks. Iosef listened politely.

Tanya saw it first and gasped. To the west, just above the horizon, a greenish ball appeared in the sky. We stared at it, transfixed by this spectral intruder. It grew and came lower and lower. I found myself standing, my heart beating faster. We hurried to the road that led out into the fields, toward the village and the refugee encampment. The comet dipped below the horizon.

Suddenly it reappeared, bursting through the trees lining the hill crest that ran north to south nearly a mile away. The trees exploded in flame and the object sparked with burnt debris and came down, down, and I shouted, my hand reaching out as if to stop it by force of will. It struck the ground and tore into the southern end of the village, trailing fire as it set the gorse aflame behind it. It skipped once, twice, then burrowed heavily into the earth. It sounded like the rush of a waterfall or the constant thunder of a thousand cannon. And then, still moving swiftly, it struck something. There was a deep shock and a sharp rending, a sound I have heard when a cannon ruptures and the metal peels apart. My nerves danced from the hideous screech. The thing bounded upward once more, arced a short distance, and struck the ground.

The fields caught fire. Part of the tree line on the distant crest blazed. My village burned. In the dark, order escaped us, but still we managed to assemble work parties to fight the fire—Iosef proved himself once more very capable in this regard—and to help the injured. So much to do!

And from the crashed comet itself, bringer of revolution, so I now thought for in that panicked night I could believe anything, came a keening sound none of us had ever heard before. All through the night it underscored our labors. It was dawn before we could take the time from the dead and dying to go look at it.

Iosef, Ilya, Tanya, some soldiers and peasants bearing water buckets, and I approached the crater in which it lay. It was a great twisted thing, like a whale with its belly slit. Later we found that it had struck a buried outcrop of granite, though I wonder if it did not already have a flaw which this chance encounter merely exposed. No matter. It had struck the rock with great force and had been torn open even as it hurtled once more into the air. Within the crater, around the wreck, lay bits and parts of machinery, huge pistons, ball bearings, other devices twisted out of shape or broken and unrecognizable.

Blood glistened everywhere and I looked closely for the injured and dead. At first we did not see them. Then there was movement and I pointed to a brown limb. It twitched convulsively for a few moments, then lay still. It seemed unconnected to a body. Another movement, more fluid, caught my attention and this time I made out the shape. The jointless limb attached to a base from which several such limbs extended, which joined a bloated sack that was crisscrossed by wounds that oozed thick red blood. Not until a large, dark eye opened sluggishly in the sack did I realize that this was the body of a passenger from the ruined comet. Once recognized it was easy to see the others, torn and mangled though they were. Most were dead. The few survivors would not live long. The machine still gave off heat. Several of the corpses appeared burnt.

As I looked down at these things I felt that an unbridgeable abyss lay between us. Not physically; they were but yards away. The abyss of Difference. We feel it when we encounter an animal in nature that we have never before seen and we must find a way to recognize it so that it makes sense as part of our world. With these creatures that was not possible. They were not of the world, they could not be made to fit into it. Never before had I felt such profound separateness, and never had I felt any degree of separateness to be natural. Until now. And in that moment the world I instinctively vowed to defend from these invaders passed away and was lost to me. Revolution had come.

The day brightened and there was work to do. Our own dead to find and bury, the injured to comfort, the rest to reassure and care for. I busied myself, not wanting to think of Moscow and that such creatures might be there now, only alive and active. Then, too, Mikhail had been gone over a day, going south, into danger.

Midmorning I stopped, exhausted, and walked out to sit not far from the wreck and stare at it and its now dead passengers. Presently someone sat down beside me. Iosef.

"Where could they have come from?" I asked, not expecting an answer.

"Mars," he said. I looked at him but he did not smile. He nodded. "Truth. After I left the seminary I took a post in the observatory in Tiflis. I worked there until last month. I was a clerk. Just before I left, the astronomers became excited about a new observation. They wouldn't tell me, but I kept the records, it wasn't difficult to find out. Besides, I carried the dispatches to the telegrapher to be sent to other observatories for confirmation. I didn't believe what I read, though, so one night I looked for myself. Giant plumes of gas were being thrown off the surface of Mars, one each night. None of them knew what to make of it, but I know the trace of a cannon when I see one." He smiled wryly. "I left shortly after. I was near Orol when I saw one come down."

"You said you were on your way to Pskov. Why did you come here?"

He narrowed his eyes at the crashed machine. "My reasons for going changed."

We buried the creatures the next day, far from the graves of their victims. More refugees arrived. Major Sekhim returned with wagons of blankets, more soldiers, and more news from other places. All word had stopped from Moscow, nor had anything been heard from St. Petersburg for three days. A fragmentary report from Orekhovo-Zuyevo told of *shtativii* advancing on emplacements of artillery. Then one phrase—*cherny dym,* black smoke—and silence.

For two more days refugees found their way to us, and then, but for a few singly or in pairs, no more. There were perhaps three thousand in the camp by then. Major Sekhim went once more to Tula, but returned soon from Shchyokino to tell us that the telegraph had been cut to Tula.

By the end of that first week a red fungus spread from the wreck. It moved swiftly and nearly covered the bare fields within a few days. The peasants attacked it, beat it back, ripped up the soil in a line from the edge of the village to the manor house. Within another week it was dying of its own unsuitability to this world.

Major Sekhim prowled the house, the estate, toured the village and the camp, drilled his men daily, inspected them, maintained discipline, but I did not think he did this out of any rational impulse. Habit and the need to feel useful in his profession drove him to enact these rituals even when we clearly had no use for them. But perhaps that isn't fair. The *muzhikii* derived a sense of security from it all, though even they could see that Major Sekhim was defending his own well-being more than theirs. In this we shared motive, because for days all I had done was for my own peace of mind.

If not for Iosef's foraging expeditions the camp would have crumbled into chaos and disaster. Major Sekhim, however, did not approve. Theft is theft, he insisted, and even in time of war certain laws must be obeyed. My letter forgave nothing in his eyes—the property owners never saw it. Iosef did not care what he said, and told him so, pointing out that Major Sekhim and his men were eating from the same stolen stocks as all the rest. But Major Sekhim was preparing for a confrontation. If he could not fight the invader, he would find another target. Iosef provided him the only alternative. Each time Iosef left, the major lectured him on law, and when he returned Sekhim met him at the edge of the encampment and berated him from horseback. Through it all Iosef ignored him. I considered Major Sekhim's position ridiculous, almost criminal. People needed to be fed, needed to be protected. Iosef managed to accomplish the first and Major Sekhim promised the second. It ought to have been a perfectly acceptable arrangement. However, if there had been a jail on Yasnaya Polyana, Major Sekhim would have attempted to lock Iosef in it.

In any case, Iosef left for longer and longer periods, ranging farther afield. It seemed clear that soon the available forage would become dangerously scarce. He had hesitated to go south—Mikhail had not returned—but his options were decreasing. One night at dinner he announced that he would go south in the morning.

"More stealing?" Major Sekhim said.

Iosef remained quiet for a time, then said, "You know, to insist on legal niceties when there are courts and police makes some sense. But now?"

"Civilization—"

"Is wrecked, Major."

Major Sekhim did not reply. He wandered off, his shoulders slightly bowed. I felt sad for him.

"You are a revolutionary," I said to Iosef.

He continued to watch Major Sekhim and shook his head. "Not anymore." His eyes shifted to me. "And neither are you, *dvoryantsvo*. We are all overthrown."

In the morning Major Sekhim did not lecture him when he left. Instead he only watched the wagons head off in the sharp after-dawn light. The fields were covered in thick patches by the pale, dead detritus of the red plant. When the foragers were out of sight Major Sekhim ordered sentries a mile or more out to keep watch for their return.

Late in the afternoon two of Sekhim's horsemen came at a gallop. Iosef's wagons were returning already. Major Sekhim mounted a squadron and rode off to give escort. By dusk they appeared and rode back into the encampment. The wagons were empty. Iosef jumped to the ground.

"Shtativii," he said. "I don't think they saw us, but they are coming this way. We saw two of them, wandering the country-side."

"We will meet them if they come," Major Sekhim said grimly.

"And do what?" Iosef asked. "They are giants, they'll step right over you."

Major Sekhim glared. "We will meet them!"

Iosef shrugged. *"Nui chto zh.* Do what you want."

"I will do my duty!"

"And I will do what is necessary."

They parted that way and never spoke again. By morning Iosef had gone, along with a few others, fellow foragers. But then our attention focused on something more immediate.

The night turned unusually chill and the sun rose on mist. Faintly at first, but growing louder and clearer, came a sound of a train whistle echoed through mountains. At least, so it seemed at first. The louder it became, though, the stranger it was, a shrill warble that scoured our nerves and tightened our hearts with fear. To the south the morning light glinted pale yellow off a tall metal cupola. It moved, left to right, then back.

During the night Major Sekhim had his men polish their steel, buff their boots, shine their saddles and buttons, and now they rode out to meet the invader, glittering and gallant, almost forty of them on horseback, sabers drawn and gleaming. I remembered such charges in my youth, remembered the stammer in the heart, the surge of blood, the pride, and anticipation. I had thought myself well past such feelings, but I watched them anxiously, the nostalgia of struggle and victory turning in my mind. It was sense-less. The *shtativ* advanced across the field, its three legs just as Iosef had said, holding its head high above its enemies, sounding its awful wail.

At two hundred yards Major Sekhim ordered the charge. The

horsemen, stretched in a single line abreast, spurred forward, screaming.

The *shtativ* staggered awkwardly a few more steps, then stopped. Beneath the cupola hung mechanical arms. One set raised a thing that could only be a weapon. It seemed to aim at the cavalry charge and I waited for the inevitable death. But the blow never came. The machine stopped, the arms dangled, its terrible wailing ceased, and all we heard was the pounding of the horses, the battle cries of the Cossacks, and nothing else.

Major Sekhim reached it first, rode under the legs, and swung his saber. The blow rang sharply and Major Sekhim's cry became a shout of triumph. The horsemen rode around the *shtativ*, striking at it, their swords ringing off the metal legs.

When the giant did not react, they stopped the attack, circling it warily. Tanya held my left arm while I walked out into the field. Others quickly followed. I stopped beneath it and peered up. Toward the rear of the cupola a hatch was partially open. Tentacles hung limply, similar in appearance to those dead creatures from the comet. I reached out and struck the leg with my cane. It sang with a crystalline delicacy. The machine did not move. I laughed. "Hah! Bronchitis!" Major Sekhim still sat his horse, staring up at it, puzzled. "Perhaps, Major, you frightened it to death. But obviously they are dying. Let them die. There's work to do."

In the weeks since we have had word from all over Russia that the *zakhvatchik* is dying. Yasnaya Polyana has become a place of focus for the survivors. Everyone seems to be mingled here. Peasant, bureaucrat, noble—they all need to eat, need shelter, need to feel safe. With each group we learn how much has been lost. It feels as though Russia has died. But it can be revived.

Yesterday I found my copy of the new novel, the one Sofya remained in Moscow to oversee. Moscow, we learned, has indeed been burned down. It is worse than Napoleon; even the Kremlin is gone. With this in mind I read what I had written. It was a silly book. It spoke of things that are now gone, along with so much else. The things that were so important for me to address with it have changed. This is no longer the same world, it cannot be. Russia—the world—does not need another novel about humankind's barbarity to itself, at least not from me. Early this morning I burned it. I wonder what Iosef would say to that. Have I done a necessary thing? Perhaps, like me, like Major Sekhim, he could not say. His world is gone, too.

I must close now, Vladimir Grigoryevich. I will write to you again when I have heard from you and know that you have survived. For now, there is work to do.

Your friend
Lev Nikolayevitch Tolstoy

From: Pavel Pobodonostsev, dep. arch., Tolstoy Institute, Univ.
       St. Petersburg, Tula
To: Karyn Alexander, asst. arch., Oxford Univ., Dept. Cultural
       Studies

Karyn: Thank you! My God, what a find! We have always known Count Tolstoy experienced the war—the refugee camp at his estate, Yasnaya Polyana, was at one point the largest community in Russia—but this is the first account of it in his own hand. The book he mentions is the "lost" Tolstoy. We only know the title—"Resurrection"—he never tried to recover it, and since he wrote no more fiction after the war we don't even have tantalizing hints. He threw all his efforts into the Global Cooperative Movement. He was seventy-two at the time and this was the effort that killed him three years later.

Of course, the people mentioned are all familiar—Major Sekhim, later governor of the region, then first Georgian Cossack elected to the bicameral duma; Sergey Lvonovitch Tolstoy, who became the first president of the Russia Monarchic Republic; Lev, who became the writer in the family; Tolstoy's wife and daughters and Strakhov, the family lawyer, all of whom died in Moscow.

However, one name mentioned has us puzzled. The man from Tiflis—present day Tblisi—Iosef Vissarionovich. We were able to trace the employment records of the Observatory—they became part of the university archives—so we're sure that this was one Iosef Vissarionovich Dzhugashvili. Up till then he'd been a seminary student, then a clerk at the Observatory. He became involved with a prodemocracy group called the *Mesame Dasi,* then disappeared. What became of him after he left Yasnaya Polyana we have no idea.

This is a treasure. Of course I would like to work with you on a presentation. I am looking forward to seeing you at the next conference anyway. It will be in Constantinople, which ought to be much better than last year's in Dresden. Keep in touch.

Yours, Pavel
Tula, 1943 A.D.

Jules Verne

PARIS CONQUERS ALL

GREGORY BENFORD AND
DAVID BRIN

I commence this account with a prosaic stroll at eventide—a saunter down the avenues of *la Ville Lumière,* during which the ordinary swiftly gave way to the extraordinary. I was in Paris to consult with my publisher, as well as to visit old companions and partake of the exquisite cuisine, which my provincial home in Amiens cannot boast. Though I am now a gentleman of advanced age, nearing my seventieth year, I am still quite able to favor the savories, and it remains a treat to survey the lovely demoiselles as they exhibit the latest fashions on the boulevards, enticing smitten young men and breaking their hearts at the same time.

I had come to town that day believing—as did most others—that there still remained weeks, or days at least, before the alien terror ravaging southern France finally reached the valley of the Seine. *Île-de-France* would be defended at all costs, we were assured. So it came to pass that, tricked by this false complaisance, I was in the capital the very afternoon that the crisis struck.

Paris! It still shone as the most splendid exemplar of our progressive age—all the more so in that troubled hour, as an ambiance of tense anxiety seemed only to add to the city's loveliness—shimmering at night with both gas and electric lights, and humming by day with new electric trams, whose marvelous wires crisscrossed above the avenues like heralds of a new era.

I had begun here long ago as a young attorney, having followed into my father's profession; yet that same head of our family had also graciously accepted my urge to strike out on a literary road, first in the theater and later down many expansive voyages of prose. "Drink your fill of Paris, my son!" That is what the good man told me, when he saw his son off from the Nantes railway station one spring day. "Devour these wondrous times. Your senses are keen. Share your exceptional insights. The world will change because of it."

Without such help and support, would I ever have found within myself the will, the daring, to explore the many pathways of the future, with all their wonders and perils? Ever since the Martian invasion began, I had found myself reflecting on an extraordinary life filled with such good fortune, especially now that *all* human luck seemed about to be revoked. Now, with terror looming from the south and west, would it all soon come to naught? All that I had achieved? Everything humanity had accomplished, after so many centuries climbing upward from ignorance?

It was in such an uncharacteristically dour mood that I strolled in the company of M. Beauchamp, a gentleman scientist, that pale afternoon less than an hour before I had my first contact with the horrible Martian machines. Naturally, I had been following the eyewitness accounts which first told of plunging fireballs striking the Earth with violence that sent gouts of soil and rock spitting upward, like miniature versions of the outburst at Krakatau. These impacts had soon proved to be far more than mere meteoritic phenomena, since there soon emerged, like insects from a subterranean lair, three-legged beings bearing incredible malevolence toward the life of this planet. Riding gigantic tripod mechanisms, these unwelcome guests soon set forth with one sole purpose in mind—destructive conquest!

The ensuing carnage, the raking fire, the sweeping flames—none of these horrors had yet reached the fair country above the river Loire . . . not yet. But reports all too vividly told of villages trampled, farmlands seared black, and hordes of refugees cut down as they fled.

Invasion. The word came to mind all too easily remembered. We of northern France knew the pain just twenty-eight years back, when Sedan fell and this sweet land trembled under an attacker's boot. Several Paris quarters still bear scars where Prussian firing squads tore moonlike craters out of plaster walls, mingling there the ocher life-blood of Communards, royalists, and bourgeois alike.

Now Paris trembled before advancing powers so malign that, in contrast, those Prussians of 1870 were like beloved cousins, welcome to town for a picnic!

All of this I pondered while taking leave, with Beauchamp, of the École Militaire, the national military academy, where a briefing had just been given to assembled dignitaries, such as ourselves. From the stone portico we gazed toward the Seine, past the encampment of the Seventeenth Corps of Volunteers, their tents arrayed across trampled grass and smashed flower beds of the ironically named *Champ-de-Mars*. The meadow of the god of war.

Towering over this scene of intense (and ultimately futile) martial activity stood the tower of M. Eiffel, built for the recent exhibition, that marvelously fashioned testimonial to metal and ingenuity . . . and also target of so much vitriol.

"The public's regard for it may improve with time," I ventured, observing that Beauchamp's gaze lay fixed on the same magnificent spire.

My companion snorted with derision at the curving steel flanks. "An eyesore, of no enduring value," he countered, and for some time we distracted ourselves from more somber thoughts by arguing the relative merits of Eiffel's work, while turning east to walk toward the Sorbonne. Of late, experiments in the transmission of radio-tension waves had wrought unexpected pragmatic benefits, using the great tower as an *antenna*. I wagered Beauchamp there would be other advantages, in time.

Alas, even this topic proved no lasting diversion from thoughts of danger to the south. Fresh in our minds were reports from the wine districts. The latest outrage—that the home of Vouvray was now smashed, trampled and burning. This was my favorite of all the crisp, light vintages—better, even, than a fresh Sancerre. Somehow, that loss seemed to strike home more vividly than dry casualty counts, already climbing to the millions.

"There must be a method!" I proclaimed as we approached the domed brilliance of *les Invalides*. "There has to be a scientific approach to destroying the invaders."

"The military is surely doing its best," Beauchamp said.

"Buffoons!"

"But you heard of their losses. The regiments and divisions decimated—" Beauchamp stuttered. "The army dies for France! For humanity—of which France is surely the best example."

I turned to face him, aware of an acute paradox—that the greatest martial mind of all time lay entombed in the domed citadel nearby. Yet even he would have been helpless before a power that was not of this world.

"I do not condemn the army's courage," I assured.

"Then how can you speak—"

"No, no! I condemn their lack of imagination!"

"To defeat the incredible takes—"

"Vision!"

Timidly, for he knew my views, he advanced, "I saw in the *Match* that the British have consulted with the fantasist, Mr. Wells."

To this I could only cock an eye.

"He will give them no aid, only imaginings."

"But you just said—"

"Vision is not the same as dreaming."

At that moment the cutting smell of sulfuric acid wafted on a breeze from the reducing works near the river. (Even in the most beautiful of cities, rude work has its place.) Beauchamp mistook my expression of disgust for commentary upon the Englishman, Wells.

"He is quite successful. Many compare him to you."

"An unhappy analogy. His stories do not repose on a scientific basis. I make use of physics. He invents."

"In this crisis—"

"I go to the moon in a cannonball. He goes in an airship, which he constructs of a metal which does away with the law of gravitation. *Ça c'est très joli!*—but show me this metal. Let him produce it!"

Beauchamp blinked. "I quite agree—but, then, is not our present science woefully inadequate to the task at hand—defending ourselves against monstrous invaders?"

We resumed our walk. Leaving behind the crowds paying homage at Napoléon's Tomb, we made good progress along rue de Varenne, with the Petit Palais now visible across the river, just ahead.

"We lag technologically behind these foul beings, that I grant. But only by perhaps a century or two."

"Oh surely, more than that! To fly between the worlds—"

"Can be accomplished several ways, all within our comprehension, if not our grasp."

"What of the reports by astronomers of great explosions, seen earlier on the surface of the distant ruddy planet? They now think these were signs of the Martian invasion fleet being launched. Surely we could not expend such forces!"

I waved away his objection. "Those are nothing more than I have already foreseen in *From the Earth to the Moon,* which I would remind you I published thirty-three years ago, at the conclusion of the American Civil War."

"You think the observers witnessed the belching of great Martian cannon?"

"Of course! I had to make adjustments, engineering alterations, while designing my moon vessel. The shell could not be of steel, like one of Eiffel's bridges. So I conjectured that the means of making light projectiles of aluminum will come to pass. These are not basic limitations, you see"—I waved them away—"but mere details."

The wind had shifted, and with relief I now drew in a heady breath redolent with the smells of cookery rising from the city of cuisine. Garlic, roasting vegetables, the dark aromas of warming meats—such a contrast with the terror which advanced on the city, and on our minds. Along rue St. Grenelle, I glanced into one of the innumerable tiny cafés. Worried faces stared moodily at their reflections in the broad zinc bars, stained by spilled absinthe. Wine coursed down anxious throats. Murmurs floated on the fitful air.

"So the Martians come by cannon, the workhorse of battle," Beauchamp murmured.

"There are other methods," I allowed.

"Your dirigibles?"

"Do not be ignorant, Beauchamp! You know well that no air permeates the realm between the worlds."

"Then what methods do they employ to maneuver? They fall upon Asia, Africa, the Americans, the deserving British—all with such control, such intricate planning."

"Rockets! Though perhaps there are flaws in my original cannon ideas—I am aware that passengers would be squashed to jelly by the firing of such a great gun—nothing similar condemns the use of cylinders of slowly exploding chemicals."

"To steer between planets? Such control!"

"Once the concept is grasped, it is but a matter of ingenuity to bring it to pass. Within a century, Beauchamp, we shall see rockets of our own rise from this ponderous planet, into the heavens. I promise you that!"

"Assuming we survive the fortnight," Beauchamp remarked gloomily. "Not to mention a century."

"To live, we must think. Our thoughts must encompass the entire range of possibility."

I waved my furled umbrella at the sky, sweeping it around and down rue de Rennes, toward the southern eminence of Montparnasse. By chance my gaze followed the pointing tip—and so I was among the first to spy one of the Martian machines, like a monstrous insect, cresting that ill-fated hill.

There is something in the human species which abhors oddity, the unnatural. We are double in arms, legs, eyes, ears, even nipples (if I may venture such an indelicate comparison; but remember, I am a man of science at all times). Twoness is fundamental to us, except when Nature dictates singularity—we have but one mouth, and one organ of regeneration. Such biological matters are fundamental. Thus, the instantaneous feelings of horror at first sight of the *threeness* of the invaders—which was apparent even in the external design of their machinery. I need not explain the revulsion to any denizen of our world. These were alien beings, in the worst sense of the word.

"They have broken through!" I cried. "The front must have collapsed."

Around us crowds now took note of the same dread vision, looming over the sooty Montparnasse railway station. Men began to run, women to wail. Yet, some courageous ones of both sexes ran the other way, to help bolster the city's slim, final bulwark, a line from which rose volleys of crackling rifle fire.

By unspoken assent, Beauchamp and I refrained from joining the general fury. Two old men, wealthier in dignity than physical stamina, we had more to offer with our experience and seasoned minds than with the frail strength of our arms.

"Note the rays," I said dispassionately, as for the first time we witnessed the fearful lashing of that horrid heat, smiting the helpless trains, igniting railcars, and exploding locomotives at a mere touch. I admit I was struggling to hold both reason and resolve, fastening upon details as a drowning man might cling to flotsam.

"Could they be like Hertzian waves?" Beauchamp asked in wavering tones.

We had been excited by the marvelous German discovery, and its early application to experiments in wireless signaling. Still, even I had to blink at Beauchamp's idea—for the first time envisioning the concentration of such waves into searing beams. "Possibly," I allowed. "Legends say that Archimedes concentrated light to beat back Roman ships, at Syracuse. . . . But the waves Hertz found were meters long, and of less energy than a fly's wingbeat. These—"

I jumped, despite my efforts at self-control, as another, much *larger* machine appeared to the west of the first, towering majestically, also spouting bright red torrents of destruction. It set fires on the far southern horizon, the beam playing over buildings, much as a cat licks a mouse.

"We shall never defeat such power," Beauchamp said morosely.

"Certainly we do not have much time," I allowed. "But you put my mind into harness, my friend."

Around us people now openly bolted. Carriages rushed past without regard to panicked figures who dashed across the avenues. Horses clopped madly by, whipped by their masters. I stopped to unroll the paper from a Colombian cigar. Such times demand clear thinking. It was up to the higher minds and classes to display character and resolve.

"No, we must seize upon some technology closer to hand," I said. "Not the Hertzian waves, but perhaps something allied . . ."

Beauchamp glanced back at the destructive tripods with lines of worry creasing his brow. "If rifle and cannon prove useless against these marching machines—"

"Then we must apply another science, not mere mechanics."

"Biology? There are the followers of Pasteur, of course." Beauchamp was plainly struggling to stretch his mind. "If we could somehow get these Martians—has anyone yet seen one?—to drink contaminated milk . . ."

I had to chuckle. "Too literal, my friend. Would you serve it to them on a silver plate?"

Beauchamp drew himself up. "I was only attempting—"

"No matter. The point is now moot. Can you not see where the second machine stands, atop the very site of Pasteur's now ruined Institute?"

Although biology is a lesser cousin in the family of science, I nevertheless imagined with chagrin those fine collections of bottled specimens, now kicked and scattered under splayed tripod feet, tossing the remnants to the swirling winds. No help there, alas.

"Nor are the ideas of the Englishman, Darwin, of much use, for they take thousands of years to have force. No, I have in mind physics, but rather more recent work."

I had been speaking from the airy spot wherein my head makes words before thought has yet taken form, as often happens when a concept lumbers upward from the mind's depths, coming, coming . . .

Around us lay the most beautiful city in the world, already flickering with gas lamps lining the prominent avenues. Might that serve as inspiration? But no, the Martians had already proved invulnerable to even the foul clouds which the army tried to deploy.

But then what? I have always believed that the solution to tomorrow's problems usually lay in plain sight, in materials and concepts already at hand—just as the essential ideas for submarines, airships, and even interplanetary craft have been apparent for decades. The trick lies in formulating the right combinations.

As that thought coursed my mind, a noise erupted so cacophonously as to override even the commotion farther south. A rattling roar (accompanied by the plaint of already frightened horses) approached from the *opposite* direction! Even as I turned round toward the river, I recognized the clatter of an explosive-combustion engine, of the type invented not long ago by Herr Benz, now propelling a wagon bearing several men and a pile of glittering apparatus! At once I observed one unforeseen advantage of horseless transportation—to allow human beings to ride *toward* danger that no horse on Earth would ever approach.

The hissing contraption ground to a halt not far from Beauchamp and me. Then a shout burst forth in that most penetrating of human accents—one habituated to open spaces and vast expanses.

"Come on, you gol-durned piece of junk! Fire on up, or I'll turn ya into scrap b'fore the Martians do!"

The speaker was dressed as a workman, with bandoliers of tools arrayed across his broad, sturdy frame. A shock of reddish hair escaped under the rim of a large, curve-brimmed hat, of the type affected by the troupe of Buffalo Bill, when that showman's carnival was the sensation of Europe some years back.

"Come now, Ernst," answered the man beside him, in a voice both more cultured and sardonic. "There's no purpose in berating a machine. Perhaps we are already near enough to acquire the data we seek."

An uneasy alliance of distant cousins, I realized. Although I have always admired users of the English language for their boundless ingenuity, it can be hard to see the countrymen of Edgar Allan Poe as related to those of Walter Scott.

"What do you say, Fraunhofer?" asked the Englishman of a third gentleman with the portly bearing of one who dearly loves his schnitzel, now peering through an array of lenses toward the battling tripods. "Can you get a good reading from here?"

"Bah!" The bald-pated German cursed. "From ze exploding buildings and fiery desolation, I get plenty of lines, those typical of combustion. But ze rays zemselves are absurd. Utterly absurd!"

I surmised that here were scientists at work, even as I had prescribed in my discourse to Beauchamp, doing the labor of sixty battalions. In such efforts by luminous minds lay our entire hope.

"Absurd how?" A fourth head emerged, that of a dark young man, wearing objects over his ears that resembled muffs for protection against cold weather, only these were made of wood, linked by black cord to a machine covered with dials. I at once recognized miniature speakerphones, for presenting faint sounds directly to the ears. The young man's accent was Italian, and curiously calm. "What is absurd about the spectrum of-a the rays, Professor?"

"There *iss* no spectrum!" the German expounded. "My device shows just the one hue of red light we see with our naked eyes, when the rays lash destructive force. There are no absorption lines, just a single hue of brilliant red!"

The Italian pursed his lips in thought. "One *frequency*, perhaps . . . ?"

"If you *insist* on comparing light to your vulgar Hertzian waves—"

So entranced was I by the discussion that I was almost knocked down by Beauchamp's frantic effort to gain my attention. I knew just one thing could bring him to behave so—the Martians must nearly be upon us! With this supposition in mind, I turned, expecting to see a disklike foot of a leviathan preparing to crush us.

Instead, Beauchamp, white as a ghost, stammered and pointed with a palsied hand. "Verne, *regardez!*"

To my amazement, the invaders had abruptly changed course, swerving from the direct route to the Seine. Instead they turned left and were stomping swiftly toward the part of town that Beauchamp and I had only just left, crushing buildings to dust as they hurried ahead. At the time, we shared a single thought. The commanders of the battle tripods must have spied the military camp on the *Champ-de-Mars*. Or else they planned to wipe out the nearby military academy. It even crossed my mind that their objective might be the tomb of humanity's greatest general, to destroy that shrine, and with it our spirit to resist.

But no. Only much later did we realize the truth.

Here in Paris, our vanquishers suddenly had another kind of conquest in mind.

Flames spread as evening fell. Although the Martian rampage seemed to have slackened somewhat, the city's attitude of *sang-froid* was melting rapidly into frothy panic. The broad boulevards that Baron Haussmann gave the city during the Second Empire proved their worth as aisles of escape while buildings burned.

But not for all. By nightfall, Beauchamp and I found ourselves across the river at the new army headquarters, in the tree-lined Tuilleries, just west of the Louvre—as if the military had decided to make its last stand in front of the great museum, delaying the invaders in order to give the curators more time to rescue treasures. While a colonel with a sooty face drew arrows on a map, I found my gaze wandering to the trampled gardens, backlit by fire, and wondered what the painter, Camille Pissarro, would make of such a hellish scene. Just a month ago I had visited his apartment at 204 rue de Rivoli, to see a series of impressions he had undertaken to portray the peaceful Tuilleries. Now, what a parody fate had decreed for these same gardens!

The colonel had explained that invader tripods came in two sizes, with the larger ones appearing to control the smaller. There were many of the latter kind, still rampaging the city suburbs, but all three of the great ones reported to be in northern France had converged on the same site before nightfall, trampling back and forth across the *Champ-de-Mars,* presenting a series of strange behaviors that as yet had no lucid explanation. I did not need a military expert to tell me what I had seen with my own eyes . . . three titanic metal leviathans, twisting and capering as if in a languid dance, round and round the same object of their fierce attention.

I wandered away from the briefing, and peered for a while at the foreign scientists. The Italian and the German were arguing vehemently, invoking the name of the physicist Boltzmann, with his heretical theories of "atomic matter," trying to explain why the heat-ray of the aliens should emerge as just a single, narrow color. But the discussion was over my head, so I moved on.

The American and the Englishman seemed more pragmatic, consulting with French munitions experts about a type of fulminating bomb that might be attached to a Martian machine's kneecap—if only some way could be found to carry it there . . . and to get the machine to stand still while it was attached. I doubted any explosive device devised overnight would suffice, since artillery had been next to useless, but I envied the adventure of the volunteer bomber, whoever it might be.

Adventure. I had spent decades writing about it, nearly always in the form of extraordinary voyages, with my heroes bound intrepidly across foaming seas, or under the waves, or over ice caps, or to the shimmering moon. Millions read my works to escape the tedium of daily life, and perhaps to catch a glimpse of the near future. Only now the future had arrived, containing enough excitement for anybody. We did not have to seek adventure far away. It had come to us. Right to our homes.

The crowd had ebbed somewhat, in the area surrounding the prisoners' enclosure, so I went over to join Beauchamp. He had been standing there for hours, staring at the captives, our only prizes in this horrid war, lying caged within stout iron bars, a dismal set of figures, limp yet atrociously fascinating.

"Have they any new ideas?" Beauchamp asked in a distracted voice while keeping his eyes focused toward the four beings from Mars. "What new plans from the military geniuses?"

The last was spoken with thick sarcasm. His attitude had changed since noon, most clearly.

"They think the key is to be found in the master tripods, those that are right now stomping flat the region near Eiffel's spire. Never have all three of the Master Machines been seen so close together. Experts suggest that the Martians may use *movement* to communicate. The dance they are now performing may represent a conference on strategy. Perhaps they are planning their next move, now that they have taken Paris."

Beauchamp grunted. It seemed to make as much sense as any other proposal to explain the aliens' sudden, strange behavior. While smaller tripods roamed about, dealing destruction almost randomly, the three great ones hopped and flopped like herons in a marsh, gesticulating wildly with their flailing legs, all this in marked contrast to the demure solidity of Eiffel's needle.

For a time we stared in silence at the prisoners, whose projectile had hurtled across unimaginable space only to shatter when it struck an unlucky hard place on the Earth, shattering open and leaving its occupants helpless, at our mercy. Locked inside iron, these captives did not look impressive, as if this world weighed heavy on their limbs. Or had another kind of languor invaded their beings? A depression of spirits, perhaps?

"I have pondered one thing, while standing here," Beauchamp mumbled. "An oddity about these creatures. We had been told that everything about them came in threes . . . note the trio of legs, and of arms, and of eyes—"

"As we have seen in newspaper sketches for weeks," I replied.

"Indeed. But regard the one in the center. The one around which the others arrayed themselves, as if protectively . . . or perhaps in mutual competition?"

I saw the one he meant. Slightly larger than the rest, with a narrower aspect in the region of the conical head.

"Yes, it does seem different, somehow . . . but I don't see—"

I stopped, for just then I *did* see . . . and thoughts passed through my brain in a pell-mell rush.

"Its legs and arms . . . there are *four*! Its symmetry is different! Can it be of another race? A servant species, perhaps? Or something superior? Or else . . ."

My next cry was of excited elation.

"Beauchamp! The master tripods . . . I believe I know what they are doing!

"Moreover, I believe this beckons us with opportunity."

The bridges were sheer madness, while the river flowing underneath seemed chockablock with corpses. It took our party two hours to fight our way against the stream of panicky human refugees, before the makeshift expedition finally arrived close enough to make out how the dance progressed.

"They are closer, are they not?" I asked the lieutenant assigned to guide us. "Have they been spiraling inward at a steady rate?"

The young officer nodded. "*Oui, monsieur*. It now seems clear that all three are converging on Eiffel's tower. Though for what reason, and whether it will continue—"

I laughed, remembering the thought that had struck me earlier—a mental image of herons dancing in a swamp. The comparison renewed when I next looked upward in awe at the stomping, whirling gyrations of the mighty battle machines, shattering buildings and making the earth shake with each hammer blow of their mincing feet. Steam hissed from broken mains. Basements and ossuaries collapsed, but the dance went on. Three monstrous things, wheeling ever closer to their chosen goal . . . which waited quietly, demurely, like a giant metal *ingénue*.

"Oh, they will converge all right, lieutenant. The question is—shall we be ready when they do?"

My mind churned.

The essential task in envisioning the future is a capacity for wonder. I had said as much to journalists. These Martians lived in a future of technological effects we could but imagine. Only through such visual-ization could we glimpse their Achilles' heel.

Now was the crucial moment when wonder, so long merely encased in idle talk, should spring forth to action.

Wonder . . . a fine word, but what did it mean? Summoning up an inner eye, which could scale up the present, pregnant with possibility, into . . . into . . .

What, then? Hertz, his waves, circuits, capacitors, wires—

Beauchamp glanced nervously around. "Even if you could get the attention of the military—"

"For such tasks the army is useless. I am thinking of something else," I said suddenly, filled with an assurance I could not explain. "The Martians will soon converge at the center of their obsession. And when they do, we shall be ready."

"Ready with what?"

"With what lies within our"—and here I thought of the pun, a glit-tering word soaring up from the shadowy subconscious—"within our capacitance."

The events of that long night compressed for me. I had hit upon the kernel of the idea, but the implementation loomed like an insuperable barrier.

Fortunately, I had not taken into account the skills of other men, especially the great leadership ability of my friend, M. Beauchamp. He had commanded a battalion against the Prussians, dominating his cor-ner of the battlefield without runners. With more like him, Sedan would never have fallen. His voice rose above the streaming crowds, and plucked forth from that torrent those who still had a will to contest the pillage of their city. He pointed to my figure, whom many seemed to know. My heart swelled at the thought that Frenchmen—and Frenchwomen!—would muster to a hasty cause upon the mention of my name, encouraged solely by the thought that I might offer a way to fight back.

I tried to describe my ideas as briskly as possible . . . but alas, brev-ity has never been my chief virtue. So I suppressed a flash of pique when the brash American, following the impulsive nature of his race, leaped up and shouted—

"Of course! Verne, you clever old Frog. You've got it!"

—and in vulgar but concise French, he proceeded to lay it all out in a matter of moments, conveying the practical essentials amid growing excitement from the crowd. With an excited roar, our makeshift army set at once to work.

I am not a man of many particulars. But craftsmen and workers and simple men of manual dexterity stepped in while engineers, led by the Italian and the American, took charge of the practical details, charging about with the gusto of youth, unstoppable in their enthusiasm. In fevered haste, bands of patriots ripped the zinc sheets from bars. They scavenged the homes of the rich in search of silver. No time to beat it into proper electrodes—they connected decanters and candlesticks into makeshift assortments. These they linked with copper wires, fetched from the cabling of the new electrical tramways.

The electropotentials of the silver with the copper, in the proper conducting medium, would be monstrously reminiscent of the original "voltaic" pile of Alessandro Volta. In such a battery, shape does not matter so much as surface area, and proper wiring. Working through the smoky night, teams took these rude pieces and made a miracle of rare design. The metals they immersed in a salty solution, emptying the wine vats of the district to make room, spilling the streets red, and giving any true Frenchman even greater cause to think only of vengeance!

These impromptu batteries, duplicated throughout the *arrondissement,* the quick engineers soon webbed together in a vast parallel circuit. Amid the preparations, M. Beauchamp and the English scientist inquired into my underlying logic.

"Consider the simple equations of planetary motion," I said. "Even though shot from the Martian surface with great speed, the time to reach Earth must be many months, perhaps a year."

"One can endure space for such a time?" Beauchamp frowned.

"Space, yes. It is mere vacuum. Tanks of their air—thin stuff, Professor Lowell assures us from his observations—could sustain them. But think! These Martians, they must have intelligence of our rank. They left their kind to venture forth and do battle. Several years without the comforts of home, until they have subdued our world and can send for more of their kind."

The Englishman seemed perplexed. "For more?"

"Specifically, for their families, their mates . . . dare I say their *wives?* Though it would seem that not *all* were left behind. At least one came along in the first wave, out of need for her expertise, perhaps, or possibly she was smuggled along, on the ill-fated missile that our forces captured."

Beauchamp bellowed. "Zut! The four-legged one. There are reports of no others. You are right, Verne. It must be rare to bring one of that kind so close to battle!"

The Englishman shook his head. "Even if this is so, I do not follow how it applies to this situation." He gestured toward where the three terrible machines were nearing the tower, their gyrations now tight, their dance more languorous. Carefully, reverentially, yet with a clear longing, they reached out to the great spire that Paris had almost voted to tear down just a few years after the Grand Exhibition ended. Now all our hopes were founded in the city's wise decision to let M. Eiffel's masterpiece stand.

The Martians stroked its base, clasped the thick parts of the tower's curving thigh—and commenced slowly to climb.

Beauchamp smirked at the English scholar, perhaps with a light touch of malice. "I expect you would not understand, sir. It is not in your national character to fathom this, ah, ritual."

"Humph!" Unwisely, the Englishman used Beauchamp's teasing as cause to take offense. "I'll wager that *we* give these Martians a whipping before your lot does!"

"Ah yes," Beauchamp remarked. "Whipping is more along the lines of the English, I believe."

With a glance, I chided my dear friend. After all, our work was now done. The young, the skilled, and the brave had the task well in hand. Like generals who have unleashed their regiments beyond recall, we had only to observe, awaiting either triumph or blame.

At dawn, an array of dozens and dozens of Volta batteries lay scattered across the south bank of the Seine. Some fell prey to rampages by smaller Martian machines, while others melted under hasty application of fuming acids. Cabling wound through streets where buildings burned and women wept. Despite all obstacles of flame, rubble, and burning rays, all now terminated at Eiffel's tower.

The Martians' ardent climb grew manifestly amorous as the sun rose in piercing brilliance, warming our chilled bones. I was near the end of my endurance, sustained only by the excitement of observing Frenchmen and women fighting back with ingenuity and rare unity. But as the Martians scaled the tower—driven by urges we can guess by analogy alone—I began to doubt. My scheme was simple, but could it work?

I conferred with the dark Italian who supervised the connections.

"Potentials? Voltages?" He screwed up his face. "Who has had-a time to calculate. All I know, m'sewer, iz that we got-a plenty juice. You want-a fry a fish, use a hot flame."

I took his point. Even at comparatively low voltages, high currents can destroy any organism. A mere fraction of an Ampere can kill a man, if his skin is made a reasonable conductor by application of water, for example. Thus, we took it as a sign of a higher power at work, when the bright sun fell behind a glowering black cloud, and an early mist rolled in from the north. It made the tower slick beneath the orange lamps we had festooned about it.

And still the Martians climbed.

It was necessary to coordinate the discharge of so many batteries in one powerful jolt, a mustering of beta rays. Pyrotechnicians had taken up positions beside our command post, within sight of the giant, spectral figures which now had mounted a third of the way up the tower.

"Hey, Verne!" the American shouted, with well-meant impudence. "You're on!"

I turned to see that a crowd had gathered. Their expressions of tense hope touched this old man's heart. Hope and faith in my idea. There would be no higher point in the life of a fabulist.

"Connect!" I cried. "Loose the hounds of electrodynamics!"

A skyrocket leaped forth, trailing sooty smoke—a makeshift signal, but sufficient. Down by the river and underneath a hundred ruins, scores of gaps and switches closed. Capacitors arced. A crackling rose from around the city as stored energy rushed along the copper cabling. I imagined for an instant the onrushing mob of beta rays, converging on—

The invaders suddenly shuddered, and soon there emerged thin, high cries, screams that were the first sign of how much like us they were, for their wails rose in hopeless agony, shrieks of despair from mouths which breathed lighter air than we, but knew the same depths of woe.

They toppled one by one, tumbling in the morning mist, crashing to shatter on the trampled lawns and cobblestones of the ironically named *Champ-de-Mars* . . . marshaling ground of the god of war, and now graveyard of his planetary champions.

The lesser machines, deprived of guidance, soon reeled away, some falling into the river, and many others destroyed by artillery, or even enraged mobs. So the threat ebbed from its horrid peak . . . at least for the time being.

As my reward for these services, I would ask that the site be renamed, for it was not the arts of *battle* which turned the metal monsters into burning slag. Nor even Zeus's lightning, which we had unleashed. In the final analysis, it was *Aphrodite* who had come to the aid of her favorite city.

What a fitting way for our uninvited guests to meet their end—to die passionately in Paris, from a fatal love.

H. P. Lovecraft

TO MARS AND PROVIDENCE

DON WEBB

Exactly twenty-nine days after his father had died of general paresis—that is to say, syphilis—in the local asylum, the boy observed the cylinder land upon Federal Hill. On some level this extramundane intrusion confirmed certain hypotheses that he had begun to form concerning the prognosticative nature of dreams. He had been dreaming of the night gaunts for three years. They had—the horrible conclusion now obtruded upon his reluctant mind as an awful certainty—come for him. As befit a gentleman of pure Yankee stock, and the true chalk-white Nordic type, he had but one option: He must venture forth to meet and if possible defeat these eldritch beings.

He was eight years old.

The initial and certainly most daunting difficulty would be getting past his mother and aunts. His grandfather, Whipple Phillips, might be an ally in this quest, since he had often kept Howard entertained with tales of black voodoo, unfathomed caves, winged horrors, and old witches with sinister cauldrons. But Grandfather Whipple was in Idaho, and his mother, though normally indulgent of such whims, would not allow his questing into the night air. Howard therefore adopted extreme stealth in the acquisition of his bicycle. He actually *carried* it several yards from the house before mounting it in quest of adventure.

Down College Hill across the river and then hard work up toward St. John's Church on Federal Hill, which is where he judged the cylinder had fallen. The neighborhood, alive with nameless sounds that vied with morbid shriekings, seemed to have taken notice of the cylinder's fall. There was a general lighting of candles, lanterns, torches, and the like. By the time he reached St. John's a rugged ring of light surrounded the shiny cylinder. He could not stand to force his way through the crowd, so he entered the church proper and climbed up to the bell tower. Opening a small window in the bell tower, he watched the scene below with growing horror and fascination.

A portion of the cylinder had begun to turn. No doubt the entity or entities therein sought the relieving air of the night as a counter to the searing heat of their bulkhead. The crowd grew fervent with their prayers—prayers to an entity Howard knew to be no more real than the Santa Claus he had abandoned at age five. The lid fell free, and a tremendous fungoid stench assailed Howard's nostrils.

The great leathery wet glistening squamous head of the cylinder's occupant lunged out, pulsing and twitching obscenely. Its vast liquid eyes, whose terrible three-lobed pupils spoke of the being's nonTerran evolution, gazed with glittering contempt upon the sea of humanity surrounding the smoking crater. Some brave soul, perhaps hoping to get a better look at the horror, shined a bull's-horn lantern at its eyes. It recoiled from this unwanted stimulus, making a great hooting cry which would be difficult to render phonetically. The creature ducked back into the cylinder, only to reemerge with a weapon of some sort. Suddenly a flash of blue lightning so intense that it made all the other light a darkness flashed from the weapon. Amidst the screams, Howard fainted.

When Howard returned to consciousness, it was a return from a dream of being medically examined by the panting, wheezing, fumbling, drooling Martians. He was—to his intense surprise—in his bed at 545 Angell St. Susan Lovecraft, his mother, was standing above him.

"I see that my little Abdul has wakened. I trust your materialism will be thoroughly shaken by the miracle which saved you from the Martians."

"Martians?"

"One edition of the *Gleaner* made it out before the terror disrupted the city. Everyone has fled. We, however, will remain until Grandfather Whipple comes for us."

Howard could begin to smell the burning city. His mother couldn't be this calm, if what she were saying was true. This must be some sort of game, like when she fixed an Oriental corner in his room when he took the name Abdul Alhazred when he was five. He would play along; after all there was the fact that he had arrived back at his home.

"You said something about a miracle?"

"The Martians killed everybody near the cylinder. Some men at the university watched it all with binoculars. One of the Martians climbed up the side of the church, to the bell tower's open window and pulled you out. It carried you down inside the cylinder. I suppose it thought you were one of their own. You are a very ugly child, Howard, people cannot bear to look upon your awful face. When the second cylinder fell, the Martians hurried out of the first to aid in the other's arrival. One of the brave men of the Brown Library, Armitage, I believe his name was, ventured all the way there to find you. He knew you because you had pestered him with questions on Cicero. You were there in the cylinder 'sleeping peacefully,' he said."

"How long?"

"You've been asleep three days."

There was something in his mother's eyes that wasn't right. Perhaps the "Martian" invasion had unhinged her highly strung nervous system. He must obtain nourishment and newspaper quickly, and then scout out the city.

"Could you bring the copy of the *Gleaner,* Mother?"

"Certainly, Howard."

The paper had huge headlines. EARTH INVADED BY MARS. The cylinders had fallen in London, Paris, St. Louis, even Texas.

How ironic, thought Howard, that the Martians would have chosen to land in the Italian section of Providence, since it was Giovanni Schiaparelli who had discovered Mars's canal system.

Mother brought him a sandwich for breakfast. The bread was stale and the house quiet.

He asked after his aunts.

Mother's face went blank and dreamy. "They've gone west to speak with your grandfather concerning the invasion. I believe they took the train."

Howard knew that one of the first things the Martians would have done would be to destroy trains, telegraphs, and roads. Mankind would panic if it lost its ability to reassert its pathetic reality by its continuous idiot god mutterings. What happy cows they would become in a few days, happy to be herd animals. He could feel the contempt he had seen in the three-lobed eyes of the Martian, a burning contempt that an older and more perfect civilization must feel against the apelike humans.

He would have to meet them again. He could feel a pull toward the cylinder near St. John's Church. An actual physical attraction like iron filings to a lodestone. Perhaps his mother was right and there was something in him that was like the Martians.

He began surveying the town from his window. Great paths of black ash cut obscene angles across the landscape. The Martians' traveling machines respected neither human habitation nor the barriers of river or hill. What marvelous creatures these Martians were to fashion machines to replace bodies. To become pure brains able to cross the cosmos! What starry wisdom they must have accumulated!

He saw the glint of metal, and reached for his telescope. A great walking machine was traversing Federal Hill moving toward St. John's. He could see the pit in front of the church quite clearly. A strange red vegetation covered the pit's sides. The red weed seemed to move slowly of its own accord, for surely no ash stirred with any breeze. The walking machine brought the Martian alongside the bell tower. The Martian placed a small golden box within.

At that moment his mother rushed into the room and pulled Howard from the window. She closed the curtains. She told him she was making hot chocolate. He should come to the parlor to enjoy some.

He felt sad for his mother, but guessed that it was perhaps a blessing that the human mind is unable to correlate its contents. Howard went down into the parlor and did partake of hot chocolate. His mother talked of trivial things as though no horror waited outside of the curtained windows.

Everything was still, very still, and Howard surmised that the city was deserted. Then a great ululation so horrible that surely no human mouth could utter nor mind conceive smashed the stillness of the air as a monolith of terror upon a plain of endless desolation. Mother nearly dropped her tiny white teacup, a proud relic of the family's past. Golly, thought Howard, something needs to be done. Mother talked rapidly and quietly. Once again the Martian cry resonated obscenely in the Terran atmosphere.

Howard excused himself. Mother didn't seem to notice. He went to his grandfather's medicine chest. Grandfather Whipple fought his pernicious insomnia with a powerful sleeping powder. Howard believed that he could easily mix it in the malted milk that his mother favored as an evening meal.

Waiting out the afternoon was torture. Something pulled Howard to St. John's Church. He could almost see the bell tower room when he closed his eyes. Knowing that the mystery was there was making him do and think things he had never thought. Mystery, he decided, was the great *transformatrice*. She effected a change in one's self by simply *being*.

The evening meal proved worse. He had had to argue with Mother so that he could prepare her malted milk. She would have to be sedated if he were to quest further. This time he must *not* faint and be subject to removal before viewing whatever horror his destiny had chosen for him.

Mother drank her malt. She joked gently that he did not know how to prepare it. He watched her carefully, making sure that she drank all of it rather than pouring it down the kitchen drain. She retired to the parlor afterward, where her fear kept her from lighting candle or lamp. As it grew darker, her words grew fainter and fainter. He listened long and hard to be sure that the whisperer in the darkness did indeed sleep, then tiptoed out of the house.

Outside deep twilight held the city in its gray-purple embrace. Only the topmost windows reflected the glorious sunset. The enchanting and beautiful twilight almost concealed the great ashen pathways of desolation that the Martians had left in their wake. Only one of the once many proud bridges still spanned the river. Howard began to run toward it. The sense of movement made him feel watched; Howard was the only thing moving on College Hill. The Martian's siege had stolen the comforting noises of the ancient city, leaving it as still as the vast void of darkling space through which they had traveled, and as foul smelling as the odor of plague-stricken towns and uncovered cemeteries.

As Howard crossed the bridge he looked upon the ancient city with eyes of memory preferring not to see the havoc of war. He looked upon the entrancing panorama of loveliness, the steepled town nestling upon its gentle hills.

Howard's run slowed to a panting walk as he climbed Federal Hill. When he reached the crater he near swooned from the Oriental sweetness that the undulating carmine growth censed through the still air, but the distant cry of a Martian, mixed with the terrified cry of the human herd, reminded him of his mission. He entered the dark church and made for the bell tower.

Beneath the bells, on a small table, the object lay. It was a garnet crystal in the shape known to science as a trapezohedron. It shone with faint ruddy light—the light of Mars, which the Babylonians (Howard reflected) called Nergal and the Northmen Tyr. By the small table stood a small chair that would exactly fit an eight-year-old boy.

He knew the shining trapezohedron must be the focus for some sort of communication. But could he withstand the daemonical truth such communication—dare he think it—*communion* could bring?

He reached out and picked up the stone. It tingled; some energy was contained within and began to have a direct effect on his nerves. At once he became aware of a vaster sensory range than his human evolution had prepared him for. Firstly the tiny chamber in the steeple, which had been fairly dark, now blazed with light. Secondly he could hear a sweet distant breathing or perhaps the sounds of flutes playing a magical but incoherent pattern. Thirdly he became aware—as much through the sense of *taste* as of sight—of a colour which floated in the air above him. He could not name this colour, it was not a colour of Earth, not belonging to the neat spectrum Newton's prism had revealed. This colour moved within itself, fashioning itself by rules not native to Earth, but of another part of space. It was sentient, and somehow *informed* or taught those possessed of it. It must be the medium through which the Martians communicated with one another. It sensed that Howard *sensed* it and it became violently agitated. Suddenly it shot a tentacle into Howard's brain. It pulled his soul free from its moorings.

For a moment he was suspended in the colour out of space. He could hear the colour, taste the colour, think *as the colour.*

The colour asked him, "Are you one of us?"

"I do not know what you mean."

"We prepared for the invasion by sending forth the minds of the greatest telepaths of our race. They dwelt among men as spies living in the bodies of men. Most returned to us, but some lost memory of their being enchanted by the revelations received in human flesh. Are you one of us?"

Howard did not know. He had felt that there was much from outside of the world of men in him.

The colour began to pulsate, pushing him along. He wondered that he had sensation separate from his body.

"You are in a body of your thoughts. When we have transported you to Mars it will be made semimaterial for two purposes. You will be able to handle and sense physical objects, and we will be able to examine your true mental form."

Howard considered that he might be a Martian. He had always felt that the day-to-day world partook of a phantom character. The only things that seemed real to him had been his dreams, certain tales in *The Arabian Nights,* and certain suggestions of a grander world which he saw in certain architectural features revealed in sunsets. Surely Mars was a sunset world, gold and red in its martial glory. What wonders a civilization older than mankind might possess. The colour, sensing his thoughts, began to show him images.

The "Martians" had come from another world to settle in this solar system. Eons ago they had crossed space in cylinders like those they had so recently employed. They settled upon Mars and Earth's South Pole. The latter colony had vanished, perhaps succumbing to the violent climatic changes that Earth had suffered. The former began a specialized eugenics program. Worshiping no god save their own intellects, they sought to eliminate all of the glands which cause emotion (save for fear, the emotion necessary for survival), and remove all enzymes which cause aging. The Martians had likewise eradicated all forms of microbial disease, leading to a practical immortality. The coming of immortality necessitated a specialized training of the will. The Martians had to cultivate those intellectual and aesthetic pursuits which could sustain an interest that would span the strange eons through which they would live.

This training of the will had an unexpected side effect; the Martians discovered that some of the stronger minds of their race could project themselves across the void without mechanical aid. These astral travelers came in contact with the various races of the solar system including the feebleminded men who dwelt upon the noisome green world of Earth and a race of what could be best described as fungoid beings inhabiting a planet on the rim of the solar system.

The Martians traded with the fungi, and Martian civilization reached its height of material prosperity. The Martians covered the ruddy surface of their world with labyrinthine Cyclopean structures, whose sole function was to express certain aesthetic, mathematical, or metaphysical formulae. The Martians waxed great in pride. Surely no race had reached such success.

This golden age gave way to a certain decadence. One of the first symptoms of this decline was a decrease in reproductive powers. The Martians had long since given up sexual reproduction in favor of a less distracting asexual budding. Fewer and fewer Martians came into being. Art became debased, and the objective art of the past was increasingly replaced by an outrageous subjectivity.

Perhaps the Martians would have gone into a long and steady decline had it not been for the discovery of the vast underground vaults at Syrtis Major.

The "Martians" discovered that uncounted eons ago, an almost godlike race had dominated their planet. The fungi confirmed this, claiming that they were in fact not dead, but had entered into a sort of undead sleep, waiting for a certain modulation of cosmos rays that would allow them to resume their play in glory and terror. The "Martians" were neither the oldest nor the last of Mars's masters.

Great energy was turned toward the excavation and destruction of the vaults, but despite their mighty heat-rays and lightning machines the Martians were unable to cut through the curious metal of the vaults. The dread of the creatures who would return was heightened by the discovering of their image carved into certain remote peaks which overlook the haunted deserts, whose baleful influence the Martians had shunned for millennia.

These elder gods with their long ghoullike face and star-destroying eyes were soon all the Martians could think of. For a season unreason held sway, and the normally logical Martians destroyed as many images of these horrors as they could find. But reason returned and the remaining specimens of statues were gathered at the capital, and controlled debate on the course of action began. A decision was made to invade Earth, and safely leave Mars for the elder gods.

A few minds had crossed to Earth to observe its affairs, and the Martians reasoned that he might be one of their own—since his mind had the strength to activate the shining trapezohedron.

The colour seemed to be exerting less pressure, and Howard realized that he would soon be on the surface of Mars. He had found his people. His long exile from those around him would be ended! Soon their superior skill in psychology and surgery would free him to walk among his own kind—his vast pulsating brain attached to the shiny metal machine!

Movement stopped and the unearthly colour began to fade. Howard found himself at the gates of a huge red building whose wings stretched in all directions—perhaps covering the planet. The slowly moving red weed covered the ground. From within he heard the mathematically perfect music of the Martians.

He went through the great gate into a hall filled with the great brains whose tentacles worked every strange device, whose construction clearly revealed their kinship to the technology which had produced the heat-ray. But as soon as Howard had entered the hall a great cry went up. The Martians were not shambling toward him in greeting as he had imagined. Instead they began a disorderly march to the exits. Howard looked about for the source of their fear.

There on the other side of the hall, through a trapezoidal doorway, came the figure of one of the elder gods. The Martians had not had time to relocate to Earth. Howard advanced toward the figure; perhaps he could slow its progress by engaging in hand-to-hand combat.

But soon came the shock that sent his mind hurtling back to Earth, a revelation about the nature of the elder gods and the time and form of their return. This shock deprived Howard of all clear memories of this adventure; indeed years later he was one of the skeptics who maintained that the Earth had not been invaded at all—for when he reached out toward the eldritch figure of the elder god, his hand had encountered *a cold and unyielding surface of polished glass.*

(For Pat Hardy)

Mark Twain

ROUGHING IT DURING THE MARTIAN INVASION

DANIEL KEYS MORAN AND JODI MORAN

> . . . this is a matter for thought, and for serious thought. And it is full of a grim suggestion; that we are not as important, perhaps, as we had all along supposed we were.
>
> —Mark Twain, "Man's Place in the Animal World"

We were on the open sea, returning from Britain; and despite the odd shower of meteorites we had seen over the previous week, nothing in our prior experience had led us to anticipate Martians.

"By God," the dwarf exclaimed, in an accent I had not heard him use before. "Would you look at that!"

I looked only at the dwarf, my eyebrows pulling together in a frown. We stood side by side at the forward bow of the *Minnehaha;* and we had been gazing, previously, at the dark smudge that would become New York City.

This is, I suppose, what comes of traveling in a ship called the *Minnehaha*. There had been nothing humorous about the trip and the only small thing I had encountered had been the dwarf.

"Ah." The dwarf resumed his phony accent. "You missed it. It is gone."

"You, sir, are a low-down dirty Cajun liar."

The dwarf, who went by the name of Francois Maitroit, turned to me. "And you are *not* a liar?"

"I'm a storyteller." I added quickly, lest the dwarf, a tricky fellow, try to equate "storyteller" with "liar," "I get *paid* for my stories."

Francois Maitroit's eyes twinkled. "To tell the truth, monsieur, I usually get paid for mine, too."

When the dwarf said "the truth," it came out as a flatly Louisiana Cajun "de trut," as opposed to the lisping Parisian "ze tooth" he had been using over the course of our two-week voyage from England.

I shook my head. "I'm baffled, Mr. Maitroit. Why would any man of worth choose to pass himself off as a bloody Frenchman?" I had, through much of the long ocean journey, suspected that the small man was some kind of con man—but by God, what was wrong with being an *American* con man?

"It's the British." The dwarf shrugged. "One makes far more money, dealing with the British, presenting oneself as a gentleman of noble French extraction, than one makes as a banjo-playing Louisianian dwarf—I've tried both routes."

From behind us, Livy asked, "You play the banjo?"

It was typical of my wife that she had ignored every other aspect of the conversation she had overheard; Francois and I turned from the railing. "All Louisianians play the banjo," Francois assured her.

"Of course they do." Livy smiled at the small man.

I did not much approve of the friendship that had sprung up between the Cajun and my wife. Other men's wives made friends with other men's wives, but not Livy. We were traveling together, we Clemenses, Olivia and myself and our daughters, the light of my life, Clara and Jean—and still Livy, in a spare two weeks, despite the attentions and company of our daughters, had arranged to take a liking to a four-foot-tall lying cardsharp of French descent.

Livy said to me, "*Did* you see that?"

"See what, my dear?"

"Well, it was like a spider, with very long legs, but made of metal, and it was skating across the top of the water."

"No," Francois answered for me. "He missed it. I *told* him to look, but he didn't."

"He's a willful man," Livy conceded. "Pity—it was skating quite well. Quite quickly."

I sighed. "I did not see it, dear."

"Oh, well." She smiled at me. "It was headed toward New York. Perhaps we'll get another chance to see it there."

————

We did not get another chance to see it there; in fact we never got to New York. A week later we were in New Orleans, and—

But I am getting a large step ahead of myself. I should explain; it is what I do, and I fancy I am good at it—explaining, that is.

Doubtless you know what awaited us. In the waters off New York we were privileged, if that is the word, to witness the final battle between the United States Navy and the invading Martians. It was short, it was awful, it was to the point. When it was over one surviving battleship steamed away into deep water—and there the Martians did not follow. (We did not know at that time, of course, that they were Martians.) Once the fight was done, and only the sinking hulks of the American ships were all that was left around them, the walkers turned back to shore—

The moment still grips me with a chill, when I think back upon it. We had thought them vessels, you see, seagoing constructs of one sort or another, though unfamiliar to us—

As they approached the shore, the walkers rose up out of the water— ten feet, twenty, forty . . . a hundred. They towered up over the sky-line of New York City, and stood before it as though they owned it. Then one of the walkers swung back out toward us—

"About!" Captain Davis cried. "Hard about!"

The *Minnehaha* steamed south.

Aboard the *Minnehaha* a tremendous argument raged. We had gathered in the main dining room—many of the sailors, Captain Davis and his first officer, and most of the male passengers.

"We are at war," Francois said. "We must learn more of the situation, and to do that we must go ashore!"

Captain Davis seemed personally affronted by the whole affair—he commented that we ought to have stayed in England, where we would have been safe. Then talk turned to the issue of assigning guilt. "The Spanish, do you think?"

"No." I lit myself a cigar, to give myself something to do—the captain edged away slightly. I shook my head. "If you live long enough, Captain Davis, perhaps your taste in cigars will improve—why, these are forty-cent cigars!" I drew on the cigar.

"Forty cents a barrel," said Francois. "I think it's the Germans—"

"The French," I said around my cigar. "And they're thirty-three cents a barrel, to come clean—that includes the barrel. I second the dwarf's plan—let's find a safe dock somewhere and go ashore, and find someone who knows something of these walkers."

"Did you see the damage those walkers caused half a dozen of the navy's best? How can you ask me to take a commercial vessel into *that?* I can't ask one of my men to go into that."

"I'll go," I said. "Have some courage, man! Let's go ashore and learn the facts."

"Mr. Clemens, you're sixty-five—"

"Sixty-four," I said dryly, "and not in my dotage yet; and I daresay this dwarf has the courage to brave the shore with me—"

The first officer, a strapping fellow name of Stephen Bradshaw, spoke up. "I'll go ashore with them, Cap'n. We'll get the lay of the land and report back promptly."

"If we're going to send anyone it ought to be some of the seamen—"

"No," I said, shaking my head, "that will not do; for when it comes to learning the truth, and reporting it flawlessly, they have not had my training."

Down around South Carolina we closed in on the shore again.

Walkers patrolled along the length of the beach. One of them turned toward us and strode out into the ocean, making a hooting noise that was eerie, indeed unearthly. Though we saw no weapon discharged toward us, the sea about us began to flash into steam, and then to bubble and simmer—

Captain Davis turned ship again and ran, with the boilers in the red.

At Florida we saw more of the Walkers, as we were now calling them, with the word audibly capitalized. One of the Walkers waded out into the water after us—and did not stop when its hood was at the level of the water. The hood dropped below the sea, and Captain Davis turned the ship and ran at full steam, a day and a night, into the Gulf of Mexico, before conceding we had outrun the beast.

Two days later we made port at New Orleans, at the mouth of the great Mississippi River.

It was plain, entering the harbor, that things were not well; the mouth of the river was choked by some terrible red growth, a growth that gave off a vile and somewhat decayed odor; the air above the city was smoky with burning buildings. Captain Davis sent the other passengers back to their cabins—I, trading shamelessly on my fame and age, convinced the captain to allow me to stay up top, though I sent Livy below with our daughters. Francois Maitroit simply took up position next to me, assuming, I imagine, that nobody would hustle him back to his cabin—no one did.

The harbor was empty of traffic; an astonishing sight. "I am of a mind to put back to sea," Captain Davis muttered to me. "But we are low on fuel, and will soon be low on food."

I watched the city. Buildings of wood were mostly burned down; the brick buildings were mostly still standing, though here and there they looked as though they had been smashed to bits with cannon fire.

We saw no Walkers. The ship held motionless, at the mouth of the Mississippi, boilers stoked, for half a day before Captain Davis had the temerity to make shore.

Over Livy's objections and the captain's dithering, Francois and Stephen Bradshaw and I went ashore in the French Quarter—in its original incarnation the Spanish part of the city. Bradshaw carried a rifle, and Francois a revolver; I declined a weapon.

"We'll be back shortly," I told the captain. "If you see signs of trouble, cast off; you're to take no chances with the lives of my wife and daughters."

The captain assented—a little readily, I thought, but just as well, in the circumstances; I could not much object to a coward of a captain, when that cowardice would protect my wife and daughters.

It was a hot day and sweltering, as sultry as only Louisiana gets at the height of summer, before we set foot on land. Our plans were not distinct; they involved finding someone still alive, and then questioning that person before he, or she, could be made otherwise by one of the Walkers.

The French Quarter stank. It always stinks, to give it its due justice, but this was a new stink, a different stink and highly improved; of decay and death, rather than the stench of perfume and rotting food. We walked down the center of the road. The wrecks of carriages were scattered here and there; the decaying bodies of dead horses were still yoked to a couple of them. The horses looked as though they had been burned—

"Fire," said Francois. "Fire everywhere. All the wood has burned, the brick is scorched and in some places melted—the city has been attacked by fire."

"The Germans," I conceded finally, "I think you are right. Not that the French would be above this; it is precisely the sort of crime those malignant little soldiers delight in; but the science behind this—the skill—it reeks of German engineering." We neared a cross street, and I slowed as we entered the intersection. For the first time we saw human corpses—fresh ones, dead no more than a day or so. Two adult men lay sprawled in the center of the intersection, one facedown, the other faceup. Both had been burned hideously—

The motion caught my eye, off to the north, and I turned to look.

It was the first Walker—the first Martian war machine, as we shortly learned—that we had seen up close. It walked on three metallic legs, and it was a hundred feet tall, with a hood-shaped platter atop it. It was a mile or more distant, I reckoned, and even at that distance it looked huge. It hesitated briefly, then seemed to catch sight of us and turned swiftly and began lumbering down the street toward us at an amazing speed, faster than any landbound creature I had ever seen—

It gave me an energy that would have astounded and delighted me, under other circumstances; it is impressive, the things a man can do with appropriate encouragement, even an old man such as myself.

We ran like the wind.

The dwarf ran remarkably well; he kept up with me easily enough. We ran south, and then cut east, out of the monster's immediate line of sight, looking for a place to hide; I knew that Francois and I could not possibly outrun that monstrosity; and Bradshaw was no longer an issue.

Bradshaw had left us, back at the intersection where we had first sighted the Walker; taken up his stance, and aimed his rifle at the approaching Walker. I glanced back over my shoulder, slowed to a halt, and yelled, "Bradshaw! Don't be—"

Something reached out and touched Stephen Bradshaw. It tore him apart and his blood sprayed twenty feet to splatter against my coat. In retrospect, sitting in the cellar with time to think about it, the moment seemed dim and blurred—the first officer coming apart like a mouse struck by the edge of a hoe. Even today, all these years later, I but barely remember the next few moments—we could hear the clang of the monster's metal feet moving down the cross street toward us, could see the flames dancing over what was left of Stephen Bradshaw, could smell Bradshaw's blood where it had spattered me—

"Here! In here!" Hands grabbed us and pulled us down into darkness.

In the darkness of the cellar I said, "Damn fool." I was so shaken I could not even think up anything witty to say, or even repeat a witticism stolen from someone else. I have seen men die before, some quantity, but not like that, not sliced in half by an invisible beam.

"Shhhh!"—came a fierce whisper in my ear. "Not a sound until it passes!" In the abrupt stillness I heard the clinking steps of the Walker—louder and louder, until each step sounded like sledgehammer blows against the surface of the cobbled city street. There came a huge sound then, an explosion that rocked the cellar and sent dust sifting down from the cellar's ceiling. An Irish-sounding voice whispered from somewhere off to my right, "Blew up the house next door, I bet," followed by the sound of flesh smacking flesh, and another "Shhhh!"

Some interminable time later, a candle was lit. I looked about the cellar and found myself in the company of a well-dressed Negro; a barrel of a man of perhaps fifty, Irish at a guess; a boy I guessed to be that man's son, and the source of the earlier whisper; and a beautiful dark-haired girl dressed in what I took to be Gypsy clothing.

A motley lot—I was extraordinarily grateful that I had left Livy aboard the *Minnehaha*—I know her, having been married all those long decades, and though she is a good woman, she would have taken to these people.

In short order the crowd had filled me in on the events of the last several weeks. The Gypsy girl started off. "First they came shooting out of the sky, crashing to the ground—one of them smashed the old St. Louis Hotel, and killed everyone in it, including a priest and two musicians. Martians, we were told, not long after that. Then they opened up and got up on their legs and started killing people. They had set fire to the remains of the hotel, and the firemen came to put out the fire; they slaughtered the firemen first—"

"Dreadful!" I exclaimed.

"Then the police came and they slaughtered the police."

"Indeed, indeed."

"Then the army came and they slaughtered the soldiers—"

"I see a drift here," said I, "a trend."

"Then the city government collapsed—"

"Fled," said the Irish boy—Paddy, a redhead of about fifteen.

The elderly Negro—well, about my age, which is elderly, in most men, those lacking my energy and charm—I do not mean to sound boastful, but my possession of those qualities is well known—this Negro said with a pronounced and attractive Southern accent, "Gone, sir, the police, the soldiers, dead or gone; indeed, most of the city has fled the city; I doubt there are five hundred humans left alive in all of New Orleans."

"The psychic pinhead," the Gypsy girl said in a profound voice, "predicted this. Back in early 1894."

I glanced at her sourly. "What psychic pinhead?"

"Oh, it doesn't matter." The girl waved an arm airily. "She's dead. Died in *late* '94."

Francois and I exchanged a look—we each recognized a liar when we were speaking to one.

"This pinhead," Francois asked. "Was she a Gypsy?"

"Oh, no, no, indeed not, Gypsies don't have pinheaded children. We're all especially good-looking."

I declined to comment on that—it was true enough, in this young lady's case; though I had known more than one ugly Gypsy, over the years. "So in 1894, this pinhead predicted that metallic monsters would take over the world at the turn of the century?"

"Well, no, she said Martians would *invade* at the turn of the century. The metallic monsters won't really take over for another few decades. And they'll come from Detroit, not Mars."

"They'll be rollers, not Walkers." That was Paddy again.

"I told him that," the Gypsy girl informed us.

"Talia thinks she's the source of all knowledge." Paddy sneered at the girl—she was probably only a few years older than Paddy, but was acting as if she were in charge of the whole cellar.

I tried valiantly to drag the conversation back on track. "Have you any kind of plan to deal with these beasts? Or are we merely hiding out until we're found and killed?"

"Don't be silly, man." The Irish father, one Mister Connor Turley, offered me a fierce look, augmented by a grandly fierce mustache—he would never have my hair or my brow, but one had to admire the facial hair. "This cellar is a hotbed of resistance," Mr. Turley continued. "We've brought down three of the devils already. In Ireland I fought the English; and here in this grand city of New Orleans, I'll fight the Martians to the death."

As the denizens of the cellar took a moment to appreciate this declaration, Paddy added, "*Their* death, he means"—evidently he didn't want anyone to think his father was contemplating either martyrhood or defeat.

"I hate the English," Mr. Turley added.

"They're a cheap lot," Francois concurred.

"I despise the French," I offered, and added, for Francois's benefit, "though Americans of French descent are rarely scoundrels. It's principally a cultural villainy." In another effort to stay on course, and to return to Livy and my daughters before some Martian fire-beamed them out of existence, I asked, "How exactly did you bring three of them down?"

"Well," said Paddy, "the first one we had help with—this Englishman, Christopher, decent sort for an English, he come up with the idea of digging a pit to catch one of them—then we painted a man and a horse, both of them, bright green, and when the Walker caught sight of them, off it went after them and ran across the hole we dug and fell in."

"And then a dozen *more* Walkers come along and slaughtered everyone who was involved with that," said the father. "We just barely got away."

"Since then," said the elderly Negro, in his deep, distinguished voice, "we've been using dynamite buried at the intersections, set off by percussion caps when the Walkers step on them—New Orleans is a dangerous place for tourists."

I eyed him. "I don't believe we've been introduced yet, sir—though you sound a native of these parts, unlike the others."

"Not quite—I was born a slave in the land of Georgia. Freed by Mr. Lincoln and given a job in the offices of this fine city."

"You're a clerk," I guessed, from the man's suit.

"I am a civil servant—Peter Grayson, at your service." The man's dark eyes gazed at me neutrally. "And you, sir, are Mark Twain."

"Samuel Clemens." I held out my hand and after a moment the other man took it. "And my companion is Francois Maitroit. We arrived by boat this morning, having crossed the Atlantic, and traveled down the coast and around Florida. Aboard the *Minnehaha*."

"Ah." Grayson smiled slightly. "Thus explaining the amusing small man."

"There's fewer than there was," said Connor Turley, speaking swiftly to cut off Francois's response. "Of the Martians, I mean. Must be some others been knocking them down as well—there was dozens of them roaming the city at one point, and now there's only just the few."

"I think they're sick," said Talia. "We've seen a couple staggering around, shooting at nothing—"

Francois glowered at Grayson, still smarting from the man's joke—he made a small gesture with the revolver. "*I'm* liable to shoot at something."

"I think," said I quickly, "we should go back to the ship."

"No! If—"

"No! We—"

"*No!*" said Grayson. "Not until dark, sir. Not until dark."

———

We waited in the cellar until dark fell.

I sat quietly for the most part, sick with worry—to be sure, I had faith in Captain Davis's cowardice, but not his competence; if one of the Martians attacked, who knew if the man would manage to get under steam in time? The *Minnehaha* had a pair of Gatling guns, and rifles and revolvers, but she was hardly a military ship, and I knew she wouldn't last long in a duel with one of the Walkers.

Only Francois managed to distract me from my worrying. He took me off in a corner and spoke in a low voice:

"The Walkers aren't the Martians themselves," Francois said. "So Paddy tells me—the Martians are inside them; the Walkers are just transportation."

"Of course," said I, "plainly the Walkers are mechanisms. So?"

"So," said Francois persuasively, "the Martians are *ugly*. Terribly, terribly ugly—tentacles and such—"

"Pretty bad."

"—green skin—"

"Indeed?"

Francois hesitated. "So Paddy tells me."

"He's Irish," I warned Francois. "They're known to stretch their details some."

"I adjusted for that—he says Martians are more frightening than a Christian Scientist working his theology—"

"I've had the honor of that sight—Paddy is wrong."

"—and uglier than a Capitalist."

"It seems extreme," I admitted. "Uglier than 'Jo-Jo the Horse-Faced Boy'; that sounds plausible, that sounds about right. You could put it on a poster. But uglier than a Capitalist . . . there would be skepticism, Francois, healthy skepticism."

"You know what we need?" demanded Francois. "Live specimens. If they *are* falling sick, if the invasion is failing—well, there's opportunity here, if we grab it."

"Grab a Martian, you mean. For display?" I said doubtfully. "I doubt it would pay, Francois. We might make a million, selling it to Barnum and Bailey perhaps, and that assumes no one else has had any luck getting himself a Martian to show, and that some circus, somewhere, will pay us what a Martian is worth." I shook my head. "The low level which commercial morality has reached in America is deplorable. We have humble God-fearing Christian men among us who will stoop to do things for a million dollars that they ought not to be willing to do for less than two million. In fact—"

"*No,*" hissed Francois, cutting me off, keeping his own voice low so that we would not be overheard. "Not one Martian for display—*two* Martians . . . a breeding pair." Even in the dimness of the candlelit cellar, I could detect the gleam in Francois's eyes. "A breeding pair."

I stared at him, a slow smile appearing below my mustache. *A dwarf after my own heart,* I thought.

I couldn't help thinking that it sounded like the setup for a joke, probably a poor one—what do you get when a Negro, two Irish, a Gypsy, a dwarf, and a world-famous writer go out for a nighttime stroll?

We did not stroll, in fact. We scurried. From place to place, cover to cover. My suit, my very good white suit, had been darkened with coal dust, and my long white hair blackened also. We made our way back to the docks without encountering another Martian, and my heart leapt at the sight of the *Minnehaha,* apparently unharmed, still tied up at the dock—

We ran down the dock, and arrived at the ship—I was out of breath from all the running and hiding, and had had about enough of it.

Only Captain Davis was up top when we arrived—the ship was darkened.

"Cast off!" called I as we crossed the boarding planks. "Cast off!"

Captain Davis sat on one of the deck chairs—he leaned forward. "Mr. Clem—Clem—Twain? Is that you, Twain?"

"Cast off, man! We're back!"

Davis shook his head gloomily, settling back into his chair. "I can't, sir. Can't do it, can't."

I could tell from the sound of the man's speech that he was roaring drunk, four or five sheets to the wind. I looked about—

"Where are the passengers? Where are the crew?"

"Oh, the passagers," said Davis dismissively. "They're b'low, they're alive, more or less." He raised a small flask to his lips, drank from it. "The crew, now, that's another story. Another story—"

"Where are they?"

"They fled!—the dogs."

"You impugn the dogs"—I said automatically—"noble creatures, dogs—and perhaps the men, too. To where did they flee?"

"They headed off along the coast, sir. For Alabama. They took the boats."

"You *do* impugn them," said I severely. "Their flaw was merely one of judgment, not character—they assumed Alabama was preferable to death. Promptly they learn of their mistake, they'll be back. In the meantime, we must sober you up, we've a project—"

By just the next day it was plain that the Martians had indeed fallen sick. The Walkers were seen less frequently—late that afternoon one of them staggered out onto the Mississippi, waded a ways into it, and then fell, and apparently drowned; at least it sank beneath the water and did not surface again.

The crew, having learned the truth about Alabama, returned to face the Martians the following day. Captain Davis seemed more relieved than angry, at the sight of them returning in the lifeboats. He lined them up for a speech:

"You have abandoned ship once or twice before this, most of you men. It is all right—up to now. I would have done it myself in my common-seaman days, I reckon, if I'd returned to the States to find Martians invading and the cities in flames. Now then, can you stand up to the facts? Are we rational men, manly men, men who can stand up and face hard luck and a big difficulty that has been brought about by nobody's fault, and say live or die, survive or perish, we are in for it, for good or bad, and we'll stand by the ship if she goes to Hell!"

The men gave up a tolerably decent cheer then, and the captain seemed to gain a little stature again with that; and added, "And there's a profit, too, men, Mr. Clemens swears it—"

There was a larger cheer at *that*.

The next morning we went out and captured a Walker.

That night was spent in planning—plotting and considering and devising, laying out tactics and strategies; schemes were proposed and modified and perfected, resources counted and estimated—no group of soldiers had ever gone about taking a city with more clarity of purpose than I and Francois and the captain and Peter Grayson and the two Irishmen and the Gypsy woman went about planning for the capture and care of a Martian breeding pair. We had plenty of dynamite, we had the ship's Gatling guns; we had twenty stout seamen who had been chastised by their failures in Alabama and were prepared to follow orders once more. The plans evolved and developed until it was clear that there were two plans with good support behind them; mine, which I supported, and Francois's plan, which everyone else supported. I proposed they dig a pit, and lead a Walker over it—with a green man aboard a green horse, as the Englishman Christopher had done earlier; I conceded I was not above appropriating someone else's good idea, though perhaps for variety's sake it would be better to paint the man, or the horse, or both, red or blue rather than green, the Martians having seen a green horse at this point. Francois accused me of plagiarism and suggested that we try lassoing one of the Walkers, using one of the *Minnehaha*'s two anchor-chains—how the lasso was to be thrown or made tight about the Walker was a minor detail, and not worked out yet. Finally Peter Grayson proposed we put the matter to a vote, and I pointed out that it was nearly daylight, and we had lost an entire night's pit digging; it wasn't safe to go digging in the daytime, I said severely, it wasn't fair to the seamen, brave fellows if a little unclear on their geography, to force them out to do hard manual labor on a sweltering Louisiana summer day—and with the threat of immolation from fire-beams on top of that, I added as it occurred to me.

The sky to the east was lightening with the first hint of morning when Francois suggested we put it to a vote. I lit a cigar to gain time—I knew a losing hand when I saw one; certainly the seamen weren't going to vote in favor of pit digging—

About twenty minutes after dawn a Walker fell over at the West End, not far from Lake Pontchartrain.

By midafternoon, scouring the city, we had found three fallen Walkers. There appeared to be none still moving. Whatever illness had struck them down had done likewise to the red weed that had so choked the Mississippi; the river was cleansing itself; clumps of the red weed were being torn free and deposited, as the river has always cleansed itself of that which it is not pleased with, in the depths of the Gulf of Mexico.

By evening we had cleared out a hotel on the banks of the Mississippi, and had eight living Martians behind bars—the sailors pulled them from their fallen Walkers, picked them up in canvas lifts, and transported them to the hotel in a sailor-drawn carriage, there being no horses alive that we had yet found.

It was my first sight of the Martians themselves—a thing no human who saw them, while they were still alive, is likely to forget. They were as ugly as their reputations—ugly as a Capitalist, and a sight uglier than Jo-Jo the Horse-Faced Boy had ever been. They have been described frequently enough since then, by a variety of word scribblers; I shall not waste time on it here, except in brief; grayish-green, with two sets of tentacles beneath the mouth; each of them was somewhat larger than a man.

I will mention their eyes at somewhat greater length. They were large and expressive; they seemed somehow both mournful and calculating, as though figuring the statistics on their situation. They were not human eyes, but there was no doubt in me that they were the eyes of sapient creatures, of creatures as intelligent as any man, including perhaps myself. When I met the eyes of the first of our captured Martians, I had the sense that I was meeting the gaze of a being wiser, and older, and colder, than any bishop who had ever lived.

Two of the sailors returned from their searching, near evening, with a story that caused us some concern. They claimed to have seen a pair of Walkers, their walking-legs bent double beneath them, kneeling at the edge of the Mississippi; and a vessel of some sort, half submerged beneath the river's flow, taking on half a dozen Martians, or more, all apparently healthy—they were not specific on this subject, due to the difficulty they had had, trying to observe while fleeing in the other direction.

By nightfall we had seven living Martians behind bars—by midnight it was down to six.

"It's the gravity killing them," Francois insisted. "I've read on this subject, Clemens, I tell you it's the gravity. Their world is colder than ours, and lighter."

I shook my head. "I grant you, the heat's not fit for man or Martian—but there's no electricity, Francois; I doubt there's a working ice-maker within a hundred miles of here."

"We could put one of the Martians in the river," Francois suggested. "Perhaps it would float, relieving the weight upon it?"

It drowned. We were down to five.

Two more died the following day. It left us with three.

I spent that night with the Martians.

The three of them looked listless.

They had trouble moving, and nothing I had arranged for them seemed to suit their appetites—they hadn't touched the beef, or the greens, or the beer, or the fruits or vegetables or eggs. I suspected that at least one of them had drunk some of the water—I'd drowsed, sitting in the padded chair the sailors had brought from the ship, and when I awoke, the water bowl was lower than it had been.

Watching them, I knew I had been a fool to think they could be bred; my optimism had gotten the better of me. I had no more idea if any two of them could make up a breeding pair than I'd have had dealing with snails, or sharks. "For all we know," I told Francois when he came by, near three that morning, "they are all three men, or women, or another sex entirely; perhaps they reproduce by division, or require ten mates—"

Francois nodded, and seated himself in the chair beside mine. We sat in a companionable silence, in the cool night air, watching the cage the three Martians had been imprisoned in. The Martians stirred occasionally, moving slowly and with evident pain.

"The sailors have ranged up the river a ways," Francois said at length. "They've found a steamship, run aground about six miles upriver. It's damaged some—"

It perked my interest. "Badly?"

"The texas deck is scarred by that weapon, they say, but otherwise it looks river-worthy." Francois looked at me sideways. "That bunch of Martians that headed upriver, Sam, they were healthy. So the men said."

"They did say that." I withdrew a cigar from its case, offered it to Francois—the small man shuddered and refused politely. I lit it slowly, turning it for a smooth draw. I had the distinct impression that the largest of the three Martians was watching me.

"It seems a long way to come, to die in a cage," said Francois.

I found myself gazing into the eyes of the large Martian, watching it as it died. "I would not feel too sorry for them—they are God's creatures, no doubt, as we are; and therefore doomed and without hope. If there is a Hell, and if they have the Moral Sense humans are blessed with, they will doubtless go there for their sins here on the Earth; if there is no Hell, then death is nothing but release, and they go into a great dark." I shrugged. "Hardly a thing to fear."

The large Martian crept forward a bit, and drank from the water bowl as I watched.

"Man is the Reasoning Animal," I said. "Such is the claim—I find it open to dispute, though. Any cursory reading of history will show that he is the Unreasoning Animal. It seems plain to me that whatever Man is he is not a reasoning animal. His record is the fantastic record of a maniac. These poor monsters had no chance—if the gravity and heat and disease had not killed them, we would have done it ourselves, I think."

"A riverboat, Sam," the dwarf said persuasively. "An empty riverboat."

"Fifty-five or -six years ago," I said softly, "it was my greatest ambition, as it was of all the boys in my village, to travel down the Mississippi—the majestic, the magnificent Mississippi, to escape Hannibal and ride down that mile-wide ribbon of water to the sea, to New Orleans."

"I've read your work," said Francois. "Most of it, I think, at one time or another."

I took a good drag, letting the smoke settle in my lungs. I spoke as I exhaled, and watched as the Martian drank again. "I expect they'll be dead before morning."

"I expect," said Francois, not taking his eyes from me.

I turned to examine him. "You want to go up the river."

"Yes, yes, I do," he said in that low, intense voice. "Let's take the guns from the *Minnehaha*, fix whatever's wrong with that riverboat the men found, and go after the Martians who fled. For profit, for revenge—"

"The river is beautiful in the summer," I said. "It's harder upriver than down, though; you must hug the banks to avoid the current. You'd need a pilot, a good one, navigating those shallows, and I confess, I'm a bit rusty." I let the smoke trickle through my nostrils—though I did not like to confess it, the idea appealed to me; there was a symmetry in it. That young boy had wanted to go down the river, had wanted it more than anything; and with the world as it was, unsettled and dangerous, and I an old man, I might never have another chance to navigate its waters—

"I'll do it," I said finally. "Let's follow them up the river."

The last Martian died just after dawn.

Joseph Conrad

TO SEE THE WORLD END

M. SHAYNE BELL

At Kinchassa, on the Kongo River, Kongo Free State, Africa, 1890. Ten years before the Martian Invasion.

The two Belgians stood to leave the hut. Carlier, a riverboat captain whose greatest skill lay in the unassisted consumption of bottle after bottle of Antwerp brandy, lifted back the hide hung across the opening for Camille Delcommune, Managing Director of the Great Civilizing Company. Carlier followed Delcommune out and let the hide flap back against the mud walls. I was too sick to follow them—and was not sure I would have followed them anymore had I been well.

They had brought me no water, food, or medicine. They let a fly into the hut, and I regretted that most of all. I heard it buzzing above me in the shadows, and I knew it would crawl on me. I was too weak to brush it off.

The Belgians must have thought I could not hear them. They stood just outside the opening and whispered about me. "Conrad will die in one or two days," Carlier said.

"Then he is a waste of time. Why does the company persist in sending frail wrecks to us? We need strong men for the work out here."

"He is not one of us," Carlier said.

Carlier was right. I had never been one of them: I had never wanted that. They started walking away. I called out to them for water, but if they heard me they did not slow their pace. "He'll cost the company plenty," Delcommune said, distantly. "He carries a manuscript of a *novel*, of all improbable things, that we'll have to send back with everything of his we decide not to keep. The weight of it will cost the company, and he'll leave us no money to cover the cost."

I listened to their retreating footsteps. If they came back, it would be only after a few days to see if I was dead.

I resolved not to give them that pleasure.

But I could do nothing to help myself then. I would have to help myself later. I felt sleep descending over me, and I could not move even to wipe the sweat out of my eyes or to brush the fly off my right arm. I would dream shortly, and I knew who I would see there. All the while I had had this fever in Africa, I had dreamt only of her.

Of my mother. In the dream that day, I was a five-year-old boy again, standing with Mother and our three trunks of clothes, blankets, dishes, and twenty-seven books on the steps of the way station in Vologda, Arctic Russia. It was the first day of hundreds we spent in that city so far from the Poland my parents had tried to free from Russia. The Russians had exiled Father, and Mother took me and we went with him into exile. A dense and shadowed pine forest surrounded Vologda, and the heavy scent of pines burned in the air. The muddy road lay rutted with wheel and horse tracks, and Mother pulled me back from walking in the mud to follow the meltwater that flowed in silvered streams down the tracks our carriage had left. Time passed, and the daylight waned. That far north, evening and night had no clear division. The day eased gently into a starry darkness.

The police had taken Father to question him and assign us a place to live. Mother and I waited for him in the cold. Snow fell lightly and dusted our trunks and my mother's black coat with white. We did not know what else to do but wait. We could not leave the way station without police permission, and we knew no one in Vologda. I asked Mother if she thought the Russians would keep Father much longer, but she did not answer me. She watched down the road for him.

I grew hot with fever and sat on a trunk. I touched the white snow on the trunk, and it melted on my fingers. I rubbed the cool water on my forehead.

And felt cool water on my forehead that day in Africa, and rough fingers there, brushing back my hair and dabbing water over my forehead, eyelids, and dry lips.

An old African woman had come to me. Her face looked kindly, but tired. "Water," she said, in French. She held up a gourd for me to see, as if I had not understood her one word. Water dripped down the sides of the gourd. I had gone a whole day without water. I tried to sit up, but she had to help me. I gulped down all the water, and the woman went to the river for more. I listened to the buzzing fly circle the ceiling of the hut, and I tried to see the fly, but it kept to the shadows above me. Suddenly, I heard not just the fly but the woman's breathing. She had returned, and I had not heard her draw back the skin and enter the hut. She dabbed more water on my lips.

"Did Monsieur Delcommune send you?" I asked. I thought the Belgians had sent her to help me.

"Your mother sent me," she said.

I did not understand. "Mother died in exile in Russia when I was six years old," I said. This African woman was somehow mistaken.

"Where are the Belgians?" she asked me. "Why are *they* not here to help you?"

"They did not send you?"

"Your mother sent me," she repeated, more firmly.

I could not understand and did not try, then. A sick riverboat captain would make the Belgians no money, and that is what they valued most: money. Money was the sum of their ethics. I did not tell the old woman that, or that the Belgians would not come back till I had died or gotten well. I was of no consequence to them sick.

For a time I could not speak to the woman at all. My thoughts came only in Polish, and this African woman spoke to me in French with an accent that made the French sound alien and exotic and I could not speak French then. But I could say one word I knew she would understand: the Lenje word for thank you. "Thank you," I told her. I must have said it many times, because she put her hand over my mouth to make me stop.

"I will come back to you tomorrow for your mother's sake," she said.

I will crawl to the river tomorrow for my own sake, I told myself. I will collect my own water, get well again, and go back to England.

I did not tell myself I would be going *home*. I had left home at five when Mother and Father took me with them into exile. I had had no home since then. The Russians did not know they sentenced me to a life of wandering when they exiled Father. I had lived whole years on the stateless sea.

When I opened my eyes again, the woman was gone. She had left feathers scattered around me on the floor in a pattern I could not discern: random groupings of four feathers with a sharpened stick placed across them. It was a protection. Evil would come to me from somewhere or some time counted in fours: four days, or four years, or from four lands away. Maybe she believed my fever would climax in four days: the stick warded away the coming evil, whatever it was or wherever it came from. I let the feathers and sticks lie where she had left them.

The fly buzzed around and around the ceiling. It never rested, but kept flying there, searching for what I could not tell.

I did not want to dream of Vologda again, but I did. Mother opened one of our chests and called me to her on the way-station platform. "Joseph," Mother said. "Let me wrap this around you, then sit here with me."

She wrapped me in a blanket and felt my forehead. It was night. The police had not yet let Father return to us.

The way-station attendant blew out the lamp in his office. We had sat in the light that shone in four squares through his one window, but now there was only light from the stars and snow. The attendant locked his door and walked up to us. He was a big man with a long, brown beard and strong arms and legs, yet he took soft, almost apologetic steps toward us, as if he did not want to startle us. I was not afraid of him.

"This interrogation is taking too long," he said.

Mother nodded.

"I have waited as long as I could. I will drive by the police station to tell them they must hurry this matter for your sakes. You need to get indoors out of the night."

"May we ride with you to the police station?" Mother asked.

The man looked about. Even as a child, I knew he must have been trying to decide whether the police would be angry with him if he helped us. "I will take you," he said finally, and he brought his wagon and drove us to the station. He did not just leave us there, but waited for us and Father, to drive us to our new house. I liked him even more. The police made Mother and me come into their building. The police did not look like good men. Father was not in the room they took us to. A policeman sat there at a desk we stood in front of. "What is your name?" the policeman asked me. He was young, maybe my mother's age, with black hair and a black mustache. I did not answer him. He looked up. "What is your name?" he asked me again. I could not answer him. I was too afraid to speak. He reached across his desk and shook me. "Where is my father?" I shouted.

I felt hands on my face, and looked up in shadows at an African woman's face above me. The policeman was gone. I knew I had been dreaming again, but the transformation in what I thought I saw was so sudden I lay there startled. The woman repeated a harmless question, but I could not answer her. "What is your name?" she asked me a third time, in French.

I shook my head.

"Try," she said.

I had to think: should I tell her my English name, the name I used because no one in the land where I lived could pronounce my Polish surname? Or should I say the Polish? I settled on that. "Joseph Korzeniowski," I said.

She did not repeat it. It seemed she had mostly wanted me to speak to her, that my name did not really matter. She kept her hands on my face. If she were blessing me, I needed her blessing. I let her keep her hands on me.

"What is your name?" I asked her.

"Sililo," she said.

I knew enough Lenje to know that her name meant *born during a relative's funeral*. "Who died when you were born?" I asked.

She took her hands away and looked at me. "Drink," she said.

She helped me sit up, but it was not water she gave me: it was dark tea with feathers floating in it and black bark on the bottom of the gourd. It tasted bitter and the liquid was gritty, but I drank what I could because it was liquid and cool, then I lay back down. She walked to the river to rinse the gourd, then filled it with water and set it next to me.

"Eat this," she said. She pressed a slice of African fruit to my mouth: something bright red, almost bloodred, and sweet. I did not know the name of that fruit, and I never saw it or ate it again after the day she fed it to me. So much in Africa was new to me: after six months I felt I was still getting only glimpses of the rich life it held. She passed me pieces of the fruit, and I ate them all.

"No one died," she said.

For a moment I did not understand what she was talking about, then

I remembered her name. "Why did your mother call you Sililo?" I asked her.

"A wise woman of my people held me first when I was born, before even my mother. She told Mother I would see the world die, so Mother named me Sililo."

I was quiet for a time. The wise woman had been, in a way, correct. The world Sililo had been born to was dying—was already dead in much of Africa. It had not been able to resist the coming of the Europeans. What had happened to her people was probably much like what had happened to mine when the Russians took over Poland. "What has happened to your family?" I asked her.

"The Belgians cut off my husband's ears because he did not bring them as much rubber as they wanted him to, though he is an old man. My son went with the Belgians up the river and has not returned. The son of my good friend who did return told me the Belgians cut off two of my son's left fingers because he ate a handful of the Belgians' food after he had gone three days without food. Last year, the Belgians took my two grandsons to the coast, and they have not returned. I must go to them."

I said nothing to her. I could think of nothing to say. We had too much in common.

"I must bring my grandsons out and follow my son up the river before the world ends," she said.

I looked at her. She did not think that all she had suffered in her land occupied by a foreign power was an end: the end she waited for was still to come. "What world will end for you, if it has not already?" I asked.

"This world where people do not live as they believe. A judgment is coming on all who live that way."

I thought how people had waited through all time for that day. I believed we had a long time yet to wait.

"I have listened to your missionaries," she said. "They talk of being kind to others, of treating others as you would want to be treated, but they and all the Belgians have not done that here. Your mother told me how the people with power did not do that in your land, either. The strong of this world do not believe what they say they believe: they have oppressed the weak, but soon they themselves will be oppressed. I must bring my grandsons out before then—with everyone else who will come with me—and go into the forest. Only there is safety."

"Why do you talk of my mother? She has never been here to speak with you."

"We talk in dreams. Your mother knows what is coming." Sililo pulled back the hide and walked out. The hide flapped back against the side of the hut. I lay there thinking of dreams and judgments and my mother who died in exile in a cold land, foreign to her, so many years before.

For two weeks, Sililo brought me water and food and blessings. My strength returned. Soon I could sit up without her help to eat and drink. When I could walk to the river, she stopped bringing me water but still brought food. She sat and talked with me while I ate. She did not have to do any of these things. She was just being kind, and I loved her for it, even if she claimed to speak to my dead mother and to know the future.

In those days of healing, I left my hut early in the morning to sit in grass on the riverbank before the heat of the day. Hippopotami wallowed in an eddy upstream. They grunted there, contented, like great pigs in mud. The far banks of the Kongo were dim and shadowy green.

One morning I fell asleep in the grass and dreamed the last time in Africa about Mother. It was the day the police forced Mother to leave her brother Thaddeus's, my uncle's, estate in Volhynia. The police had granted Mother a three months' leave to go there, and she had taken me with her. They ignored all pleas of her illness: she had to go back to exile with Father at the appointed time.

On that day, she whispered with Uncle Thaddeus in the long hallway, and they did not know I was on the stairs and could hear them. "I'll look out for the boy," he told Mother.

She said something I could not hear. Then Uncle Thaddeus said Father "might surprise us: he might live a long time."

"My son will," she said. "He will do great things."

They stepped quickly down the hall, and before I could move they saw me on the stairs. We looked at each other and said nothing at first, then I ran to Mother and hugged her. She and Uncle had been talking as if she and Father would die. I was too young then to understand all that that would mean for me, but I did not want to find out.

The dream shifted, and Mother and I were in the police carriage. Mother looked straight ahead, to hide her tears, but I turned around in the seat and waved at everyone standing in the driveway—Uncle Thaddeus, my cousin Josephine, and Grandmother, who had come from Polish Russia to see Mother.

Then Sililo walked onto the veranda, dressed in a white dress and red shawl.

"Sililo!" I shouted and waved, but she did not wave back. She looked worried and pointed up at the sky. I looked up and saw only the sun there, and clouds. She kept pointing up, and I watched the sky long after the carriage entered the main road and I lost sight of Uncle's estate and everyone Mother and I loved there.

I woke gently and looked at the sky and clouds. Mother died four months after the day I dreamed about. Father died four years later. I remembered Sililo's four feathers, and thought how my troubles had much to do with the number four. I heard the grass stir and looked. Sililo sat there. She held out a sweet fruit. "Eat," she said.

As soon as I could, I walked unsteadily into Kinchassa. I bathed in the Belgian compound. No one spoke to me. I said nothing to the Belgians. There was nothing more for me to say to them. I found Camille Delcommune sitting in his office cooled by fans circling in shadows above him. Flies flew among the blades, which struck the flies one at a time and knocked them dead onto Delcommune's desk and papers. He brushed them to the floor as they fell. Always, more flies replaced those the fans had killed. "We do not pay men for days spent sick in huts," Delcommune said, before I could say a word.

"Then I need the work the company promised me." I did not tell him I would work only as long as it took to save money to buy my passage to England.

"You were sick too long. I gave your commission to Captain Carlier. You must wait now till another appears."

I stared at him. The Belgians expected no new boats on the river for a year. I would be out of work that long.

"I will honor my company's contract with you," Delcommune said, "then."

I left his office without another word. I had money to buy a canoe and food, and did so. "There are the rapids below us!" said the man who sold me the canoe. "You will never reach the coast."

"I am a better captain than that," I said.

Sililo met me at the river, bundles in her arms. "I am sorry," I told her. "I did not know what was happening here in your country when I took this work. I will not stay another day in it."

"Take me to the coast," she said.

I took her arm. "I will help you free your grandsons from the Belgians."

"You will escape the coming judgment," she said.

I held the canoe while she climbed in, then I shoved it out on the river and jumped in. I was weak physically, but determined to leave.

The river lay dark and powerful before us. I felt the raw strength of it as the current seized the canoe and sped us west toward the coast.

I wanted Sililo to be right. I wanted a judgment to come on the strong of our world, a judgment that, like this river, would bear all the oppressed away to a better place and leave behind, irrelevant, the oppressors.

Ten years later at Matadi, the mouth of the Kongo River, Kongo Free State, 1900. Four weeks after the Martian Invasion drove us from England.

Only the darkness of a new moon saved us. Matadi lay black and quiet, and as we first steamed toward it we thought the city government might have ordered all lights out at night to not attract Martians—but we had not expected Martians in this part of Africa yet.

Jessie, my English wife of four years, took my hand. "We have come so far," she said. We spoke softly.

I turned to the men around me. "Cut the engines," I said. Two men rushed to do so. The sudden quiet seemed at once more ominous and more convincing of danger near us. Matadi lay utterly quiet. Not even a dog barked there. No birds called from treetop nests. The air was thick with smoke, though the city had not burned.

"Let the ship drift back into the shadows," I said. "We'll anchor under the trees."

Sudden movement, if the Martians had observed us, would prove our end. Movement attracted them, and they could move quickly to attack, even through the sea—this river would mean nothing to them. One week before, we had seen two of their great craft stride out through the deepening sea from São Tiago, in the Cape Verde Islands, to train their heat-rays on the hundreds of vessels fleeing south from Europe. That we did not die then was not from lack of trying on the Martians' part: they burned the Portuguese *Mãe de Deus* sailing slightly ahead of us, then a French warship heading north probably to protect France itself, and the sudden cloud of smoke from the two doomed vessels rose up to hide us from the Martians, who turned to fire on ships behind us.

We rescued five men from the Portuguese ship—the only survivors to escape before it sank—and sailed on. The Martians did not pursue us. We found Accra and Lagos brightly lit and alive—and panicked at reports of Martians in the Sahel, Martians at sea, Martians in the Ethiopian uplands and heading west. No one knew where to run to escape them.

Except me. I remembered Sililo's words: "I must bring my grand-sons out before [the world ends] and go into the forest. Only there is safety." And I remembered her feathers placed to protect me from something to do with the number four: when I first read about the Martian Invasion, all I could think of was that Mars is the fourth world from the sun. When it came time for us to flee, I found work on a ship in Dover and brought my Jessie, little Borys—then only two years old—and all these others from dying England to a place I knew filled with fevers, and disease of all kinds, yet rife with a vigorous life hidden under vast forests—and one woman who had maybe seen what was coming and thought her great forest would protect us.

With Sililo, or at least in her forest, we might survive for a time. That had been my hope.

We floated under a canopy of great trees spreading out over the river and gently lowered the anchor. The ship ceased all movement. The night was very still. I felt water on my face, then on my arm. I looked at the branches above us, and saw clouds moving above them, blowing in from sea. Rain spattered the surface of the river. Everyone pulled on coats and hats or took cover. Jessie touched my arm. "There," she said, pointing.

Starlight glinted off the gleaming metal of a Martian machine strid-ing toward Matadi from upriver. It explained the city's silence. The Martians had undoubtedly sprayed their black smoke over Matadi. Nothing lived there now.

If the Martian had seen us or heard us, we would not have lived long either.

Everyone on board stepped quietly to the railing to watch. The Mar-tian stopped in the harbor and rotated there, surveying the black land. Its heat-ray pointed at us, then swung away in a wide arc, burning nothing. It must have heard us, but evidently could not detect us now. It stood there waiting, I believed, for us to move. It could wait there till first light, I realized, when it would see us under the shadows.

Yet we could not move. Distinct sound would bring it upon us, and everyone there understood that. No one on deck moved. I heard water lap against the side of our ship, and the falling rain, and nothing more for some time. Perhaps the Martian will go back upriver from where it had come, from whatever work we had stopped it from rushing toward, I thought. If it left, we could slip back out to sea and wait there—for what I did not know. We had nowhere to run now.

"Joseph."

Someone spoke my name. I looked around. Everyone on deck looked back at me, wondering. "Joseph," the voice said again.

The voice came from shore. I walked to the shoreward railing and looked into the shadows under the trees there. I saw nothing distinguishable in the deep blackness—then a flash of white, the sound of movement in the water, the dipping of paddles—and a canoe gliding up to our ship. Sililo sat in it, dressed in a white robe, with men around her guiding the canoe. I recognized her two grandsons from the day I helped them escape the Belgians; I thought the man without fingers on his left hand must be her son.

"I came back for you," she said.

I did not question how she knew I would come. We spoke softly, and the rain covered the sound. "I remembered your words," I said.

"Bring your people," she said. "And bring your writings. Come with me to see the world end."

For her the end had not *yet* come: London destroyed, Paris— probably Brussels. Matadi a lifeless shell, and still she waited for the true end of the world. I could not imagine what she thought it would be.

I took off my shoes, tied the laces together, and hung them around my neck. Everyone on deck did the same. Three or four of us at a time stepped quietly into the wooden canoe and went to shore. After a time, all seventy-nine of us were walking in the great forest away from the Martian. No one spoke. I carried my writings, as Sililo had asked: an unpublished manuscript about her land, *Heart of Darkness;* an unfinished novel, *Lord Jim,* among others. I felt the pages expanding in the humidity, and when I touched them the ink smeared. I did not know if I could preserve them—or if it mattered anymore.

Sililo seemed in no hurry. She led us at a leisurely pace, walking arm in arm with Jessie and carrying Borys for a time. With dawn we saw what the Martians had done to her land. They had burned away vast stretches of forest. Sililo led us along a sooty trail, stopped above a ravine, and pointed into it: a downed Martian machine boiled there, steam still rising from where it lay, its feet caught in vines and logs. "They can't walk through the forest," she said. "They tried burning a way through, but it was too slow. They walk up the rivers, but we keep a watch and move back from them. They have not gone past the rapids yet."

We walked on, hidden under a leafy canopy, into the heights the

Kongo flowed through, past the rapids Sililo and I had fought our way through ten years before. In breaks in the forest, we looked out over the broad land below, smoky with the Martians' fires. Smoke wafted out over the sea and obscured the great river. It was a surreal walk that day, with an old woman I somehow expected to meet here.

"You have a part to play in the world's end, Joseph," she told me. She touched my manuscripts, and I wondered.

After two weeks of walking, we climbed a hill and saw Kinchassa. The Martians had not reached it yet, as Sililo had said. The city had grown in the ten years since I left Africa, blighting the land along the river with the temporary shacks of Europeans come here for money and nothing else. Vast though it was, it seemed impermanent. This cannot last, I thought.

Kinchassa was filled with Europeans anxious for any news we brought from Europe, none of it good. Camille Delcommune still worked there. He looked at me through jaundiced eyes. "Africa almost killed you before," he said. "Death drew you back, for certainly the Martians follow you."

But they did not. I had hoped to go on into the forest, but the Africans let no European leave Kinchassa. Thousands of Africans surrounded the city, camped in armed groups, and they brought from upriver every Belgian.

"You have been like Martians to us," Sililo told them. "When they have gone, you must go."

When she said that, I began to understand how the world would end. I worried that the Belgians would panic and fight, and tried to shame them from it. I told anyone who would listen the stories of what the Russians had done to my family and to Poland. Others told similar stories—a man from Alsace-Lorraine, a Moroccan trader whose family remembered Andalucía, a German Jew with grandparents murdered in a pogrom. Some read *Heart of Darkness* in manuscript, turning the pages carefully to keep the ink from smearing, and afterward they looked at the Africans among us, troubled.

We knew the Martians, after all. We knew them well. They did no new thing among us, and to them all the great nations meant nothing more than Poles, Jews, Moors, or Africans had meant: the Belgians, English, Chinese, and Russians were now peoples to be swept aside. I began to hope that the shock of what the Martians had done to us was so great that, if we somehow survived, we could no longer treat each other that way. The world would truly have ended then, for the Earth would be a new place.

Four weeks later, Kinchassa, Kongo, 1900. After Earth's bacteria killed the Martians.

Sililo came to me early in the morning. "It is over," she said. "The Martians are dead, and all of you must go now."

Twenty of us followed her to the coast to see. We found the Martians rotting in their machines, a vast destruction along the coast. Everywhere the forest had been burned. The European cities were leveled, but under trees near Matadi I found the boat, undamaged. We flagged a passing ship, whose captain told us the same thing had happened in South Africa and Angola. We could only assume it had happened, or was happening, everywhere.

We hurried back to Kinchassa, for the last time. I took Borys in my arms when I got there. "Come out," I said to the Europeans. "The world we knew has ended. A better one must now be born."

Some followed Sililo and me to the coast because they were ashamed of what men had done to each other and knew it must stop. Others came because the Africans surrounded them by the thousands, but they all came.

The land was healing as we walked through it. Green grass rushed up through the ashes, and everywhere flowers bloomed. We made temporary camp on the coast, and shortly I took the first boatload of Belgians back to Ostend.

Sililo stood with Jessie and me that morning, and she held Borys for the last time and smiled at us all. "The world has ended," she said.

"I hope so," I said.

"You will see. The Belgians are first to change. Your England will follow, then all others."

She handed Borys to Jessie, and we boarded the ship.

Near Berdichev, Poland, 1908. Eight years after the Martian Invasion.

I almost wrote that the new world was born more quickly than Sililo could have imagined, but she somehow knew so much that I doubt that. Jessie spent our first weeks back recopying my manuscripts, trying to reconstruct pages damaged in the tropical wetness, while I wrote accounts of Sililo and what we had seen in Africa. My stories played a part in the Great Change, and the stories of all the oppressed played their part and sundered the world from its violent past. Earth is not perfect yet—there are still many wrongs to right—but in the years since the Martian Invasion, I have wondered what this world would have been like, what horrors it would have known, if the Martians had not come to shame us into living according to our highest ideals.

Jessie and I live most of the year in rebuilt London, where I sit as free Poland's delegate to the Council of Earth, but we have a house in Poland, outside Berdichev, near the house my parents rented when I was born. The first night in that house, I dreamt of Mother.

She held Borys and walked with me along a quiet road shaded by tall trees, and I remembered in that dream that when I was a baby she walked with me there often. Now I was a man taller than she. She smiled and took my hand, and we came to a place in the road that led down to a beautiful valley and the white houses there. Not far down the road, Sililo stood with Father, Grandmother, Uncle Thaddeus, and so many others I had loved and lost to death.

"I want to go with you," I told Mother.

She kissed Borys and handed him to me. "Take your son back to the new world," she said. I watched her walk to Father and Sililo and all the others, and they went on into their beautiful valley. I turned with Borys to go back and saw that the valley behind us had become just as beautiful.

Jack London

AFTER A LEAN WINTER

DAVE WOLVERTON

Pierre swept into Hidden Lodge on Titchen Creek late on a moonless night. His two sled dogs huffed and bunched their shoulders, then dug their back legs in with angry growls, hating the trail, as they crossed that last stubborn rise. The runners of his sled rang over the crusted snow with the sound of a sword being drawn from its scabbard, and the leather harnesses creaked.

The air that night had a feral bite to it. The sun had been down for days, sometimes hovering near the horizon, and the deadly winter chill was on. It would be a month before we'd see the sun again. For weeks we had felt that cold air gnawing us, chewing away at our vitality, like a wolf pup worrying a shard of caribou bone long after the marrow is depleted.

In the distance, billowing thunderclouds raced toward us under the glimmering stars, promising some insulating warmth. A storm was chasing Pierre's trail. By agreement, no one came to the lodge until just before a storm, and none stayed long after the storm began.

Pierre's two poor huskies caught the scent of camp and yipped softly. Pierre called "Gee," and the sled heeled over on a single runner. Carefully, he twisted the gee-poles, laid the sled on its side next to a dozen others. I noted a heavy bundle lashed to the sled, perhaps a moose haunch, and I licked my lips involuntarily. I'd pay well for some meat.

From out under the trees, the other pack dogs sniffed and approached, too tired to growl or threaten. One of Pierre's huskies yapped again, and Pierre leapt forward with a dog whip, threatening the lean beast until it fell silent. We did not tolerate noise from dogs anymore. Many a man would have pulled a knife and gutted that dog where it stood, but Pierre—a very crafty and once prosperous trapper— was down to only two dogs.

"S'okay," I said from my watch post, putting him at ease. "No Martians about." Indeed, the frozen tundra before me was barren for miles. In the distance was a meandering line of weazened spruce, black in the starlight, and a few scraggly willows poked through the snow along the banks of a winding frozen river just below the lodge. The distant mountains were dark red with lush new growth of Martian foliage. But mostly the lands were snow-covered tundra. No Martian ships floated cloudlike over the snowfields. Pierre glanced up toward me, unable to make out my form.

"Jacques? Jacques Lowndunn? Dat you?" he called, his voice muffled by the wolverine-fur trim of his parka. "What news, my fren'? Eh?"

"No one's had sight of the bloody-minded Martians in two weeks," I said. "They cleared out of Juneau."

There had been a brutal raid on the town of Dawson some weeks before, and the Martians had captured the whole town, harvesting the unlucky inhabitants for their blood. We'd thought then that the Martians were working their way north, that they'd blaze a path to Titchen Creek. We could hardly go much farther north this time of year. Even if we could drag along enough food to feed ourselves, the Martians would just follow our trail in the snow. So we dug in, holed up for the winter.

"Ah 'ave seen de Marshawns. Certayne!" Pierre said in his nasal voice, hunching his shoulders. He left the dogs in their harness but fed them each a handful of smoked salmon. I was eager to hear his news, but he made me wait. He grabbed his rifle from its scabbard, for no one would walk about unarmed, then forged up toward the lodge, plodding toward me through the crusted snow, floundering deeper and deeper into the drifts with every step, until he climbed up on the porch. There was no friendly light behind me to guide his steps. Such a light would have shown us up to the Martians.

"Where did you spot them?" I asked.

"Anchorawge," he grunted, stamping his feet and brushing snow out of his parka before entering the warmer lodge. "De citee ees gone, Jacques—dead. De Marshawns keel everybawdy, by gar!" He spat in the snow. "De Marshawns es dere!"

Only once had I ever had the misfortune of observing a Martian. It was when Bessie and I were on the steamer up from San Francisco. We'd sailed to Puget Sound, and in Seattle we almost put to port. But the Martians had landed, and we saw one of their warriors wearing a metal body that gleamed sullenly like polished brass. It stood watch, its curved protective armor stretching above its head like the chitinous shell of a crab, its lank, tripod metal legs letting it stand gracefully a hundred feet in the air. At first, one would have thought it an inanimate tower, but it twisted ever so insignificantly as we moved closer, regarding us as a jumping spider will a gnat, just before it pounces. We notified the captain, and he kept sailing north, leaving the Martian to hunt on its lonely stretch of beach, gleaming in the afternoon sun.

Bessie and I had thought then that we would be safe back in the Yukon. I cannot imagine any other place than the land near the Circle that is quite so relentlessly inhospitable to life, yet I am intimate with the petty moods of this land, which I have always viewed as something of a mean-spirited accountant which requires every beast upon it to pay his exact dues each year, or die. I had not thought the Martians would be able to survive here, so Bessie and I took our few possessions and struck out from the haven of San Francisco for the bitter wastes north of Juneau. We were so naive.

If the Martians were in Anchorage, then Pierre's tidings were mixed. It was good that they were hundreds of miles away, bad that they were still alive at all. In warmer climes, it was said, they died quickly from bacterial infections. But that was not true here by the Circle. The Martians were thriving in our frozen wastes. Their crops grew at a tremendous rate on any patch of frozen windswept ground—in spite of the fact that there was damned little light. Apparently, Mars is a world that is colder and darker than ours, and what is for us an intolerable frozen hell is to them a balmy paradise.

Pierre finished stamping off his shoes and lifted the latch to the door. Nearly everyone had already made it to our conclave. Simmons, Coldwell, and Porter hadn't shown, and it was growing so late that I didn't anticipate that they would make it this time. They were busy with other affairs, or the Martians had harvested them.

I was eager to hear Pierre's full account, so I followed him into the lodge.

In more congenial days, we would have had the iron stove crackling merrily to warm the place. But we couldn't risk such a comforting blaze now. Only a meager lamp consigned to the floor furnished any light for the room. Around the lodge, bundled in bulky furs in their unceasing struggle to get warm, were two dozen stolid men and women of the North. Though the unending torments of the past months had left them bent and bleak, there was a cordial atmosphere now that we had all gathered. A special batch of hootch warmed on a tripod above the lamp. Everyone rousted a bit when Pierre came through the door, edging away enough to make room for him near the lamp.

"What news?" One-Eyed Kate called before Pierre could even kneel by the lamp and pull off his mittens with his teeth. He put his hands down to toast by the glass of the lamp.

Pierre didn't speak. It must have been eighty below outside, and his jaw was leather-stiff from the cold. His lips were tinged with blue, and ice crystals lodged in his brows, eyelashes, and beard.

Still, we all hung on expectantly for a word of news. Then I saw his mood. He didn't like most of the people in this room, though he had a warm spot in his heart for me. Pierre had Indian blood on his mother's side, and he saw this as a chance to count coup on the others. He'd make them pay for every word he uttered. He grunted, nodded toward the kettle of hootch on the tripod.

One-Eyed Kate herself dipped in a battered tin mug, handed it to him. Still he didn't utter a word. He'd been nursing a grudge for the past two months. Pierre Jelenc was a trapper of almost legendary repute here in the North, a tough and cunning man. Some folks down at the Hudson Bay Company said he'd devoted a huge portion of his grub-stake to new traps last spring. The North had had two soft winters in a row, so the trapping promised to be exceptional—the best in forty years.

Then the Martians had come, making it impossible for a man to run his traplines. So while the miners toiled in their shafts through the dark winter, getting wealthier by the minute, Pierre had lost a year's grub-stake, and now all of his traps were scattered in their line, hundreds of miles across the territory. Even Pierre, with his keen mind, wouldn't be able to find most of those traps next spring.

Two months ago, Pierre had made one desperate attempt to recoup his losses here at Titchen lodge. In a drunken frenzy, he started fighting his sled dogs in the big pit out behind the lodge. But his dogs hadn't been eating well, so he couldn't milk any fight out of them. Five of his huskies got slaughtered in the pit that night. Afterward, Pierre had left in a black rage, and hadn't attended a conclave since.

Pierre downed the mug of hootch. It was a devil's concoction of brandy, whiskey, and hot peppers. He handed the cup back to One-Eyed Kate for a refill.

Evidently, Dr. Weatherby had been reading from an article in a newspaper—a paper nearly three months old out of southern Alberta.

"I say, right then," Dr. Weatherby said in a chipper tone. Apparently he thought that Pierre had no news, and I was of a mind to let Pierre speak when he desired. I listened intently, for it was the doctor I had come to see, hoping he would be able to help my Bessie. "As I reported, Dr. Silvena in Edmonton thinks that there may be more than the cold at work here to help keep the Martians alive. He notes that the 'thin and rarefied air here in the North is more beneficial to the lungs than air in the South, which is clogged with myriad pollens and unhealthy germs. Moreover,' he states, 'there seems to be some quality to the light here in the far North that causes it to destroy detrimental germs. We in the North are marvelously free of many plagues found in warmer lands—leprosy, elephantiasis, and such. Even typhoid and diphtheria are seldom seen here, and the terrible fevers which rampage warmer climes are almost unknown among our native Inuit.' He goes on to say that 'Contrary to speculation that the Martians here will expire in the summer when germs are given to reproduce more fervently, it may be that the Martians will hold forth on our northern frontier indefinitely. Indeed, they may gradually acclimatize themselves to our air, and, like the Indians who have grown resistant to our European measles and chicken pox, in time they may once again venture into more temperate zones.'"

"Not a'fore bears grow wings," Klondike Pete Kandinsky hooted. "It's cold enough to freeze the balls off a pool table out thar this winter. Most like, we'll find them Martians all laid out next spring, thawing in some snowbank."

Klondike Pete was behind the times. Rumor said that he'd struck a rich vein in his gold mine, so he'd holed up in the shaft, working eighteen-hour days from August through Christmas, barely taking time to come out for supplies. He hadn't attended our previous conclaves.

"Gads," Dr. Weatherby said, "I say, where have you been? We believe that the Martians came here because their own world has been cooling for millennia. They're seeking our warmer climes. But just because they are looking for warmer weather, it doesn't mean they want to live on our equator! What seems monstrously cold to us—that biting winter that we've suffered through this past three months—is positively balmy on Mars! I'm sure they're much invigorated by it. Indeed, the reason we haven't seen more of the Martians here in the past weeks seems blatantly obvious: they're preparing to migrate north, to our polar cap!''

"Ah, gods, I swear!" Klondike Pete shook his head mournfully, realizing our predicament for the first time. "Why don't the army do somethin'? Teddy Roosevelt or the Mounties ought to do somethin'."

"They're playing at waiting," One-Eyed Kate grumbled. "You know what kinds of horrors they've been through down south. There's not much the armies of the world can do against the Martians. Even if they could send heavy artillery against the Martians in the winter, there's no sense in it—not when the varmints might die out this coming spring, anyhow."

"There's sense 'n it!" one old-timer said. "Folks is dyin' up here! The Martians squeeze us for blood, then toss our carcasses 'way like grape skins!"

"Yeah," One-Eyed Kate said, "and so long as it's the likes of you and me that are doing the dying, Tom King, no one will do more than yawn about it!"

The refugees in the room looked around gloomily at one another. Trappers, miners, Indians, crackpots who'd fled from the world. We were an unsavory lot, dressed in our hides, with sour bear grease rubbed in our skin to keep out the weather. One-Eyed Kate was right. No one would rescue us.

"I just whist we 'ad word on them Martians," old Tom King said, wiping his nose on the sleeve of his parka. He looked off into a corner with rheumy eyes. "No news is good news," he intoned, the hollow-sounding supplication of an atheist.

None of us believed the adage. The Martian vehicles that fell in the southern climes were filled only with a few armies and scouts. Thirty or forty troops per vehicle, if we judged right. But now we saw that these were only the advance forces, hardly more than scouts who were meant, perhaps, to decimate our armies and harass the greater population of the world in preparation for the most massive vehicle, the one that fell two months later than the rest, just south of Juneau. The mother ship had carried two thousand Martians, some guessed, along with their weird herds of humanoid bipeds that the Martians harvested for blood. The mother vehicle had hardly settled when thousands of their slaves swarmed out of the ships and began planting crops, scattering otherworldly seeds that sprouted nearly overnight into grotesque forests of twisted growths that looked like coral or cactuses, but which Dr. Weatherby assured us were more likely some type of fungus. Certain of the plants grew two hundred yards high in the ensuing month, so that it was said that now, one could hardly travel south of Juneau in most places. The "Great Northern Martian Jungle" formed a virtually impenetrable barrier to the southlands, a barrier reputed to harbor Martian bipeds who hunted humans so that their masters might feast on our blood.

"If no news is good news, then let us toast good news," Klondike Pete said, hoisting his mug.

"Ah've seen dem Marshawns," Pierre said at last. "En Anchorawge. Dey burned de ceety, by *gar*, and dey are building, building—making new ceety dat is strange and wondrous!"

There were cries of horror and astonishment, people crying out queries. "When, when did you see them?" Dr. Weatherby asked, shouting to be heard above the others.

"Twelve days now," Pierre said. "Dere is a jungle growing around Anchorawge now—very thick—and de Marshawns live dere, smelting de ore day and night to build dere machine ceety. Dere ceety—how shall I say?—is magnificent, by *gar*! Eet stands five hundred feet tall, and can walk about on eets three legs like a walking stool. But is not a small stool—is huge, by *gar*, a mile across!

"On de top of de table is huge glass bowl, alive with shimmering work-lights, more varied and magnificent dan de lights of Paris! And under dis dome, de Marshawns building dere home."

Dr. Weatherby's eyes opened wide in astonishment. "A dome, you say? Fantastic! Are they sealing themselves in? Could it keep out bacteria?"

Pierre shrugged. "Ah 'uz too far away to see dis taim. Some taim, maybe, Ah go back—look more closer. Eh?"

"Horsefeathers!" Klondike Pete said. "Them Martians couldn't raise such a huge city in two months. Frenchie, I don't like it when some pimple like you pulls my legs!"

There was an expectant hush around the room, and none dared intervene between the two men. I think that most of us at least half believed Pierre. No one knew what the Martians were capable of. They flew between worlds and built killing death rays. They switched mechanical bodies as easily as we change clothes. We could not guess their limitations.

Only Klondike Pete here was ignorant enough to doubt the Frenchman. Pierre scowled up at Pete. The little Frenchman was not used to having someone call him a liar, and many honest men so accused would have pulled a knife to defend their honor. A fight was almost expected, but in any physical contest, Pierre would not equal Klondike Pete.

But Pierre obviously had another plan in mind. A secretive smile stole across his face, and I imagined how he might be plotting to ambush the bigger man on some dark night, steal his gold. So many men had been taken by the Martians, that in such a scenario, we would likely never learn the truth of it.

But that was not Pierre's plan. He downed another mug of hootch, banged his empty mug on the lid of the cold iron stove at his side. Almost as if magically summoned, a blast of wind struck the lodge, whistling through the eaves of the log cabin. I'd been vaguely aware of the rising wind for the past few minutes, but only then did I recognize that the full storm had just hit.

By custom, when a storm hit we would set a roaring blaze and lavish upon ourselves one or two hours of warmth before trudging back to our own cabins or mine shafts. If we timed it properly, the last of the storm would blanket our trail, concealing our passage from any Martians that might fly over, hunting us.

Still, some of us were clumsy. Over the past three months, our numbers had been steadily diminishing, our people disappearing as the Martians harvested us.

My thoughts turned homeward, to my own wife Bessie, who was huddled in our cabin, sick and weakened by the interminable cold.

"Storm's here, stoke up the fire!" someone shouted, and One-Eyed Kate opened the iron door to the old stove and struck a match. The tinder had already been set, perhaps for days, in anticipation of this moment.

Soon a roaring blaze crackled in the old iron stove. We huddled in a circle, each of us silent and grateful, grunting with satisfaction. During the storms, the Martian flying machines were forced to seek shelter in secluded valleys, it was said, and so we did not fear that the Martians would attack. The bipeds that the Martians used for food and as slaves might attack, I suspected, if they saw our smoke, but this was unlikely. We were far from the Martian jungles, and it was rumored that the bipeds held forth only in their own familiar domain.

After the past two weeks of damnable cold, we needed some warmth, and as I basked in the roaring heat of the stove, the others began to sigh in contentment. I hoped that Bessie had lit our own little stove back in the old mining shack we called home.

Pierre put his gloves back on, and the little man was beginning to feel the effects of his drinks. He weaved a little as he stood, and growled, "By *gar,* your dogs weel fait mah beast tonait!"

"You're down to only two dogs," I reminded Pierre. He wasn't a careless sort, unless he got drunk. I knew he wasn't thinking clearly. He couldn't afford to lose another dog in a senseless fight.

"Damn you, Jacques! Your dogs weel fait mah beast tonait!" He pounded the red-hot stove with a gloved fist, staggered toward me with a crazed gleam in his eyes.

I wanted to protect him from himself. "No one wants to fight your dogs tonight," I said.

Pierre staggered to me, grabbed my shoulder with both hands, and looked up. His face was seamed and scarred by the cold, and though he was drunk, there was a cunning glint in his eyes. "Your dogs, weel fait, my *beast,* tonait!"

The room went silent. "What beast are you talking about?" One-Eyed Kate said.

"You looking for Marshawns, no?" He turned to her and waved expansively. "You want see a Marshawn? Your dogs keeled mah dogs. Now your dogs weel fait mah Marshawn!"

My heart began pounding, and my thoughts raced. We had not seen Pierre in weeks, and it was said that he was one of the finest trappers in the Yukon. As my mind registered what he'd brought back from Anchorage, as I realized what he'd trapped there, I recalled the heavy bundle tied to his sled. Could he really have secured a live Martian?

Suddenly there was shouting in the room from a dozen voices. Several men grabbed lanterns and dashed out the front door, the dancing light throwing grotesque images on the wall. Klondike Pete was shouting, "How much? How much do you want to fight your beast?"

"I say, heaven forbid! Let's not have a fight!" Dr. Weatherby began saying. "I want to study the creature!"

But the sudden fury with which the others met the doctor's plea was overwhelming.

We were outraged by the Martians for our burnt cities, for the poisoned crops, for the soldiers who died under Martian heat beams or choked to death in the vile black fog that emanated from their guns. More than all of this, we raged against the Martians for our fair daughters and children who had gone to feed these vile beasts, these Martians who drank our blood as we drain water.

So great was this primal rage that someone struck the doctor—more in some mindless animal instinct, some basic need to see the Martian dead, than out of anger at the good man who had worked so hard to keep us alive through this hellish winter.

The doctor crumpled under the weight of the blow and knelt on the floor for a moment, staring down at the dirty wood planks, trying to regain his senses.

Meanwhile, others took up the shout. "There's a game for you!" "How much to fight it? What do you want?"

Pierre stood in a swirling, writhing, shouting maelstrom. I know logically that there could not have been two dozen people in the room, yet it seemed like vastly more. Indeed, it seemed to my mind that all of troubled humanity crowded the room at that moment, hurling fists in the air, cursing, threatening, mindlessly crying for blood.

I found myself screaming to be heard, "How much? How much?" And though I have never been one to engage in the savage sport of dogfighting, I thought of my own sled dogs out in front of the lodge, and I considered how much I'd be willing to pay to watch them tear apart a Martian. The answer was simple:

I'd pay everything I owned.

Pierre raised his hands in the air for silence, and named his price, and if you think it unfairly high, then remember this: We all secretly believed that we would die before spring. Money meant almost nothing to us. Most of us had been unable to get adequately outfitted for winter and had hoped that a moose or a caribou would get us through the lean months. But Martians harvested the caribou and moose just as they harvested us. Many a man in that room knew that he'd be down to eating his sled dogs by spring. Money means nothing to those who wish only to survive.

Yet we knew that many would profit from the Martian invasion. In the South, insurance hucksters were selling policies against future invasions, the loggers and financiers were making fortunes, and every man who'd ever handled a hammer suddenly called himself a master carpenter and sought to hire himself out at inflated prices.

We in this room did not resent Pierre's desire to recoup his losses after this most horrible of winters.

"De beast has sixteen tentacles," he said, "so Ah weel let you fight heem with eight dogs—at five t'ousand doughlars a dog: Two t'ousand doughlars for me, and de rest goes for de winner, or de winners, of de fait!"

The accounts we'd read about Martians suggested that without their metallic bodies, they moved ponderously slow here on Earth. The increased gravity of our world, where everything is six times heavier than on Mars, weighed them down greatly. I'd never seen a bear pitted against more than eight dogs, so it seemed unlikely that the Martian could win. But with each contestant putting in $2,000 just for the right to fight, Pierre would go home with at least $16,000—five times what he'd make in a good year. All he had to do was let people pay for the right to kill a Martian.

Klondike Pete didn't even blink. "I'll put in two huskies!" he roared.

"Grip can take him!" One-Eyed Kate said. "You'll let a pit bull fight?"

Pierre nodded, and I began calculating. If you counted most of my supplies, I had barely enough for a stake in the fight, and I had a dog I thought could win—half husky, half wolfhound. He'd outweigh any of the other mutts in the pit, and he pulled the sled with great heart. He was a natural leader.

But I caught that sly gleam in Pierre's dark eyes. I knew that this fight would be more than any of us were bargaining for. I hesitated.

"By gol', I'll put in my fighter," old Tom King offered with evident bloodlust, and in half a moment four other men signed their notes to Pierre. The fight was set.

The storm raged. Snow pounded in unbounded avarice, skirling across the frozen crust of the winter's buildup. One-Eyed Kate lugged a pair of lanterns into the blizzard, held them over the fighting pit. At the north end, a bear cage could be lowered into the pit by means of a winch. At the south end, a dog run led down.

Klondike Pete leapt in and flattened the snow, then climbed back up through the dog run. Everyone unhitched, brought their dogs from the sleds, then herded them down the run. The dogs smelled the excitement, yapped and growled, stalking through the pit and sniffing uneasily.

Someone began winching the big cage up, and the dogs settled down. Some of the dogs had battled bears, and so knew the sound of the winch. One-Eyed Kate's pit bull emitted a coughing bark and began leaping in excitement, wanting to draw first blood from whatever we loosed into the pit.

It was a ghoulish mob that stood around that dark pit, pale faces lit dimly by the oily lanterns that flickered and guttered with every gust of wind.

Four men had already lugged Pierre's bundle around to the back of the lodge. The bundle was wrapped in heavy canvas and tied solidly with five or six hide ropes of Eskimo make. A couple of men worried at the knots, trying to untie the frozen leather, while two others stood nearby with rifles cocked, aimed at the bundle.

Pierre swore softly, drew his bowie knife, and sliced through the ropes, then rolled the canvas over several times. The canvas was wound tight around the Martian six turns, so that one moment I was peering through the driving snow while trying to make out the form that would emerge from the gray bundle, and the next moment, the Martian fell on the ground before us.

It burst out from the tarpaulin. It backed away from Pierre and from the light, a creature frightened and alone, and for several moments it made a metallic hissing noise as it slithered over the snow, searching for escape. At first, the hissing sounded like a rattlesnake's warning, and several of us leapt back. But the creature before us was no snake.

For those who have never seen a Martian, it can be difficult to describe such a monstrosity. I have read descriptions, but none succeed. My recollections of this monster are imprinted as solidly as if they were etched on a lithographic plate, for this creature was both more than, and less than, the sum of all our nightmares.

Others have described the fungal green-gray hue of the creature's bulbous head, fully five times larger than a human head, and they have told of the wet leathery skin that encases the Martian's enormous brain. Others have described the peculiar slavering, sucking sounds that the creatures made as they gasped for breath, heaving convulsively as they groped about in our heavy atmosphere.

Others have described the two clumps of tentacles—eight in each clump, just below the lipless V-shaped beak, and they have told how the Gorgon tentacles coiled almost languidly as the creature slithered about.

The Martian invites comparison to the octopus or squid, for like these creatures, it seems little more than a head with tentacles. Yet it is so much more than that!

No one has described how the Martian was so exquisitely, so gloriously alive. The one Pierre had captured swayed back and forth, pulsing across the ice-crusted snow with an ease that suggested that it was acclimated to polar conditions. While others have said that the creature seemed to them to be ponderously slow, I wonder if their specimens were not somehow hampered by warmer conditions—for this beast wriggled viciously, and its tentacles slithered over the snow like living whips, writhing not in agony—but in desperation, in a curious hunger.

Others have tried to tell what they saw in the Martian's huge eyes: a marvelous intelligence, an intellect keen beyond measure, a sense of malevolence that some imagined to be pure evil.

Yet as I looked into that monster's eyes, I saw all of those and more. The monster slithered over the snow at a deceptively quick pace, circling and twisting this way and that. Then for a moment it stopped and candidly studied each of us. In its eyes was an undisguised hunger, a malevolent intent so monstrous that some hardened trappers cried out and turned away.

A dozen men pulled out weapons and hardly restrained themselves from opening fire. For a moment the Martian continued to hiss in that metallic grating sound, and I imagined it was some warning, till I realized that it was only the sound of the creature drawing crude breaths.

It sized up the situation, then sat gazing with evident maleficence at Pierre. The only sound was the gusting of wind over the tundra, the hiss of frozen snow stinging the ground, and my heart pounding.

Pierre laughed gleefully. "You see de situation, mah fren'," he addressed the Martian. "You wan' to drink from me, but we have de guns trained on *you*. But dere ees blood to drink—blood from dogs!"

The Martian gazed at Pierre with calculating hatred. I do not doubt it understood every word Pierre uttered, every nuance. I imagined the creature learning our tongue as Pierre talked to it and his dogs on the lonely trail. It knew what we required of it. "Keel dem if you can," Pierre admonished the creature. "Keel de dogs, drink from dem. If you ween, Ah weel set you free to fin' your own kind. Ees simple, no?"

The Martian expelled some air from its mouth in a gasp, an almost mechanical sound that cannot adequately be described as speech. Yet the timing of that gasp, the pitch and volume, identified the beast's intent as certain as any words uttered from human lips. "Yes," it said.

Haltingly, with many a backward glance at us, the Martian slithered over the ground on its tentacles, entered the bear cage. Klondike Pete went to the winch and lifted the cage from the ground, while Tom King swiveled the boom out over the floor of the pit; then they lowered the cage.

The dogs sniffed and yapped. Snarls and growls mingled into a continuous sound. One-Eyed Kate's pit bull, Grip, was a grayish creature the color of ash, and it leapt up at the cage as it lowered, growling and snapping once or twice, then caught the alien's scent and backed away.

Others were not so circumspect. Klondike Pete's dogs were veterans of the ring, used to fighting as a team, and their teeth snapped together with metallic clicks as we lowered the Martian into the pit. They jumped up, biting at the tentacles that recoiled from them.

When the cage hit the floor of the pit, Klondike Pete's huskies snarled and danced forward, thrusting their teeth between the pine-wood bars at each side of the bear cage, trying to tear some flesh from the Martian before we pulled the rope that would open the door, freeing the Martian into the ring.

The dogs attacked from two sides at once, and if it had been a bear in that cage, it would have backed away from one dog, only to have the other tear into it from behind. The Martian was not so easily abused.

It held calmly in the center of the cage for half a second, observing the dogs with those huge eyes, so full of malevolent wisdom.

Klondike Pete pulled the rope that would spring the door to the cage, releasing the Martian to the pack of dogs, and what happened next is almost too grisly to tell.

It has been said that Martians were ponderously slow, that they struggled under the effects of our heavier gravity. Perhaps that was true of them when they first landed, but this creature seemed to have acclimated to our gravity very well over the past few months.

It became, in an instant, a seething dynamo, a twisting, grisly mass of flesh bent on destruction. It hurled against one side of the cage, then another, and at first I believed it was trying to demolish the cage, break it asunder. Indeed, the Martian was roughly the size and weight of a small black bear, and I have seen bears tear cages apart in a fight. I heard timbers crack under the monster's onslaught, but it was not trying to break the bars of its cage.

It was not until after the Martian had hurled itself against the bars of its cage that I realized what had happened. Each of a Martian's tentacles is seven feet long, and about three inches wide near the end. With several tentacles whipping snakelike in the air, striking in precision, the Martian had snatched through the bars and grabbed one husky, then another, and pulled, pinning the dogs helplessly against the sides of the bear cage where it held them firmly about their necks.

The huskies yelped and whined to find themselves in the Martian's grasp, and struggled to pull away, desperately scratching at the beast's tentacles with their forepaws, tugging backward with their considerable might. These were not your weak house dogs of New York or San Francisco. These were trained pack dogs that could drag a four-hundred-pound sled over the bitter tundra for sixteen hours a day, and I believed that they would easily break free from the Martian's grasp.

The door to the cage began to drop open, and with one tentacle, the Martian grasped it, twined the tentacle about the door, and held it closed as securely as if it were held by a steel lock, and in this manner it kept the other dogs somewhat at bay.

The other dogs barked and snarled. The pit bull lunged and experimentally nipped the tentacle that held the door closed, then danced back. One or two dogs howled, trotted around the pit, unsure how to proceed in their attacks. The pit bull struck again once—twice, and was joined quickly by the others, and in a moment three dogs were snarling, trying to rip that one tentacle free of the door. I saw flesh ripped away, and tender white skin, almost bloodless, was exposed.

The Martian seemed unconcerned. It was willing to sacrifice a limb in order to sate its appetite. Holding the two huskies firmly against the cage, the Martian began to feed.

It must be remembered that Pierre had held this Martian for nine days without food, and any human so ill-treated perhaps would also have sought refreshment before continuing the fight. It has also been reported that Martians drink blood, and that they used pipettes about a yard long to do so. From other accounts, one might suppose that such pipettes were metallic things that the Martians kept lying about near their vehicles, but this is not so.

Instead, from the Martian's beak, a three-foot-long rod telescoped, a rod that might have been a long white bone, except that it was twisted, like the horn of a narwhal, and its tip was hollow.

The Martian expertly inserted this bone into the jugular vein of the nearest husky, who yelped and snarled ferociously, trying to escape.

A loud, orgasmic slurping issued from the Martian, as if it were drinking sarsaparilla with an enormous straw. The dog's death was amazingly swift. One moment it was kicking its hind legs convulsively, bloodying the snow at its feet in its struggles to escape, and in the next it succumbed totally, horribly, and it slumped and quivered.

The tiniest fleck of blood dribbled from the husky's throat as it ceased its frantic attempts at flight.

In thirty seconds, the feeding over, the Martian twisted with a snapping motion, inserted its horn into the second husky, and drank its blood swiftly. The whole process was carried out with horrid rapidness and precision, with as little thought as you or I might give to the process of chewing and swallowing an apple.

By now, the other dogs had gotten a good portion of the flesh on the Martian's tentacle chewed away, and as the Martian fed upon the second of Klondike Pete's prize fighting huskies, the Martian struck with several tentacles, pummeling the dogs on their snouts, frightening them back a pace, where they snarled and leapt back and forth, seeking an opening.

The Martian stopped, regarded Klondike Pete balefully, and tossed the body of a dead second husky a pace toward him. The look in the creature's eyes was chilling—a promise of what would happen to Klondike Pete if the Martian got free.

The Martian exhaled from its long white horn, and droplets of blood sprayed out over our faces. The sound that this exhalation—this almost automatic cleaning of the horn—made was most unsettling: it sounded as a trumpeting, ululating cry that rang through the night, slicing through the blizzard. It was a mournful sound, infinitely lonely in that dark setting.

At that moment, I felt small and mean to be standing here on the edge of the pit, urging the dogs to finish their business. For their part, the other six dogs backed away and studied the monster quietly, sniffing the air, wondering at this awe-inspiring sound that it made.

A biting gust of wind hit my face, and for the first time during that fight, I realized just how cold I was. The storm was blowing in warmer air. Indeed, I looked forward to the next few days under the cloud cover. But the wind was brutal. It felt as if ice water were running in my veins, and the bitter weather drove the breath from me. I hunched against the cold, saw how the dogs quivered with anticipation in the pit, the breath steaming hot from their mouths.

I wanted to turn, rush inside to the warm stove, forget this grisly battle. But I was held by my own bloodlust, by my own quivering excitement.

There were six strong dogs in the ring, dogs bred to a life of toil. They growled and menaced and kept their distance, and the Martian retracted its horn back under that peculiar V-shaped beak and flung open the doors of the bear cage, surging forward. Its appetite for blood had been sated, and now it was ready for battle.

In a pounding, quivering mass it rolled forward over the ice, staring into the eyes of the dogs. There was a look of undaunted majesty in those eyes, an air of mastery to the creature's movements. "I am king here," it was saying to the dogs. "I am all you aspire to be. You are fit only to be my food."

With a coughing bark, Grip lunged for the Martian, its gray body leaping silent as a spectre over the snow. It jumped in the air, aiming a snapping bite at the Martian's huge eye. I was almost forced to turn away. I did not want to see what happened when that pit bull's monstrous, viselike jaws bit into that dark flesh of the Martian's eye.

In response, the Martian dropped down and under the dog with incredible speed. It became a whirling dynamo, a vortex, a living force of incredible power. Reaching up with three tentacles, it caught the pit bull by the neck in midair, then twisted and pulled down. There was an awful snapping as the pit bull hit the ground, bounced twice. The pit bull slid a few feet over the snow, its neck broken, and lay panting and whining on the ice, unable to get up.

But the huskies were undaunted. These were the cousins to wolves, and their bloodlust, the primal memories passed through generations, overcame their fear. Four more dogs lunged and bit almost simultaneously, undaunted by the spectacle of strangeness and power before them. As they latched onto a tentacle, twisting, trying to rip and tear at the Martian as if it were some young caribou on the tundra, the Martian would convulse, pull its limb back rapidly, drawing each dog into its clutches.

In seconds, the Martian had four vicious, snarling dogs in its grasp, and its tentacles wound about their necks like a hangman's ropes.

There was a flurry of activity, of frantic writhing and lunges on the part of the dogs. The growls of attack became plaintive yelps of surprise and fear. The eager savage cries of battle became only a desperate pawing as the four worthy huskies, these brothers of the wolf, tried to escape.

The Martian gripped with several tentacles to each dog, as a squid might grasp small fishes, and choked the fight and life from the dogs while we ogled in horrid fascination.

Soon the startled yelping, the labored breathing of dogs, the frantic tussle as the huskies sought escape, all became a stillness. Their heaving chests quieted. The wind blew softly through their gray hair.

The Martian sat atop them, slavering from its exertions, heaving and pulsating, glaring up at us.

One dog was left. Old Tom King's husky, a valiant fighter that knew it was outmatched. It paced on the far side of the pit, whimpered up at us in shame. It was too smart to fight this strange monster.

Tom King hobbled over to the dog run, grunted as he lifted the gate that would let his dog escape the pit. Under normal circumstances, this act of mercy would not be allowed in such a fight, but these were anything but normal circumstances. We would not be amused by the senseless death of this one last canine.

Klondike Pete raised his 30-30 Winchester, aimed at the Martian's head, right between its eyes. The Martian stared at us fiercely, without fear. "Kill me," it seemed to say. "It does not matter. I am but one of our kind. We will be back."

"So, mah fren'," Pierre called to the Martian. "You have won your laif. As Ah promis', Ah weel let you go now. But mah companions here," he waved expansively to the rest of us around the pit, "Ah no t'ink weel be so generous, by *gar*. Mah condolences to you!"

He turned his back on the Martian, and I stared at the indomitable creature in the pit, lit only by the frantic wavering of our oil lamps. The storm was blowing, and the fierce cold gnawed at me, and for one moment, I wondered what it was like on Mars. I imagined the planet cooling over millennia, becoming a frozen hell like this land we had all exiled ourselves to. I imagined a warm house, a warm room, and I thought how I, like the Martian, would do anything for one hour of heated solace. I would plot, steal, kill. Just as the Martian had done.

Time seemed to stop as Klondike Pete took aim, and I found myself croaking feebly, "Let it live. It won the right!"

Everyone stopped. One-Eyed Kate peered from across the pit. Pete cocked his head and looked at me strangely.

The Martian turned its monstrously intelligent eyes on me and gazed, it seemed, into my soul. For once there was no hunger in that gaze, no disconcerting look of malevolence.

What happened next, I cannot explain, for words alone are inadequate to describe the sensation I received. There are those who assume that the Martians communicated through clicking sounds of their beaks, or through the waving of tentacles, but the many witnesses who observed the monsters in life all agree that no such sounds or motions were evident. Indeed, one reporter in London went so far as to suggest that they may have shared thoughts across space, communicating from one mind to another. Such suggestions have met with ridicule in critical circles, but I can only tell what happened to me: I was gazing into the pit, at the Martian, and suddenly it seemed as if a vast intelligence was pouring into my mind. For one brief moment, my thoughts seemed to expand and my intellect seemed to fill the universe, and I beheld a world with red blowing desert sands so strikingly cold that the sensation assaulted me like a physical blow, crumpling me so that I fell down into the snow, curling into a ball. And as I beheld this world, I looked through eyes that were not my own. All of the light was tremendously magnified and shifted toward the red spectrum, so that I beheld the landscape as if on some strange summer evening when the sky shone more redly than normal. I looked out across a horizon that was peculiarly concave, as if I were staring at a world much smaller than ours.

A few red plants sprouted in this frigid waste, but they were stunted things. Martian cities—walking things that traveled through great mazelike canyons as they followed the sun from season to season—were marching in the distance, tantalizing, gleaming. I craved their warmth, the company of my Martian companions. I hungered for warmth, as a starving man might hunger for food in the last moments of life.

And above me, floating like a mote of dust in the sea of space, was the shining planet Earth.

One. We are one, a voice seemed to whisper in my head, and I knew that the Martian, with its superior intellect, had deigned to speak to me. *You understand me. We are one.*

Then above me—for I had fallen to the ground under the weight of this extraordinary vision—a rifle cracked, the sound of it reverberating from the cabin and the low hills. Klondike Pete cocked the gun and fired three more times, and the stinging scent of gunpowder and burnt oil from the barrel of his gun filled the air.

I got up and looked into the pit at the Martian. It was wriggling in its death throes, twisting and heaving on the ground in its inhuman way.

Everyone stood in the freezing, pelting snow, watching it die. I looked behind me, and even Dr. Weatherby had come out to witness the monster's demise.

"Right then, I say," he muttered. "Well, it's done."

I brushed the snow from me, and looked down into the pit. Tom King was watching me with rheumy eyes that glittered in the lamplight. He pulled at his beard and cackled. " 'Let 't live,' says he!" He turned away and chuckled under his breath. "Young whippersnap-per thinks he know ever'thing—but he don't know gol'-durned nothin'!"

The others hurried into the warm lodge for the night, and in mo-ments I was forced to follow.

That was on the night of January 13, 1900. As far as I know, I was among the last people on Earth to see a living Martian. In warmer climes, they had all passed away months before, during that hot August. And even as we suffered that night through the grim storm, the huge walking city in Anchorage began a tedious trek north, and was never seen again. Its tracks indicate that it came to the frozen ocean, tried to walk across, and sank into the sea. Many believe that there the Martians drowned, while others wonder if perhaps this had been the Martians' intended destination all along, and so we are forced to wonder if the

Martians are even now living in cities under the frozen polar ice, waiting to return.

But on the night I speak of, none of us at Hidden Lodge knew what would happen in months to come. Perhaps because of the Martian's malevolent gaze, perhaps because of the nearness of the creature, or perhaps because of our own feelings of guilt for what we had done, we feared more than ever an ignoble death in the tentacles of the Martians.

After we had warmed ourselves for a few moments in the lodge, the men all scurried away. Dr. Weatherby agreed to accompany me to my cabin under the cover of the storm, so that he might look in on Bessie. More than anything else, it was her need that had driven me to the lodge this night.

We left Hidden Lodge during the middle of the storm, let the snows cover our trail until we reached the cabin and found Bessie gone. The front door was open, and an armload of wood lay on the floor just inside. I knew then that the Martians had gotten her, had snatched her as she tried to warm herself. I tramped through the snow until I found her frozen, bloodless corpse not far outside the cabin.

I was overcome with grief and insisted on going out, under cover of darkness, and burying her deep in the snow, where the wolves would not find her. I did not care if the Martians took me. Almost, I wanted it.

The Arctic night was brutally cold, the stars piercingly bright. The aurora borealis flickered green on the northern horizon in a splendid display, and after I buried Bessie, I stood in the snow for a long hour, looking up.

Dr. Weatherby must have worried at why I stayed out for so long, for he came out and put his hands on my shoulders, then stared up into the night sky.

"I say, there it is—isn't it? Mars?" He was staring farther south than I had been watching, apparently believing that I was studying events elsewhere in the heavens. I had never been one to study the skies. I did not know where Mars lay. It stared down at us, like a baleful red eye.

After that, Dr. Weatherby stayed on for a week to care for me. It was an odd time. I was brooding, silent. On the woodpile, the good doctor set out petri dishes full of agar to the open air. Small colored dots of bacteria were growing in each dish, and by watching these, he hoped to discover precisely what species of bacteria were destroying the Martians. He insisted that cultures of such bacteria might provide an overwhelming defense in future wars. I was intrigued by this, and somehow, of all the things that happened that winter, my numbed mind remembers those green splotches of mold and bacteria better than just about anything else.

After the doctor left was the most difficult time of my life. I had no food, no warmth, no comfort during the remainder of that winter. Sometimes I wished the Martians would take me, even as I struggled to stay alive. Before the end of the winter, I ate my dogs and boiled the leather from my snowshoes at the last. I struggled from day to day under each successive frozen blast from the North.

I lived.

And slowly, like the march of an enfeebled man, after the lean winter, came a chill spring.

Emily Dickinson

THE SOUL SELECTS HER OWN SOCIETY: INVASION AND REPULSION: A CHRONOLOGICAL REINTERPRETATION OF TWO OF EMILY DICKINSON'S POEMS: A WELLSIAN PERSPECTIVE

CONNIE WILLIS

Until recently it was thought that Emily Dickinson's poetic output ended in 1886, the year she died. Poems 186B and 272?, however, suggest that not only did she write poems at a later date, but that she was involved in the "great and terrible events"[1] at the turn of the century.

The poems in question originally came to light in 1991,[2] while Nathan Fleece was working on his doctorate. Fleece, who found the poems[3] under a hedge in the Dickinsons' backyard, classified the poems as belonging to Dickinson's Early or Only Slightly Eccentric Period, but a

[1] For a full account, see H. G. Wells, *The War of the Worlds*, Oxford University Press, 1898.

[2] The details of the discovery are recounted in *Desperation and Discovery: The Unusual Number of Lost Manuscripts Located by Doctoral Candidates*, by J. Marple, Reading Railway Press, 1993.

[3] Actually a poem and a poem fragment consisting of a four-line stanza and a single word fragment* from the middle of the second stanza.

  * Or word. See later on in this paper.

recent examination of the works[4] has yielded up an entirely different interpretation of the circumstances under which the poems were written.

The sheets of paper on which the poems were written are charred around the edges, and that of Number 272? has a large round hole burnt in it. Martha Hodge-Banks claims that said charring and hole were caused by "a pathetic attempt to age the paper and forgetting to watch the oven,"[5] but the large number of dashes makes it clear they were written by Dickinson, as well as the fact that the poems are almost totally indecipherable. Dickinson's unreadable handwriting has been authenticated by any number of scholars, including Elmo Spencer in *Emily Dickinson: Handwriting or Hieroglyphics?*, and M. P. Cursive, who wrote, "Her a's look like c's, her e's look like 2's, and the whole thing looks like chicken scratches."[6]

The charring seemed to indicate either that the poems had been written while smoking[7] or in the midst of some catastrophe, and I began examining the text for clues.

Fleece had deciphered Number 272? as beginning, "I never saw a friend—/I never saw a moom—," which made no sense at all,[8] and on closer examination I saw that the stanza actually read:

"I never saw a fiend—
I never saw a bomb—
And yet of both of them I dreamed—
While in the—dreamless tomb—"

[4] While I was working on *my* dissertation.

[5] Dr. Banks's assertion that "the paper was manufactured in 1990 and the ink was from a Flair tip pen," is merely airy speculation.*

   * See "Carbon Dating Doesn't Prove Anything," by Jeremiah Habakkuk, in *Creation Science for Fun and Profit*, Golden Slippers Press, 1974.

[6] The pathetic nature of her handwriting is also addressed in *Impetus to Reform: Emily Dickinson's Effect on the Palmer Method*, and in "Depth, Dolts, and Teeth: An Alternate Translation of Emily Dickinson's Death Poems," in which it is argued that Number 712 actually begins, "Because I could not stoop for darts," and recounts an arthritic evening at the local pub.

[7] Dickinson is not known to have smoked, except during her Late or Downright Peculiar Period.

[8] Of course, neither does, "How pomp surpassing ermine." Or, "A dew sufficed itself."

a much more authentic translation, particularly in regard to the rhyme scheme. "Moom" and "tomb" actually rhyme, which is something Dickinson hardly ever did, preferring near-rhymes such as "mat/gate," "tune/sun," and "balm/hermaphrodite."

The second stanza was more difficult, as it occupied the area of the round hole, and the only readable portion was a group of four letters farther down that read "ulla."[9]

This was assumed by Fleece to be part of a longer word such as "bullary" (a convocation of popes),[10] or possibly "dullard" or "hullabaloo."[11]

I, however, immediately recognized "ulla" as the word H. G. Wells had reported hearing the dying Martians utter, a sound he described as "a sobbing alternation of two notes[12] . . . a desolating cry."

"Ulla" was a clear reference to the 1900 invasion by the Martians, previously thought to have been confined to England, Missouri, and the University of Paris.[13] The poem fragment, along with 186B, clearly indicated that the Martians had landed in Amherst and that they had met Emily Dickinson.

At first glance, this seems an improbable scenario due to both the Martians' and Emily Dickinson's dispositions. Dickinson was a recluse who didn't meet anybody, preferring to hide upstairs when neighbors came to call and to float notes down on them.[14] Various theories have been advanced for her self-imposed hermitude, including Bright's Disease, an unhappy love affair, eye trouble, and bad skin. T. L. Mensa suggests the simpler theory that all the rest of the Amherstonians were morons.[15]

None of these explanations would have made it likely that she would

---

[9] Or possibly "ciee." Or "vole."

[10] Unlikely, considering her Calvinist upbringing.

[11] Or the Australian city, Ulladulla. Dickinson's poems are full of references to Australia. W. G. Mathilda has theorized from this that "the great love of Dickinson's life was neither Higginson nor Judge Lord, but Mel Gibson." See *Emily Dickinson: The Billabong Connection,* by C. Dundee, Outback Press, 1985.

[12] See Rod McKuen.

[13] Where Jules Verne was working on *his* doctorate.

[14] The notes contained charming, often enigmatic sentiments such as, "Which shall it be—Geraniums or Tulips?" and "Go away—and Shut the door When—you Leave."

[15] See *Halfwits and Imbeciles: Poetic Evidence of Emily Dickinson's Opinion of Her Neighbors.*

like Martians any better than Amherstates, and there is the added difficulty that, having died in 1886, she would also have been badly decom-
posed.

The Martians present additional difficulties. The opposite of recluses,
they were in the habit of arriving noisily, attracting reporters, and blasting at everybody in the vicinity. There is no record of their having
landed in Amherst, though several inhabitants mention unusually loud
thunderstorms in their diaries,[16] and Louisa May Alcott, in nearby Con-
cord, wrote in her journal, "Wakened suddenly last night by a loud
noise to the west. Couldn't get back to sleep for worrying. Should have
had Jo marry Laurie. To Do: Write sequel in which Amy dies. Serve her
right for burning manuscript."

There is also indirect evidence for the landing. Amherst, frequently
confused with Lakehurst, was obviously the inspiration for Orson
Welles's setting the radio version of *War of the Worlds* in New Jersey.[17]
In addition, a number of the tombstones in West Cemetery are tilted at
an angle, and, in some cases, have been knocked down, making it clear
that the Martians landed not only in Amherst, but in West Cemetery,
very near Dickinson's grave.

Wells describes the impact of the shell[18] as producing "a blinding
glare of vivid green light" followed by "such a concussion as I have
never heard before or since." He reports that the surrounding dirt
"splashed," creating a deep pit and exposing drainpipes and house
foundations. Such an impact in West Cemetery would have uprooted
the surrounding coffins and broken them open, and the resultant light
and noise clearly would have been enough to "wake the dead," including the slumbering Dickinson.

That she was thus awakened, and that she considered the event an
invasion of her privacy, is made clear in the longer poem, Number

---

[16] Virtually everyone in Amherst kept a diary, containing entries such as "Always
knew she'd turn out to be a great poet," and "Full moon last night. Caught a
glimpse of her out in her garden planting peas. Completely deranged."

[17] The inability of people to tell Orson Welles and H. G. Wells apart lends credence
to Dickinson's opinion of humanity. (See footnote 15.)

[18] Not the one at the beginning of the story, which everybody knows about, the
one that practically landed on him in the middle of the book which everybody
missed because they'd already turned off the radio and were out running up and
down the streets screaming, "The end is here! The Martians are coming!"*

  * Thus proving Emily was right in her assessment of the populace.

186B, of which the first stanza reads: "I scarce was settled in the grave— When came—unwelcome guests— Who pounded on my coffin lid— Intruders—in the dust—"[19]

Why the "unwelcome guests" did not hurt her,[20] in light of their usual behavior, and how she was able to vanquish them, are less apparent, and we must turn to H. G. Wells's account of the Martians for answers.

On landing, Wells tells us, the Martians were completely helpless due to Earth's greater gravity, and remained so until they were able to build their fighting machines. During this period they would have posed no threat to Dickinson except that of company.[21]

Secondly, they were basically big heads. Wells describes them as having eyes, a beak, some tentacles, and "a single large tympanic drum" at the back of the head which functioned as an ear. Wells theorized that the Martians were "descended from beings not unlike ourselves, by a gradual development of brain and hands . . . at the expense of the body." He concluded that, without the body's vulnerability and senses, the brain would become "selfish and cruel" and take up mathematics,[22] but Dickinson's effect on them suggests that the overenhanced development of their neocortexes had turned them instead into poets.

The fact that they picked off people with their heat-rays, sucked human blood, and spewed poisonous black smoke over entire counties, would seem to contraindicate poetic sensibility, but look how poets act. Take Shelley, for instance, who went off and left his first wife to drown herself in the Serpentine so he could marry a woman who wrote monster movies. Or Byron. The only people who had a kind word to say about him were his dogs.[23] Take Robert Frost.[24]

The Martians' identity as poets is corroborated by the fact that they

---

[19] See "Sound, Fury, and Frogs: Emily Dickinson's Seminal Influence on William Faulkner," by W. Snopes, Yoknapatawpha Press, 1955.

[20] She was, of course, already dead, which meant the damage they could inflict was probably minimal.

[21] Which she considered a considerable threat. "If the butcher boy should come now, I would jump into the flour barrel,"* she wrote in 1873.

    * If she was in the habit of doing this, it may account for her always appearing in white.

[22] Particularly nonlinear differential equations.

[23] See "Lord Byron's *Don Juan*: The Mastiff as Muse" by C. Harold.

[24] He didn't like people either. See "Mending Wall," *The Complete Works,* Random House. Frost preferred barbed wire fences with spikes on top to walls.

landed seven shells in Great Britain, three in the Lake District,[25] and none at all in Liverpool. It may have determined their decision to land in Amherst.

But they had reckoned without Dickinson's determination and literary technique, as Number 186B makes clear.[26] Stanza Two reads:

"I wrote a letter—to the fiends—
And bade them all be—gone—
In simple words—writ plain and clear—
'I vant to be alone.' "

"Writ plain and clear" is obviously an exaggeration, but it is manifest that Dickinson wrote a note and delivered it to the Martians, as the next line makes even more evident: "They [indecipherable][27] it with an awed dismay—"

Dickinson may have read it aloud or floated the note down to them in their landing pit in her usual fashion, or she may have unscrewed the shell and tossed it in, like a hand grenade.

Whatever the method of delivery, however, the result was "awed dismay" and then retreat, as the next line indicates:

"They—promptly took—their leave—"

It has been argued that Dickinson would have had no access to writing implements in the graveyard, but this fails to take into consideration the Victorian lifestyle. Dickinson's burial attire was a white dress, and all Victorian dresses had pockets.[28]

During the funeral Emily's sister Lavinia placed two heliotropes in her sister's hand, whispering that they were for her to take to the Lord. She may also have slipped a pencil and some Post-its into the coffin, or Dickinson, in the habit of writing and distributing notes, may simply have planned ahead.[29]

[25] See "Semiotic Subterfuge in Wordsworth's 'I Wandered Lonely as a Cloud': A Dialectic Approach," by N. Compos Mentis, Postmodern Press, 1984.

[26] Sort of.

[27] The word is either "read" or "heard" or possibly "pacemaker."

[28] Also pleats, tucks, ruching, flounces, frills, ruffles, and passementerie.*

   * See "Pockets as Political Statement: The Role of Clothing in Early Victorian Feminism," by E. and C. Pankhurst, Angry Women's Press, 1978.

[29] A good writer is never without pencil and paper.*

   * Or laptop.

In addition, grave poems[30] are a well-known part of literary tradition. Dante Gabriel Rossetti, in the throes of grief after the death of his beloved Elizabeth Siddell, entwined poems in her auburn hair as she lay in her coffin.[31]

However the writing implements came to be there, Dickinson obviously made prompt and effective use of them. She scribbled down several stanzas and sent them to the Martians, who were so distressed at them that they decided to abort their mission and return to Mars.

The exact cause of this deadly effect has been much debated, with several theories being advanced. Wells was convinced that microbes killed the Martians who landed in England, who had no defense against Earth's bacteria, but such bacteria would have taken several weeks to infect the Martians, and it was obviously Dickinson's poems which caused them to leave, not dysentery.

Spencer suggests that her illegible handwriting led the Martians to misread her message and take it as some sort of ultimatum. A. Huyfen argues that the advanced Martians, being good at punctuation, were appalled by her profligate use of dashes and random capitalizing of letters. S. W. Lubbock proposes the theory that they were unnerved by the fact that all of her poems can be sung to the tune of "The Yellow Rose of Texas."[32]

It seems obvious, however, that the most logical theory is that the Martians were wounded to the heart by Dickinson's use of near-rhymes, which all advanced civilizations rightly abhor. Number 186B contains two particularly egregious examples: "gone/alone" and "guests/dust," and the burnt hole in 272? may indicate something even worse.

The near-rhyme theory is corroborated by H. G. Wells's account of the damage done to London, a city in which Tennyson ruled supreme,

[30] See "Posthumous Poems" in *Literary Theories that Don't Hold Water*, by H. Houdini.

[31] Two years later, no longer quite so grief-stricken and thinking of all that lovely money, he dug her up and got them back.*

 * I told you poets behaved badly.

[32] Try it. No, really. "Be-e-e-e-cause I could not stop for Death, He kindly stopped for me-e-e." See?*

 * Not all of Dickinson's poems can be sung to "The Yellow Rose of Texas."**

 ** Numbers 2, 18, and 1411 can be sung to "The Itsy-Bitsy Spider." Could her choice of tunes be a coded reference to the unfortunate Martian landing in Texas? See "Night of the Cooters," by Howard Waldrop, p. 97, this volume.

and by an account of a near-landing in Ong, Nebraska, recorded by Muriel Addleson:

We were having our weekly meeting of the Ong Ladies Literary Society when there was a dreadful noise outside, a rushing sound, like something falling off the Grange Hall. Henrietta Muddie was reading Emily Dickinson's "I Taste a Liquor Never Brewed," out loud, and we all raced to the window but couldn't see anything except a lot of dust,[33] so Henrietta started reading again and there was a big whoosh, and a big round metal thing like a cigar[34] rose straight up in the air and disappeared.

It is significant that the poem in question is Number 214, which rhymes[35] "pearl" and "alcohol."[36] Dickinson saved Amherst from Martian invasion and then, as she says in the final two lines of 186B, "rearranged" her "grassy bed—/And Turned—and went To sleep."

She does not explain how the poems got from the cemetery to the hedge, and we may never know for sure,[37] as we may never know whether she was being indomitably brave or merely crabby.

What we do know is that these poems, along with a number of her other poems,[38] document a heretofore unguessed-at Martian invasion. Poems 186B and 272?, therefore, should be reassigned to the Very Late or Deconstructionist Period, not only to give them their proper place as Dickinson's last and most significant poems, but also so that

[33] Normal to Ong, Nebraska.

[34] See Freud.

[35] Sort of.

[36] The near-rhyme theory also explains why Dickinson responded with such fierceness when Thomas Wentworth Higginson changed "pearl" to "jewel." She knew, as he could not, that the fate of the world might someday rest on her inability to rhyme.

[37] For an intriguing possibility, see "The Literary Litterbug: Emily Dickinson's Note-Dropping as a Response to Thoreau's Environmentalism," P. Walden, *Transcendentalist Review*, 1990.

[38] Number 187's "awful rivet" is clearly a reference to the Martian cylinder. Number 258's "There's a certain slant of light" echoes Wells's "blinding glare of green light," and its "affliction/Sent us of the air" obviously refers to the landing. Such allusions indicate that as many as fifty-five* of the poems were written at a later date than originally supposed, that and the entire chronology and numbering system of the poems needs to be considered.

   * Significantly enough, the age Emily Dickinson was when she died.

the full symbolism intended by Dickinson can be seen in their titles. The properly placed poems will be Numbers 1775 and 1776, respectively, a clear Dickinsonian reference to the Fourth of July,[39] and to the second Independence Day she brought about by banishing[40] the Martians from Amherst.

NOTE: It is unfortunate that Wells didn't know about the deadly effect of near-rhymes. He could have grabbed a copy of the *Poems*, taken it to the landing pit, read a few choice lines of "The Bustle in a House," and saved everybody a lot of trouble.

---

[39] A holiday Dickinson did not celebrate because of its social nature, although she was spotted in 1881 lighting a cherry bomb on Mabel Dodd's porch and running away.*

  * Which may be why the Martian landing attracted so little attention. The Amherstodes may have assumed it was Em up to her old tricks again.

[40] There is compelling evidence that the Martians, thwarted in New England, went to Long Island. This theory will be the subject of my next paper,* "The Green Light at the End of Daisy's Dock: Evidence of Martian Invasion in F. Scott Fitzgerald's *The Great Gatsby*."

  * I'm up for tenure.

Jules Verne

AFTERWORD: RETROSPECTIVE

GREGORY BENFORD AND DAVID BRIN

In reflecting back, the terrible year described in these accounts can be seen as a fulcrum. The pivot, indeed, of modernity. IF we rise above ourselves.

About that hinge it tipped the fate of two worlds, two darkly different destinies. It led to a far better one for humanity than might have been, had the tripods never come. With the balm of three decades to heal the pain, one can perceive benefits—though bought at dear cost— in the tragic way that Mars first encountered Earth.

Above all, by uniting humanity against a shared foe, the Martians deflected our festering nationalist energies, which had seemed aimed toward a Twentieth Century in which our finest tools would be used for beastly ends. Instead, the invaders made us join together, redirecting all ingenuity and will toward a common cause.

So it is that we now have the world of marvels that you, the reader, and I, your humble editor, now inhabit. We blink in fulsome awe at palatial floating airships, at Cunard's ornate, gothic tourist-submersibles, at pneumatic tubes carrying mail rapidly from town to town— even when our many, still muddy roads thwart the steam-busses and cable lorries—so that even in the worst winter storms we all remain linked in a united world.

And of course there are the Great Cannons of Canaveral, Sumatra, Kourou, and Kenya—those behemoths of iron who regularly bellow loud enough to be heard even in distant lands, filling the sky with mirror-semaphores and other delights of the modern age.

A further benefit lies in literature. Our conviction that the world is illimitable and will obey reason, so that Man can improve upon it, has resurged. This is remarkable in light of the waning decades of the Nineteenth Century, which saw futuristic thinking, especially in the hands of Mr. Wells, darker in texture and sullenly pessimistic at least in implication.

So it is in a reflective mood that I enter these very words onto the kinetoscope screen of my tabula rasa—the latest of the electron-driven wonders. It is two weeks before my hundredth birthday. Never would I have thought that I could reach the fantastical year of 1928!

I have just been contemplating the news received hours ago by Hertzian wave from the first human interplanetary argonauts, scouts of the grand flotilla meant to return that "visit" we received a generation—and an age—ago.

Mars proves, as we suspected, a sad and wounded place, ancient and dry. In the terms used by an alienist, one can well imagine why a bitter, paranoic way of thinking would evolve there. Relayed carbon-stripe images of Martian cities show structures of exquisite grace and beauty, unencumbered by earthly gravity. The same gravity that will make our warriors seem as titans when they land . . . unless the Martians finally drop their wretched, prideful silence.

They *MUST* agree to speak! They must help bridge the mental gulf between our races, yawning as wide as the straits between our worlds— or else we shall have no choice. Our actions will be fore-ordained and there will be an end to them.

Despite some lingering wrathful unforgiveness on the part of some, it is mostly with reluctance that we ponder that genocidal option. For in learning to decipher their machines—and through dissection, their organic forms—there has grown among countless humans an unquenchable desire to fathom the inner splendor and grace of these hideous but strangely compelling beings. There are even fetishists, small in number but leaders in recent fashion, who seek to emulate the styles, speech, and even the eerie ways of thought that some interpolate from salvaged Martian records.

To be sure, many disapprove this effort at exaggerated empathy, but with my renown I assail such intolerance. Clearly, our celestial neighbors suffer from an inflexibility that cripples them far more than it ever harmed us—millions of deaths notwithstanding. If it is possible to cure them of this mortal flaw, it will only happen if youthful, flexible humankind manages to meet them more than halfway.

If I had my way, I would save as many of the poor creatures as I could from the two-legged wrath now descending toward the red world. If need be, I would have everyone *go Martian* just a little.

In this, I recall what one of my own favorite characters, Captain Nemo, once said—

The true price of war is borne by mothers.

Or in the words of my young friend and collaborator, Herbert George Wells—

Ignorance has caused more calamity than malignity.

Ponder the relations of the advanced nations of Europe and the Americas, and the vaster multitudes still enduring poverty and nescience around the rest of our troubled globe. We of the West have in a true, cultural sense defeated the empires of ancient ignorance. They now cower in our shadow.

In the oblique manner of lived history, we must now grasp that it is better to contemplate eventual reconciliation, world linked to world. The Western world must reach out, here, to the rest. And so it must come in parallel, on Mars.

An astronomical whole would be greater by far than the sum of our separate parts. We should not stride as conquerors, lonely in our righteous, vengeful vindication. We should not stand on the dry red plain of ashes that we have won. We should go to Mars to learn, even from the defeated.

—Jules Verne
Amiens, France
October 1928